early reviews

"A funny, empathetic novel about family, frustration, and the perils of miscommunication. Maggie's blogging misadventures are familiar to us all, and her voice is irresistible."

Joanna Weiss
Boston Globe columnist and author of *Milkshake*

"I am so glad overwhelmed suburban mom Maggie Kelly wasn't writing about me in her vent-gone-viral blog 'Maggie Has Had It,' but am so thrilled Meredith O'Brien indeed has written about her. Dig right into this very satisfying parfait of fiction that reads keenly as fact happening behind the closed curtains right next door to you, marital drama harshly exposed to the light of day via this smart, sharp and funny look at what happens when one woman's personal TMI world explodes."

Suzanne Strempek Shea
Author of *Becoming Finola* and *Selling the Lite of Heaven*

"Meredith O'Brien uncovers the messy underbelly of modern motherhood, throws in resentment, anger and of course, blogging, and turns it into a thoroughly entertaining read. Put on a video for the kids and treat yourself to *Mortified*."

Jen Singer
Author of *You're a Good Mom (and Your Kids Aren't so Bad Either)*

MORTIFIED

a novel about oversharing

MORTIFIED

a novel about oversharing

MEREDITH O'BRIEN

Mortified:
A Novel About Oversharing
By M.E. O'Brien

ISBN: 978-1-939288-03-5

Library of Congress Control Number: 2013932789

How To Save A Life
Words and Music by Joseph King and Isaac Slade
© 2005 EMI APRIL MUSIC INC. and AARON EDWARDS PUBLISHING
All Rights Controlled and Administered by EMI APRIL MUSIC INC.
All Rights Reserved International Copyright Secured Used by Permission
Reprinted by Permission of Hal Leonard Corporation

Wyatt-MacKenzie Publishing
DEADWOOD, OREGON

Wyatt-MacKenzie Publishing, Inc.
www.WyattMacKenzie.com
Contact us: info@wyattmackenzie.com

Publisher's Cataloging-in-Publication data

O'Brien, Meredith.
   Mortified : a novel about oversharing / Meredith O'Brien.
   p.cm.
   ISBN 978-1-939288-03-5
1. Marriage — Fiction. 2. Blogs — Fiction. 3. Social media — Fiction.
4. Internet — Fiction. 5. Boston — Fiction. I. Title.

PS3615.B7628 M67 2013
813.6 —dc23   2013932789

To Gayle, the best pal and sassy sounding board for which anyone could ever ask,

and to Scott, Jonah, Casey and Abbey with boundless love and affection.

The worst humiliation is only someone else's
momentary entertainment.
— KAREN CROCKETT

Be not thy tongue thy own shame's orator.
— WILLIAM SHAKESPEARE, *The Comedy of Errors*

One man's transparency is another's humiliation.
— GERRY ADAMS

CHAPTER ONE

Snow had completely coated the windshield of the SUV during the brief time Maggie had been inside the hotel. Instead of clearing it off, Maggie roughly brushed the snow off the door handle, unlocked the vehicle, slid onto the driver's seat and quickly turned on the ignition, clumsily dumping her purse, hat and coat in the general direction of the passenger seat. After wrenching her scratchy scarf off her neck and letting it fall to the damp floor, Maggie turned the heater up as high as it would go, closed her red, puffy eyes and leaned her aching back into the seat. In the distance, she heard the grinding metal-on-pavement sound of a snowplow, perhaps clearing a side street, or even the highway. She couldn't be sure of its location as she sat in a borrowed truck that was parked illegally in front of a hotel at nearly 8:30 at night days before Christmas, after sneaking past hotel staff to speak with a man who didn't want to hear from or see her. The love of her life. Her cell phone was brimming with scalding unheard voicemail messages from her mother-in-law who would've likely preferred that Maggie just pull the SUV into oncoming traffic and be done with it. Maggie deleted the messages—12—without listening to them while wondering if Alfred or Courtney had seen her when she ran through the lobby sobbing and noisily blowing her nose.

Some of the snow around the perimeter of the SUV's front window had now returned to liquid form and was starting to streak down the windshield leaving behind glossy trails on the slightly fogged windows. Maggie watched the droplets push their way through the snow which had been providing her with a camouflage of sorts, shielding her face from passersby, not that there was anyone out at that time and in that weather, save for a plow driver or, perhaps Alfred if he ever decided to look away from the web sites he was now surfing and notice the SUV parked in the fire lane.

Restless, she tried to think of something she could do to pass the time and keep her mind occupied, to stop herself from trying to bargain with God about what she'd do (or not do) if her marriage survived this. Seeing nothing in the way of amusements in the front seat — George had no magazines, CDs, newspapers in his vehicle, unlike Maggie's highly cluttered minivan — Maggie turned on the radio, flipping through the stations until she got to a pop station which was playing the latest tune from a singer whose life was being engulfed by a downward spiral of drinking and drugs. It was soothing to Maggie, in a twisted sort of way, to listen to this cotton candy confection of a song by a seemingly broken young woman and to think that somewhere out there someone had a more screwed up relationship and life than she did. A song by a new boy band came on, followed by one from a band comprised of guys who'd soon be collecting Social Security, then the station played a grating Christmas song that was so awful that it had no business being broadcast in public.

By now, the rest of the snow on the windshield had liquefied and Maggie had grown tired of the pop station. She tuned in a static-y independent college radio station from New Hampshire. "Who out there hates 'Dominick the Italian Christmas Donkey' as much as I do raise your hand," the DJ asked as the signal faded in and out.

Maggie, who could now see clearly through the window, raised her right hand.

"Well then I've got a better Christmas-y song to play for you, the late Jeff Buckley's 'Hallelujah.' Okay, so it's not technically a Christmas tune but hey, the snowstorm's about over folks, let's all say, 'Hallelujah' together. Keep warm and enjoy this non-donkey, non-chipmunk, non-grandma-got-run-over-by-a-reindeer song." The haunting voice of the deceased singer filled the stuffy SUV air, coupled by the simple strums of a guitar. Before she realized it, Maggie was sucked into the song's melancholy. Tears again pooled at the corners of her eyes and leaked down Maggie's face forming more salty streaks through her haphazardly applied makeup. As the singer repeated the word, "hallelujah" over and over with increasing emotion, Michael appeared at the driver's side door, without a jacket, his face just as red as Maggie's, his eyes just as bloodshot, his heart beating just as hard. Maggie — who'd yet to regain her composure — didn't open the window. Or the door. If she just stayed where she was, she thought, nothing could end. Everything would remain frozen in place.

Confused and impatient, Michael opened the unlocked door, rested his left forearm on it, glowered at his wife and then looked down at his feet. He raised his head slowly and haltingly said, "I . . . I, I've missed us too." He paused again, placed both of his warm hands against the roof of the SUV and leaned forward allowing the steamy heat from inside the vehicle to radiate against his chest and thighs. "I never knew . . . never expected that you . . . that you could be so cruel, that you said those things, felt them about me. That you were so angry."

A lengthy silence idled between them as Michael's face contorted with anguish. "I didn't know you were so miserable," his voice broke, "with . . . me. Am I such a bad guy? A bad husband?"

He sharply inhaled and paused, affording Maggie an opportunity to jump in, an opening which she was too scared to take.

DRUNK BLOGGING'S ALL RIGHT WITH ME
File under: I'm in a sucky mood, how 'bout you?

The Invisible Man didn't come home for dinner again.

The Invisible Man has too much work with some really, super important dudes who rule the universe, therefore, when he spends time with them, he's kinda ruling the universe too.

And the Invisible Man, who secretly wants to be king of the universe, didn't make it home to see his subjects again. What's that for, like, I dunno, 47 nights in a row? But who's really counting, right?

The Invisible Man . . . or should I call him the Wannabe-King, since he's not quite the king at his place of work yet? I think I should call him Wannabe-King given that he's now meeting and drinking with really "important people," much more important than me, or, uh, his two kids. I'm going for it, henceforth I declare that he's going to be called EITHER the Invisible Man or the Wannabe-King, depending on how I'm feeling like at any given moment . . . but where was I?

Oh, yeah, the Wannabe-King did, in fact make contact with his people to tell his lady in waiting (I like this royal metaphor stuff, it works for me . . .) he wouldn't be home until whenever the "important people" who actually rule the universe are damned well good and done. Oh, and he'll show his face AFTER they've had drinks, which is what they usually do because what good is having a meeting with "important people" if you can't have a beer later? After informing me he was blowing off dinner again, the Wannabe-King hung up the phone because he was done and his time is important, dammit! That's right folks, the Wannabe-King HUNG UP on yours truly, the LIW (that's Lady in Waiting for those of you following along at home).

He fucking hung up. He was probably terrified I'd reach through his BlackBerry — which is like his second dick that he fiddles with all day — and rip his head off. (Pun intended.)

He is, after all, the Wannabe-King, so apparently he gets to do what HE wants to do and I'm just supposed to shut the fuck up and deal with it . . . while Thing II is literally pissing into potted plants around the Wannabe-King's kingdom. Really, the kid did. And no, I did not clean up the plant that the kid really pissed on just a little while ago. How would you even do that, clean the plant? I guess wipe off the leaves? But I'm not going to. I'm not even going to attempt such a feat. As a penalty for treating his LIW so shitty, I'm considering moving the pissed-on plant into the Wannabe-King's office. "Just trying to brighten your room, my lord, it's right here next to your throne." Thing I is, as I type this, shoving Thing II against the wall with her Ragu-covered hands in the living room. They're both shrieking and acting like their usual heathen selves. This is what MY evenings are like, listening to the wee little Wannabe-King's subjects scream and act like maniacs while refusing to eat the dinner that I, everyone's LIW, prepared for them. I have no idea what The Ungratefuls are fighting about this time. She probably touched her brother with her bare feet or something and he freaked out because he has an unnatural aversion to naked feet. Frankly, I don't care. I'm going to ignore them unless one of them suddenly starts bleeding or becomes unconscious.

The Wannabe-King thinks that I, his LIW, will just sit back and take this (almost a year since his number of meetings exploded and he started regularly missing dinner, rendering absolutely everything domestic and pediatric to me). He, in his master of the universe mode, is bringing home all of the dough (now I'm really mixing metaphors, but mixing metaphors works really great with the bottle of white wine I'm polishing off). True, I'm just making small-time money with my anemic career as a Memory Makers scrapbooking consultant . . . that is when I can fit MY work into the family's schedule in between the Wannabe-King's work and getting a babysitter, which, his highness argues costs more per hour than I make, so therefore I should just give it up and be his geisha girl because it'd be more cost effective that way. Oh and I should continue to keep my complaints to myself. Yeah. He's a freakin' peach these days.

Is this what we've come to: He who makes the money calls the shots? When the fuck did this happen? This is a guy who got me into bed oh so many years ago by treating me like I really was a queen, who he worshiped. He'd play my favorite CDs (when people were buying CDs and not burning MP3s, you know, the Stone Ages), cook me all kinds of awesome food and call me in the middle of the day just to tell me some dumb joke. Now, well now, the Wannabe-King's too good for me, the slovenly woman who's been demoted from Queen to a LIW, the moron who waits, and waits, and waits for him to start showing up and share his life with her instead of leaving her to pick up and clean up shit all by herself. Now he only calls, WHEN he calls, to tell me he's going to be late, not to share a funny with me.

This is not what I signed up for. And when the Wannabe-King comes home later tonight and TRIES to even speak to me (that's assuming he wants to speak to me) it's gonna be mighty cold. Ice, ice, baby.

$\wp$

"Tommy pissed in a plant?"

"Oh my God! He did! I was in the middle of making pasta — yeah, I *know*, pasta again, please don't say anything about that . . . *anyway*, I was cleaning up the mess I'd made, red sauce all over myself. I'd just heard from Michael and felt like I wanted to murder someone. And he said, like, maybe, a dozen words to me during our whole conversation, rushed me off the damned phone without apologizing for leaving me hanging about when he was coming home. The kids were acting like little animals when Jackie ran into the kitchen and went, 'He peed! He peed in the plant!' You know that ficus tree we have, the tall one by the front door?" Maggie leaned way back as she sat atop the wooden stool next to the kitchen island and peered into the darkened hall to glance where the two-foot-tall plant, which had been barely clinging to life well before it was saturated in Tommy's urine, was standing. "It *would* drive him crazy," Maggie said, as a hint of mischief crept into her voice. Cradling the phone between her shoulder and chin, she walked down the hall, momentarily slipping on the frayed maroon hall rug (the tape that once secured it in place had been ripped off the floor by the constant rumblings of Tommy's fleet of Tonka trucks), grasped the plant and walked it into Michael's well appointed office — which looked like a Staples catalog all in black and white — adjacent to the kitchen. The pristine room, where even the paper shredder was free from dust and debris, was off limits to the kids, though everything of Maggie's, of course, was open season to their sticky, malevolent hands.

"What's that grunting? . . . Maggie, what are you doing?" Diane, Maggie's former college roommate, asked, as she leafed through a pile of bills that had stacked up on her desk during the past week. Sunday was usually bill paying night in the Kimball house but Diane was getting a jump on it by pulling out some of the junk. She absentmindedly flipped through a two-month-old L.L. Bean catalog that she, for some reason, didn't remember why she hadn't yet tossed yet.

"I'm . . . moving the plant. Shit! Got some dirt on the floor!"

"That smell WILL drive him crazy! Remember my friend Shelly? The one with the twin boys? They're now in, what, fifth or sixth grade, now? I'm not sure. Well, when they were in kindergarten or preschool, must've been preschool, that sounds right, well they dumped poop into the bottom of the dehumidifier in their basement playroom. They put it in that, you know, that water part on the bottom where the water goes before you dump it out."

"Ewww."

"Well, Shelly went down to the playroom one day. Said it smelled God awful. She said was indescribable. Nearly made her puke. She looked everywhere to try to figure out where the smell was coming from, cleaned the walls with bleach, rented a steam cleaner and even brought all the boys' toys outside and hosed them down when it was below-zero. Because it was winter she wasn't in the habit of emptying the dehumidifier every day. Then, after all that, she finally thought to look inside the bin for water. She was so ticked. How long do you think it'll take Michael to figure out what the smell is?"

"If Jackie doesn't say anything about Tommy peeing, which reminds me, I'll need to bribe her to keep her mouth shut? Hmm. I don't know, couple days maybe, if it starts to smell," Maggie bent down and sniffed the plant. "It only has a faint smell right now at the top of the plant here. I'm about a foot away from it." She squatted down and breathed deeply, about an inch away from the soil and gasped aloud. "Oh yeah, if I smell the dirt, it stinks." She plunked the plant next to Michael's black wire trash can next to his black desk, flicked some of the papers askew just a little because the finicky tidiness annoyed her, and left, shutting the door behind her so that the smell would be trapped inside the office.

Her conversation with Diane, as always, proved calming to Maggie who no longer felt the burning desire to ransack all of Michael's belongings after he'd bailed on dinner with the family because of work and had abruptly ended his phone call with Maggie, to which Maggie responded by chucking the black handset against the living room wall, leaving behind a sizable, jagged chip of yellow paint on the floor lying next to the remains of the phone. But despite the satisfaction she got from hurling the phone at the wall, Maggie was still all worked up and needed to direct her anger somewhere, not at her 3-year-old son and 6-year-old daughter who'd abandoned their pasta dinners on the table.

Maggie had retrieved the bottle of chardonnay from the fridge and poured herself a generous glass. Her battered black beach flip-flops slapped loudly against the dry, cracking soles of her feet as she retrieved her laptop computer, covered with pink "Girls Rock!" stickers, and placed it next to the green wine bottle on the island in the kitchen. The computer whirred to life and Maggie tapped on the keyboard, describing her version of the evening for the regular readers of her blog *Maggie Has Had It*.

Once she'd published her latest post and received positive feedback from Diane, Maggie couldn't seem to wipe the smirk off her face. She basked in the reflective glow of her laptop as she re-read the entry, very pleased with herself. *Maggie Has Had It* had been launched the year before on a whim after Diane had forwarded her a news article about the uptick in the number of personal blogs on the Internet. The news story featured one blog written by a guy who had "in-laws from hell," something with which Diane thought Maggie could relate. "This would be perfect for you," Diane wrote. "You'd make a great blogger, Mags! Dorothy gives you plenty of material."

When Maggie started the blog, she was still fairly busy with her work for a Minnesota-based company, Memory Makers, which sells scrapbooking materials via home sales parties, like Tupperware, only for photographs. Maggie not only had been booking three sales events per week, but had been promoted to the post of New England coordinator, something which provided her a nice bump in her paycheck in addition to her commission. Just as her scrapbooking business was taking off, Michael's slate of night meetings with various local boards for the big highway project he was spearheading at work, had begun to dramatically increase, meaning he wasn't available to watch the kids as he and Maggie had originally planned when she started working for Memory Makers to keep from going stir-crazy. Babysitting came almost exclusively in the form of her mother-in-law Dorothy (not Dot, not Dotty, not any nickname whatsoever; Maggie was to call her "Mom Kelly," per Dorothy's explicit request, though Maggie avoided calling her by any name). Michael gave Maggie a hard time when she said she wanted to find a regular, paid babysitter because he said he couldn't justify paying someone if his mother was a half-hour drive away from their Greenville home and would babysit for free. However to Maggie, having Dorothy babysit cost her a hefty price because it meant she had to endure an acerbic, running commentary on how everything Maggie did as a mother, a wife and a woman sucked every way to Tuesday. Having her mother-in-law babysit meant Maggie would have to run around buying food and cleaning the house before Dorothy arrived, lest Maggie have to endure the well-meaning verbal treatises on how having fresh fruits and vegetables in the house at all times creates "a lifetime of good habits," the middle school nurse would preach, and why scouring the bathroom with bleach — at least twice a week — keeps the flu and other illnesses at bay. It was proving difficult, virtually impossible, to find reliable, cost effective child care alternatives on which Maggie and Michael could agree. Backed into a corner between money and having to see her mother-in-law multiple times a week which left always left Maggie feeling lousy about herself, Maggie reluctantly relinquished the New England coordinator post and reduced the number of scrapbooking sales parties rather than have to put up with Dorothy's scrutiny, in person, all the time.

This was all happening at the same time when Maggie and Michael were having trouble getting Tommy, who was just two at the time, to sleep through the night. He'd repeatedly get up and walk around the house loudly wailing in the hallway near the doors to the three bedrooms at their Maple Road home. Michael made the case that he couldn't get up to deal with Tommy and spend all that time coaxing him back to sleep because he had to be up early, work late hours as the lead environmental guy on the team for Boston-based Ernest, Newton & Young (ENY), a traffic/environmental consulting agency, and he needed the rest. ("You don't want me to fall asleep at the wheel while driving on the Turnpike to work? Do you?" he asked Maggie.) So the responsibility fell to Maggie to get up with Tommy each night and either sing him the same lullaby her mother Molly used to sing or read aloud one of her favorite Dr. Seuss books, often multiple times a night. Even though she enrolled Jackie in preschool five mornings a week, Tommy's brief morning nap didn't afford

Maggie sufficient time to catch up on her sleep.

During one particularly dark day, while in the throes of marital frustration and sleep deprivation, Maggie re-read Diane's e-mail about blogs and decided to try it. She used to keep a diary when she was a teenager, the traditional kind where she put pen to actual paper in an actual book with a little lock on it so her younger brother Luke wouldn't be able to read it. Maggie started keeping it when she was 14, soon after her mother died in a car accident and no one seemed like they wanted to talk about it, not her dad, certainly not her younger brother, and none of her school friends. In between the pages of that diary was the only place where Maggie felt she could safely let out all the angry, unkind things she felt about the world, about the fact that her father Rob had been reduced to a specter, that she was now expected to raise her younger brother and be the family's domestic servant. She certainly couldn't unload on her dad, who seemed too fragile to withstand hearing her complaints, and not to anyone who went to school with her. She stopped journaling once she entered college, finding that she was too busy to write each day and she just didn't feel the need to do it anymore.

Yet here she was, a decade-plus later, wondering if chronicling her thoughts and feelings in such an open forum, like writing a public diary on the Internet, might be just what she needed, some free therapy so she wouldn't feel as though she was the only woman who was disillusioned with what had become of her life and how she felt swallowed up by everyone else's needs while hers languished. After a bit of Internet surfing, Maggie quickly learned that she could start a blog for free. This had the potential to provide her with a jolt of excitement, she thought, because actual people, strangers, could read what was going on and chime in on what she wrote. No one could do that with her diary entries that sit there, lifeless, in a book hidden under a pile of bra and panties in her underwear drawer. This could be a dynamic, living breathing virtual diary . . . one that talked back. Dubbing her blog, *Maggie Has Had It*, Maggie blanched at the notion of listing her last name, hometown or providing other personal info. Even though she fully intended on revealing very intimate details of her life in her daily entries, she felt it would be too revealing to identify Michael, Jackie and Tommy by name. She decided her online handle would be "Maggie from Mass." who lived in the Boston area and had two kids — who she referred to as Thing I and Thing II in order to protect their anonymity — and a husband, who went by a variety of nicknames. Her mother-in-law Dorothy, well, she too was called a variety of names in the blog, many of them profane.

"At the very least," Maggie told Diane on the phone after she'd written and published her first entry, "it will be like a release. I'll get all my pissed-off-ness out on the blog, not at Michael or the kids. They don't deserve to deal with all my shitty feelings all the time." Her very first blog post consisted of a lengthy description of the previous night when Dorothy, who'd been babysitting, cleaned out Maggie's refrigerator, re-arranged her cabinets and threw out tons of "bad food" which she believed was unhealthy for her grandchildren, such as Doritos, Pringles and Maggie's stash of months-old Easter candy. Maggie e-mailed the link to her premiere entry to Diane, the only other person who knew that she was blogging. In short order, Maggie was shocked to learn that *Maggie Has Had It* had gained a modest readership comprised of at least 3,000 people from all over the United States, two in Australia and one in London, people who seemed enamored by her no-holes-barred commentary on everything from suburban life, TV and politics, to the Red Sox and sex.

The occasionally graphic blog entries, where she complained about her less-than-thrilling sex life, were the most widely read posts. Readers would publish their comments at the bottom of her blog entries saying that it was a relief to read that not everybody was having mind-blowing interludes with their spouses, that the sex recommendations from the women's magazines and daytime talk shows were patronizingly stupid and that Maggie's candor was refreshing. The plaudits her readers showered upon her made Maggie feel as though she was clearly onto something, as if she'd struck a vein of suburban mom commentary that had been left largely untapped. Among her readers' favorite entries in those early months of blogging: Her vivid description of a "Goddess Party" she attended at Diane's house, where a consultant sold "marital aides" (re: sex toys) to giggly thirty- and forty-something moms — including one attendee who asked if the warming, personal lubricant (which Maggie described as feeling like applying an Altoid to one's nether regions) came in a Coors Light flavor, her husband's favorite — and Maggie's brutal dissection of a silly article from a woman's magazine about how to stoke the flames of one's sex life "after the baby."

Maggie had her critics though, fierce and vocal ones, ones who could regularly be counted on to post nasty remarks, telling her that she didn't deserve her husband and that someone "as nasty as this ho" should've been sterilized and "never been allowed to breed." One particularly irate reader told Maggie that she planned to search all over Massachusetts to locate Maggie's "poor husband" and show him what a "good woman" really was after Maggie published a post lamenting the fact that her husband hadn't given her an orgasm in four months:

"I spend weeks on end caring for his two kids, including one still in diapers, with absolutely no help from him at all. I've been out running around to stores searching for the 'perfect' Mother's Day gift for his damned picky mother, when my mother is long gone. I also have had to get ready for a kickass brunch for HIS family, never mind Mother's Day for me. Who the fuck cares about Mother's Day for the mother who's actually in the act of raising kids right now . . . And he hasn't even noticed this small detail that I haven't had an orgasm in 16 weeks? I think it's been six months since I've gotten any oral action

for God's sake. I don't know whether sayin' something will hurt his feelings or make him less likely to do it. This isn't the sort of subject you bring up at the family dinner table. I'm not sure what to do about this. And no, don't suggest lingerie. Tried it. Hasn't worked."

In addition to the stalker who vowed to find Maggie's husband, there had been other angry commenters who called her "dirty and skanky, and probably have junk that smells as shitty as you write" and one who said that Maggie deserved to "choke on that brunch you spoiled little bitch." However for every vitriolic comment, there were two supportive ones from women who told their own tales of sexual frustration and who offered tales on how they overcame them with their husbands. They urged Maggie to hang in there, that once the hands-on work of parenting passed, things would change. Regardless of the Internet "trolls" — a moniker bloggers assigned to people who leveled personal attacks and harassed bloggers — Maggie felt buoyed by the support she received from the online strangers who seemed to understand her and made her feel as if she was part of a community where people didn't BS one another and where people were real, unlike in her real, flesh-and-blood neighborhood where she felt many people were frequently phony. By dumping her visceral angst into the blog entries, Maggie felt detoxified, cleansed of the base, ugly emotions welling up inside her. More often than not, as Maggie's disappointments and feelings of powerlessness mounted, so did the level of animus in her posts. "Better to channel it to the Internet," Maggie said to Diane, justifying her increasingly dark and profanity-laden blog entries, "than toward Michael, who's just as frustrated as me."

"Do ya ever worry though," Diane added, a hint of nervousness lurking in the back of her voice, "that he'd be wicked pissed if he read any of this stuff?"

"Naw," Maggie said, "he doesn't have time to screw around with the Internet. He'd never find it anyway."

CHAPTER TWO

Maggie wrenched her neck at an awkward angle while trying to get a glimpse of the clock sitting on her cluttered nightstand next to a store brand box of tissues, four brown stretched-out elastic hair bands, six dog-eared magazines, two remote controls (TV and DVD player), a bottle of unscented hand lotion and a full cup of water that had been sitting there for a few days and by now likely had a thin layer of dust floating across the surface. The clock read six-twenty-two. "Shit," she said quietly, realizing she'd have to get up soon. One of the kids would inevitably race into the room and demand something — breakfast, TV, a game of Candy Land — at any minute. She rolled over, yanked down her blue cotton tank top that had ridden up on her during the night, and looked at Michael who was still asleep. His hair was sticking out all over his head at odd angles. He kind of resembled one of those troll dolls she used to carry around when she was a kid, the ones with the hair that shot straight up toward the sky and came in shades which Mother Nature never intended, only Michael's hair wasn't as long as the trolls' locks. She could detect a smidgen of his clean-smelling cologne that he'd applied the previous day lingering in his dense chest hair. The scent was filtered through the ripped neckline of his crimson Boston University T-shirt, circa freshman year, 1991. That shirt reminded her of their early dating days when, just months after he graduated from BU, they'd met at ENY. She was happy back then. Michael would take her to BU basketball games, to his favorite college haunts, order micro-brewed beer for the both of them when it was just starting to become a big thing and they'd pretend to be sophisticated urbanites.

Maggie brushed his hair back with her fingertips, as though she were petting a dog, forgetting, just for a moment, that she was still angry with him for blowing her off again. His hair was quasi-prickly from gel, particularly in the front.

"I thought you hated me," Michael said, his eyes still closed. He tried to direct his rancid morning breath away from Maggie, who never seemed to have the same morning breath problems he did upon waking. This was a nagging worry of his, that his bad breath would turn off his wife. It was one of a mountain of fears that he kept to himself.

"I do," she said, edging closer next to him, putting her head on his chest and wishing to pause the world in this very moment. "I'm just directing my loathing into more productive places right now."

"Oh *real-ly*," he replied, eyes still closed as he stretched his right arm out to pull her closer. "What kind of places?"

"Evil, evil places," she said. Maggie awkwardly climbed on top of him, accidentally yanking the red quilt along with her. They watched as it fell to the floor. "You always steal the covers."

"No, YOU do my dear. Then you blame me . . . Hey, why don't you go lock the door?" he asked with a playful glint in his eyes.

Knowing that she would need him to do her a favor for her later — by getting home early so she could get to her Memory Makers house party by 6 p.m. — Maggie agreed to leave their comfortable bed in order to lock their bedroom door so that little people wouldn't suddenly appear at an awkward moment. Pains also had to be made to place pillows and/or blankets along the bottom of the door because small persons in the Kelly family had been known to camp out by the door, lie on the ground and try to peer through the gap between the door and the floor in an attempt to see what was happening inside the locked sanctum. Occasionally, when they grew tired of waiting for their parents to emerge from the room, the children would shove things, one by one, under the door — Legos, slim books, toothbrushes — and then loudly insist that the items be returned, as if their parents had stolen them in the first place. So when Maggie leapt out of bed, she did so very quietly hoping not to wake Jackie, who was a light sleeper. She lifted the door handle slowly, closed the door then pushed the button on the handle to lock it. Spying a basket of clean but wrinkled laundry on the floor next to the door (laundry baskets were *always* there, except when company came over and the baskets were shoved into a closet), Maggie snagged a few towels and spread them out along the narrow gap between the floor and the door, leaving with them the clothing she had on. She jumped back into bed, where Michael had already made fast work of ditching his T-shirt and his green chili pepper boxer shorts which read, "Hot Stuff" across the rear. (Not his style, but it was a Valentine's Day gift from Maggie. What could he do?) Morning interludes were mostly stolen, quick moments, very efficient because time was very limited, unpredictably so. Unfortunately for them, on this morning, their time was more limited than they thought. Maggie was just rounding the bend, about to arrive at her blissful place when Jackie's voice pealed through the door as if she were using a bullhorn, "Maaaa-mmmaaaa! We don't have any more waffles!"

Maggie and Michael exchanged pained looks. "Pretend you don't hear them," Michael said in that low, jagged bedroom voice of his that Maggie adored, as he put Maggie's hands over her own ears so he could get her to finish before he did. The pounding of two sets of little fists upon the bedroom door was followed by what sounded like tiny bodies slamming against the wood. "MAH-MEE, DAD-DEE!" Tommy shouted in such a sing-song voice. Anyone listening could tell he was smiling. "Ihungry! Comeonouddadere!"

"They're holograms," Michael said fruitlessly. "Just background noises. Annoying kids from the Disney Channel."

Disappointment flooded Maggie's chest as she brusquely shoved Michael's hands off of her, and pulled the sweaty sheet across her body. "Damn it! Damn it! Damn it! Damn it!"

Michael kissed her wide face on both sides, right where her high cheekbones made little, round apples, as the children continued to shout various, taunting inanities. "We'll be out in a few minutes, go play in Jackie's room!" Michael called sternly.

"Well," Maggie said, shoving Michael on his back, "this doesn't have to be a total loss."

"No, no, Mags, we don't have to . . . you didn't . . ."

"Shush! No use in us both being frustrated."

A while later, after the kids and Michael had breakfast and Maggie tried to satiate herself with freshly brewed coffee and a slightly stale lemon poppy seed muffin, Michael and Maggie retreated to their bathroom that was drenched in sunlight. Holding her purple coffee mug, Maggie sat on the red counter wearing her now soiled tank top and white daisy patterned "full coverage" briefs while she watched Michael, fresh from the shower, get ready for work. The kids were happily watching Nick Jr. on TV, which bought Maggie and Michael a bit of time to carry on a cogent conversation using full sentences and multi-syllabic words while they were both still lucid and not yet thoroughly irritated by the day's events.

"Now you remember, you need to be HOME, not *leaving* for home, nor thinking about home, but actually over-the-threshold HOME by 5:30 tonight so I can make it to the Linda Sampson's for 6 to set up for the night, right?"

"Yes Mags. I put it into my BlackBerry. It's on my work schedule on the desk top at the office, and I've told the admin staff, Sue specifically, that I'm leaving at 4:30 today. I worked late last night, so it shouldn't be a big deal. I'll just have to bring some work home with me tonight."

"That's fine, I won't be here tonight so I won't be able to

threaten to do naughty things to your BlackBerry until you pay attention to me." She grabbed his bottle of hair gel just as he was going to use it.

"Come on, I've gotta get going."

"No," she said, eluding his grasp by holding the bottle out of his reach. She opened the cap and poured a liberal amount onto her fingers, "*I'm* going to do it."

"That's too much! Too much!" he protested watching her dispense well more than the recommended quarter-size amount of gel into her hands. But he decided to let her do it, seeing that she was smiling and, at least for now, didn't seem annoyed with him. He'd let her mess with his hair, even if it looked bad. It would please her, he thought. Good husbands please their wives. He'd just fix it later at the office if he needed to; she'd never know.

Maggie smiled provocatively and pulled him in between her thighs by the belt of his emerald green bathrobe. Michael was momentarily distracted by the shining spot of gel that she'd left on the bathrobe's belt when she commanded his attention. "Now, let's see, should we go George Clooney from *ER*, the early days?" she asked as she flattened his hair forward against his forehead and fashioned it into a Caesar hairstyle. She laughed as he looked over her shoulders at his reflection in the mirror and slowly shook his head, "No."

"How about Pee-Wee Herman, *before* the unfortunate incident in the movie theater?" she suggested, smoothing his hair down very severely.

"Or," she said in a flirty voice, "we could go Michael Douglas from *Wall Street*, a golden oldie." She slicked his hair back as if he'd been caught in a fierce windstorm of hair gel at the Vidal Sasson factory.

"Greed is good," Michael quipped in a low, gruff stage voice that sounded nothing like Michael Douglas. He grabbed his hairbrush from the counter and, despite his original intention to let Maggie style his hair, he couldn't resist brushing it just so, with the little tuft pointing toward the ceiling in the front, the way he liked it. Maggie watched as he groomed himself, waiting for him to apply the final touch, the subtle cologne that she'd picked out for him for their last anniversary, the one that had a carnal effect on her once it hit his skin, even when she was wildly furious with him.

She leaned in to plant a passionate kiss on his lips but caught only the side of his mouth because, at that same moment, Michael was turning to leave the room. "Please don't forget about tonight," she hollered as she drew the clear, plastic sea horse shower curtain closed behind her, "even if Sam Young or someone else from work calls. It could be a good night for my sales. I could really use a good month of orders right before the school year starts. The summer has been really slow."

"What did I tell you?" Michael asked, poking his head around the shower curtain, kissing her on the bridge of the nose. "You don't have to worry. I'll take care of it."

Maggie wasn't always like this, someone who, when she wasn't weaving intensely revealing tales for the world's consumption, was incongruously spending time in women's homes (and the occasional bland hotel meeting room) peddling heartwarming family scrapbooks and all the various accoutrements to make them pretty, like pens, embossed stickers, decorative papers and tools, like an overpriced stick used to relocate misplaced stickers without ripping the pricey gummy beauties. Following the six-week premature birth of her oldest child and the baby's subsequent one-month stay in the Neonatal Intensive Care Unit, Maggie fully intended to go back to work in Human Resources once Jackie was deemed healthy enough to attend daycare. Maggie had Jackie's spot at the top-notch daycare facility on the same block as ENY in Boston, all lined up having put her name on the daycare's waiting list once she and Michael had seen an image of their baby on an ultrasound mid-way through the pregnancy.

When Jackie was healthy and strong and started daycare, Maggie was able to return to her quirky little corner of the HR department where her desk was covered with funky items like pens with bright fuzzy tops on them and eyes that rattled when you shook the pen, vivid pink paper clips, an array of playful pushpins decorating her corkboard in the shape of flowers, cupcakes and puppy heads, and humorous pictures featuring Bart Simpson. On her first day back at work after having Jackie, Maggie felt like her own person again, not like a milk-making machine covered in crusty spit-up who had to serve at the baby's every beck and call. By 8 months old, Jackie had adjusted beautifully to daycare, was sleeping through the night and frequently laughed in ebullient, infectious bursts which prompted everyone within earshot to respond with smiles and laughter. Only those possessing the coldest of hearts could possibly resist smiling, at least a little bit. Maggie couldn't believe how this whole motherhood thing, of which she'd initially been skeptically resistant, was turning out. She got to have regular lunches with Michael at work where they'd enjoy lively discussions about the Red Sox or the day's news, followed by quality time as a family of three after work. She was beloved by her ENY colleagues who enjoyed her bawdy sense of humor, which she'd frequently deploy over a cup of coffee. Her kooky "welcome" baskets that she would bestow in theatrical fashion upon new hires — which included a book of Dilbert cartoons, chocolates, Red Bull and a coffee mug from the comedically subversive workplace flick *Office Space* — became legendary.

But one unusually cold spring morning altered her perfectly balanced, work-life equation. At about 10:30, just after Maggie had polished off her second cup of java and related a joke she'd heard on *The Simpsons* to her supervisor Francie, she received a call from the daycare center. Jackie had spiked a fever of 104 degrees, and the not-worth-mentioning cough the child had been battling had suddenly mushroomed into a wheezing, dangerous-sounding cough. "You need to bring her to the ER. Now!" Jackie's pediatrician told Maggie during the panicked cell phone call Maggie made while running from her office down the street to fetch her daughter. Jackie had contracted a serious respiratory infection which landed her in the hospital. Maggie took a temporary leave of absence from work and spent weeks driving the 45-minute commute from the new house they'd just bought in Greenville to the hospital in downtown Boston, spending every day with her child, praying to God that she'd regain her health. Maggie became peaked, sported unsightly bags under her eyes and shed 15 pounds from worry. Maggie just drank coffee, sucked on breath mints and stared at her sickly baby. At night, when Maggie couldn't sleep in the quiet house, she sat in the nursery and stared at the empty crib. After nearly a month, Jackie, although still relatively weak, came home.

"Jackie can't be exposed to the germs and colds that fester in daycare centers," Michael said before dinner a week after Jackie had been released from the hospital. Wine, lots of it, could only help him make his case. He could hear his mother Dorothy's words, reinforced by the daily conversations he had with her on his cell phone while he was driving home from work — ricocheting around inside his head like a small, bouncy Super Ball. ("Michael, that child cannot go back to daycare. Absolutely not! It probably caused her to be sick in the first place. She was already so delicate when Margaret stuck her in there at 12 weeks old," Dorothy audibly sighed, "given that she was premature and all. She was such a tiny baby, Michael. She's still so delicate. You have to convince Margaret that she needs to do something else, work part-time, be at home. Jacqueline needs to be cared for by family, like you and Joseph were, with Nana Sophie while I was working, not some stranger who doesn't wash her hands, surrounded by babies and toddlers whose mothers stick them in daycare when they're already sick, and then those women just bolt from the building. I see that all the time at the school. Parents send their kids to class even when a blind man could see that the children are sick, just so the work-a-holics can get in a few hours worth of work before school nurses like me have to call them and ask them to take their sick children home. They're not fooling anyone.")

Michael placed his hand over Maggie's warm, thick fingers and started to massage them. "I know that you . . ." he started to say softly, in that breathy way he had of speaking, which people sometimes thought sounded as if Michael was talking down to them, patronizing them, or that he was slightly congested.

"I get it! I know what you're gonna say!" Maggie snapped, yanking her hand away, whipping her head to the side to face the window overlooking their wooded, picturesque backyard. She grabbed the glass of wine, still refusing to look in Michael's direction, and filled her mouth with the ruby colored liquid, trying to remember if she'd eaten dinner or not. Most likely not. Wine was her dinner. From her chair, Maggie started to really look around at their house. It was a far cry from the tiny, rented, studio apartment in Boston's South End that they'd lived in before. This house, in a relatively new subdivision in a sleepy yet growing suburb, had three decent-sized bedrooms and a large family room with a wood burning fireplace that she adored. Their neighborhood was teeming with very young children and their at-home moms. And here he was, the man with whom she fell in love while working at a job she loved, asking her (without directly asking her, as was his passive-aggressive wont in such touchy situations) to join the ranks of the non-working Maple Road mommies. She doubted that her income would cover the cost of an in-home nanny. If she looked at the economics of what she knew Michael was going to propose, she thought they *could* make it on Michael's salary if she left her job, only *temporarily* she thought, though she'd have to be a little more careful about what she bought at the grocery store. When Maggie and Michael bought the house, Michael suggested that they use his income to determine if they could handle the mortgage payments and still live comfortably without having to scrimp. His income was the only one listed on the loan application. "Was this his plan all along?" Maggie wondered as she took another sip of the spicy wine trying to figure out how long she'd need to spend at home until she returned to ENY.

Michael had wanted to avoid this conversation and, in fact, never thought he'd have to have it. He loved that Maggie worked. She was confident and sexy when she was at ENY. She wore stylish shoes and told stories which made everyone laugh. She was the one whose opinion everyone wanted to hear when something weird happened on the latest install-ment of *Survivor*. And now here he was trying to persuade his wife to give up her job, and the time they spent together during lunch hours, and stay home with their baby. He felt like Fred Flintstone. All he was missing was Fred's oversized club and a leopard-skin dress. When Maggie was pregnant, Michael had wholly bought into the idea that they could make it all work, that they could both have flourishing careers and have a happy home life, until Jackie got sick. That was the game changer. The moment he saw his fair-skinned, dark-haired baby daughter hooked up to IV lines, oxygen and heart monitors was the moment he decided, in his heart, that things could no longer remain the same. Jackie shouldn't go back to daycare, he thought. If his mother was retired, he would've suggested having her watch the baby, even though Maggie would've erupted at the mere thought of having her mother-in-law in the house every day. But since his mother wasn't retired, that wasn't in the cards. The only realistic option he could think of to keep his baby safe was for Maggie, who made laughably less money than he did, to stay home with Jackie.

"This wouldn't be forever," he said. "Jackie will become stronger. And you'll be able to go back to ENY. Maybe when

Jackie's, say, in preschool. Don't they start at around 3 or 4?"

Maggie glared at him. Her brownie-colored eyes — which everyone agreed were her most striking feature — burned. Michael folded his hands on their hand-me-down kitchen table and looked waiflike. "There," Maggie thought, "is a sweet guy, who rarely asks for anything, puts up with my moods, finds *me* and my flat, frying pan face attractive."

"I can't just 'be home' you know, like those chicks down the street, doing Pilates and baking homemade bread," she began, as Michael nodded in frantic agreement, trying not to overplay his hand. "I'm going to have to do something else. Some work. Something with a paycheck, maybe something from home, or something I can do when you're at home. I cannot let it become like it was when I was back at home pretending to be my mom and had no life. We're not going to repeat that. I won't do it."

"No, no, no," Michael said, softly grabbing her by the shoulders and folding her into his firm embrace, "it won't be like that. Whatever you want. We'll find sitters or have my mom help out to save some cash . . ."

"Dorothy?!" Maggie said, her body noticeably stiffening.

"Come on Mags, I don't mean all the time, but just so we know Jackie's cared for and safe, and so you can get you to your . . . your . . . I don't know . . . your part-time work or whatever you wind up doing done. We can use her as a means to an end." He knew that his mother, who was a natural with children, would leap at the chance to look after Jackie in the after-school hours. By giving Dorothy more access to Jackie, she would see for herself that Maggie wasn't the "no class, completely selfish mother" she believed her daughter-in-law to be, an opinion which she shared with her eldest son on occasion. He and Maggie would find a babysitter, Michael was certain. He just had to get Maggie to agree to stay home.

A month after that conversation Maggie left ENY for good. She never went back, though that wasn't her original intent when she told Francie she would call her when Jackie was ready for preschool. Years later, Maggie kept thinking about that cheesy 1990s George Michael song "Freedom" over and over as she drove to Enrollment Day at the preschool she'd picked for Jackie. Maggie planned on calling Francie as soon as she got her hands on the preschool calendar to schedule her return to the world of working adults. But upon entering the gymnasium where the school administrators and faculty were processing the preschool students' paperwork as well as meeting the students and parents, Maggie found herself overwhelmed by nausea. She vomited in the trash can right next to the "Welcome Preschool Families!" sign, no doubt impressing the staff and new preschool moms with her retching skills. Maggie wrote the incident off as the penalty for eating some sliced roast beef beyond a reasonable period of freshness. "How long ago did I buy that roast beef? Two weeks?" she asked herself while dabbing the corners of her mouth with a dampened, rough paper towel, the cheap, gray industrial kind she found in the school bathroom adjacent to the gym. Maggie was apt to eat anything in the fridge even if it had been sitting around for who knows how long because, "You just can't waste it!" she'd lecture Michael, who was a by-the-books toss-leftovers-after-24-hours kind of guy. "You never grew up in a house where we couldn't afford to throw stuff out."

Ten days after preschool registration, Maggie continued to find herself scrambling for any available wastebasket or toilet to vomit, prompting Michael to ask one night, after the odor of lasagna made her sick, "You sure you're not pregnant? When was your last period?"

Denial, at least for Maggie, was a potent drug. She had not even allowed herself to let the mere glimmer of the possibility that she might be pregnant enter her mind even though it made all the sense in the world. "Shut up! It's not *that* you moron!" Pregnancy would mean she likely wouldn't be going back to ENY any time soon. There was no way she'd be able to persuade Michael to put another baby into daycare. She'd be stuck in mommy hell. She wouldn't get her exit Visa for another four years, minimum.

"You didn't answer me. When was your period?"

Anxiety clutched her around the back of her neck as nausea grabbed at her stomach. Maggie only had a rough idea of when her period was supposed to arrive, although she was pretty sure it was supposed to have arrived already. Failing to remember something like the date of your last period — something on which mature, adult women of reproductive age are supposed to keep tabs —would make her look and feel foolish in front of Michael, who meticulously recorded practically everything in his ubiquitous BlackBerry. For all she knew, he could've inputted the date of her last period in the BlackBerry's calendar. "It's not *that*," she repeated, unconvincingly, as though if she kept repeating it, she could make it be true.

The more Michael thought about the possibility of a new baby — maybe a boy! — the more excited and hopeful he became. Though Maggie had made it clear that she didn't want any more children — four months earlier, she had started sending Michael e-mails about how quickly and simply a vasectomy could be done, complete with illustrations from medical web sites (which didn't help convince Michael) — Michael was certain he did indeed want more children. He just hadn't figured out exactly what he needed to say and do in order to successfully wage his campaign for baby number two. Skilled at crafting arguments bolstered by research and political spin like he routinely did professionally when talking about potential new developments in front of licensing boards and mobs of annoyed citizens, Michael envisioned staging a series of subtle discussions over the course of a few months, culminating with Maggie coming to the conclusion that having another baby was her idea.

The morning after Maggie regurgitated the lasagna she'd attempted to eat, Michael had gotten up early, left a voice mail at work saying he'd be late, dashed to Dunkin' Donuts where he bought Maggie's favorite (a jelly doughnut), along with a big iced coffee with cream and two sugars (it was decaf, but he wasn't going to tell her that) and a couple of jelly doughnut holes for Jackie. He also picked up a pregnancy test at the drug store next door to the doughnut shop, which he nonchalantly placed on the kitchen counter next to the white wax paper sack containing the highly-caloric goodness.

Jackie heard Michael bustling about in the kitchen and squealed upon seeing the pink and orange doughnut shop logo on the bag which promptly woke Maggie, whose mouth felt dry and tasted nasty. Throwing on her ancient gray, oversized Framingham State College hooded sweatshirt over her black T-shirt, she pulled on a pair of black yoga pants (she never took yoga a day in her life) and trudged down to the kitchen to find out why Michael hadn't left for work yet.

"Jesus Michael!" Maggie said when she spotted the test. Defiantly, she stuffed nearly half of her jelly doughnut into her mouth. Powdered sugar coated her lips and the tip of her nose. Loudly slurping some coffee to wash down the doughnut, she dug her fingernails into the test, grabbed the box and stomped off to the downstairs bathroom.

"Jackie-Jay," Michael cooed to his daughter as he picked her up, twirled her around in his arms and kissed one of her plump cheeks, which, like her mother, also wore a thin layer of powdered sugar, "would you like to be a big sister?"

The girl, her thin bob haircut curling around her face providing a parenthetical frame, smiled. "I lika be a big sistah," she said, nodding affirmatively.

"Good!"

Maggie returned to the kitchen 10 minutes later. She walked over to the block of fancy knives — an ironic wedding gift from her in-laws — pulled out a serrated bread knife and pretended to plunge it into her gut, then melodramatically fell to the floor with a loud, uneven thud. She capped it off with overly-theatrical gurgling.

"Mama okay?" Jackie asked, panic creeping into her squeaky voice. She wriggled out of her father's arms and crawled over to her mother's side.

Michael laughed and joined his girls on the floor, an irrepressible, silly grin on his face. He rolled over and gave Maggie a cartoonishly loud kiss and awkwardly threw his arm across her waist. "I love you," he said. "And you have no idea how happy this is going to make everyone. Right Jackie? She just told me she wants to be a big sister."

Jackie, her Pull-Up diaper emitting a crinkling sound as she rolled from Maggie's side to Michael's, chirped, "Dis is fun. Can we have bwefis here?"

Michael grew giddy as he sprawled out in the middle of the floor amidst the crumbs and clumps of dust, of which, remarkably, he didn't take note. Jackie sloppily fed him doughnut holes. Maggie just lay there in a faux catatonic state. Michael couldn't stop himself from kissing Maggie and Jackie, each in turn until Maggie unexpectedly sat up, put her hand over her mouth and ran to the bathroom again. "Did you have an onion bagel or something?" she yelled through the open door after she threw up the jelly doughnut. "Uck. You can't eat any onions until this crap is over!"

CHAPTER THREE

Michael was stuck in a snarled mass of idling vehicles trying to make his way home from yet another in a long series of site visits to the small town of Westbrook, population 5,000. He had trekked through a wetlands area called "The Cove," one of the many swampy tracts of land through which state officials wanted to situate a proposed highway called the Central Mass Bypass, a pet project of the governor's on which ENY's traffic and environmental pros had been contracted to work. Summoned to Westbrook by members of the local Conservation Commission who wanted to show him all manner of fowl, small mammals and plants whose existence would allegedly be disrupted if ENY's design was approved, Michael wasted hours standing in muck and feeling ridiculous because he was ill-prepared to be making a site visit. Sure, he was in his tan, tattered work boots that he kept in his car trunk, but he was also wearing a dark brown suit, white shirt with the cuff links (a gift from his mother) and a textured terra cotta colored tie. He was swarmed by mosquitoes who, like Maggie, were drawn to his cologne and copious amount of hair gel. (Had he known he'd be walking through this before he left for work, he would've skipped the cologne.) Michael had arrived at the Westbrook Town Hall at noon, as he'd been requested to do, but one of those annoying, brief summer thunderstorms had moved into the area bringing with it a torrent of tepid water. The two Conservation Commissioners, who acted like they had a combined age of about 247, insisted that all three of them sit around in the Westbrook Planning Office and "shoot the shit" until the rain passed. Two hours later when the rain finally ceased, they drove to the site in Michael's teal, hyper-tidy Honda Accord, at Michael's insistence, convinced that it would take the glacially slow moving Bud Collins and Hank Monroe too long to drive there and back. However Michael wound up being trapped at the site when Bud and Hank demanded extra time to thoroughly examine a thorny section of underbrush where Bud insisted that he had spied an insect that he hadn't seen in this particular swamp area before and he absolutely refused to leave until he collected a sample. It took diligent persuading to get the commissioners to leave the site. They didn't have wives at home waiting for them to relieve them from child caring duty. In fact their wives wanted them out of the house and busy for as long as possible, so the men didn't feel the urge to hurry.

It was 4:45 when Michael pulled out of the Westbrook Town Hall parking lot. Almost as soon as he got onto the highway to race home, and hopefully avoid a speeding ticket, he found himself in a mammoth traffic jam that the radio reporter said wouldn't end any time soon because a truck filled with mangoes had overturned, prompting local talk show hosts to crack wise with all manner of tropical fruit jokes, most of which were pretty bad. "If I don't get home on time for the fourth night in a row, she will kill me," Michael thought, ticked off that no matter how hard he seemed to try, he always wound up looking like an uncaring jackass in his wife's eyes. If he called to tell her that he was going to be late, she'd just breathe fire through the phone and he didn't relish getting screamed at while suffering through miles and miles of bumper-to-bumper traffic where he had to look at the back of a dirty yellow, rusty hatchback with a peeling anti-President Bush bumper sticker on the trunk. "Best to delay *that* for as long as possible," he said quietly. "Nothin' I can do about it now."

He slouched, dejected, in the seat and listened to the traffic report on the radio:

"*. . . and if you're on the Mass Pike, you'd better sit back and enjoy this newscast because you aren't going ANYWHERE, not for a while anyway. That mango truck turnover has now caused rubber neck delays in both directions of at least 15 miles as state police have closed off all but one lane of westbound traffic. For those traveling in the north-south direction on I-495 and Route 93, it's clear sailing for this last week of summer . . .*"

"North-south is clear," Michael repeated aloud. He grabbed his cell phone and quickly dialed his mother hoping maybe she could zip down to his house and watch the kids for Michael until he got there so Maggie could get to her Memory Makers event on time.

"Hello."

"Mom! Whew! Glad you're there."

"Michael? You're calling a little early today. Did you leave work early? Is everything all right?"

"Yeah, everything's okay Mom. It's just that I promised Maggie I'd be home by 5:30 so she could run a Memory Makers home party in Stockton, but there's no way I'm gonna make it home on time. Any chance you're free and could watch the kids for a while until I get home? I'm stuck on the Pike."

"Behind that mango truck spill?"

"Yeah, isn't that bizarre? A truck full of mangoes."

Dorothy glanced at the wooden clock on the wall, the one that Frank had made 10 years ago. "I can do it. No problem. I'll be there. Now don't stress out Michael. You've been working so late these past few nights. Take your time getting home. Stop off somewhere. Get out of that traffic. Grab something to eat. I'll watch Jackie and Tommy, give them a bath, read them a bedtime story and put them to bed. Don't you worry."

"Mom, thanks," Michael said. His shoulder muscles slackened a tad. "You're a lifesaver. Call you later."

Tossing his BlackBerry onto the passenger seat — where

it landed on top of several rolls of plans — Michael turned up the AC, turned off the news radio station and put in one of his classic rock mix CDs and unwound for the first time since the coitus-interruptus this morning, allowing the cool air and the music wash over him. He'd have to make up for the interruption with Maggie later tonight. If she did well at her home party and sold more products than at her last scrap-booking party, she'd be in a good mood. And the kids would be in bed. Asleep. Maybe he'd even pick up a bottle of wine now that he had time.

At that same moment in Greenville, Maggie had given up on tidying the living room. It was covered by a sprawling Tinker Toy, Mega-Block and Lego "city" (a metropolis which looked as though it'd been designed by a madman with a death wish) that she and the kids had built that afternoon. She'd also abandoned dinner prep when she couldn't decide on a meal that both Jackie and Tommy would willingly eat without her pinning them down and force-feeding them. They had pasta yesterday. There was no more peanut butter in the house. They were out of milk, so they couldn't have cereal, but then again, Maggie thought, they'd had Cheerios for lunch. "Michael will be here soon, he can deal with it," she thought. Instead, she concentrated on getting herself ready, curling and brushing her shoulder-length hair, the color of black coffee, which had absolutely no body or curves of its own, just like Maggie's body. She opted to wear her hair down for a change instead of up in a ponytail secured by a plain brown elastic band, the kind which she bought in bulk at BJs because her thick mane frequently strained the bands to the point that they snapped. Carefully framing her hair around her face and then coating it liberally with hairspray so the curled ends would keep their shape, she then spent a lot of time applying a new plum eye color she'd picked up at Stop & Shop while grocery shopping the other day, hoping it would accentuate her wide-set eyes when she enthusiastically raised her eyebrows during her presentation.

"It's simple, *really*, so easy to preserve your family's memories in a way that's so totally personal," she said, practicing her spiel in front of the bathroom mirror while applying a second coat of mascara. Maggie was big on second or third coats of everything, hairspray, mascara, paint, nail polish, cake frosting. "I mean, come on, *look* at me." She unleashed her inner Vanna White and drew both her hands to her chest as she scrunched up her shoulders, then slowly unfurled her arms and moved her hands along the front of her body, hovering just above the surface not touching her off-white terry cloth robe that had long ago lost its suppleness and was now actually a bit scratchy, its pockets filled with used tissues and crumpled Dora the Explorer Band Aids. "I'm not a real craft-making kinda mom who always does everything perfect. I'm just jealous of those who are. When I left my house tonight, I wondered if the EPA would declare it some kinda waste site. I'm kind of a piss-poor housekeeper." Maggie paused and counted to three in her head, approximately about the amount of time she hoped the women would laugh at her self-deprecating joke. "No really," she paused again, but this time, only for about one beat. "My kids had cereal for lunch. And they might have even had it again for dinner tonight, except there's no more milk in the house. I still haven't bought all the 87 bazillion things on my daughter's first grade class supply list and school starts on Wednesday. I don't have a backpack for my little boy's first day of preschool. So if *I* can make a scrapbook for *my* family, so can you. It's simple. I try to scrap once a month, usually on a weekend afternoon when my husband Michael takes the kids to see his parents — a great way to get out of going to the in-laws' by the way, while you're" she made air quotes with her index and middle fingers "'preserving memories.' I spread everything out in the living room, put on some On Demand shows on TV and knock off a bunch of pages. I make sure to write 'Scrapbooking' on the calendar each month. In ink. And I tell my husband it's non-negotiable."

Maggie stepped back from the mirror and smiled at her reflection. Her "I'm-a-slacker-mom-who-scrapbooks" attitude generally went over well, particularly after the moms had been mildly liquored up with wine and sated with rich brownies and cheesecake, all of which she planned on buying en route to Linda's house. Guilt about potentially losing one's family's memories by leaving photos languishing in shoeboxes, coupled with Maggie's low-pressure salesmanship, made her a natural. She skillfully soft-peddled the guilt, knowing that, in fact, it was guilt that prompted people to buy products from her, even if the moms never cracked open the scrapbook material once they got home. Another plus in Maggie's favor was that other mothers didn't tend to perceive her as some kind of threatening Super Mom archetype like many of the other women who typically ran home parties selling things like cookware, candles, books or makeup. Maggie usually wore the same type of clothing to all her scrapbooking sales pitches: Low-rise jeans (paired with powerful underwear that kept her pregnancy-stretched abdomen in check), a pair of clunky high-heeled shoes and a fitted, long T-shirt that dipped two inches below her jeans' waistband so no one would spot her stretch marks or Spanx. She favored shirts that featured sarcastic sayings like, "You Didn't Marry Your Mother," "Mommy Needs a Time-Out" and "A Comedy of Errors, Otherwise Known as My Life." She was the gal from the 'burbs with whom you could drink few cocktails, tell dirty jokes AND scrapbook. When she finished primping, the look she projected was one of casual indifference, though that casualness took more work for Maggie to pull off than she was willing to muster on a daily basis, when she opted for loose-fitting tops and high-waisted pants that didn't require special, uncomfortable underwear designed by NASA.

The Kelly front doorbell chimed at 5:35. "Why is he ringing the bell?" Maggie muttered. She raced down the bare wooden stairs, leaving the kids behind in her bedroom where they were now watching *Sesame Street*. They'd made a little fort on her bed out of toss pillows and throw blankets and were peering at the TV through a narrow opening. Maggie was unprepared to find Dorothy at her door bending over on the front stoop checking out the faded "Welcome" mat while slightly wrinkling her brow.

"Mom Kelly . . ." Maggie said slowly. "Were you in the neighborhood? Uh . . . oh . . . come in, come in."

Dorothy read Maggie's T-shirt — "Stop Whining & Make Your Own Freakin' Dinner!" — and rolled her eyes. "Is that really appropriate for a mother of two young children?" she thought as she walked into the house and felt as though she'd walked into a cloud of stale, noxious-smelling . . . *something*. "Michael hasn't called you yet?" Dorothy said as she tried to discretely put her hand over her mouth so she wouldn't gag, wondering if soiled diapers were responsible for the pungent smell. She planned on pinpointing the odor's source as soon as Maggie left.

"Huh?" Maggie mumbled, confused, as the phone rang.

"That must be him," Dorothy said as she moved deeper into the house. "I told him to relax because I'd take care of everything. He probably pulled off the highway to get a Starbucks. That mango truck. Terrible." Dorothy tried not to visibly flinch as she walked into the kitchen and saw that the sink was positively overflowing with dirty dishes, cups, plastic spoons and Cheerios. Wads of multi-colored Play-Doh, along with dried out Play-Doh crumbs were scattered across the kitchen table. The kids' "city" of toy blocks and plastic building material covered the floor all the way from the dining area in the kitchen to the living room.

Momentarily stunned, Maggie was still holding the door open as the words "mango truck" lingered in the air. "What is Dorothy doing here?" she wondered, staring at the woman whom she viewed as militant when it came to housekeeping, with standards Maggie had always found incredibly high. The phone was on its third ring and Maggie still hadn't moved.

"Margaret, the phone," Dorothy said sternly as she rolled

up the sleeves of her pale yellow blouse and got to work on the dishes.

The answering machine on the desk in the kitchen picked up the call and Michael's voice echoed while Maggie hunted around for the second handset, the other having been rendered a heap of barely functioning plastic and wires courtesy of her tantrum the previous day.

"Hey . . . hey, Michael, I'm here," Maggie said, hearing the sound of her own voice accompanied by loud static coming out of the answering machine as she got too close to it with the handset, which she'd located in the kids' Lego "jail." She turned the machine off and ran up the stairs, two steps at a time, and darted into Jackie's empty bedroom so she could speak privately with her husband.

"Why is your mother here? Where are you?" she whispered roughly.

"Didn't she tell you?"

"What do you mean didn't 'she' tell me? You're the one who's supposed to be walking through our front door right now, not HER. I get no call, no warning and then she's there. Walks right in. You knew an hour ago, 40 minutes ago even, that you wouldn't be walking through the door on time, why are you just calling me NOW? The house is a complete wreck. I could've used some warning. We've got NOTHING, do you hear me, NOTHING good for the kids to eat. If I'd known she was coming I would've at least run out to get some milk."

Disappointed, Michael put his half-empty venti Starbucks latte down next to the copy of the day's *Boston Journal* that he'd just finished reading. Most of the time, the *Journals* spent the day inside his briefcase, with the idea that Michael would read the paper later, but "later" rarely came. Yes, he could've phoned Maggie right after he spoken with Dorothy; he knew that. But he *did* arrange for child care. The kids would be fine. Maggie could still go out. Her work could proceed. He didn't see what the big deal was. He just wanted a moment or two to himself. It's been a shitty couple of days, he thought, and he was exhausted from the late nights, not that Maggie cared about things like that anymore.

"Look, she's going to feed the kids and put 'em to bed. I got delayed in Westbrook with those geezer Conservation guys who wanted to walk through the wetlands all afternoon. For the third time. Plus they insisted on looking at some predatory beetles or something like that, that they found and think are new to the area. It's all good."

"No!" she said, retreating into Jackie's closet, climbing on top of pile of junk including a pair of green plastic rain boots that still had that new boot smell, assorted mismatched pink and purple socks, a menagerie of stuffed animals and the *Green Eggs & Ham* book Maggie had been looking for the other day. "It's not 'all good.' We've got no food. The kids are covered in crap, Play-Doh, maple syrup and I have to leave. If I'd known she was coming over, I could've been at least a little prepared. I don't need to give her another reason to think that I'm a knucklehead who's not good enough for her son. If you'd just given me some notice . . ."

"Mags, really, it's fine. Don't be so hard on yourself. You're making a federal case out of nothing. Forget about trying to please her. Have a kick-ass party tonight. Sell lotsa stuff and I'll see you when you get home. No rush though. Enjoy yourself. 'Kay?"

"ARGH!" was her reply as she hung up the phone, wishing the gesture could've been more dramatic like in the days when everyone rented those solid, rotary phones from the phone company. You could make a thunderous statement when you slammed down one of those receivers. THAT was hanging up on someone. Pressing a little "off" button that emitted a soft "beep," no matter how hard you hit the button, just didn't have the same panache.

SURPRISE VISIT FROM THE TORTURER-IN-CHIEF
File under: My MIL should work in Guantanamo Bay

So I was getting ready for a big Memory Makers home party (made a good chunk o'sales wouldn't ya know, diva of sales that I am). The Wannabe-King was supposed to be home on time for a change so that I could go out and earn some of my own money. He promised. And at the exact moment The Wannabe-King was supposed to be home who walked through my front door? The Torturer-in-Chief, the MIL. The Wannabe-King had called her. He, I later learned, was busying himself with majorly important work like, I dunno, chillin' at Starbucks and eating espresso brownies, flirting with the cute baristas, swingin' his thing around . . . whatever . . . meanwhile I was scraping kid-shit off of me so I could look halfway decent before I was given a day pass out of Alcatraz. He's got it damned tough, or so the Torturer-in-Chief informed me after berating me about the condition of my house. (She was right, as much as I hate to admit it. The house was a foul dump when she got there, but in my defense, I didn't know she was coming over. I would've picked up if I'd known her arrival was imminent.)

"He works hard MARGARET," the Torturer-in-Chief said, refusing, yet again, to call me by my name of choice. Maybe I should start calling her by a name I select for her for a change. Maybe, Stalin? Mussolini? Maybe I should have a naming contest . . .

What gross violations of privacy did the Torturer-in-Chief (also known as The Wannabe-King's Excuse-Maker-in-Chief) bestow upon yours truly, the cost of trying to have a life outside of my home? She threw out a bunch of leftovers and other stuff we had in the fridge — a lot of sauces and stuff which I adore — with no explanation. AGAIN! (Yes, I've complained about this before. I've even asked her to stop doing this but she doesn't give a fuck what I think, about my own house.) The plastic containers of the duck and hoisin sauces and hot mustard that came with our Chinese take-out a few days ago were in the garbage this morning, (I recycle those containers, yo!) along with a half-empty container of Betty Crocker vanilla frosting, in the kitchen trash can. (Who doesn't like to eat frosting from the container, I ask you?) I know she hates that I have that canned frosting in the house because she once yelled at me that it's "loaded with chemicals! Have you read the label? Just make your own you lazy ass daughter-in-law! It's much better for the kids" when I was putting the finishing touches on cupcakes for Thing II's birthday. Okay, she didn't call me a "lazy ass," but the sanctimonious bitch said the rest of it. Oh, and my half-eaten hot fudge sundae from Friendly's that was in the freezer also got the boot into the trash.

She did a couple of loads of laundry and left the clothing neatly folded piles in everyone's bedrooms. I found a couple of my and The Wannabe-King's older pairs of underwear in the trash next to the duck sauce and my melted sundae. And what did I happen to leave in the washing machine when I left the house, you ask? My thong underwear. The one and only thong I own. And SHE had to see the garment. Handle it. Excellent. When I realized what she'd done, touched the thong underwear (and put them on TOP of my clean laundry pile like some kind of exclamation point), I burned it. Literally. No lie. Out in the driveway after The Wannabe-King was asleep last night. Had a chilled bottle of beer while I watched the black fabric disintegrate. (It smelled pretty nasty when it burned. Ick. That photo above, that's what remains of the thong.) The Wannabe-King who never has to do any cleaning, cooking, shopping or child care, of course, saw absolutely no problems with his mom's behavior, "She's just helping us. She's family. We don't have to hide anything. Just be yourself." But I could never again wear that particular pair of under-pants knowing she'd touched them, because, after all, I only wear them when I'm trying to entice The Wannabe-King. I knew that if I'd kept the thong, the next time I put it on, instead of thinking about doing my husband, I'd be thinking about the fact that the Torturer-in-Chief had folded the underwear, then there'd be no carnal relations.

This morning, the morning after the invasion of the Torturer-in-Chief, after The Wannabe-King left for work — he swore he'd be home early tonight (I'm not holding my breath), the Friday before Labor Day weekend — I asked Thing I and Thing II what their Nana had done with them when I was out. They were all excited to tell me that they baked oatmeal cookies together and that, according to the 3-year-old, "Nanny said we should tell Mama to clean the house more because it's good 'en healfie for us." "Oh," added the 6-year-old, "she said we need more fruit."

On top of all of this, before the Torturer-in-Chief even arrived, I'd been promised by the Wannabe-King that I was gonna get some after I got home from my Memory Makers event, but the mere fact that the woman had inhabited every room in the house, including the bedroom, sucked all the oomph out of me. She's like a negative force field, that woman. The human equivalent of Salt Peter. (For those who don't know what that is, look it up HERE by clicking on this link.) Maybe her presence doesn't make The Wannabe-King lose his sex mojo (which raises all sorts of uncomfortable Freudian questions itself), but she sure as hell kills mine . . . for at least a few days, until I can wipe down every surface that the judgmental hands have touched and the kids stop parroting her words.

Now about that contest idea: I'm getting a little sick of calling my MIL "Torturer-in-Chief." It doesn't really roll off the tongue. I need a clever new nickname for her. So I'm opening it up to all of you. Please post your suggestions in the comments section below. Be as nasty as you want. I will mail the winner of the snarkiest nickname — as selected by me, of course — my unused gift certificate for merchandise that's peddled by that bitchy Queen Bee and her perky little you-can-clean-too-you-stupid-ass-wipe sayings that try to make cleaning look easy and fun. Which, it isn't. On either count. You're not fooling anyone Queen Bee. Cleaning sucks. Annnywaay, the Torturer-in-Chief gave me that gift certificate for my birthday and I'll be damned if I'm going to use it. All the better to give it away to the person who's most willing to mock the Torture-in-Chief.

If you need a recap to help jog your memory about previous Torturer-in-Chief stories (and to count yourself lucky that she's not YOUR mother-in-law), you can look under all of the previous "My MIL should work in Guantanamo Bay" blog posts I've written since Maggie Has Had It began (link to the entries is HERE). Now, let's get creative, shall we?

CHAPTER FOUR

Michael absolutely hated it, when Maggie put him in the middle between her and his mother. Although at first glance, he was willing to admit that Dorothy could look somewhat severe to some people. She wore her shiny silver hair in a chin-length bob with razor sharp bangs which went straight across her forehead just grazing Dorothy's eyebrows. The sharpness was accentuated by a short nose that came to a narrow point, like a bird's beak. But to Michael she was all radiance and rounded corners, full of the best intentions, the women who loved him unconditionally, frequently telling him how he was "one of the best things that ever happened" to her. As far as Michael was concerned, Dorothy was motivated solely by her boundless affection for him and her fierce overprotective nature. Although he knew his mother wasn't exactly Maggie's biggest fan and said critical things about his wife, everything Dorothy did came directly from her heart, Michael believed. Her ultimate goal: To assure his happiness, not to be indiscriminately cruel, as Maggie claimed. She just wanted to help, Michael thought, acknowledging that Maggie could use a little help in the people skills department.

"That girl had no mother around to raise her right," Dorothy said six months into Michael and Maggie's relationship. "Her father wasn't really there, was too 'busy' working at the DPW. Her brother too. He didn't even go to college, just like his father. She's surrounded by men, boys really, who do nothing but drink beer out of the can and smoke and watch sports on TV. And she's just like them, and she blabbers out the most inappropriate things. She says all kinds of things that she shouldn't, private things that she has no business talking about, like making fun of you during Mother's Day and how your card was so sweet, or when she told us she couldn't eat my salmon casserole because it gave her gas. She said that in front of my sister. That girl has no social graces and no idea of what boundaries are. Oh, and did you see what she brought to our family Fourth of July barbecue? Ritz crackers in the box with the price tag still on it and a block of cheese still in the plastic wrapper. Just plopped it down and said, 'Here ya go.' No serving utensils, no plate, no platter, nothing. Who *does* that? If ever anyone needed a mother, it's this girl."

Despite Dorothy's vigorous lobbying efforts, Maggie and Michael continued to grow closer. Dorothy had once secretly hoped that, as a kind of tribute to her, her sons would've found wives who were more like her and could serve as substitutes for the daughters she never had, pals with whom she'd be able to swap recipes and gardening tips and chat with about old, sappy movies of which her husband and sons made fun. However when it became clear that no matter what she said, Michael was irretrievably besotted with "that Margaret Finn," Dorothy decided it wouldn't be wise to create a permanent wedge between herself and the only son who cared enough to live close to her. (Her youngest son Joseph had moved out of the area the first chance he got. After graduating from Boston University like his older brother, Joseph moved to upstate New York and rarely called home or visited. It was an unhealed, festering sore spot for Dorothy, who viewed it as a public and personal rebuke. And if there was one thing Dorothy hated, it was being embarrassed, like when her neighbor Shirley asked at the neighborhood block party last summer in the middle of a group of people when Joseph had last been home for a visit, knowing full well that he hadn't been home for over a year because Dorothy, in a moment of weakness, had confessed that information to her that the week before. "She asked about Joseph just to humiliate me!" she angrily complained to her husband Frank later, vowing to neither forgive nor forget Shirley's transgression.

When Michael and Maggie eventually announced their engagement, Dorothy opted to make the best out of things and tried to pull a *My Fair Lady*. "I'm going to mold Margaret into a good wife, even if it kills me," she informed her colleagues at Franklin Middle School in Norton, New Hampshire where she'd been the school nurse for decades. Thus, shortly after Michael and Maggie were wed, Dorothy commenced her crusade which her husband had code-named, "Mission: Maggie." Dorothy, who adored cooking, tried to teach and encourage her new daughter-in-law in the fine art of culinary excellence. She would e-mail Maggie themed, "quick and easy" menus from cooking web sites. She also mailed Maggie actual recipe cards, decorated with little cooking mice donning quaint aprons, detailing how to prepare some of Michael's favorite dishes, always accompanied by cheerful words of encouragement written on Dorothy's signature stationery — heavy stock, crisp white paper with an image of ivy climbing along the left-hand margin. "This recipe is so easy!" Dorothy would write. "It was Michael's favorite when he was a growing boy. I'll bet it'll become one of your favorites too." If she was sharing a recipe with Maggie that she'd never tried before, Dorothy would try to make it a game, writing, "The recipe says it only take 30 minutes to prepare. Let me know how it works out. I'll make it this week too and we can compare stories!" The Sunday afternoon after Maggie had received a recipe packet in the mail, Dorothy would call to see how Maggie's recipe turned out. Maggie would see "Dorothy and Frank" pop up on the Caller ID and back away from the phone as though it was radioactive and either let it go to voicemail or make Michael answer it. When Maggie was guilted to the phone — after Michael, hand clasped over the receiver, pleaded in an urgent whisper for her to "talk for just a minute" — she would resolutely refuse to employ white lies and pretend as though she'd tried out the recipes just to pacify "that lunatic." Maggie was who she was and that was that. No Eliza Doolittle she.

"Margaret, oh, I'm so glad you picked up. It's so hard to reach you sometimes. You and Michael don't answer the phone a lot. I just *had* to call. Dad Kelly and I just enjoyed that delicious sesame noodle dish, that recipe I sent you from the *Boston Journal's* food section. It was so good that I've decided to put it in our regular recipe rotation. It had just the right amount of spice. How was yours?"

"Sorry Dorothy . . ."

". . . Um, it's 'Mom Kelly,' if you wouldn't mind dear."

"Sorry . . . *Mom Kelly*," Maggie said exaggeratedly as she paused and coughed, holding up her left middle finger toward the ceiling in silent protest, "I haven't had the chance to get to the store to buy the ingredients for the sesame noodles. Maybe Michael can pick them up some time next week. You know *Michael* is a really good cook. *He* loves to cook."

Dorothy ground her teeth and pressed on in a light-hearted and determined albeit strained tone, as though she believed she could charm Maggie into submission. Or wear her down. Eventually. "How about the chocolate mousse? I whipped it up in the food processor and Dad Kelly and I just ate it up. Our friends, the Martins, said it was delicious when they were here Saturday night."

"Nope, haven't tried that either," Maggie replied, getting a perverse kick out of this routine, which rarely varied with the exception of the names of dishes. She was curious as to when Dorothy was going to finally give up on trying to transform Maggie into something that she wasn't. "We eat out a lot. We *did* get take-out from this small, family restaurant in the North End the other night. Michael picked it up on the way home from work. Puttanesca. It was unbelievable. Michael actually called the restaurant later to ask for the recipe so he could try to make it here. Maybe he'll make it for you and Frank, oh, sorry . . . you and *Dad Kelly*, the next time you visit."

When her culinary efforts failed, Dorothy tried to help improve things on the housekeeping front, particularly after Michael and Maggie moved to the Greenville house, and Maggie left her ENY job and became an at-home mom. Each time Dorothy visited their home, she was stunned at what Maggie considered a "clean" house. Maggie didn't seem to notice or care that the house was frequently unkempt, though Michael once admitted to Dorothy that Maggie's disinterest in cleaning did bother him a great deal, although he expected that once the kids got older, keeping the house clean would become an easier endeavor. "Poor boy," Dorothy said to him. "You work hard for your family and shouldn't have to come home to *that* or have to put up your own supper."

"Mom, it's okay," he said breezily, trying to head off another anti-Maggie riff. "Maggie has many talents and amazing traits. *Really*. She's just not into cooking or cleaning. And I'm okay with that most of the time. She tells great stories, keeps me laughing. Great with Jackie too. She taught Jackie to read, took her to see the Dr. Seuss sculptures in Springfield after Jackie read *The Cat in the Hat* out loud for the first time. She makes everything, birthdays, holidays, bigger than life and lots of fun. House and cooking stuff isn't on her agenda."

Undeterred, Dorothy asked some of the thirtysomething teachers at her school who had small children how they managed to keep their homes clean — and these were full-time working mothers to boot, she thought — and they suggested visiting a web site called Queen Bee, which offered no-nonsense tips on how to de-clutter and organize one's life, one small step at a time. Logging on to the Queen Bee site that night, Dorothy looked at the quirky cartoon Queen Bee character logo — the Queen Bee had an oversized head, bright red lipstick on voluptuous lips, exaggeratedly lush eyelashes and a yellow and white gingham print apron tied around the rotund black and yellow striped body — and thought a cartoon character might appeal to Maggie's off-beat sensibilities. So she signed Maggie up to receive e-mailed housekeeping tips from the Queen Bee, which always included the reminder that having a clean house should start with having a clean shower, which, by the way, the Queen Bee claimed is easy to maintain after one rigorous cleaning. Maggie, however, likened the folksy Queen Bee e-mails to an insect infestation cropping up in her inbox that required swift extermination. Weeks after Dorothy registered Maggie for the Queen Bee tips, Maggie grew so irritated by the daily e-mails and at having to delete the swarm of hints — she couldn't find the option to "unsubscribe" from the Queen's e-mail list — that she put a block on the Queen Bee newsletters. Though Dorothy never copped to being the one who signed Maggie up for the Queen Bee e-mails, when Maggie then started receiving "anonymous" e-mails extolling the virtues of a clean home from a web site called, "Hints from Someone Who Cares" (marketed as a site that would send anonymous e-mails to people with bad habits they needed to break, such as breath problems, BO, etc.) Maggie knew her mother-in-law had to be the one behind all of it.

The list of ways in which Dorothy attempted to help her daughter-in-law was legion, at least among Maggie's friends, and later, to her blog readers. Her inability to move Maggie one inch closer to acting like a "responsible, mature woman," was deeply dispiriting to Dorothy, who, when everything she tried seemed to fail, verged on despair. "I wish my mother were here to give me some advice on how to handle Margaret," she said one evening after wrapping up yet another unproductive, 60-second telephone conversation with Maggie, who'd mentally cursed herself for forgetting to check the Caller ID before picking up the phone. "Frank, what am I doing wrong? I just can't seem to get through to that girl. I wanted to be like my mother so badly when I was her age, make a beautiful home, good meals for my husband, my children. When she taught me about cooking and, I don't know, smaller basic things like how to remove grass stains, I felt so close to her and when I carried on her traditions it was like she was still with me. And Maggie, well, Lord only knows *what* she wants to be other than sarcastic and slovenly. Our son lives in filth. What should I do? I thought she'd welcome a mother figure in her life."

Frank — Dorothy's very tall husband and her high school sweetheart who'd retained a youthful look in his face though his head of thick, hair had turned fully white when he was in his early thirties — put down the latest biography he'd picked up at the book exchange at the Norton transfer station, a governmental euphemism for "the town dump." (He nurtured a minor obsession with biographies about American historical figures and was rarely without a book to read.) He directed a kind, loving glance at his wife, whom his oldest and dearest friends had affectionately nicknamed, "The Bulldog." Because he was a low-keyed kind of fellow who didn't really have a strong opinion about most things that went on in his house, Frank usually let Dorothy rule over the Kelly Kingdom of Norton. In the event of a dispute or disagreement, it was almost always Frank who was the first one to apologize and he didn't mind that, really, because he preferred peace to war, especially in his home. As long as he could get up each morning, head out to his decades-held job as the head engineer at the neighboring former mill town, Taylor — which was reshaping itself into a would-be hub of small biotech firms along the New Hampshire/Massachusetts state line, somewhat awkwardly morphing from a blue collar to a white collar town — Frank was content. He would clock in a reasonable day and head home by 5 o'clock. Dorothy would already have returned from school and would be preparing dinner, filling the kitchen with tantalizing aromas. Frank's evening routine consisted of perusing whatever parts of the newspapers (the local *Norton News* and the *Boston Journal*) that he hadn't already read during the day, dining on a home-cooked meal, enjoying pleasant conversation with his whip-smart wife, and then retiring with a book or watching a ballgame on TV after dinner. About once a month, he'd go to his neighbor Paul's house to play low-stakes poker with a handful of men he'd known for years, maybe indulge in a cigar (which Dorothy hated although she pretended she didn't notice the cigar stench on his clothing when she washed it) and listen to the guys tell some off-color jokes which he'd never share with his morally upstanding, responsibly serious wife. But mostly, Frank liked things quiet, peaceful and simple. Just before they got married, Frank had told Dorothy that one of his life's goals, as much as he could help it, was to have a home that was largely free from drama. Therefore, when Dorothy got riled up about a subject, Frank usually chose from one of two options: Appeasement or impassivity. It was only on a handful of occasions, however, when Frank would go rogue and amuse himself by intentionally contradicting his wife and watch the anger manifest itself on her face only to have him swoop in and commence the making-up "process."

For example, Frank didn't share Dorothy's epic frustrations with their daughter-in-law. On the contrary, he found Maggie highly amusing. She reminded him in a vague way of a 1920s flapper he'd read about in a book years ago. The flapper — who, coincidentally also went by the name Maggie — liked to hide a flask of homemade hooch in her girdle and reveled in flouting the puritanical dictates of the time, unperturbed by social scorn and the societal expectations for her gender. Maybe it was all in his daughter-in-law's attitude, or that deep laugh of hers which was distinctly unfeminine, at least to Frank, emanating from way down inside her belly someplace. Or those flippant T-shirts Maggie wore a lot which Dorothy called "tacky and unnecessarily provocative."

Frank's perspective on the Maggie and Michael pairing — not that anyone had asked for his opinion — was that Maggie could lighten up the baby-faced Michael's super-serious outlook on life, inject vitality and risk-taking into his eldest son's days. Although Dorothy bragged to everyone that Michael was the spitting image of Frank, "minus the white hair and bookish glasses," who had followed his dear old dad into the engineering field, it was clear that Michael was his mother's son when it came to maintaining general order, doing things in a certain "right" way and being generally super-clean. When Maggie entered the scene, she forced Michael to relax his standards and really focus on enjoying the small moments instead of over-thinking them, like soaking in the electricity of the Fenway Park crowd when a Red Sox player hit a homer in the bottom of the ninth to win the game, really laughing out loud at a hilarious line from a solid comedy or appreciating the rich, creaminess of melted mozzarella that's oozing off of a piping hot piece of pizza even when your face and fingers get all messy from the grease. Frank thought Maggie's influence on these fronts was positive because Michael could be such a staid, buttoned-down soul that it worried him that sometimes his eldest son's life would pass him by before he'd even lived it.

Whenever Dorothy would complain that Maggie lacked manners and grace, Frank would simply allow his wife to vent until she'd exhausted herself. He'd smile, his skin crinkling around his soft eyes behind the thin wire rims of his glasses, nod affirmatively and then, when she felt satisfied that her views had been validated, he'd return to the quiet comfort of his books. He'd silently count his blessings that he was in this marriage where both spouses were comfortable in their roles. He likened their relationship to a well-oiled clock that efficiently ticked along, something for which Frank took credit, although only in his own mind.

But this was one of those rare moments when Frank was being directly asked what his wife "should do" about Maggie. And, feeling wry, he decided to instigate his petite spouse, the one wearing the sensible black flats and standing about as tall as the middle schoolers to whom she ministered. "Why don't you just pull back a little bit hon? Give Maggie some space. Maybe she'll come around to your suggestions, but on her own time. Sometimes you push her too much and she doesn't react well to that, gets stubborn, snappish, you know that. Doesn't like feeling cornered. Kind of like a caged animal."

Dorothy raised her eyebrows so that they disappeared beneath her curtain of silver bangs. She aggressively placed her hands on her hips, her fingers fanned out over her navy linen trousers. She slowly walked across the tan sisal rug in the kitchen over to Frank and stared directly into his eyes as he donned a droll, teasing look. He was hoping that after he apologized for his provocations, they'd have make-up sex.

"What? Did? You? Say?" she asked, her voice rising with a staccato-like punch with each word she uttered.

He snickered in a way Dorothy always found demeaning, then thrust his arms out and said, "Come here Sweetie."

She stood immobile, eyes narrowing, eyebrows still hidden by her bangs.

"Okay. Have it your way. I'LL come to you," Frank said, standing up fully, so that his trim 6-foot-4 inch frame towered over Dorothy's diminutive 5-foot-2 stature. He gave her a long, full-bodied hug and said, "Whatever you want to do hon, I'll support you. I know you just want what's best for the family. I love you. You know that."

Dorothy resisted her urge to liquefy into his arms. Hugs of this variety were her one true weakness, that, and an ice cold gin and tonic with a fresh, juicy slice of lime. But Frank hadn't yet uttered the magic words, "I'm sorry," so he was getting nothing from her until he complied. He knew the drill. Standing ramrod straight, arms pinned to her sides, she said, "You didn't even answer my question."

"I *did* too, but you know what?" he paused and cupped his large hands around the edges of her angular face, just beneath her ears and along her jaw line, "I'm sorry I offended you. I have confidence that whatever you do with Maggie will eventually help everyone. What's that phrase I heard Lisa say on Channel 4 the other night, 'You go girl?'"

Dorothy laughed against her will. Whenever Frank tried to make hip, contemporary references, invoking a new slang term he'd picked up from an intern at town hall, she had to chuckle because he usually used them incorrectly. She knew the correct usage of the latest slang because she heard it from the middle school students every day in the hallways. In this case, however, his use was spot-on.

"All right then," she said, allowing her body to soften into his. "But just remember, it's for our son's own good. He doesn't always see clearly when it comes to her. I've got to look out for him. It's *my job* to help."

"Okay hon, okay." He took one of her hands and placed it in his. With his other hand he gestured toward their bedroom, winked mischievously and asked, "Shall we?"

"You!" Dorothy said as she smiled in spite of herself. "You big idiot!"

SERIOUSLY LADY, BACK THE FUCK OFF!
File under: My MIL should work in Guantanamo Bay

A few questions for all those parents out there to ponder: Do you have time to A) Grow your own garden B) Potty train your toddler C) Keep your toddler from running out into traffic D) Make all your food from scratch E) Try to do some paid employment (of any kind) AND F) Shave, shower, wash your clothes, straighten your hair, apply make-up and wear only the chicest of clothing, all at the same time? Me neither. So why is the Torturer-in-Chief pushing so fucking hard and riding my ass all the time about all of those things? Good Lord do I need a breather.

She called the house this afternoon (I didn't answer & just let the machine take it) to not only remind me of how appalled she was by the condition of my house the other day — when I wasn't expecting her — but to offer her 'help' so I won't seem so stressed out by my 'busy life' (a phrase which, coming from her lips, was dripping with sarcasm). She wanted to tell me that she has e-mailed me a grocery list of what she called 'healthy shopping options' to stock my house with all sorts of golly, gee, happy, handy food stuff that I can have regularly delivered via an Internet grocery shopping/delivery service so that I won't be so freaked out all the time and run out of things and not starve her precious grandchildren and son. Not only did she offer to cover all the grocery delivery costs if I promised to follow her pre-determined menu and have the ~~rock-gut~~ healthy food sent to my house on a weekly basis, but she also said she'd foot the bill if I went to a salon every six weeks to get my hair dyed and get my legs waxed (man, a slam out of nowhere). She said she noticed gray hairs on my head — 'You're too young for that' — and that my legs were 'rather stubbly.' Oh, and in the e-mail (for which I haven't looked) I was promised links to web sites about how to start planning for a garden for next year so that I won't ever be without fresh fruit and veggies which my growing children need. No word on a weekly wine delivery service though.

To add insult to injury, the Wannabe-King just called and was saying similar crap. Must've been fed his lines by his mommy. Clearly the two of them talked because he told me he thinks that ordering groceries online is a marvelous idea and that his mother suggested that, if I don't want to follow her menus, he will do the ordering from his work computer. (Of course he won't be home to prepare the food, never mind eat it, but who the fuck cares about that, right? Details, details.) Plus he's all into the garden idea (ditto on the not being around part and how he's just adding shit to my To Do list).

Tell me this: When did my life become the property of other people? When did everyone else get to decide what I, a grown woman, does? You don't see me calling up the Torturer-in-Chief and telling her that her haircut is about as up-to-date as VHS tapes and that just because she's wearing 'new' L.L. Bean clothes doesn't mean they're fashionable. I haven't e-mailed her and then called HER husband to reinforce the point that no one, I repeat, NO ONE likes her spinach dip or her green bean casserole, even the Wannabe-King who she *thinks adores it. I'm not getting into her business, so why can't she just stay out of mine? And why does her son have to carry her water for her?*

So many questions, so little wine . . .

CHAPTER FIVE

Maggie had decided to shake things up on a garden variety Wednesday night in the Kelly house in the middle of October, opting to go retro and declaring it "Prince Spaghetti Day." She had fond memories from her childhood of watching the TV ads featuring a boy named Anthony who ran around an Italian neighborhood in Boston, the North End, so he could get home in time to enjoy his mama's authentic spaghetti and meatball dinners on Wednesday evenings. To make this particular meal of pasta (they had pasta multiple times a week) a quasi "event," Maggie found the actual Prince Spaghetti Day ad online and played it for the kids as she made dinner, with some Frank Sinatra tunes providing a melodious soundtrack. Jackie and Tommy repeated the little Anthony spaghetti ad over and over again while Maggie finished preparing the meal and setting the table. Tommy was enthralled by Anthony and decided that he had to shout, "Annnthonneeee!" out the kitchen window just like the mom did in the ad, though Tommy sounded more like a pint-sized Stanley Kowalski than a cheerful Italian mother summoning her child from the streets of Boston. He did this repeatedly until Jackie slugged him in the upper arm and he sat back down in front of Maggie's laptop and quietly whimpered.

"Why is that little boy walking in Boston all alone on the street?" Jackie asked, mouth full of shards of baby carrot sticks. Maggie hadn't seen Jackie assault her sibling.

"There were different rules then. Mothers weren't led away in handcuffs for not watching their kids all the time. Kids could actually go outside and have fun together with other kids," Maggie replied, realizing that she probably shouldn't have said those things out loud to a 6-year-old who liked to repeat things. Twisted by a first grader's mind, a botched translation of Maggie's words could very well come back to haunt her at an inopportune moment.

"Distract, distract, deflect," Maggie thought.

"Hey guys, quick! Go wash your hands. I hear Daddy's car pulling into the garage." Michael's car wasn't actually pulling into the garage, but she knew that by invoking his name, the kids would immediately leave the kitchen and stop asking Anthony-related questions.

Twenty minutes later, when Michael had indeed arrived and the family of four were all seated together at the table, the kids continued to chatter about Prince Spaghetti Day and tell their father about the TV ad. "And Daddy, this boy ran around Boston with no grown-ups with him!" Jackie said, sounding scandalized.

"Kids used to be able to do that," Michael said. "People thought it was safer then than it is now. They weren't as afraid of bad things happening."

Maggie's eyes widened. "But you guys aren't going to be alone, running around the streets because that wouldn't be safe for you. Not until they're older, *right*, Daddy?"

Flashing an "I get it" look at Maggie, Michael got on board, "Yeah, right now, when you guys want to play outside you can have a grown-up or a babysitter with you. When you get a little older then you can play by yourselves." Michael hoped that Jackie wouldn't press him for specifics on what "older" meant as he and Maggie hadn't had that conversation yet.

"You know I used to have Prince Spaghetti Day on Wednesdays when I was a little boy," Michael said, trying to change the subject. "Your Nana Kelly and Great Nana Sophie used to make really yummy Italian food, recipes Great Nana Sophie got from her family in Italy. And every Wednesday, and then Sundays too, we'd have big Italian meals with lots of meat sauces, like with hamburger and sausages, fresh breads and all different kinds of pasta in different shapes."

The kids, however, could've cared less about the family history lesson. "But couldn't Anthony have gotten hurt by himself in Boston? What would happen to him if he got hurt? Did he have a cell phone?" Jackie asked, rolling a meatball around her plate that she clearly wasn't going to eat.

"No," Michael said. "There were no cell phones. And besides, back then everybody knew their neighbors. They all hung out together. Today people work farther away from their houses and don't see their neighbors as much."

"They just stick anonymous, nasty notes demanding that you weed the mulched area in your mailbox," Maggie muttered.

"I wuv Pwince Sketti Day!" Tommy blurted, raising his hands above his head triumphantly, in the process, knocking over his blue plastic dinosaur cup full of milk in between his plate and Jackie's. Tommy and Jackie remained still, watching, as the milk started to breach their thick, foam ABC placemats, then ran like a cresting river toward the glass vase of slightly wilted yellow mums, and then through the crack in the middle of the table where one could add extra table leaves to seat more people.

"Put your napkins on it!" Maggie shouted as she leaned over and fruitlessly dropped her own napkin on top of the puddle. "Don't just stare. Help Mommy and Daddy!"

Michael, who had fetched several sheets of paper towels, was already under the table on his hands and knees wiping up the wood floor when he noticed remnants of tortilla chips, granola bars and crushed cereal bits scattered about. He opted to say nothing about the debris and continued cleaning, scraping the sticky gunk out from between the grooves of the wooden floor planks as he made a mental note, as much as he didn't want to, he needed to open up the kitchen table to clean the space between the table leaves. The kids, oblivious, continued to eat their spaghetti from their chipped blue and white dinner plates. Jackie still wasn't having any part of the meatballs as she continued to wonder aloud about what "that Spaghetti kid Anthony's" favorite color was and whether he liked drawing with apple scented magic markers.

"Oh! Mama! Mrs. Stone said I gotta send back my reading log. You hafta sign it and she got you a note," Jackie said, getting up from her chair — nearly knocking over her own plastic cup of milk decorated with a soccer ball pattern. Michael, who'd just emerged from beneath the table, saved the cup from tipping over just in time. Jackie loudly scampered over to her bright red backpack and fished out a crumpled, ball of paper. "Here!" she said, handing it over to Maggie.

"For me?"

"Mmhmm," she said, nodding as she stuffed a large fork full of pasta into her mouth.

Maggie threw out the rest of the soiled paper towels and plopped back down on her chair. She flattened out the paper and saw that it was a form letter, half typed and half handwritten in Jackie's scrawl. It said:

"Dear Mommy," (This was typed out.)

"Puleez rememer snak tomrw." (This was in Jackie's handwriting.)

"I need to have a healthy snack each day so I can have energy to learn." (This was typed out.)

"Lv, Jackie." (Jackie's writing.)

"I don't understand," Maggie said. Huffing audibly, she stomped over to Jackie's backpack, unzipped the small front pocket — one of about 10 zippered compartments in the backpack — and pulled out an intact Ziplock bag of graham crackers and a juice box whose attached straw had fallen off. "Here's your snack. Why didn't you eat it?"

"You didn't put it in the right place Mama. I told Mrs.

Stone I couldn't find it and she helped me with this note."

Maggie fell back into her kitchen chair, still clutching the bag of graham crackers. "Why does it say, 'Dear Mommy?' You have TWO parents! Daddy could've packed this snack."

Jackie slumped slightly in her chair, half-heartedly examining a carrot stick on her plate. "You're the one who gets our snacks most days Mommy. Don't you like the note?"

Maggie tried to suppress her ire. She squatted next to Jackie, smoothed down her daughter's dark bob then gave her a warm hug and a half dozen kisses. "Don't worry kiddo. You didn't do anything wrong," she said as she placed one last light kiss on the soft edge of her left ear. "Just please look through EVERY part of your bag first before you tell Mrs. Stone that there's no snack there, okay?"

"Okay," Jackie said. She put her hand over her stomach. "My belly doesn't feel good."

"Maybe you ate your spaghetti too fast sweetie," Maggie replied. "You were taking huge bites."

"Can I be 'scused and go upstairs?" Jackie asked.

"Me too?" Tommy added.

"Yep. Go get your PJs on. We'll be up to read in a few minutes. Pick out two books each. 'kay?"

Once the kids were out of earshot, Maggie unloaded. "What the hell is that bullshit? 'Dear Mommy.' First of all, it's sexist, assuming the mom's doing all the snack prep. Second of all, it's also bullshit that the teacher would assume that I fucked up without even checking Jackie's backpack first to make sure there was no snack there. And, even if there wasn't one, what's the big deal? It's not like Jackie would die from hunger if she missed a snack one day. Jesus! You'd think I'd just starved the kid. Aren't all the pediatricians sayin' kids are too fat nowadays anyway? It's just a snack, for Christ's sake."

Unfazed, but feeling grateful that the note didn't say, "Dear Daddy," Michael spooned more marinara sauce and two more meatballs atop of his second helping of spaghetti.

"Well aren't the majority of the parents who are packing snacks the moms anyway, especially in this town?" he asked.

"It doesn't matter!" Maggie said, now indignant. "The majority of moms with young kids are working in one form or another. And I'm working part-time. Besides, I don't like them giving the kids the message that only the mom takes care of all the child care stuff. You've packed snacks for school before."

"Well you *are* doing that, taking care of the kids and their stuff, most of the time so aren't you sending them that message every day, with your day-to-day life?"

Maggie fiercely slammed down her glass of wine from which she was about to take a big sip, and glared at Michael. "You can't be serious. You're going to equate my staying home with the kids, something you begged me to do, with perpetuating sexism? I'M sending them a sexist message? I AM working ya know, though maybe not full-time like your mom did . . . Come to think of it, didn't she come home from work and take care of all of your and Joseph's school things, all the meals and the stuff around the house? Frank didn't do any of that, so wasn't SHE setting a bad example even though she was working full-time, that it's a woman's job to keep the home?"

"Actually, Nana Sophie was at home when we got home from school, but Mom got home right after Joseph and I did. Nana and Mom would make dinner together and even clean together once Nana moved in, sometime after Joseph turned, oh, I don't remember exactly, when Joseph turned around 4 or 5? Something like that. That means I was about 7 or 8."

"Well, isn't that so all-American as apple pie? I'm glad you had a *Leave it to Beaver* childhood Michael, but that isn't what we decided our life together was going to be like. *We* were supposed to have an equal marriage. We were both working, had careers, even after we had Jackie, at least initially. *We* were supposed to be telling our kids that partners share these chores together. That's what we decided when we got married, not that we were going to try to copy what you had growing up. When I was still working at ENY, we took turns filling the diaper bag. It wasn't always me. Are you defending this?" Maggie shook the paper in the air, lost hold of it and watched as it slid under the table, out of sight. "Do you think it's okay for a teacher who I haven't even met to assume that, in the 21st century, it's the *mom* who forgot to pack the snack, even though I didn't forget the snack in the first place?"

"No," he stammered, "I'm not saying that. I don't even know what we're talking about anymore. How did we get sidetracked on my mother? Why did you drag her into this? I was just pointing out the facts, that's all. I wasn't trying to start something . . . You're not going to do anything, with this note, right?"

"Like what?"

"Like scream at Mrs. Stone. Or write something nasty to her. Jackie just started school. I don't want her to start off on the wrong foot and have her teacher hate us."

"You mean hate *me*," she said. Maggie despised it when she felt he was being cowardly, backing down from a fight. He wasn't this way at work when a hundred people stood up in a room, mocked that bit of upswept hair at the front of his head by nicknaming him "Gel Boy," or said he was a destroyer of the environment for wanting to put a new highway through a swamp. He wasn't afraid then. He didn't back down from a heated discussion in that context, so why did he seem afraid of the first grade teacher? She concluded that it was something to do with not bucking his mother's authority and the fact that she also worked at a school, something that people with a lot of letters after their name would have to figure out.

"I'll handle it Michael, don't you worry your pretty little head about it." She rose from the table and picked up her plate and the children's plates. "Why don't you go upstairs with the kids? You haven't seen them all day. I'll clean up here and join you afterwards."

As soon as Michael left, Maggie fetched her laptop and

fired off an e-mail to Mrs. Stone:

"Dear Mrs. Stone,
Please make sure that Jackie checks EVERY pocket of her back-
pack for her daily snack. She might find that her snack is in there, like
it was today, before she starts blaming her parents, or her mother
specifically, for forgetting to pack one. She sometimes doesn't look
thoroughly and accidentally puts blame where it doesn't belong.
Thanks for looking out for her.
Sincerely,
Margaret Finn Kelly"

"Ah," she said, finishing off her glass of wine and pressing the "send" button, "much better."

Maggie had stalled in the kitchen long enough. She'd cleaned it so well that even the Queen Bee would've given her two thumbs up, or two antennas up or whatever a bee would raise to indicate success. No longer steamed at Michael, that third glass of wine helped, Maggie slowly crept up the stairs and overheard Michael singing Tommy his nightly lullaby. She sat down on the top stair and listened to her husband's hushed, somewhat off-key rendition of the tune that was a staple of Maggie's childhood.

"Daddy I wuv you and wish you were here all da time," Tommy said, making a loud smooching sound. "I miss you."

"Me too buddy. I love you."

Michael didn't notice Maggie, who was greatly moved listening to the two of them, when he left Tommy's room and walked across the hall to their bedroom. Maggie waited a second or two, then slipped into the kids' rooms to kiss them goodnight, removing Tommy's second blanket from his bed so he wouldn't wake up in a pool of sweat in the mild autumn weather. When she retired to her bedroom, Michael had already shed his work clothes and was sitting atop the bed wearing black boxer shorts and yet another selection from his voluminous collection of BU T-shirts. The sitting on the bed part, Maggie liked. What she didn't like was the fact that he was in bed with his BlackBerry and his briefcase, which was open.

She stood next to her white painted wooden bureau — another hand-me-down, her mother's actually — with a slightly worn oval mirror mounted on the back. As she looked at her own reflection, she started thinking about her mother, who would've just turned 56. Maggie only allowed the thought to linger in her mind for a second, before she went to the master bathroom to splash her face with cold water. "Forget about it," she told herself sternly. She had other plans for tonight. Mourning her mother who died 18 years ago was not one of them. Maggie quickly brushed her teeth with her spicy cinnamon toothpaste and had to spend more than the usual amount of time brushing the snarls out of her hair. (Tommy had accidentally dropped a glue stick on the side of her head earlier.) She sprayed her citrus-infused perfume on the back of her neck, down the front of her shirt, at her wrists and pumped a blast on her legs. She returned to her dresser to pull out her softest cotton pajama bottoms, the ones with the drawstring which provided Maggie with the illusion of a waist, and selected a thin, green camisole top with spaghetti straps. ("It is Prince Spaghetti Day," she thought, cringing at her own bad pun as she adjusted the straps.) She changed her clothes in the bedroom in a slow, obvious and showy way, hoping to catch Michael's attention.

He noticed nothing. He was concentrating on the tiny screen in front of him, sending someone a time sensitive ("Everything is 'time sensitive,'" she thought) e-mail. If she'd asked him to please put the BlackBerry down so they could talk, she was 99 percent sure his response would be, "Just a minute. I just need to do this one more thing . . ."

She hopped onto the bed, a cherry sleigh bed, which matched nothing in the room, and was also inherited from her parents, her mom's side of the family. She leaned over her rickety nightstand and fumbled through her CDs in search of one she'd made and called, "Night Mix 2," for occasions such as this. As a slow-jam played, Maggie slowly began removing Michael's work items from the bed, one by one, placing them in a neat pile on the floor. First the black three-ringed binder, "the bible" for the variance ENY and the Massachusetts Highway Department were filing for the proposed Central Mass Bypass. Next she slid a giant roll of plans ("Did he really think he'd be unrolling these all over the bed?" she thought.) and placed them next to the binder. The briefcase soon joined them. He still hadn't noticed that Maggie had moved his stuff to the floor, as she eyed the last item, the BlackBerry, which was still in his hands. To get this item out of the bed area, Maggie opted to climb on top of her husband and place her legs on either side of his lap. Recognizing that the window of time he had to use BlackBerry was rapidly closing, he started typing faster without looking up, holding up a single index finger as he said, "One sec, I'm almost done."

Normally, Maggie would've reacted very negatively to Michael choosing to continue to use his BlackBerry instead of paying attention to his wife who had just mounted him. On most days, he would've been on the receiving end of an angry outburst followed by the silent treatment for the rest of the night. But tonight she was feeling persistent. Maggie started rolling her hips clockwise in slow, wide circles. Slowly. Very slowly. That got his attention. "Okay it's gone," he said abruptly, putting the BlackBerry on his nightstand and focusing fully on his wife. She put her face right in front of his, mere inches away, so she could feel his breath on her skin and smell the marinara sauce he'd had for dinner. He tried to kiss her but she gently swerved her head to the left and began to kiss his ear, gradually moving her lips down the side of his neck, to his face, all the way to his chin where she could feel his rough stubble sting her lips. Her kissing became more forceful while her hands sought out the edge of his T-shirt and lifted it up over his head and hooked it around his shoulders, exposing them. She firmly grabbed a bare shoulder in each hand and pulled them forward as she pushed her hips into him like he was a human rowing machine. After rhythmically pulling and thrusting for 30 seconds, Maggie resumed rotating her hips while she lightly caressed his light brown chest hair. (She adored his chest hair and whenever he asked her whether she thought he should wax his chest and do some "man-scaping," she admonished him to never remove something she said, "screamed manliness.") In one quick move, she seized one of his hands and plunged it down the front of her already loosened pajama bottoms, guiding his hand with hers as she pressed her camisole-clad breasts into his face. "That's it," she murmured, "oh . . . oh . . . right there. Yes. *There.* Like that." When he no longer needed her assistance, she put her own hand down the front of his boxers as he emitted his own murmurs of pleasure.

A loud shriek from the bedroom next door suddenly pierced through them, followed by an indeterminate but distinctly not-good sound. They froze in place.

"Mommmm!!" they heard Jackie shriek, followed by a retch.

Maggie leapt into action, abruptly withdrawing her hand from Michael's boxers so fast that it made a loud *thwap* sound as the elastic waist band snapped back hard, and rather uncomfortably, against him and his erection. She slid off his lap and fled the room. Michael, suddenly feeling self-conscious, grabbed a red pillow and placed it on top of his lap. He heard another retch. Then another. Followed by Maggie screaming, "Oh! Oh God!"

"Right words," Michael thought, "wrong place."

What seemed like a feature length-film later, Maggie

appeared in the doorway. Jackie had her arms wrapped around Maggie's right shoulder. Her legs encircled Maggie's right hip. Red vomit, courtesy of Prince Spaghetti Day, was dripping off of Maggie's left shoulder, off her camisole and the peak of her left breast. Michael saw red splotches on Maggie's pants, the ones Michael had planned to remove less than a minute ago. Wearing a look of resignation, Maggie asked, "Which do you want to clean up, the kid or the bedroom?"

Michael, embarrassed, held the pillow firmly in place. "Bedroom," he said, adding, "I don't ever want Prince Spaghetti Day again."

MARINARA SAUCE IS DEAD TO ME
File under: Gross kid stuff

Is this some kind of twisted Karma? I bash the Torturer-in-Chief for offering to pay the delivery charges for groceries to be sent to my house each week (which some of my favorite Internet trolls — 'MassMan' specifically' — said was exceedingly generous of her and that I am a "pampered whore" who's "an entitled elitist cunt" for complaining about it) and I get not only marinara sauce ruined for me, but also the possibility of a good fuck (preceded by a funky lap dance given by yours truly) taken away?

Well you folks who think I was a bitch about her offer can celebrate today because, just when the Wanna-Be King and I were about to get it on last night, Thing I came down with a stomach bug and puked spaghetti and red sauce all over her bed, the bathroom, herself and me. (I guess I can be grateful that she didn't want to eat the meatballs after all.) As I took care of her all night on the bathroom floor and clutched my own curdling stomach hoping that I wouldn't get it, I imagined that a couple of the Internet haters would be so happy for me to be sitting amidst vomit. Score!

Just thought I'd share the posh glamorousness that is my life with y'all, and to tell you that you should consider yourselves thankful I didn't share the gross puke images that are permanently seared into my brain with you here. It's only 'cause I love you guys. Except for "MassMan." You can suck it buddy.

CHAPTER SIX

"So which one are you going to pick?" Diane asked as she stuffed a blueberry bagel into her mouth, chasing it down with a gulp from the biggest cup of Dunkin' Donuts coffee that they had on sale. Her youngest child, her baby Lily, napped in her stroller, white powdered sugar dotting her left cheek and coating the ends of her straw-colored bangs after Diane had let her suck on a small piece of a powdered doughnut hole. Diane and Maggie had decided to meet up at the doughnut shop located roughly equidistant from their houses, giving them time to drop their kids off at preschool and first grade — they both had first graders and preschool-aged kids — drive to the coffee shop, gab, then dash back to their respective preschools and public schools with barely enough time to pick up their kiddos before the staff started getting annoyed and placed nasty phone calls to their homes and cell phones asking where the hell they were and when were they going to get their offspring.

"Which what?" Maggie asked, assessing her medium vanilla coffee and questioning whether she should've gotten the super-sized tub of java like Diane. Since Wednesday's Prince Spaghetti Day debacle, Jackie had seemed surprisingly healthy. She perked up some three hours after interrupting Michael and Maggie but Maggie had decided to keep the girl home from school on Thursday just to be sure she was okay because she didn't want to be *that* mother who sent her child to school sick. Maggie spent all of Thursday babying Jackie, serving her flat ginger ale and chicken soup while commencing an ambitious mom-and-daughter project: Reading the whole Harry Potter book series aloud. This morning, Friday, however, Maggie decided that Jackie was well enough to return to school.

"Your contest for the blog," Diane said, then, realizing she shouldn't have said "blog" so loudly. She leaned over as she tucked a stray dark, wavy hair back into the elastic gathering at the nape of her thin neck, and whispered, "You know, the Torturer-in-Chief nickname contest. The winner gets that Queen Bee gift certificate? I wouldn't mind getting that gift certificate myself. Do you like any of the entries? I looked through the comments. You got 107 of them as of last night. There were some really good ones and really awful ones too. You might want to delete some of 'em."

"Yeah, I saw those, liked a bunch, actually. Haven't been able to decide which one should win. By the way, didya see the comment from 'YouSuck2001' who was like, 'You're too skanky and probably too fat to wear a thong' and 'must live like a sick pig who's lucky to have a husband and mother-in-law who'll put up with your shit?' That was really nice. Made me feel all warm and tingly. At least 'MassMan' didn't comment on that post."

The baby's head slumped over to the right as she sunk deeper into her quiet slumber in the stroller. Diane gingerly slid the fleece blanket away from Lily's face, trying not to wake her.

Maggie lowered her gaze, taking in all of Lily's infant cuteness. "I remember when Jackie started sleeping with her Blankie-Blank, you know, the purple baby blanket, the one you gave her that's just like the one Lily has. She was about 1 and it was the only thing she wanted in her crib. Needed it to get to sleep. Didn't want a binkie. Just that purple blanket. The first time we lost it, I think I left it at a Dunkin' Donuts or something, Jackie flipped out. I went online that night and ordered six of 'em — literally — so we wouldn't have to deal with that crap again. But Lily looks so content there, with hers."

Maggie leaned back in the uncomfortable, hard plastic coffee shop chair and noticed a bulge of belly flesh protruding along the waistband of her jeans as the front of her forest green hoodie rose in the front. The fleshy ridge disappeared when Maggie sat up straight, but its sudden appearance when she slouched troubled her. "My pregnancy with Jackie was the beginning of THIS," Maggie said, pinching her stomach flesh.

"What? What was the beginning of what?" Diane asked, sighing, girding herself for a long tirade. She thought to herself, "When's the last time she asked about my family, or about George?"

"When Jackie was a baby and I left ENY, started being an at-home mom, I stopped going to the gym to save money. I was supposed to walk around the neighborhood with Jackie in the stroller for, like, exercise. That was the original plan. But it was always too cold or too hot, I was worried about Jackie getting sick again and I never got around to doing it. God, there are, like, a bazillion reasons why I loved working, like the gym in the ENY building. I could go right after work. It was really convenient. I think I must've gained like 15 to 20 pounds since I stopped going there." She poked at her belly and said, "I didn't have THIS. Then after I had Tommy too, I threw a few more pounds on top of the weight from Jackie."

The usually even-keeled Diane wasn't feeling her normal, supportive gal pal self at this moment and she decided she wasn't going to hide it for a change. "So just join a gym. Tommy's in preschool now. Jackie's in school all day. You've got the time. And aren't you making more money now with Memory Makers? Use that money to fund your gym member-ship. There's a new Body Sculptures that opened up at The Roseway shopping plaza near your house. George and I are trying to cut back too, so I've started power-walking every morning with my neighbor Jane. We get up before our husbands leave for work, sometimes I even take Lily in her stroller . . ."

"I guess I *could* join a gym," Maggie interrupted. "Start eating better. I've been so damned tired all the time. Do you think that's why Michael looks through me like I'm transparent? He's always looking at his BlackBerry. He barely listens to me."

"Seriously Mags, you just need to prioritize what you want. If you want more energy, want to feel more energy, then suck it up and join a gym. And, you know what? I just think Michael's just busy, not blowing you off. You guys did just have that 'funky lap dance' thing you mentioned on the," she paused and leaned in toward Maggie again, lowering her voice, "blog. *Before* Jackie started puking. It sounds like, from what you wrote, that he was definitely noticing you."

"Only because I sat on top of his lap, gyrating like some stripper to get him to put his BlackBerry away."

Diane frowned and pretended that she needed to re-tie Lily's baby shoes. She spoke without looking at Maggie's face, "Well, all I know is that ever since Jane and I started walking, I've felt, like, a million times more energetic, even though Lily's still not quite sleeping through the night yet. You might try it. Isn't there someone who lives near you who you could walk with?"

"Nope," Maggie said, picking at the sesame seeds on what remained of her bagel. "I have no friends in my neighborhood. They're all too Stepford for me. There's no one around that I have anything in common with."

"Do you even WANT to fit in? Do you even try?" Diane asked sternly. "I can't believe there's nobody you could walk with. You never had a problem with making friends when we were at Framingham State, or at ENY."

Maggie looked bemused. "Why do you ask that? You know I tried after we first moved in. Michael and I went to that first cocktail hour party at a neighbors' house and all the families were there. I don't know what it was that I said or did, but we didn't get invited back to any cocktail hours after that. No purse parties or stamping parties. And they didn't respond to my e-mails offering to run a Memory Makers party at their houses. I asked a couple of them for coffee and they were always busy with PTA whatevers. What more could I have done? Thrown myself on their front lawns while holding baskets of freshly baked muffins and begging to be let into their little social mafia? I don't think so."

Diane placed both her hands flat on the table and looked at Maggie. "I know you don't like all this stuff," she began, "the being at home stuff, the mommy stuff, the power walking in the morning, the PTA and you think less of me because I actually DO like it even though I thought I never would. It's obvious that you just want to go back to work. You want to run screaming from your neighborhood because you hate all those women who you don't even know and go back to work where you seemed in your element, and you have a lot of blog readers who share your viewpoint on that. But I *like* the women in my neighborhood. I go walking with them, belong to a book club, have coffee with them. Maybe I'm different than I was when we were in college. Maybe you are. I don't know anymore. Sometimes I wonder whether you'd even like me if we'd met right now at this point in our lives, rather than when we were teenagers at Eastborough High."

"You know, we've made the same choices, except for that power-walking thing. Oh, God, I'd rather take out my eyes with a spoon than do *that*. And that PTA stuff, which I think is just make-work stupidness to keep bored people busy, no offense Diane. Look, I know there's lots of good things the PTA does to support the classrooms, you know, my Memory Makers clients are moms and I sell them scrapbooking supplies. I don't hate moms. I don't hate you. I love you. You're my best friend. We've just been seeing things differently since we've had our kids."

"See, there you go with that 'make-work stupidness' crack. I happen to think what we do at PTA has a very important impact on our children's education, helps the teachers out so they don't have to pay for things out of their own pockets, improves and supplements the curriculum. You don't have to like the PTA groups, but I *do* like them. Maybe you don't feel like you fit in because you send out this really strong judgmental vibe that they pick up on. It's pretty loud, even when you're not saying anything, the kind of vibe you say Dorothy sends you. But that's fine, Maggie. Being an at-home mom isn't for everybody. And that's," she paused, took in a deep breath, stretched out her long, trim legs and kissed Maggie on the forehead as she gathered her things, "that's why I love you. You're one of a kind. I gotta go. Talk to ya later."

Diane stood, poised behind Lily's stroller then added, "Try not to be so hard on Michael. His project is enormous. It's in all the papers. There's a lot of pressure on him right now. He's got to maintain a good public image and come off well during those meetings or else the project is dead."

"Yeah, yeah," Maggie said as she stroked the still-sleeping Lily's head. "See ya. Maybe I'll check out Body Sculptures or something." As Diane walked away, her blue flowered Vera Bradley diaper bag swung on her shoulder while she pushed the stroller, Maggie said quietly to herself, "Or not."

Maggie was in a snit for the rest of the day after the unusually confrontational coffee break. She wished she could sit down and chat, face-to-face with the moms who commented on her blog who were career-oriented like her but felt as trapped by life and circumstance and she did. They'd certainly be able to buoy her spirits. It bothered her when she and Diane fought. Typically, if there was obvious tension, they'd have these marathon talks, sometimes hours in length where they tentatively danced around whatever issues they were having at any given time. It was rare for them to have sharp exchanges. This one rattled Maggie. "She's too sucked into her perfect mom world to see straight," she muttered while driving to pick Jackie up from school and bring her to her dance class. Thankfully, Tommy, who she had picked up first, had already fallen asleep in his car seat, all tuckered out from a vigorous game of tag he enjoyed at recess. "Not every mom likes the shit she likes. Jesus! I don't even think she ever liked working."

Maggie quickly ran Jackie into the dance class while lugging a napping Tommy over her shoulder. The dance studio was located in one of Greenville's many tastefully appointed, brand new strip malls, the kind with the high-quality awnings and wooden signs (no neon or plastic signs allowed, per town bylaws). Body Sculptures was perched at the end of the plaza, taunting her. After Jackie, in her pale pink leotard and white tights, bounced her way into "Ballet I" to join the other girls, Maggie carried the now drooling Tommy back out to her minivan which she'd parked right in front of the dance studio. As Tommy continued to snooze, Maggie pulled out a book of humor essays from her purse in an attempt to elevate her mood. But she couldn't concentrate on the essayist's witty recollections of his quirky Midwestern childhood. (This happened to be the same book the women in her neighborhood book club were reading, or so she'd overheard at the school pick-up line. Not that Maggie — who almost always carried a book around with her — had been asked to join them, despite such energetic hinting that she thought she'd pull a muscle fishing for an invitation.) She looked through the dance studio's large plate glass window at the other moms who sat waiting for their daughters. They all seemed to be getting along well with one another, chitchatting like members of yet another club to which Maggie hadn't been asked to join, even though she wasn't sure she even wanted to join. She felt like an alien in her own skin.

That night, following a dinner comprised of turkey and

cheese subs and barbecue potato chips from D'Angelos, and after the kids had gone to bed, Maggie and Michael retreated to their bedroom to change into comfy, post-dinner clothes in preparation to sack out in front of the TV and watch a mediocre movie with an accompaniment of a couple of beers.

"Do you think I should have something done?" Maggie hollered to Michael as she stood in front of their bathroom mirror in a bra and plaid pajama bottoms.

"Like your nails?" Michael shouted, throwing his socks near the laundry hamper but not actually getting them in. For once, he let them stay there on the floor.

"No," she said. "Come 'ere."

She had pulled one of her bra straps up, elevating her left breast a good two inches higher than the right one. "Whaddya think?"

Michael looked at her lopsided chest. "I don't know what you want me to say . . . I like your bra?"

"Think I should have a boob lift?" She turned to look at her profile, then frowned upon seeing the sea of stretch marks across her abdomen which pooched out a bit at her waist line. She let her left breast return to its natural location and moved her hands to either side of her stomach and pulled the pregnancy-stretched skin upward toward her hips. "Or a tummy tuck? They've got a name for it now. They call is a 'mom job,' but not the kind where you get paid. It's the kind where you get your hotness back."

Michael leaned against the doorway, arms crossed across his bare chest, looking at her. "You never lost your hotness. That's ridiculous. Although you may want to send me in for surgery . . . career surgery. Those whack-job Templeton Conservation Commission guys, they told me, in front of someone from the Mass Highway Department and two assholes from the DEP today that I was, 'completely out of my depth,' and had, 'no clue,' what I was doing. They even called me 'Gel Boy' during a meeting, mocking my hair again. I'm worried that Sam Young's going to start agreeing with them if everybody keeps saying that I can't get this project done. This is a good project, but not if this guy" he pointed to himself "gets it killed. I can't afford to look bad. Then you'll have to schedule me for a 'dad job.'"

Michael slid his arms around Maggie's waist from behind her and they looked at their entwined reflection. He kissed the back of her neck then spun her around to face him.

"What if they're right?" he asked. "What if I do suck? What if I have no idea how to get this project done and it's my fault the project dies and the governor blames me or something?"

"It won't," Maggie said, wrapping him in an embrace, resting her head on his chest. "And you don't suck. You're a captain of industry I tell ya." In silence, she gently massaged his shoulders for a few minutes and then led him to the bedroom.

♏

YEAH, BAY-BEE
File under: Gettin' biz-ee

Sheer ecstasy. That's what Maggie's in right now, y'all. Sheer. Ex. Ta. See.

The Wannabe-King not only was home for dinner (on time!) last night, but he was there in so many ways. THERE. That's right. Down there. And he was spectacular. Beyond spectacular.

Now if I could have that kind of service twice a week, okay, once a week (I shan't be greedy here) I'd be a much happier woman. If I'm going to remain a kept woman — kept in the house with the kids, with the exception of my handful of evenings of saleswoman genius — I should at least be sexually satisfied. It would make me a much more cheerful wife. Wait. Correct that. I'd be A cheerful wife, as opposed to what I am right now, one who bitches all the time and lives off of caffeine, BBQ potato chips and TV shows on DVD.

I don't know why the Wannabe-King . . . wait, I'm feelin' generous. I'll call him, Sweet Lips for the rest of this post . . . I don't know why Sweet Lips gave me all that sex goodness last night. He'd had a bad day at work. People had mocked him, called him names, made fun of his hair in front of his boss (he hates feeling embarrassed, but I guess we all do). So maybe he just wanted to have at somebody — me! — stand up and applaud his efforts. Well I tell ya, after what he did, when I was still sprawled out on the bed, I applauded, clapped, hooted, the works. Woke up Thing II with all my shoutin' afterwards. Had to throw on a robe and tuck him back into bed (the kid, I mean), but it was definitely worth it.

Sometimes, though, you don't want to question things too much. Like why he was suddenly into all that last night. Sometimes you should just enjoy. And enjoying I still am, rolling the footage of the evening in my head over and over. And over. It makes me feel like I'm blessed that this guy loves me and I love him.

But I'm floating so happily on air right now that I'll bet this good mood'll last me all day so that when Thing I and Thing II get home from school I'll do nothing but enjoy them and play with them and be the mom I always wish I could be.

CHAPTER SEVEN

Sitting at the kitchen counter in the silent house next to an empty pot of coffee, Maggie, still in one of Michael's BU T-shirts and his plaid pajama bottoms (her own PJs were next to the laundry hamper which she was pretending she didn't notice was belching its contents onto the floor), reclined back on the stool with a satisfied look on her face. She'd just finished writing a blog entry and was still smiling over what she thought was a particularly clever turn of phrase when the phone rang.

"Mommy, where ARE you?"

It was Jackie, whom Michael had driven to school before dropping Tommy off at his school, enabling Maggie to sleep in on this warm late October morning.

"What? What's wrong? Are you sick? What happened honey?"

"Mommy, the Halloween party is starting and you're not here! Mrs. Stone said I could call you because you're the only mommy who's not here."

"I'll be right there!" she hung up the duct-taped handset. "Shit! Shit! Shit!"

Maggie ran over to the nearly foot-thick pile of papers that had been brought home from school by Jackie and Tommy. During the first weeks of school, Maggie'd had the best of intentions of keeping organized. She bought three-ring binders for each kid and, each day, she'd go through the papers in their backpacks and file them, sorting out things she needed to sign, items designated for proud display on the refrigerator and items she could toss out, like the wrapping paper fundraising packet from the PTA. When Jackie started playing soccer in September, Maggie went out and bought a separate binder for soccer stuff and placed the soccer game schedule on the front of the refrigerator next to the dates for Tommy's "Little Sport" classes at the nearby indoor sports facility. She'd marked the Red Sox-themed family calendar (also on the fridge) with all the important dates she'd been able to glean from the various schedules and school notices including: The multitude of half-days and "professional days" for Jackie, the dates of the parent-teacher conferences, the dates when Tommy was supposed to bring in snacks for his whole class and when Jackie was supposed to supply orange slices for her soccer team. With two children now in school, Maggie told herself, she needed to be more organized.

But things quickly spiraled out of control. Maggie came down with a bad case of bronchitis and couldn't sleep at night, prompting her doctor to prescribe a cough syrup with a sleep aid. During the bronchitis bout, Michael had several night meetings which kept him out of the house for long hours and Maggie just barely got through the days. Meanwhile, every little drawing Jackie or Tommy made, every worksheet they completed, all the PTA forms and daily newsletters from the preschool about what songs they sang that day had started to pile up. By the time Maggie felt like herself again, the stack had grown to such a height that it looked too daunting to tackle.

With Halloween now looming, it was easy for Maggie to blow off that stack and become preoccupied with racing around to the various stores in the metro Boston area searching in vain for the costumes Jackie and Tommy had requested. She wound up paying an extra fee to an online merchant to expedite the shipping so the costumes would arrive at her house on time because she couldn't find them in the stores. Most "organized" moms, she'd been told, snapped up their kids' costumes in early September, some even in late August. Sure, she could've just told Jackie and Tommy that they had to get other costumes because their character get-ups were no longer available in stores, as Michael had suggested, but Maggie didn't want to break their little hearts. And since she didn't have the sewing skills that her mother possessed when Molly handcrafted Maggie's Halloween costumes to Maggie's specifications, Maggie wanted to make up for it by getting her kids exactly what they wanted, even if the hunt made her crazy in the process.

In the meantime, she'd completely missed this whole first grade Halloween party thing. After Jackie's panicked phone call, Maggie approached the mass of school papers figuring that the flier for the class Halloween party was likely lurking somewhere in there. She dumped them onto the kitchen floor and spread them out, scanning for something that looked like a Halloween party invitation. Sure enough, on an orange paper decorated in all four corners with smiling jack-o-lanterns, was the announcement:

"Mrs. Stone's First Grade Class Invites You to Halloween Hollow!

Our first graders have worked really hard to create a fun, fall Halloween Hollow in Room 47. Please come see our Jolly Jack-O-Lanterns, our Wise Witches, our Gleeful Ghosts and enjoy other fall time fun.

Date: October 21

Time: 9:30AM

Location: Room 47

Please come in costume (nothing too scary!!!) so you can surprise your 1st grader.

Also, our Room Mothers, Mrs. Waldigger and Mrs Tribb are looking for volunteers to contribute food & supplies for the party and to help with the set up and clean up. See the list below for the items they need. Please e-mail them to let them know what you'll be bringing."

"Fuck! A costume?!" Maggie yelled.

Fifteen minutes later, Maggie showed up empty-handed to Mrs. Stone's class wearing a red BU T-shirt, a pair of ripped jeans (the only ones she had clean), a navy Red Sox cap and Groucho Marx glasses, a pair with fuzzy eyebrows, mustache and oversized plastic nose.

"Jackie! Look! Your mommy's finally here!" exclaimed Mrs. Stone, a twentysomething teacher dressed like a butterfly who was practically vibrating with energy. "We're so glad you could make it."

"Yeah," Maggie muttered, trying to discern if Mrs. Stone was trying to give her a hard time or not.

Jackie was wearing the Halloween costume Maggie had found online: Silvery, sequined-covered pants, an oversized bright purple tunic and sparkly rainbow ribbons in her hair that Jackie's favorite pop star, Chrissy Singer, wore on her Disney Channel TV show. Maggie was surprised that Michael remembered to put Jackie into the outfit before bringing her to school, given that Maggie had completely missed the fact that this event was even taking place. Jackie bounded up to her mother. "What ARE you?"

"Um, I'm, uh, a comic. A funny person. Kind of like a clown. Don't I look funny?"

Jackie scrunched up her nose and frowned.

"Forget it, just show me what you've made. Did you make one of those big witches on the wall? Or maybe a jack-o-lantern? You always make lots of art projects that are really colorful."

Jackie emitted a dramatic sigh as if she were bored by her mother's compliments. "I'm gonna go get another doughnut."

"Okay."

As Maggie looked around the room, she saw varying degrees of parental compliance on the costume front. One dad was in a business suit but had positioned a cock-eyed Santa Claus cap on his head. He glanced warily at the over-excited children as if they might unexpectedly leap at him and soil his pressed, thinly pinstriped trousers at any moment. Another mom was just in casual wear, loose jeans, clogs and a red turtleneck, nothing Halloweenish.

"Did you not get the invitation? Or did you just forget?" Maggie quietly asked the mom in the regular clothing, as if she was a secret agent passing along classified information.

The mother, her voice full of shame, whispered, "I forgot about the parent costume part. I can't even remember if I read the whole thing, the notice, the one that came home. I'm lucky I remembered to get here today. What are you anyway?"

Maggie laughed. "I'm dressed as a comedian, I guess. At least that's what I told my daughter anyway, but, to be honest, I never even knew about this party. Jackie just called me. My husband put her in her costume this morning. After I finally found the flier, I grabbed these glasses that we had lying around and ran out of the house."

The mom laughed. "So I'm not the only screw-up?"

"Screw-up? You were HERE. You didn't have to be summoned by your crying kid whose teacher handed her the telephone. Hey! I think you and I could be soul mates!" Maggie said, as she pulled out a tiny chair meant for elementary school students to sit next to her new mom friend. But before she could sit down, Jackie grabbed her wrist and dragged her away to the "Spooky Corner" where Mrs. Waldigger and Mrs. Tribb, the room parents dressed as Tweedledee and Tweedledum, were ladling out lemonade and fruit punch. Nearby, a father, dressed as a Red Sox star slugger, was putting on quite a show attempting to do a bit of awkward magic. What magic had to do with being a baseball star was anyone's guess. A mom — dressed like a twisted vampy, post-rehab older sister to pop star Chrissy Singer — was laughing a bit too loudly at his antics. Tweedledee and Tweedledum exchanged disapproving glances.

"Would you like some lemonade?" Tweedledee asked Maggie. "No high fructose corn syrup! Made it fresh this morning."

"Or there's fruit punch," Tweedledum said, "but, sorry Hope, I don't know if it has any corn syrup in it. Must be why I was given the Tweedledum costume!"

All three laughed uncomfortably.

"Wonder who *she's* supposed to be," Tweedledee mumbled, pointing her huge, stainless steel ladle toward the mom who was giggling at everything the magician/Red Sox dad was saying.

"A MILF?" Tweedledum suggested, feigning looking shocked by her choice of words and putting her hand over her mouth after she said it. Maggie decided she wanted no part of this conversation and decided to seek out her daughter.

"Jackie, want some lemonade?" Maggie asked as her daughter shoved a whole strawberry into her mouth.

"Yeff pweez," she said in between chews.

"What nice manners Jackie!" Tweedledee said as she served her some lemonade, overlooking the fact that chunks of berry were flying out of Jackie's mouth as she spoke. She then stuck out her hand to Maggie, "Hi, I'm Ally, Tyler's mom. That's Hope, Belinda's mom. We're the room mothers. I haven't met you before, but I've met Jackie. She's a sweetheart."

"Thanks. I'm Maggie. How do you know Jackie?"

"We've been volunteering in the classroom, helping out Mrs. Stone with language arts and computers. Your daughter LOVES books. Quite the little bookworm. She says you are reading the Harry Potter books out loud together, that's cool. She's so sweet."

"Oh, that's great to hear," Maggie said half-heartedly, suddenly feeling like a guilty, distinctly uninvolved mother in the face of these two women who, much to her chagrin, were being kind to her. They weren't giving her any ammo to skewer them in her blog. And they hadn't even made any backhanded remarks about her pathetic outfit or asked her what she was supposed to be. If only they'd make a snarky remark, Maggie thought, then she'd have a great blog entry. Taking swipes at others who deserved it always made her feel better about herself when she was in a vulnerable position.

But they didn't deserve any swipes. Tweedledee and Tweedledum were perfectly charming. In fact, none of the parents — except for Maggie herself — said a word to Maggie about being late, about not contributing any food or labor to the party, about showing up looking like she'd just rolled out of bed, which she basically had done. All of which just made her feel worse. It was much more fun, Maggie thought, to rail against perfectionist moms when they acted all self-righteous and snide than it was to have to own your screw-up and beat yourself up about it.

BAD MOMMY: HANGING MY HEAD IN SHAME
File under: I'm in a sucky mood, how 'bout you?

So I was just finishing off that last blog post, about the Wanna-Be King/Sweet Lips — being all chirpy and positive for a change! — when I got a phone call from Thing I, which was weird, because it was so early in the school day. I was worried because I immediately thought she was sick or something. But Thing I was in the middle of her classroom Halloween party. And I was supposed to be there. In costume. Like all the other good, responsible parents who were already there. Yet I was sitting at the kitchen counter still in my pajamas. I never even saw the sheet that Thing I brought home from school announcing the party. There are way too many pieces of paper that come home, if you count Thing II's stuff too. I counted one week. 72 pieces of paper. Seriously. Including Thing I's drawings (she's a prolific artiste in school), worksheets, daily updates from Thing II's preschool, etc. I wind up throwing half of them out, unread because I can only take so many updates on which little poems they read in Circle Time today.

And this is the price I paid for not reading each and every piece of dead tree that comes home in my kid's backpack, being embarrassed and letting my kid down.

I jumped in the minivan and only ran two stoplights (No cops. Yes!) on my way to what I was certain would be humiliation at the hands of the good parents whose kids didn't have to call them from the school phone to the party, helped by their kid's teacher who already thinks I don't know how to pack snacks for my kid. I'd thrown on a pair of ripped jeans, wore the T-shirt I'd slept in and added Groucho Marx glasses and a Red Sox hat. I really didn't have a "costume" per se and decided, as I slammed the minivan door and ran to the school, that I'd say I was a comedian if asked.

Of course all the other kids' parents were there in costume. Or almost everyone was in costume. There was this one mom — on who I now have a girl crush because we hit it off so well . . . I think I want to have her baby — who wasn't in a costume, along with an annoyed father in a suit wearing a Santa cap who kept messing with his Black-Berry. (I wanted to grab it away and stomp on it. But I have some very personal reasons for loathing BlackBerries in general, as you well know.) Other than those two and me, the other parents had followed the rules and were dressed up, including the two room parents who were annoyingly perfect in their Alice in Wonderland duds — Tweedledee and Tweedledum. However the humiliation I felt for appearing as the lame comedian was nothing compared to feeling as though I'd let down my kid. Again. This is becoming a bad habit of mine, I'm afraid. I'm planning on making it up to Thing 1 tonight by bringing her to the bookstore and letting her select some new books. Plus I'll read to her a little longer than usual before bedtime. Not that that'll make me feel better, but it's not all about me is it?

A question to throw out to the world: When did it become acceptable to hijack parts of an adult's day and insist that they attend an in-school Halloween party at 10 in the morning? When did it become acceptable to expect that you can explicitly demand that parents — grown adults — show up in costume to a first grade classroom or else you'll disappoint your child? The kids are going to get plenty of candy and cupcake time, plus time in costume on the actual night of

Halloween. So do we really need to require parents to don costumes and show up at school or else be considered a spoilsport? There are so many opportunities for me to fail my kids every day. And this was just one more.

Thing I was a remarkably good sport about her mother's screw-up. She just seemed relieved when I finally made an appearance. Or maybe she let me off the hook because I let her load her plate up with sweets.

UPDATE: For those of you who provided me suggestions about where to get Thing I's Chrissy Singer costume without having to sell a kidney on the black market, THANK YOU! THANK YOU! THANK YOU! Her costume arrived in the mail two days ago along with Thing II's Roger Spaceman suit. I just love my readers! You find the best bargains out there! It made having to pay extra for faster delivery a little less painful.

CHAPTER EIGHT

". . . They actually listened to me. For once. No one said obnoxious things about hair. I don't know if it's actually going to make any difference with those Highway Department guys, but I really think that altering that small area of the Bypass, moving it around this one wetlands area, will make all the difference in getting it through, getting that variance."

"You'll do it Michael," Dorothy said. "You'll convince them. You're such a good talker, so smart. I was talking to my friend Bev in Westbrook, you remember her from St. Frances, right? She and I used to run the annual St. Frances Church Thanksgiving pie sale for years and years. Anyway, Sarah videotaped that combo Selectmen-Planning Board meeting with the Conservation Commissioners last week where you made your presentation. She dropped it in the mail and your father and I watched it last night. We were both impressed. Nice tie by the way."

Michael looked down to remind himself of what tie he was wearing today — a deep maroon one with golden swirls — then looked back out at the road just in time to apply the brakes and avoid rear-ending the blue Civic in front of him that had come to an abrupt stop in stop-and-go rush hour traffic. "What tie was I wearing at that meeting?"

"The moss green one I gave you for Christmas last year. The one from Filene's . . . you know, that one that comple-ments your hazel eyes. But the camera was too far away and we couldn't really see the color of your eyes well. Too bad."

"I can't even remember what I wore yesterday. Or even what I'm wearing today without looking down at my clothes. How's Dad? Anything new in the Taylor Engineering Department? How's that intern from BU working out?"

"Intern? He hasn't said. Nothing's new though. Nothing at all. You know your father. He never complains. Speaking of Christmas . . ." Dorothy said, cradling the phone in between her shoulder and her ear while opening her black, leather day planner in front on her at her kitchen table, already cleared of the dishes from an early 5 o'clock dinner. The only other item now on the table was a glass vase full of pink roses that Frank had brought her the other day for no reason. Dorothy sipped her still scalding peppermint tea from her "World's Best Nana" mug, which bore a photo of Jackie and Tommy in their 2004 Christmas outfits, and waited for his response.

There was none.

"Well?" Dorothy said, drumming her short, well manicured nails — coated in clear nail polish — against the table loudly enough so that Michael could hear.

"What?"

"Christmas."

"What about Christmas? No one mentioned Christmas." Michael, who'd been on a rare high because of the absence of criticism from the Westbrook people, started to feel the leaden weight of what Maggie called "Holiday Hell" starting to weigh on him, wrapping around his neck like an anchor and dragging him to the ocean floor. Whenever the subject of major holidays which necessitated the purchase of greeting cards or the preparation of a big meal came up, Michael felt like an animal in captivity with no place to go. No one was ever satisfied with what he and Maggie did on holidays, especially Michael and Maggie.

"*I* mentioned Christmas when I mentioned your green tie. Anyway, I didn't want to talk about Christmas really. Thanksgiving. Thanksgiving is the holiday I first wanted to discuss." She paused, consciously trying to select the right tone of voice that wouldn't reveal her real angst, the powerlessness she felt ever since she'd had to share her son with the Finn family on national holidays. "Isn't there any way you could get out of going to the Finns' house for Thanksgiving dinner this year? Couldn't they just get together with you all on Friday? There's just Margaret's father and brother, right? Surely they wouldn't mind if their dinner was pushed back by a day. Friday's a day off for them since they work for the town. Your Aunt Sue is going to be up here visiting from Florida. She was going to spend Thanksgiving here then leave our place on Friday morning to visit our cousin Hal in Rhode Island. Your brother will be here from New York, and so will your father's brothers. We haven't seen Joseph in so long. It'll be a big gathering with lots of great, home cooked food. I'd hate for you to miss it and not see all of your family. Sue hasn't seen Jacqueline and Thomas is such a long time. Thomas was just a baby the last time she saw him I think."

For a moment, Michael allowed himself to envision Maggie's reaction if he breathed a word to her about Dorothy's tweak to their holiday plans. It'd definitely be ugly, and R-rated, due to language and violence. "I'm sorry Mom, but we've been doing this for some time now. Years. We agreed to do it this way when Maggie and I got married. We alternate Christmas, Thanksgiving and Easter. One year with the Finns, the next year with the Kellys. This is a Finn year for Thanksgiving. You get us for Christmas. And besides, there are going to be so many people at your house that you won't even miss us."

"Impossible! You're the only one with kids. Your brother hasn't even found a steady girlfriend yet. Your uncles' children live too far away and won't be here. Jacqueline and Thomas are the only children who would be there. They add so much life to the holidays, and laughter. When you aren't there, it's noticeable, believe me. It makes me so sad. I miss you so much. To have a holiday without you breaks my heart . . . Maybe you could leave the Finns' house early and come have dessert with us? If you had dinner early at the Finns', say at noontime or thereabouts, you'd have plenty of time to come to still make it to our house. That way you wouldn't be breaking your holiday promise to them."

If it came to it, Dorothy thought, maybe she'd try to bribe them with the possibility that they could stay overnight and she'd babysit so Michael and Maggie could go out, not that she wanted Michael to go out but she was willing to do what it took to get him to stay over on Thanksgiving night. She felt untold comfort when Michael was just physically in her house, in his REAL home. Even if they weren't in the same rooms, Dorothy wanted him nearby.

"Mom, dinner's already set for three at the Finns'. You know that every time we go there we go with them to the Eastborough High football game. Then we go back to make dinner, or finish whatever we hadn't done the night before. We really wouldn't be able to make it to your house in time for dessert."

Visualizing her son eating processed gravy that came from a jar, stuffing from a box ("Stove Top is where you cook not what you eat," she told Frank after she heard about what had been served at the Finns' house during Michael's first Thanksgiving there), cranberry sauce from a tin can (which always had that slight, off-putting metallic after-taste), it felt like too much for Dorothy to bear. She always made every bit of Thanksgiving dinner all on her own, from scratch, just like her mother had done, full of love and attention to detail, a culinary expression of how much she loved her family. "Just come over here later. After dinner's over. You, Margaret and the children could sleep over. You and Margaret could go out, see a movie. You could still see your aunt that evening and for breakfast before she leaves. She could visit with the children."

Michael looked at the digital dashboard clock and realized he'd only be 15 minutes late getting home today. Practically on time. He'd tuned his mother and her plans out already.

"Michael, what do you say Sweetie?"

"I'm sorry Mom, but we'll see you on Friday afternoon, like we planned. For leftovers. Please save some of your corn-bread stuffing for me though. It's my favorite. I know Joseph will try to eat it all. If you put some in an opaque plastic container near the back of the fridge, he wouldn't find it and suck it down as a midnight snack. It's just not Thanksgiving to me without having some of your stuffing."

Dorothy sighed in a showy, loud fashion. "Drive safely Michael," she said, not bothering to reign in the audible disappointment in her voice. "We'll talk tomorrow I guess, if you have the time for me."

"Told you hon," Frank said from his chair in the living room, taking a pause from the Sam Adams biography he'd been reading which weighed more than a compact car. "Leave 'im alone. We'll see him Friday! They're going to the Finns'."

"No one asked you!" Dorothy yelled sharply, protectively covering the phone with her hand. "They're going to be drinking Lite beer and eating still-frozen, mushy apple pie from Sara Lee."

"Hey! Mom! Hello?! I can still hear you," shouted Michael, picturing his father's bemused expression.

"I'm sorry Michael," Dorothy said, though she really wasn't. "I just want you to enjoy the kind of Thanksgiving you deserve. I e-mailed Margaret some recipes for Thanksgiving since I know her father and brother certainly won't be cooking." She paused again to fortify herself with another sip from her tea. "You don't know how much it pains me to not have you with me on Thanksgiving, eating the same dishes your Nana Sophie used to make for me when I was a girl. I know how depressing it is for you to go to that house, with the Finns, probably still wearing their dirty uniforms and work boots . . ."

"Mom!" Michael gently reprimanded. "That's enough. Please don't talk about them like that. You don't know what it's like to be there. Be kind."

"I only know what *you've* told me," Dorothy said. "How do you think I know what they wear to dinner, what they eat for Thanksgiving and how much of a pigpen their house is? Because *you* told me about it. I've certainly never been invited over there, even though I've extended that courtesy to the Finns a number of times. Something they've never accepted by the way. And, you know what? I lost my mother too, more recently than they lost Molly, so please don't tell me that I don't understand what they're going through. She was the center of our family, Michael. The heart."

"YOU are the heart of the family Mom. Not Nana. You. And we haven't lost you. But we all miss Nana, you're right about that."

Dorothy's eyes welled with tears, which she fiercely fought, willing them to be absorbed back into her eye sockets.

"Here." Frank appeared next to the table, dangling a light blue tissue out in front of Dorothy's face.

She reluctantly snatched the tissue from the disembodied hand looming over her head in front of her, looked away and daintily dabbed her eyes. Frank put his hands on Dorothy's shoulders and kissed the top of her head. He, personally, hated the holidays. His favorite time was just after they were done and over with, when the house was filled with leftovers, his wife was calmer and he could retreat to the living room with a big slice of pumpkin pie or maybe a mound of mashed potatoes drowning in Nana Sophie's unrivaled mushroom gravy.

"Thank you," Dorothy said.

I'VE GOT YOUR TURKEY RIGHT HERE, BUDDY
File under: My MIL should work in Guantanamo Bay

Her Excellency Benita (I'm still in love with this new MIL Mussolini reference! Star blog commenter Sassy Sally — who won the

Queen Bee certificate — you rock!) is apparently very, very concerned that I'm going to poison her son and her only grandchildren on Thanksgiving. Or else she thinks I have the brains of a doorstop. The ambition of a garden slug. What other, possible, earthly reason could explain why she continues to send me a blizzard of e-mails about how to properly cook a turkey?

I got several e-mailed recipes including one from Butterball, one from Perdue, and three others from various gourmet cooking web sites (links are HERE, HERE and HERE) for variations on a roast turkey. There was a recipe on how to cook it with oranges. There was another one mentioning a sausage stuffing. One using Macintosh apples and port wine. One even suggested slipping fresh sage leaves beneath the turkey skin before roasting. (The idea of loosening skin and shoving things underneath it makes my own skin crawl, thank you very much. I think I threw up in my mouth a little bit just thinking about it.) All of the recipes she e-mailed me included gorgeous photos of a perfect bird on a beautiful serving platter, surrounded by bright sprigs of fresh green herbs.

Earth to Benita: This ain't my first rodeo. I've been in charge of making turkeys for Thanksgiving for my father and brother since I was a teenager. My turkeys might not have a pomegranate glaze or be basted in a "nice" chardonnay as you suggested (meaning not the three-for-$10 bottles I keep on hand to cope with mother-in-law emergencies). They're very basic. But they're edible. They're classic. Kind of like the Pilgrims might've eaten in this very state of Massachusetts lo so many years ago. (But Benita's from New Hampshire. Maybe that's her problem.) And my kids happen to like the way I make their Thanksgiving turkey, only they happen to eat their turkey with an assist from the Heinz ketchup company . . . because Thing I and Thing II won't eat any meat without slathering it in what Benita has called "the Devil's condiment" . . . kidding about that. Kind of. She doesn't like ketchup, said my kids use it too often, but never assigned demonic intentions to it. That I know of.

So while I'm dealing with Benita's recipe blitzkrieg, I have to mentally get ready to go back to the house where my dad and brother live, the place you might recall that I've referred to in the past as

"Bleak House," for several reasons: The darkness (both literal and actual), the beer cans, the always-on TV, the constant haze of cigarette smoke, the fact that it's frozen in a mid-1980s style. Not much has changed since my mom ran that house. But I try to keep up appearances, do my daughterly duty and then get the hell outta there as soon as possible. There's a slight chance that, since we're staying overnight at Bleak House, Sweet Lips and I might be able to sneak out on Thanksgiving night and leave my kids with their grandfather and uncle and have a real date. (The kids'll be asleep. All the Bleak Boys would need to do in the event of an emergency would be to call 9-1-1. I think they can handle that.) Maybe Sweet Lips and I could go to the karaoke bar and I could show Sweet Lips what his missus can do. I'll be practicing in front of my bathroom mirror. I so need a date to reconnect with Sweet Lips. It'll put me in much better spirits.

CHAPTER NINE

The yellow, two-bedroom ranch-styled house sat midway down the densely populated Oak Terrace near the center of Eastborough. Its backyard was tightly hemmed in by the neighboring small Capes and other ranches, largely shaded by the towering trees. In its earliest days, Oak Terrace was filled with families where most of the fathers worked at the Wallace Paper Mill and the mothers were, by and large, at-home moms. In the 1970s, many of the women on the street started working "mother's hours" at the Eastborough Community Savings Bank, the small New England-based department store — Bellman's — in the next town over, or at the Eastborough Apothecary.

Maggie spent a large chunk of her grade school years with her neighbor across the street, Kim Plainer, a petitely compact, somewhat shy, freckled redheaded girl who almost always wore her hair in two thin braids on either side of her head. Maggie was envious of the fact that Kim had two sisters — Samantha, who was older and Becky, who was two years younger — as Luke wasn't much of a playmate. When Maggie and Kim weren't pressing the other Plainer siblings into staging a talent show — where they'd sing along with 45s played on Maggie's turquoise blue, Fisher-Price record player on the Finns' back porch and charge Oak Terrace kids five cents to attend each showing — the girls were scheming about ways to get into the *Guinness World Records* book. For two weeks one summer, Kim and Maggie were certain they'd be able to break the record for the longest time spent jumping on pogo sticks. They practiced every day, making loud, annoying, rubbery-metallic sounds on their matching blue pogo sticks while bouncing on Kim's driveway, which was in dire need of resurfacing; its rough patches regularly caused the girls to falter and fall to the ground. On the big day when they planned to try for the *Guinness* record, it rained, so they watched *Super Friends* and the *Brady Bunch* reruns instead, abandoning their record-breaking venture.

Pogo-sticking aside, during nice weather the duo could be found perched behind Kim's red wagon with wooden, removable slat sides, in front of the Plainers' house, hawking everything from lemonade (served in plastic cups that Maggie's younger brother Luke would inevitably drop onto the grass or into the dust along the side of the road, and re-use without washing) to oatmeal cookies they'd bake with Kim's mother Lizzie. As soon as the cookies cooled, Maggie and Kim would stack them on a thick, plastic plate, plop them onto the wagon and peddle them to neighbors, pocketing the cash which they'd later blow on candy, particularly bags of red Swedish fish from Simon's, the convenience store on the corner.

On warm summer evenings, Maggie's father Rob would organize a game of "SPUD" in the backyard which drew kids from all around. A shaggy-haired suburban pied piper, Rob would rake his longish, somewhat stringy bangs to the left with the fingertips of his right hand — an unconscious tic of his — so he could see everyone clearly and then he'd assign everyone a number. Once everyone knew his or her number, Rob would chuck a tennis ball high up into the air as the sweaty children crowded around him, then he'd shout out a number in his very deep voice. The kid whose number was called would try to quickly grab the ball and yell, "SPUD!" the moment she got hold of it while everyone else would scatter in all directions. Once the word "SPUD" was shouted, the players were supposed to freeze in place, though Luke frequently broke that rule with impunity. The kid with the ball would then try to hit the closest person with it. If the thrower missed, she'd be given a letter. If she hit the kid, who couldn't move his feet to avoid getting hit by the ball, the kid who got hit would receive a letter. If a player eventually got all four letters and spelled out the word "SPUD," the player would be out of the game. For hours, the children, upwards of 12 to 15 kids, played SPUD or Wiffle ball or tag with Rob, and for this, mothers up and down Oak Terrace were grateful.

When the kids grew bored, they'd file into the Finn house, bringing that gamey kid scent with them, asking Molly Finn for something to drink. Tucking her bushy, shoulder-length dirty blonde hair behind her ears, Molly would always oblige with great cheerfulness, usually doling out small paper cups filled with Kool-Aid made from a mix, sometimes handing out Popsicles as well. She wasn't a big baker like her neighbor Lizzie and preferred opening a package of cookies to dipping into the neglected tin flour and sugar canisters on her kitchen countertop to whip something up. After the kids gobbled up their snacks, Molly would shoo them back outside and join Lizzie on the back porch, the radio playing softly in the corner, while they drank vodka on the rocks out of Betty and Veronica jelly glasses, smoking their way through packs of Kent Golden Lights and exchanging scandalous tidbits of information about their friends, neighbors and celebrities which they'd gleaned from the tabloids of which Molly was fond. When the mosquitoes would get too nasty and drive them into house, they'd snack some more and eventually wind up playing cards or working on one of Molly's sewing projects.

Kim's father Jon worked at the paper mill with Rob and they'd frequently drive in together early in the mornings, hopping into either Jon's green AMC Gremlin or Rob's brown Chevy Malibu wagon. Their wives were both at-home moms until their youngest children entered kindergarten. On Luke and Becky's first day of school, Molly and Lizzie had two cups of coffee and a cigarette each in Lizzie's kitchen, then walked down to Eastborough Apothecary together to apply for part-time jobs as sales clerks on the condition that they work the same daytime shifts on alternating weekdays so that one of them would always be home when the kids got home from school. They laughed when they realized that they'd gone to the interview dressed like twins, wearing the same wrap-around denim skirts (they'd shared the pattern and a bolt of fabric with one another), brown Dr. Scholl's sandals with the buckle on top and the wooden soles, along with breezy, eyelet white blouses. While dressed alike, they didn't look alike as Lizzie — who wore her sleek blonde hair back in a high pony-tail, had high cheekbones which she accented with soft pink rouge and a classic hourglass figure — garnered the most of the owner, Ed Carr's attention when they filled out their job applications at the drug store counter. Molly, who wore little to no cosmetics and sometimes felt self-conscious about her soft, round belly and short legs when she was around the shapely Lizzie, worked hard to make up for what she saw as her physical shortcomings with an out-sized personality including her quick, contagious laugh and her ability to make conversation with anyone. Molly managed to pry Mr. Carr's appreciative eyes away from Lizzie by asking him what he thought about the Red Sox's recent close loss to Milwaukee. This prompted Mr. Carr to prattle on for some 10 minutes, detailing every mistake he believed had been made as Molly nodded, laughed and chimed in with insightful commentary in all the right places. When Lizzie and Molly left, they each had pink Eaton Apothecary employee aprons slung over their arms and the following week's work schedule in their hands.

It all seemed so perfectly grand to Maggie, a classic tomboy who had a slight but noticeable gap between her front teeth and preferred her hair to be kept in the no-fuss Dorothy Hamill/wedge style. She loved reading Judy Blume books and frequently protested having to put aside her reading in order to do whatever Girl Scout project she'd been assigned. Her mother, a reluctant troop co-leader who led the group with Lizzie, pressured Maggie into joining the Girl Scouts saying it would be "character building" and would provide her with important life skills. Then three events took place in three consecutive years, shattering Maggie's safe Oak Terrace cocoon: The first was that the Wallace Paper Mill closed in 1985. Rob was able to land one of the few open spots on the Eastborough Department of Public Works with the help of one of his buddies with whom he played softball for the Wallace Mill's men's team. While appreciative of the job, Rob felt guilty about getting it because he'd beaten out many of his former Wallace co-workers, including Jon Plainer. The mill's closure led directly to the second event: The Plainer family moved to Connecticut the following year after Jon found a job down there, and Maggie tearfully watched her best friend move away. Then in 1987, on a dark, rainy early spring afternoon, just days before Maggie's 14th birthday the third event: Molly's car hydroplaned and violently slammed into a utility pole in front of Bellman's Department Store. The police found Molly, killed on impact, slumped over the steering wheel. Maggie's birthday gift — a thick, cable knit rainbow sweater that Maggie had been coveting — had fallen out of the cherry red Bellman bag and was lying on the floor in front of the passenger seat, splattered with blood.

During the months that followed, Maggie dropped out of Girl Scouts, stopped reading in her normal voracious fashion, assumed Molly's domestic duties — cooking, cleaning, grocery shopping — and watched over her 8-year-old brother after school as Rob requested more overtime hours. As she entered high school, Maggie seemed more like a disillusioned middle-aged housewife than a young woman. By the beginning of her freshman year of high school, six months after Molly was buried, a group of the self-appointed "cool" kids started referring to Maggie as "Ghost Girl" because she'd withdrawn from social activities, stopped speaking in class and had even been avoiding making eye contact with people in the halls. The only person outside of her family with whom she spoke was Diane DiGiovanni. She sat with Diane at the school cafeteria but did little else with her. Though Maggie had initially earned some sympathy from her peers in the weeks immediately after Molly's death, the general consensus by the time high school started was that she had grown too quiet, weirdly and eerily silent. It was thought the prudent move for anyone with social aspirations at Eastborough High to keep their distance from the girl with the dead eyes who was now dressing all in black.

As a result, Maggie didn't wind up dating much. No guy would last beyond a handful of dates. Her first dating "experience" occurred during her freshman year when she reluctantly made out at the winter dance with a stout, curly-haired classmate named Phil, a drummer in the school marching band and one of Eastborough's smarter students who eventually became the class salutatorian. Phil had a crush on Maggie all through junior high, but never had the courage to do anything about it. But by high school, Phil figured no one else would ask Maggie to the winter dance because of the "Ghost Girl" thing so he decided to take a chance. He stopped by the Finns' home over Thanksgiving weekend, two weeks before the dance, and spoke with Rob, who, once he learned that Phil wanted to take Maggie to the dance, insisted that Maggie accompany Phil. "It'd be good for you to get out of the house," Rob said.

After going to the dance with Phil — their one and only date — she briefly dated the number two guy on the Eastborough varsity track team, a thin reed named Will who was a full foot taller than Maggie. Will was a senior who was obsessed with horror flicks and intrigued by Maggie's gloomy reputation. He took Maggie out on her first official date shortly after she turned 16. (She never considered going to that winter dance and allowing Phil to slobber all over her, a *real* date since her father made her go.) They went to see a horror movie, *Halloween 5* — Will's choice — and she spent the film's entire 96-minute running time avoiding looking at the gruesome gore on the screen and instead, concentrated on trying to chew the unpopped popcorn kernels at the bottom of the popcorn bucket and see how long she could grind them between her teeth before they turned to mush. (The record was 92 chews.) After the movie, they went to Friendly's with the intent of splitting a giant hot fudge sundae with a dozen scoops of mint chocolate chip ice cream and chocolate jimmies. At least they'd agreed to split it, but Will scarfed down most of it while Maggie was trying to short-circuit her ice cream headache by warming the roof of her mouth with her tongue. Maggie decided she'd had enough of Will by date number three. That night they were taking a walk, hand-in-hand, through the MacDonald School playground near Maggie's house when Will observed that Maggie's fingers were "kinda chubby." As he held her right hand up in the meager light emitted by the park's lights, Will examined her fingers and suggested, "Maybe you could do some finger exercises or something to slim 'em down." A few minutes later, as they were sitting next to one another on playground swings, the overhead light cast harsh shadows over their faces. Will cocked his head to the side and squinted his eyes as he scrutinized Maggie's face. "Were you ever hit *really* hard on the nose? Because it's a bit crooked and mushed over to one side, kind of flat," he said, exaggeratedly pressing his own nose over to one side.

When Maggie commenced her college career at Framingham State College, with Diane DiGiovanni as her roommate, Maggie was eager to shed her pathetic-kid-whose-mom-died image and threw herself into the party scene. Wanting to embrace life by its jagged edges, Maggie plunged into a series of very casual "relationships," with only a handful of them leading to sex, much to the chagrin of the guys who thought that since Maggie was liberal with her profanity, opinions, cleavage and her beer intake, she'd be just as liberal about jumping into bed with them. The men she dated with whom she deigned to have sex, inevitably found themselves abruptly jettisoned, without warning, as Maggie simply cut off all form of communication when she felt a guy was getting too close. She'd essentially disappear, refusing to answer their phone calls or respond to the knock on her dorm room door when they came to visit. If she did happen to pass by them on campus, Maggie would ignore them, leaving them to wonder what they'd done to offend the funny, warm and irreverent girl whose eyes were no longer dead.

When Michael started dating Maggie and he set foot in the Oak Terrace house for the first time, he found it to be a stark contrast to his parents' orderly, slate blue home. There were layers of dust so thick that it looked as though dryer sheets had been laid across much of the furniture. Everything seemed to bear a thin coat of powdery debris, except for the matching set of faux black leather recliners parked right in front of the TV which got more use than anything in the house with the exception of the bottle opener. The country style red and yellow striped wallpaper that was glued onto the walls of almost every room in the house — Molly had gotten a bargain it — had faded and was peeling at the seams. The white toilet bowl in the small black and white bathroom had a dark beige tinge on the inside as though it hadn't been scrubbed since the Reagan administration, only Bill Clinton was now the president. The linens on the beds were paper-thin — you could almost see through them if you held them up to the light — but were in decent condition, considering that they were almost two decades old. In not such good condition were the bathroom and kitchen towels, which, when you used them felt as though you were dragging a loofah sponge across your skin. The darkened refrigerator (the light bulb went out years ago and was never replaced) had inky newsprint fingerprints along its handle, reminding Michael of the moldy fridge he'd once seen in a frat house.

During that initial evening when Maggie cheerfully brought Michael home to introduce him to her father and brother — he was the first male she'd ever brought home, introduced as "my boyfriend" and had ever made moony eyes about — she hoped they'd all bond over pizza, beer and a Celtics game. Michael couldn't help but worry, once he was inside, that he looked like a prissy snob as he tried to avoid touching things in the house so as to not come in direct contact with items that he was certain must've been incubating bacterium by the millions.

"Want to join me on the sofa?" Maggie asked, patting her hand on the stained tan couch in the living room, which was positioned against the wall, beneath decade-old family photos. Rob and Luke had already taken up residence in their matching recliners, metal TV trays set up in front of them loaded with two cans of Lite beer each, and pepperoni and meatball pizza slices from Ricky D's, which were saturating the paper plates beneath them with grease.

Michael, who was still sitting on a wooden chair at the kitchen table in the adjoining room, looked at the couch trying to figure out when was the last time it had been vacuumed and exactly how many pounds of potato chip crumbs were caught in between the cushions. (His mother regularly vacuumed their white and blue plaid sofa and matching wing chair, on Mondays and Thursdays. Every week. He'd carried on the Kelly vacuuming tradition when he went to college, earning the nickname, "Mike the Vac" from obnoxious, though appreciative roommates who recognized the benefits of having a neat freak in the house.) "No thanks, Mags," he said, fearful that his forced cheerfulness seemed too obviously phony. "I'm going to have some more pizza here at the table." He gestured to the half-eaten, rectangular party-sized pizza. He slipped a third slice onto his paper plate, vowing to do an additional set or two of ab crunches the next morning to make up for all the extra calories he was consuming. "Plus, I think I'm going to have some of that salad we bought and I don't want to spill Italian dressing onto the couch."

"Salad?" Luke said, snapping out of his silence. Not much of a talker, the surly, 16-year-old didn't like Maggie bringing someone home, some guy who ate salad and brought a pricey, caramel-colored micro-brew six-pack that had an illustration of fruit on its label. Luke, a regular beer consumer since age 13, had one firm rule when it came to his beer drinking: No fruit.

Michael glanced at Luke, who was wearing a wrinkled, blue Eastborough High Football T-shirt and gray sweatpants, and decided that that beefy guy could absolutely destroy Michael's puny ass with his left elbow, so he left the "salad" quip alone. He'd already sensed that he wasn't winning over any fans among the Finn men, or at least with Luke. He wasn't sure about Rob though. It started off badly from the moment Michael introduced himself to Luke and stuck out his hand to share a handshake, only to have the teen blow him off and instead run his right hand through his unruly, blonde, curly hair. Maybe it was that Michael was wearing a blindingly, white, ironed Polo shirt (Dorothy had pressed it for him because he was living at home when he started working at ENY right after graduation), and Dockers khaki pants. With pleats. Also pressed. And starched.

"Mikey, you don't wanna shake my hand right now buddy," Rob said, also declining Michael's handshake offer as well, albeit politely. "I think I've still got some dirt on me from work, some oil or grease or somethin' that I just can't get off. I don't wanna get ya dirty. Wanna beer?"

"Sure," Michael said, handing a plain, brown paper bag to Rob, who'd just changed out of his work clothes and thrown on his new Levis, a red and black flannel shirt and a sweat-stained navy Sox cap. "I brought you some beer. Maggie said you and Luke love to have beer when you're watching a game."

"Oh. Well. Thanks Mike," Rob said, setting down the bag on the kitchen table next to a freshly opened red, white and blue bag of State Line Potato Chips. Rob absentmindedly grabbed a handful of chips and stuffed them in his mouth as he peered into Michael's bag and extracted a single brown bottle from the cardboard six-pack. Rob eyed the bottle with a raised eyebrow. "Mmmm. Fan-cy. Thanks, Mike! Where's it from?"

"Vermont. It's a micro-brewed blueberry beer. I thought you might like it."

"Well, thank you very much. You didn't have to do that."

Luke rolled his eyes as he fetched a Lite beer can from the fridge and exited the kitchen, leaving a guttural, "Hmph!" in his wake.

The Celtics smacking around the Lakers took some of the uncomfortable edge off the fact that Michael simply couldn't bring himself to sit on the sofa, which did not go unnoticed. The 110-82 win put Rob and Luke in good moods for the rest of the evening. Michael, meanwhile, quietly suffered from stomach pains from eating all that grease-laden pizza, never daring to tell Maggie that he would not voluntarily eat Ricky D's pizza ever again, not if he could help it.

CHAPTER TEN

CAN WE JUST SKIP ALL THIS HOLIDAY BUSINESS AND CALL IT A DAY?
File under: Holiday madness

Do we really have to do this, Thanksgiving I mean? I'm soooo not in the mood to drag my ass to the grocery store, buy all the makings for a meal that'll be eaten in silence in Bleak House, a place where I don't want to go? I predict with 100 percent certainty that Things I and II will whine through the entire day and pester me about why Bleak House smells so bad.

Why does it smell bad? Because of the cigarette smoke. I know I'm going to have at least one fight with my brother who smokes all the time and doesn't give a shit if his niece and nephew are around breathing in his fumes. (He swears like crazy as well, right in front of the kids, no filter on that guy. Sure I swear here, but not in front of the kids.) Here's how it usually goes: I ask him politely if he can stop smoking when we're there — or at least go outside — but I think that's as likely to happen as me and Her Excellency Benita joining hands and skipping while singing, "Ring Around the Rosy" together.

I know my dad will be his best, passive aggressive self, not getting in the middle between my brother and me. Just being there with him, in that house, seeing the lack of . . . what's the word, I dunno, the lack of LIFE there, is so damned depressing. I just hate it.

Maybe I can get out of the whole thing by faking an illness. Don't think I haven't given this some serious thought. I'd set it up two days beforehand (so I wouldn't have to go shopping or make anything), by complaining of stomach pains so bad that I have to lie down. I could *refuse to eat anything the day before Thanksgiving and make violent retching sounds in the bathroom. If I make sure that I look like an absolute mess on Thanksgiving Day, Sweet Lips will take pity on me and handle Thanksgiving on his own. But then again, I'd miss out on our Thanksgiving night karaoke date. Is going out on that date worth faking illness and skipping Thanksgiving altogether? Who's being passive aggressive now? (*pot, kettle, black*)*

I'm gonna have to just pull on my Big Girl panties and suck it up and get through this, if not for me, then for the sake of Thing I and Thing II who don't deserve to have their holiday ruined by a fake illness. All I want to do right now instead of getting all prepared for this day from hell is to pull those two kids close to me, snuggle with them on the couch and let 'em watch some crappy Disney movie while I hold them tightly and give my own silent thanks for having them. But no such luck, apparently.

Good night and good luck my peeps. Happy Thanksgiving.

"I've got a good feeling about today!" Rob announced optimistically, as he tried to tousle his grandson Tommy's closely shorn dark brown hair that was so short it couldn't really be tousled.

"'bout what Pop-Pop?" Tommy asked as he responded in kind, running his tiny fingers over his grandfather's thinning, shaggy gray hair.

"The Eastborough Eagles. They play their enemies today in football."

"Dad," Maggie said, voice heavy with anticipatory disapproval, as she unpacked two coolers filled with the side dishes she'd prepared for the Thanksgiving dinner, "the Lester Lions team isn't the *enemy*!" She looked directly at Tommy. "They're NOT the enemy. They're just the team that Pop-Pop's favorite team is going to play at today's game."

"So no enmee?" Tommy said, throwing a series of unco-ordinated punches at an unseen enemy opponent as he yelled, "Hi-ya!"

"No, no enemy," Maggie said, wondering if she'd left the cans of cranberry sauce behind in Greenville.

"Nomuddy's gonna die? From enmees?"

Maggie looked at her father as she said, "No, no one's dying. Why don't you and Jackie go play outside in the back-yard. Daddy brought a soccer ball and a football, I think."

Attempting to maintain the illusion of a festive mood, Maggie thought it best to keep Michael out of the house as much as possible because she knew how much he hated being there, as she eventually discovered during their first year of marriage. In the middle of an argument about the fact that a small army of tiny ants had created their own highway from the backyard to the area beneath their kitchen table near the sliding glass door, Michael yelled, "*Of course* you don't think it's a big deal that there are crumbs under the table that you never bother to clean up. You've lived in squalor for years. Your dad's place is filthy. I don't know how you stand it, how you lived there. It's repulsive."

"Well I'd rather live in a house that's relaxed and real, rather than in one where everyone has a giant floor mop rammed up their assholes and they all walk on eggshells, not that there are ever eggshells or anything on the floors there, at your mother's house, where you learned your whole anal Mr. Clean routine. Oh no! Can't be like them white trash Finns," she said.

"Come on Maggie, you know it's true. I just don't want our house to become like theirs. And now we've got ants!" He prayed Dorothy would never find out. He'd be so ashamed.

"Our house *isn't* 'filthy.' I got some cracker crumbs on the floor. We got sugar ants. Tiny ones. So what? The exter-minator guy said that it's not unusual. It doesn't mean I'm dirty! He said the treatment he used should take care of it. So shut the fuck up about it!"

"I'm not saying that *you* are dirty, you personally, your body or anything. It's that you haven't exactly had the best role models for keeping a house clean."

Maggie grabbed some of the newspapers that had been stacked on their rickety wooden telephone table next to the refrigerator, angrily balled them up and threw them at the wall in frustration, knocking a framed wedding photo off of the wall. "You're so childish," Michael said, disgusted.

"And you're such a sanctimonious ass."

"I'm leaving the kitchen until you calm down," Michael said. He left the room, then popped his head back in the doorway to say, "I just want to keep our place reasonably clean so we don't get bugs. I don't think that's too much to ask. I didn't want to get into all of this other crap." With that, he started to half-trot up the stairs to their bedroom.

Maggie recalled that argument as she picked up a Stop & Shop grocery bag from her father's crumb-covered kitchen floor. "Michael did have a point," she thought as she surveyed the once sunny room turned dank in which she was supposed to whip up Thanksgiving dinner, while Michael was outside with the kids, likely slathering their hands with antibacterial gel. Rob and Luke were pouring through the *Boston Journal's* sports section, debating the story previewing the Eagles-Lions contest. For once, Maggie had planned ahead. She'd already made the mashed potatoes, mashed butternut squash, the stuffing and the green bean casserole at home. She bought a couple of pies — apple and pumpkin — from the market, along with the rolls and two cans of cranberry sauce, which she did indeed leave at home. The only thing she had to cook in this kitchen was the turkey. She'd already cleaned, seasoned and put the bird into a roasting pan the previous night and popped it into the fridge. The plan was to put the 12½-pound turkey into the oven well before they went to the high school football game, then she'd re-heat the side dishes in the microwave and oven when they got back.

Maggie was surprised to find herself excited to go to this

Thanksgiving Day Eastborough High game. Diane had told her that not only would she and George be attending, but a number of their high school friends were going to be there too, including a few people with whom Maggie actually wanted to catch up. Diane was having an all-from-scratch Thanksgiving at her parents' house, but told Maggie that she and George would still have time to make it to the game. Michael was up for going to the game too because not only did he think the kids might like to see it — all Jackie had been talking about was trying to learn the cheerleaders' cheers — but that would mean three hours of not having to pretend he wasn't skeeved out while sitting in his father-in-law's house.

As soon as the turkey was in the oven and Maggie had deftly evaded Jackie's question about where the turkey's butt was located, she and Michael packed up the kids in the red minivan while Luke and Rob climbed into Luke's new, black Chevy pick-up. Finding parking adjacent to the high school football stadium was a challenge. Maggie had forgotten how crowded it could get for these Thanksgiving Day games, with alums and their families wearing the home team's colors of royal blue and white. After Maggie did a couple of loops through the residential neighborhoods, Michael said, "Just go into the stadium lot."

"But you have to pay to park there."

"That's fine. I don't want to have to have the kids walk a long way back and forth to the car and get all cranky."

Maggie pulled into the queue and saw a pony-tailed teen in a blue Eastborough High soccer team jacket holding a hand-painted sign aloft above her head, "Eagles Stadium Parking: $20. Support EHS Sports :)"

"Twenty bucks?! No way! I can find free parking some-where else."

"Mags, just pull in. It's no big deal. It's about as much as parking in Boston. It'll be easier. Just go in there."

"But we'll never get out of the parking lot. We'll be stuck here forever in a line of cars."

Michael placed his hand on her forearm. "Mags, we'll leave a little early. It's okay. Just trust me." In the days leading up to Thanksgiving, he'd literally seen Maggie's tension level physically ratchet up, as it typically did whenever she knew she'd be spending time in the Finn house on a major holiday. It wasn't so much that Maggie felt stressed out from planning and pulling together the makings of Thanksgiving dinner, instead, it was that leaden ache she felt as she anticipated walking into her mother's kitchen and laying her hands on Molly's carefully selected china plates (white with delicate pink roses along the edge), her faded holiday linens, her well worn pots and pans.

Even though he knew this was a difficult time for Maggie, Michael hadn't had much of an opportunity to provide her with any relief, provoke an easy laugh, surprise her with a bouquet of flowers or some of those chocolates in the fancy dark brown and gold paper that she liked. Pressure to revamp a major portion of ENY's variance application caused Michael to work until 9 p.m. for nearly three straight weeks. While he hadn't gone into the office during the two weekends before Thanksgiving — as he believed he really should have done — Michael worked most of Saturday and Sunday afternoons and evenings holed up in his home office while Maggie kept the kids at bay. (He was convinced that the odd smell that had mysteriously taken over his office was somehow a result of something Bud and Hank had done when he gave them a ride to the site and they were sitting next to Michael's brief-case and cardboard tube of plans. It had been driving him crazy, not being able to figure out how to get rid of the pungent odor.)

Even on Thanksgiving, Michael felt he needed to keep on top of the stream of e-mails being sent by Sam Young, his divorced boss who had a distaste for holidays and vacations and who, none too subtly let everyone know that he was going to be spending Thanksgiving in the office. Michael decided he needed to clandestinely check his BlackBerry from the privacy of the bathroom or when he took the kids outside in the Finns' backyard, out of Maggie's line of sight because she'd explode if she saw that he was working. He'd also stowed his laptop under the third row seats in Maggie's minivan in the event he had a chance to use it.

He also hadn't broached with Maggie his intention to alter their plans for the evening. He wanted to finish dessert early, head to his parents' house and stay there overnight. Maggie had already packed everyone's things with the intent of sleeping at the Finns' so that she and Michael could go out with Diane and George to an Eastborough bar after Thanksgiving dinner, but Michael thought he could persuade her to leave his in-laws' house. By going up to Norton, they'd get to sleep in clean beds with clean sheets and Michael could actually shower the next morning without fear of contracting a penicillin-resistant infection from the Finns' bathtub. They'd also be able to gorge on Dorothy's grade-A leftovers on Thanksgiving night *and* the following day, PLUS Michael would be able to sneak in some work in the small den/sunroom without getting yelled at because Maggie would want to simply zone out in front of the TV so as to avoid conversations with Dorothy.

But first, he had to lay the groundwork and make sure that things went smoothly for Maggie. Enjoying this football game was first on his agenda, even if that meant ridiculously overpaying to park at a high school to watch a crappy gridiron romp. Michael smiled as he handed over the $20 bill to Maggie to give to the over-caffeinated Eastborough High soccer player sporting a fake tan and unnaturally white teeth.

"Over there," Michael said, gesturing toward a parking spot close to the exit.

"But they're waving me farther into the parking lot down the first aisle, over there to the left," Maggie said, ready to follow the thin teenagers wearing orange vests who were disinterestedly waving orange sticks.

"Forget them, just pull in here. We'll be able to get out

easily when we're ready to leave," he said.

"But . . ." Maggie applied the brakes, uncertain of what to do. As off-beat and rule-breaking as she might have been perceived by the moms of Maple Road and to the women who bought Memory Makers products from her, deep down, Maggie was an angst-ridden rule follower.

"Look at them," Michael said, pointing to the students. One teen was reading a text on his cell phone while mindlessly moving his orange stick in a giant oval pattern. Another was checking out the pedestrians as they filed onto the sidewalk. "They're kids. They don't care. What are they going to do to us? Put us in detention? Parking lot jail?"

"Fine!" Maggie shouted as she maneuvered the minivan in between some orange cones that were intended to funnel traffic toward the back of the lot, and parked in a spot near the exit. The lead parking lot staffer, a high school senior who was standing next to the one collecting the cash saw Maggie and weakly yelled, "Hey! Over here!" But, upon seeing Maggie pull into the spot and that small kids were exiting from the van, he decided it wasn't worth his effort to do anything about it. The student shrugged his shoulders and read a new text he'd just received.

They found Rob and Luke already in the stands, five rows up at the 50-yard line, just high enough to see the field over the heads of the players standing next to the bench on the sidelines, and above the row of cheerleaders. Tommy climbed onto Rob's bony lap while Luke, looking like a surly linebacker in his navy blue Eagles' hooded sweatshirt and Patriots baseball cap, drained a large Styrofoam cup of Dunkin' Donuts regular coffee (very light with two sugars, his usual). He pretended not to notice his nephew and niece with whom he rarely exchanged a word. Michael and Maggie — both unintentionally wearing matching ensembles of tan pants, black turtleneck sweaters and black leather jackets — scaled the bleachers to join them. Maggie spread out a blue fleece blanket across the cold, aluminum bench seats to ward off the chill, which wasn't too harsh considering it was a New England morning in late November. The sun was out and, when the breeze wasn't blowing, it was in the mid-50s, entirely pleasant, so much so that Tommy started unzipping his red fire truck jacket and pulling off his cherry red Red Sox knit cap.

"Dad, can you please put Tommy's jacket back on? The wind can get cold."

Rob — in his worn jeans, jean jacket and black, cotton waffle shirt furrowed his brow as he pushed his gray bangs out of his eyes — glanced at Tommy, who smiled broadly back at him. "He's fine Maggie. I'll keep him warm." To reinforce his point, Rob put his arm around Tommy and pulled him close to his side, vigorously rubbing the child's back.

"Dad, please put his coat back on. He won't stay next to you for long. He's squirmy."

"Fine, fine . . . oooh, Buddy, look, here comes the team!"

The cheerleaders — in brilliant blue and white skirts and sweaters, hair severely pulled back in high ponytails perched at nearly the tops of their heads and festooned with blue ribbons (even if the girls' hair was short, their locks were pinned back and lacquered with enough hairspray that they'd withstand a Nor'easter) — roused the crowd with shouts and rhythmic clapping that Jackie, who had snuggled up close to her father, studied intently. Rob and Luke soon became alternately engrossed and disgusted by the football game, depending upon the score in the back-and-forth contest. Maggie, meanwhile, anxiously scanned the stands looking for any sign of Diane and George, or anyone she knew from high school who wasn't a pothead or a cliquish snob.

"Jackie, would you like to sit over here too, on this blanket, next to Pop-Pop?" Rob asked earnestly, extending his open arm toward his granddaughter and, for a moment, reminded Maggie of the father he was when she was a young child, the one who got all the neighborhood kids to play games in their backyard for hours until it was so dark that they couldn't see their hands in front of their faces.

Jackie, in a cheerleading-induced trance, didn't respond, which broke Maggie's heart. "Yo! Jackie Kelly! Wake up lady!" Maggie shouted.

Jackie flinched as though she'd been smacked in the head and looked as though she was about to burst into tears.

"Sweetie," Michael cooed, wrapping his arm around Jackie's watermelon pink winter coat with the fake fur collar dyed a bright combination of pink and dotted with silver threads, "Mommy was just trying to get your attention, that's all." He paused dramatically, wondering if he'd stopped the flood of tears that was threatening to flow. Trying to redirect her attention, Michael asked, "Do you have a favorite cheer-leader?"

Jackie sniffed loudly, giving her mother an angry, side-long glance. Focusing on the sidelines again, Jackie singled out a tall, thin blonde cheerleader at the far end who seemed to be an underclassman because she executed her cheers tentatively and kept looking at the other squad members for guidance. "Her. I like her the best."

"Why did you pick her?" Michael asked.

"She jumps the highest."

"Jackie, would you like to sit on the blanket over here next to your grandfather?" Maggie asked again in a polite, plaintive tone. She leaned over and whispered to Michael, "I want us to take a walk. Alone. We can leave 'em here with my dad."

Having overheard her mother, Jackie turned her nose up toward the sky, crossed her arms in front of her and emitted an irritated, high-pitched, "Hmmph!"

Sensing a potentially nasty mother-daughter showdown in the making, Michael quickly stepped in. "Hey Jackie jack o'lantern, Pop-Pop is the best person to sit next to. He can tell you all about the game. He even *knows* some of the players!"

Jackie, reluctant to respond at first, finally said, "Does he know about the cheerleaders?"

Michael stood up and said, "Pop-Pop knows all about football games. He might even know the cheerleaders, or their parents. Ask him about it. C'mon Mags. Let's take a walk." He extended his gloved hand to his wife. "Rob, do you mind watching the kids for a bit while Maggie and I take a walk to look for some of her friends?"

"No Daddy, no!" Tommy yelled, sliding off his grandfather's lap and rushing toward his father. "Don't go! Don't go!"

"No! The jacket!" Maggie hollered as she watched Tommy's fire truck coat slide off Rob's lap and slip through the gap in the bleachers. "Argh! Now we're gonna have to crawl under there! That's a brand new jacket, Tommy!"

Tommy shoved his way past his grandfather's knees in order to get to Michael and buried his face into Michael's legs, wrapping his arms around them tightly. He sniveled and got snot over Michael's carefully pressed khakis.

Maggie waited a beat to see what would happen next. Would someone offer to fetch the jacket for which she spent way too much at a fancy kid's store at the mall when she knew she shouldn't have splurged but couldn't resist its cuteness? Would Michael pitch a fit because the jacket was now likely lying in debris? Would her father intervene with Tommy so she could get a few precious minutes alone with her husband? She counted to 30 in her head. No one moved. No one said anything, save for Tommy's crying and Jackie's quiet mimicking of the cheerleader's chants.

"Fine!" Maggie thundered as she threw her hands up into the air and exaggeratedly stomped down the bleachers past a clutch of Eastborough High girls whispering and pointing at a football player. Her disappointment grew as she stormed along the sidelines looking at the crowd and seeing not a single person she knew, not even people she was planning on ignoring if she saw them. Pulling her cell phone out from the bottom of her oversized purse, she looked to see if Diane had called, because if the phone had rung she probably wouldn't have heard it from underneath all that stuff she lugged around with her. A little phone icon on the display screen indicated that she had a voicemail message. She walked behind the bleachers and leaned up against the black chain link fence so she could listen to Diane's message, hoping it contained the location of where they were sitting. She pressed the palm of her right hand over her ear while holding the phone in her left hand and crouched as she strained to hear Diane's voice mail over the roar of the crowd:

"Maggie! Don't know if you've left for the game yet, but George and I can't make it. Donna and Mary can't either. I spoke with them this morning, but we're going to meet at Shots tonight, around 8:30. Please come. They're having a karaoke night, like I told you, and you and I are due for some tunes sistah. I'm bringing that new song we love on CD so we can sing it. Maybe you and Sweet Lips will get in some slow dancin'. Good luck with dinner. Happy Thanksgiving. See you tonight."

Maggie snapped the phone shut and tossed it back into her purse. She wanted nothing more than to go home to Greenville, to forget about Thanksgiving, forget about dinner, forget about this stupid game and just crawl back into bed. But if she had to be in Eastborough, at least she had a night with Diane and George to look forward to. First though, she had to fetch Tommy's jacket. When she spotted a glimpse of red under the aluminum bleachers, she cringed. It was atop a bed of smashed Styrofoam cups coated with dried coffee and old lip gloss marks along the rim, cigarette butts, crumpled squares of tin foil that had once been wrapped around greasy burgers from the Booster Club's snack shack, and at least a dozen gum and candy wrappers. She stepped, ducked and wove her way around the bleachers' beams and bars, beneath the disappointed Eagles' fans and noticed a brown liquid dripping onto her left shoulder from above. "What, is that hot chocolate? Coffee?" she wondered as she roughly brushed it off her jacket, hoping it wouldn't leave a stain. She was reluctant to climb deeper underneath the bleachers after carefully treading through the garbage. She squatted down and stretched her arm out toward the jacket, but it was still a little more than three feet out of her reach. Maggie would just have to inch forward more, even if it meant stepping over a few used condoms, which made her shudder. If Michael had seen those, he would've insisted that they abandon the coat behind for fear that super-microbes might've been clinging to the fabric. However Maggie knew how much she spent on the size 4T jacket and figured she'd just wash it on the hottest cycle and put it through the dryer for a good long time to kill anything that survived the wash cycle.

Emerging from the underbelly of the bleachers feeling in dire need of a shower, Maggie saw Michael standing there, wrinkling his nose, revolted, as he looked at the ground.

"Are those what I think they are?" he asked, pointing near the area where Maggie saw the condoms.

Standing fully upright and holding the jacket in one hand, Maggie brushed her legs off and said, "That's right. Condoms. And other assorted gross crap. Thanks for your help by the way. Very gentlemanly of you to volunteer to go under there to get this jacket. I'm going to go put it in the back of the minivan. I've got a plastic bag in there. I'll wash it when we get to my dad's."

Worried she'd find his laptop hidden in the van — something he'd promised her he wouldn't bring with him — he offered to join her, besides, he wasn't eager to return to the company of Rob and Luke and the now whiny Tommy. "Let's bring it there together. I'll go with you," Michael said, starting to put his arm around her shoulder, then, remembering that she'd just been beneath the bleachers, he pulled it away centimeters before he touched her. Seeing Maggie frown, he said, "Sorry honey, but you were just under there with all that . . . stuff . . . I'll owe you a hug."

"Whatever," Maggie said dully as she trudged ahead of him, holding the jacket away from her body between the tips of her fingers.

Two hundred yards into the silent trudge, Maggie couldn't contain herself any longer, "What the hell? Why is this so hard? I just wanted it to be easy. I tried to get as much done as I could beforehand so I wouldn't have to do any more than cook the turkey at my dad's. I thought that coming to this game would be fun, a chance for us to spend a little time with my friends, let Dad watch the kids for a few minutes. Now everything's going to hell. Diane and my friends aren't coming. The Eagles are losing, which means Luke'll be an unbearable asshole when we get back to the house. Jackie's being impossible and Tommy's doing nothing but whimpering. I had to plow through rubbers to get this coat. And you didn't even offer to get it for me. Just stood there, watching me. Now you won't even put your arm around me."

Michael didn't respond immediately. He was trying to choose his words carefully in his head before speaking them out loud so as not to toss gasoline onto the smoldering flames otherwise known as his wife. "Sorry Maggie," he replied quietly. "Tommy was holding onto my legs tightly and it was really hard to get him off of me. He was crying. He kept saying, 'Daddy, Daddy,' and I couldn't leave him in that kind of state with your father. He wouldn't have known what to do with him, and Tommy would've fallen apart if I hadn't calmed him down. I came down here as soon as I could. I would've gotten the coat for you, but you beat me to it. I called your name, trying to tell you to wait for me, but I guess you didn't hear me. I'm sorry."

Maggie, not buying Michael's story, pulled out her enormous keychain with 18 keys along with a Swiss Army knife and a bottle opener (which Michael repeatedly told her was redundant because her Swiss Army knife has a bottle opener, to which she always responded, "Bite me.") and opened up the back of the van, rummaging around for that plastic Stop & Shop bag she'd left there this morning.

"Cut it out Michael. You wouldn't have climbed through all that crap to get the coat. You would've just let me do it, let me get dirty, because what, I have a dirty family? Then you shun me for getting dirty, doing all the dirty work, while you're all sparkly clean . . . Wait, what's this? Your laptop? I thought you promised that you wouldn't be doing any work today. For one fucking day."

Dropping the coat on the ground next to the van, she surprised Michael by swiftly reaching into the breast pocket of his jacket and extracting his cell phone. She punched in the security code and started scrolling through his most recent texts, e-mails and calls before Michael realized what she was doing.

"Hey!" he tried to grab the phone back, but Maggie turned away too quickly and ran in front of the van.

"You've been texting Sam Young! Oh . . . and you . . . you've been making calls all morning when you were supposed to be playing with the kids. What the fuck? Can't you just be with us for a second on Thanksgiving without doing ENY stuff? I knew it!"

"Look," he said, his temper rising quickly despite his earnest efforts to remain calm, "you have no idea what's going on right now with this variance. It's at a crucial point and if I don't do this stuff I'm gonna be out of the loop, considered, I don't know, not relevant, not important to the process. I've got to *seem* critical to the process for them to value me. You know that. You worked there. Sam's *working* today. He's in the office right now, and I don't want to be the only one who's not communicating with him today. I can't be AWOL. I'm not spending that much time on this Maggie. I'm here aren't I? You haven't noticed me not being around today have you? What more do you want?"

"I want you to be here . . . your mind to be here. . ." She suppressed the urge to cry. "I want you to . . ." Her voice trailed off. She turned away from him and said nothing.

"Why are we even fighting about this? I'm here. I'm at this game. We're gonna eat Thanksgiving dinner at your dad's house. We're all together. If I slip off for a few minutes on this, here and there, it's really no big deal. The kids were fine outside and you would've never known about this. It wouldn't have made any difference to you or your day if you'd never found the laptop."

She turned sharply. "So your argument is that since I haven't noticed that you've been working today it's 'no big deal?' What, what I don't know won't hurt me?"

"Yes!" Michael said firmly. "All of this is for us, for the family, to help us. The better I do at work, the better we do. I didn't tell you so it wouldn't get all complicated."

"Rrrgh!" Maggie growled. She grabbed Tommy's jacket from the ground, tossed it into the trunk and slammed the trunk door shut. "Well, at least we've got tonight. That's the only bright spot in this whole, shitty day."

"Tonight?"

"Ye-esss . . ." she said warily. "We talked about going out with Diane and George tonight. To Shots. We talked about this. More than once. You said you'd go. Don't tell me you forgot."

"Well . . ."

Feeling heat flush her cheeks again, Maggie clenched her fists in preparation for a hyper-articulate, well rehearsed response full of rational excuses that would make her blood boil, "Well what?"

"My mom . . ."

"Your mother? Oh! Here we go! What the hell does your mother have to do with tonight? What, I suppose she wanted us to blow off my dad and go up to her house today."

"Aunt Sue is up . . ."

"Here we go," Maggie repeated.

"Just listen please. Give me a sec before you go nutty. Please," Michael stuck his right hand out in front of him, palm facing forward. Then he gently lowered it as if he thought he could diffuse the situation by moving in slow motion, like he was taming a lion. "Aunt Sue is up from Florida and she's leaving for Rhode Island early tomorrow morning. If we don't go up to my mom's house tonight, we won't see her. I haven't seen her in a long time. She hasn't seen Tommy since he was a baby."

Maggie bit her tongue and tried to reply with an equal measure of calmness. "We had a deal. We switch off every other year. Last Thanksgiving, my mother's best friend, Lizzie Plainer, was in town and I haven't seen her in, what, 15 years or something, and I didn't get to see her because we were up in Norton at your family's Thanksgiving dinner as we planned. I didn't break my promise."

"But that wasn't a member of the family."

"What? My mother's best friend . . ."

"It's not . . ."

". . . comes to visit and *you* get to decide if she's worth seeing . . ."

"I'm not . . ."

". . . based on whether she's my blood relative?"

"Maggie!"

"Your mother is just looking for a way to finagle things how she wants them, even though she already agreed to this arrangement. It's not like she's not going to see us this weekend."

"I wouldn't say she agreed."

"She said she did. What, now I'm supposed to analyze what she really means when she says, 'Yes' to alternate Thanksgiving and Christmas dinners? I'm supposed to, what, call in therapists or language experts or something to see if we agree on the meaning of the word 'yes?' This is OUR family, we're talking about. Where we spend our holidays is OUR decision. Not hers."

"You're making too much of this."

"No, I'm not. You're not mad enough about her manip-ulation."

"This is not some giant Dorothy conspiracy. It's not like she called Aunt Sue and said, 'Hey, why don't you schedule your trip so that you'll only be here less than 48 hours and I can guilt Michael and Maggie into coming to my house for Thanksgiving for two years in a row.'"

"Your mother would've called me Margaret, not Maggie."

Michael smirked and stepped toward Maggie, who had her arms tightly crossed in front of her chest. He put his hands on her shoulders and tried not to balk as he thought about all the germs that were reproducing at that moment on the exterior of her jacket. He knew he had Purell in his pocket though, which he'd use when Maggie wasn't looking. "Please listen to me. I wasn't going to suggest that we cheat your family out of their Thanksgiving dinner. Here's what I was thinking. And if you hear me out, and don't interrupt, maybe we can discuss this like reasonable people. Everyone can win here."

Maggie made a fierce face — which reminded Michael of the face Jackie had made a few minutes ago after Maggie yelled at her — and glared at him. The Eastborough High crowd could be heard collectively groaning their disappointment at yet another fumble, the third in the first half.

"We go back to your dad's house. We eat. We have a lovely dessert. We go to Shots for a little while, then we drive to my parents' house late. I'll drive. I don't mind driving at night. I'll grab a coffee. My mom can have the sofa bed ready for Jackie and Tommy, who'll already be asleep. I'll get to chat with Aunt Sue, who's a night owl. And I know you don't like sleeping at your dad's any more than I do. Everyone will be happy."

"Everyone?"

CHAPTER ELEVEN

Maggie and Michael went on a double-date with Diane and George for the first time only three weeks after Maggie and Michael started seeing one another. Maggie had been gushing about Michael to Diane — who was already engaged to the sweet but oafish George after spending all four of their college years as a joined-at-the-hip couple — since the day Michael had walked into the HR office at ENY. She called Diane within an hour of meeting him.

"This guy, Michael . . . I'm at a loss for words," Maggie said, trying to covertly whisper into the phone so her HR colleagues wouldn't hear her.

"You? At a loss? So what, he's tall dark and handsome? A George Clooney?"

"No, not a Clooney. More like, well, he's not like any movie star really. More like the main star's best friend. The quiet, confident nice guy. He's not flashy or anything. He's got this, this *thing*. I don't know exactly how to describe it, a quiet but kind of, like, electric thing? Does that sound right? You know, or maybe it's a chemical thing, a chemical attraction. But he's all I've thought about since he left my office. He's got the most adorable hair, really short except near the front where he gels it up, almost like a 50s hairstyle, something out of *Grease*. I just wanted to reach out and pat his head when he asked me about his Blue Cross Blue Shield plan. He looks like he walked out of the pages of a Lands' End catalog. Very preppy, if people still use the word 'preppy' anymore."

"Did you ask him out?"

"Not yet," Maggie said, biting the edge of the nail on her right index finger, "but there's going to be this 'problem' with his health insurance that's going to require him to come see me again. Soon. Oh, and I've got a huge favor to ask."

"What?"

"Can you see if George can call his friend Matt, the one whose dad has the season's ticket to the Sox? See if he can get tickets to a game? When I walked by Michael's desk, I saw that he had a Sox mug and screensaver on his computer. I could just 'happen' to have two tickets to a game . . ."

Maggie and Michael's first date did indeed take place at a Red Sox game. They sat along the third baseline in the Loge section, some 20 rows back from the field, in George's friend's dad's seats. The Sox bested the Milwaukee Brewers, 4-2 after having lost three straight leading up to the Sunday afternoon contest. The game was highlighted by a Tim Naehring homer in the seventh, a blast sent rocketing deep into left field over the Green Monster wall. Even though Maggie's favorite player, first baseman Mo Vaughn, went 0 for 3 at the plate, by the time she got home from the game, she felt as though she'd personally fared quite well. From that point on, she and Michael talked at work every day and had lunch together whenever they could. They'd gone out on seven "official" dates — they didn't count their shared lunch times at ENY as dates — before Michael and Maggie accompanied Diane and George to Shots, an Eastborough dive featuring karaoke, a place which Diane and Maggie frequented during winter, spring and summer breaks from Framingham State. On that first night out as a foursome, Diane took a liking to Michael within five minutes of meeting him. In order to privately express her approval to Maggie as soon as possible (she didn't want Maggie — who Diane thought had a checkered past when it came to finding suitable boyfriends — to do anything to blow this relationship) Diane grabbed Maggie's wrist and announced, "We gotta go to the Ladies Room. We'll be back!" leaving Michael at the table with George, a veritable stranger.

"So, did I get a thumbs up from her, ya think?" Michael asked George, who was busily draining his plastic cup of Bud Light.

"'course," George said. "Maggie's talked about nothing else but you for weeks now. Diane just whispered to me that she thinks you two are a perfect match . . . but I probably shouldn't 've told you that. Don't say anything will ya?"

Michael laughed, exhaling with relief, appreciative of George's honesty. He spotted Maggie and Diane emerging from the lavatory located on the other side of the room. He had a fluttery sensation in his stomach as she watched Maggie, who was walking back to their table, moving in between the shadows and dim spots of light, through the smoky cigarette haze, which hung in the air, slightly blurring and softening her features from a distance.

"She's got this great laugh," Michael said, recalling how it seems to rise all the way up her body and is violently forced out of her in bursts that he can literally feel reverberate inside his chest.

"Yep," George, who'd known Maggie for as long as he'd known Diane. "And she's really feisty that one. Diane says she like a human cup of coffee, excitable, like too much caffeine sometimes."

The air in the dark bar — decorated by two dozen glowing neon beer signs, New England sports paraphernalia and framed beer ads along the wood paneled walls — vibrated with the sound of the bass line of the songs the resident DJ played at high volume. Michael noticed that the humidity level seemed to have had risen during this early summer night as he continued watching Maggie, whose determined footfalls happened to coincide with the beat of the song. Her hips swayed in her tightly-fit ripped jeans, offset by a burgundy-colored teasingly low-cut top that flared out at just below her waist. Michael caught her eye and they maintained eye contact as she sauntered up to him, pulled him to a standing position and pressed her body into his. "Let's dance," she said in a low voice, grabbing his elbow and guiding him out to the already crowded area comprised of laminate squares masquerading as a comically microscopic dance floor. While most people were swinging their hands back and forth above their heads, clapping with the beat or shaking their rumps, the front of Maggie and Michael's bodies were sweatily crushed together, as they rocked side-to-side, their hips making the bulk of the motion as their feet barely moved on the tiny patch of real estate they occupied on the dance floor.

"Did I pass inspection? Did Diane green-light us?" Michael whispered into her ear, his face so close to Maggie's that she could feel the sharpness of his stubble against her cheek. "George said . . ."

She cut him off and covered his mouth with hers, simultaneously sliding her hands from either side of his trim waist down to his lean, khaki-covered behind and softly squeezing. "Take me home," she demanded once she came up for air after a deep, lingering kiss. "Take me home now and fuck me."

"Really?" Michael asked. He'd thought he wouldn't be able to broach the subject of sex for another week or two at least. He imagined they'd have to have a serious, socially responsible discussion about when it might happen, what protection they'd use and dish about previous sexual partners. But he was pleasantly surprised that this moment occurred earlier than anticipated, and on her initiative. He ran his hands along her waist and hips and kissed her, rendering her intoxicated by his scent which took her breath away. "Let's go," he said.

It had been 10 years since that night at Shots. While nothing had changed, everything had. The bar's decor was almost exactly the same as it was on the night of the double-date, only the Red Sox posters and beer ads were faded and cracked, edges curling. A 2004 Red Sox World Series Championship banner was the only noticeable addition, plus a couple new Patriots' Super Bowl banners. Some of the neon beer signs — that once evoked a seedy, almost sultry atmosphere of dimly glowing light — were cracked and many of the bulbs were no longer operational. The cigarette smoke that had once hung in the air like a hallucinogen was a thing of the past, courtesy of a statewide smoking ban. The air was now clear, although the tavern's odor was still stale, like kegs of cheap beer gone bad.

To Michael, stepping back into the Eastborough watering hole was like walking into the Finns' house, only on Oak Terrace the smell of cigarettes still clung to everything, like a heavy wool blanket thrown over your head on a humid summer's day. The bar was nothing like he remembered it from his first visit, after which he and Maggie consummated their relationship in Maggie's sparse studio apartment on the mattress she had on the floor because she hadn't gotten around to purchasing a bed frame yet. "Red sheets," he remembered. "She had red sheets that night that smelled like fresh laundry detergent. Cottony, clean."

But any lusty memories that going to Shots might've stirred up were obliterated by Michael's bad mood which turned sour back in the Eastborough High School field parking lot. Matters had not improved as the day had progressed. Luke was as friendly and welcoming as a starving, rabid coyote. He began grousing and drinking on the ride home from the game, popping open a beer bottle in his pick-up. Once they got back to the house, Luke literally threw himself onto his recliner and, in between drinking, started chain smoking, one cigarette after another.

"Luke! Can you please not smoke when the kids are in

the house?" Maggie shouted from the kitchen while she prepping Thanksgiving dinner.

"What the hell? It's my house!" he shouted, staring straight ahead at the TV which he had tuned to the Atlanta Falcons-Detroit Lions football game.

"Luke, I don't want the kids around smoke. Can you please either not smoke or smoke outside, until we leave? We won't be here all that long, just a few hours. I'd really appreciate it. It's Thanksgiving."

"It's my house. It's not your perfect little snotty mansion with your perfect little doormat of a husband. This is my Thanksgiving dinner, and if I wanna smoke in here, I will. Mom smoked when we were kids. And if it was good enough for us, it's good enough for them."

Maggie looked at Rob, silently pleading with him to intervene. Rob avoided her gaze and stared at the floor for a few seconds before heading into the bathroom.

Figuring there was no way they were going to get Luke to refrain from lighting up, particularly given the "doormat" remark, Michael said to the kids, "Come on guys, let's go outside. We can practice some of those football plays we saw the Eagles do. And Jackie, you can show me some of those cheers you learned."

Michael and the kids stayed outside for over an hour, even though dark clouds had rolled in, sending temps plummeting into the 30s. When Tommy began shivering — as he had no coat to wear — Michael had them pile into minivan. He turned on the ignition and blasted the heat while they played with toys and colored in coloring books and he worked on his laptop in the front seat, piggybacking on a neighbor's unsecured wireless Internet connection.

As Maggie kept cooking and stealing glances out the front window, Rob returned to the kitchen to hover nearby. Rob, who didn't like to get into the middle of his kids' arguments, tried to make it up to his daughter. "Maggie, I'm sorry about Luke," he said quietly. "You know how hard he takes it when

Eastborough loses the Thanksgiving Day game."

"Dad, my kids are outside right now. Outside. On Thanksgiving, because he can't just not smoke for a few hours. He's too damned selfish."

"You know your brother," his voice sounded hollow as he flicked the edge of the battered vinyl-backed tablecloth on the kitchen table with his index finger. "But your mother would've loved to know that you were here in her kitchen . . ."

"Turkey's done," she said cutting him off as she heaved the roasting pan onto the top of the stove. It made a loud, metallic crash, louder than Maggie had intended. "I'm going to let it cool here for a bit before I carve it. I'm gonna finish heating everything else up. After we have dessert, Michael and I want to go out for a while, to Shots, not for too long, if you don't mind watching Tommy and Jackie, like we talked about yesterday. Then we're leaving. We're not going to sleep here tonight, especially not with all this smoke. And if you could work on trying to get Luke to not smoke with Michael and I are out, I could consider that an early Christmas gift."

Rob, who had started to look old to Maggie about two years ago, pursed his lips and said nothing in reply. He clasped his hands together behind his back, nodded his head then stood motionless for a few seconds before retreating to his worn recliner alongside Luke as his son cursed a bungled Lions play.

Maggie and Michael were barely on speaking terms when they left the Finns' and headed to Shots. Michael had spent a large part of the afternoon with Jackie and Tommy in the minivan while Maggie finished dinner preparation alone. "This is ridiculous," he later grumbled to Maggie. "I'm really not in the mood to go to Shots right now Maggie. And it's only seven. Diane and George won't get there until 8:30 and they're usually late. I cannot stand the idea of the kids spending any more time in this house. Why don't we just skip it?"

"We're going!" Maggie said, lightly brushing the last dregs of the pressed translucent powder from her drugstore compact across her shiny forehead, still damp from the steam from the hot water she'd used when cleaning the dishes. Her fingernails, she noticed, were in bad shape and starting to peel in several spots. "I called Diane and asked her if she and George could get to Shots earlier than we planned 'cause I said we're going to leave early and go to your mother's house. She said they'd be there soon. You'll see Aunt Sue, so the least you can do is to go to Shots for an hour or so. I want to do something *I* want to do. For me. We never go out anywhere together without the kids anymore."

As Michael predicted, Diane and George were not there when he and Maggie arrived at the jam-packed bar. There were no open tables, so Michael and Maggie had to stand behind two ample-sized middle-aged regulars in hooded sweatshirts and baseball caps. Maggie and Michael drank their draft beers mostly in silence as they stood, ram-rod straight looking uncomfortable.

"I'm sorry," Maggie blurted, feeling compelled to kill the silence and salvage what remained of the day.

"For what?" Michael snapped, still annoyed that Maggie had made him feel guilty for working. Just before leaving for the bar, Michael learned that his ENY transportation counterpart Rick Strong had physically gone into the office late in the afternoon after Thanksgiving dinner, showing him up in front of Sam Young, looking more dedicated to the company than Michael. And here he was, trapped in what looked like a scene from a low-budget independent film about burn-outs. But Maggie had no idea that he was stewing about his career's future. She likely wouldn't care even if he did tell her that he felt that he should be in the office, not drinking Bud from a keg cup, he thought.

"About everything. I hate Thanksgiving now. It sucks. The whole day sucked. Stupid bastard Luke. Fighting with you. I don't want to fight with you. We're supposed to be on the same side."

"Hmmm," Michael said, refusing to look at her while

feigning interest in the Dallas Cowboys-Denver Broncos game on the twin TVs above the bar.

"I mean it," Maggie said, as she encroached upon Michael's personal space so much so that Michael could smell Luke's cigarette smoke on her sweater. He had taken the clean shirt he planned on wearing the following day from his duffle bag and changed before leaving because the shirt he'd been wearing stunk. "I don't wanna fight. I just wanna spend a little while with you, without anyone harassing us." Still holding her beer, she put her open hand on the small of his back. "Let's dance."

"I'm not in the mood Maggie," he said, putting his beer in between them like a shield. "I really don't want to dance."

Song after song played. They continued to stand there without saying anything. When the two barstools filled by the gruff patrons in front of them emptied — they left to take a bathroom break, and because the Cowboys-Broncos game was in a commercial time-out before going into overtime — Michael quickly moved in to claim them, hoping the two guys wouldn't return and humiliate him by demanding he and his wife vacate the seats. But Maggie had other thoughts as she took Michael's beer cup out of his hand and placed it on the bar next to her cup. She started to maneuver him to the dance floor, however he openly resisted and pulled his hands out of hers abruptly.

"I said, 'No' Mags. Really," Michael said, sliding his behind onto the stool.

"I need this. Just sway back and forth with me. You don't have to do anything more than that."

She didn't seem as though she was going to relent, so he reluctantly accompanied her to the perimeter of the dance floor. She put her hands around the back of his neck and interlaced her fingers. He slouched and lazily rested his hands around her waist, watching the two men at the bar — he'd named them Nick and Bob in his head — plop themselves back onto the stools he had tried to claim. Trying to penetrate his distracted consciousness, Maggie squeezed Michael with both her arms and put her head on his chest, closed her eyes and tried to let the music dissolve her anger and disappointment away. She tried, in vain, to listen for Michael's heartbeat, but couldn't hear it above the 1980s rock anthem playing in the background.

"Do you remember the night we first came here?" she asked, a dreamy look on her face.

"What? I can't hear you. White Snake is whining too loudly."

"Do you remember the night we came here for the first time?" Maggie shouted into his dour-looking face.

"That was a long time ago," he said, wishing she hadn't made him dance. He wanted to leave, the bar, Easthorough, the Finns. He was trying to act like the cool and collected professional everyone thought he was, trying to put out of his mind that Sam Young was in the office at this very moment, working, alongside Rick who was one-upping him right now, and he was here, in a past-its-prime dive trying not to scream.

"A lifetime ago," she said. Maggie rested her head on his chest again and tried to conjure up the old, electric feelings they once shared. She remembered when, in those early days, if she accidentally touched any part of his skin with hers, her flesh would feel as though it was burning, every touch singed with desire. "We had sex for the first time that night after we came here. And it was amazing. I knew that there would be no other man for me."

Michael nodded, tormented by the fact that he couldn't even muster a modicum of fake enthusiasm. He didn't want to be inauthentic. It felt like lying. He'd made a promise to her in the afterglow of that night a decade ago that he'd never lie to Maggie about his feelings toward her.

"It was really amazing, that night," Maggie said. "Changed my life."

He nodded again.

"Can't you say something? Something more than nod? Didn't that night mean *anything* to you?"

"Mags, I'm having trouble hearing you. The music's too loud." He kissed her on the top of her head.

Maggie was having none of this. She'd plow through all of it, all of his attitude and whatever it was that was bugging him, she decided. She put one hand behind his head, pulled it toward her and plunged her tongue into his mouth when they felt the shockingly cold chill of liquid splash across their bodies.

"What the?" Michael yelled as he broke away from Maggie's kiss, whipped around and saw a goateed college student, wearing a wrinkled, black, short-sleeved T-shirt over a long-sleeved gray T-shirt, clearly under the influence of one too many draft beers. He had tripped over his own feet and sent the three plastic cups full of beer that he'd been carrying flying out of his hands. Most of the beer wound up on Michael and Maggie.

"Dude, sorry," the guy said, stumbling away toward the back of the bar.

Maggie looked at the amber-colored beer stains dotting her tan, stretch-fabric pants, which were now clinging to her like plastic wrap on a wet countertop. The beer accentuated the darker-colored gravy stain on her left thigh that she hadn't been able to remove after dinner, acquired when Rob nervously passed the basket of rolls a little too quickly toward his daughter and accidentally knocked the gravy ladle out of the gravy boat and onto her lap. The one good thing was that you couldn't really notice the beer spots on her black turtleneck sweater — it just blended in and made the sweater look darker black, not stained — so Maggie wasn't concerned that she'd look like a wet T-shirt contestant.

Michael got the worst of it, as the beer covered almost his entire left side, on his tan pants and light blue pull-over. "I've got to go try to do something about this," Michael said, pulling the wet fabric away from his body trying to shake off the excess liquid.

"So you don't wanna just keep dancing? It's only beer. Who cares?" Maggie said, hoping in vain that he'd let her dance with him and kiss him, although she knew that the fleeting bit of forced intimacy was gone.

"I'll be back," Michael barked as he stalked off to the men's room only to discover that it was a single room with one stall and he had to wait because the guy who'd dumped the beer on him was already inside, getting sick judging by the retching Michael heard.

Defeated, Maggie headed back to the bar and took the single, open stool next to "Nick and Bob," who didn't seem to have moved an inch since Maggie and Michael went to dance. She vigorously waved a $20 bill in the air to get the bartender's attention and held up two fingers, "Draft. Bud." Sitting at the bar alone, she pulled out her cell phone and it rang in her hands. It was Diane.

"Hey! Where are you guys?" Maggie shouted, afraid Diane wouldn't be able to hear her above the music and the chattering sportscasters on the TV.

"We just got here. We're in here. Where are you and Michael? I don't see you."

"Look by the bar," Maggie said as she knelt on top of the stool and vigorously waved her right arm. "I'm waving."

Diane, clad in a scoop-cut emerald green shirt that showed off her over-sized lactating breasts and skinny jeans, nodded, "I see you. George and I'll be right there."

"Sorry we're so late Mags," Diane said, wrapping Maggie in a big hug but quickly recoiling after she felt her sweater. "Ewww. You're all wet. What happened?"

"Some asshole ruined my one and only slow dance with Michael by tripping and spilling beer all over us. Michael went to the bathroom to try to clean himself up, I don't know, I guess try to use the hand dryer or something. I decided to stay here and drink." She nodded at the bartender who brought over her drafts in large cups. She threw an extra generous tip onto the sticky bar. "Take one Diane. You seriously need to catch up. You can pump and dump your breast milk later. But you already knew that. Where the hell's George?" Maggie picked up one of the cups and pressed it into Diane's hands, which, she noticed, had a professional-looking manicure which Diane most likely did herself because she believed that paying someone to get them done was a waste of money.

"George saw Ted Grint on the way in. They're friends through work or something, maybe their basketball league, I don't know. Who knew that George would know someone in Eastborough? How was Bleak House?"

"Can't even talk about it. Horror show. Plus, Dorothy wormed her way into Michael's head, got him all worked up about us leaving here early so we could drive up to New Hampshire. Tonight! Oh, and Michael brought work. He's been working all day when he thinks I didn't notice that I had to make dinner by myself and clean up alone. I've barely seen him. I tried to dance with him, kiss him. Then the beer asshole. Guess that's what I get for trying to have some PDA, a beer in the face."

"Wanna karaoke? You need some release and I need to enjoy some grown-up time. I've got our CD ready."

"Why not? Can't get much worse tonight unless I fall flat on my face on stage. I think they start in 15 minutes, that's what they announced, but I don't know if there's a waiting list already. Michael and I can't stay long, so maybe I can't sing with you after all. I don't want to listen to any more of Dorothy's shit than I already have to. If we pull in there when it's too late I'll never hear the end of it."

Diane, an enthusiastic karaoke fan, grabbed Maggie's arm. "Come on. I know the guy working the karaoke machine. Not to worry. We'll jump the line."

On the way to talk to Seth the karaoke guy with the sign-up sheet on a clipboard, Diane spotted George, in his oversized Patriots' jersey, cupped her hands around her mouth and shouted, "Michael's in the bathroom! Find him. Make sure he's watching when we karaoke. Tell him we're going to sing and he needs to root for his gal." George adjusted his red FSC baseball cap and nodded at his wife and her best friend.

A short while later — after Maggie sucked down a third draft — Diane's buddy had bumped Diane and Maggie to the top of the karaoke list and called them to the front of the stage. The two grabbed hold of the battered microphones and waited in the meager heat of the weak spotlight for the music to begin to play. Straining her eyes in the uneven light that spilled down upon the four-inch tall stage made of plywood planks that still had calculations written on them in black marker, Maggie looked for Michael in the crowd. Had he even emerged from the men's room yet? Was he going to miss it?

Diane elbowed her and pointed, "Over there. With George."

Maggie then spotted Michael, looking distinctly gloomy, in the back of the room, near the bar and the two immovable hooded sweatshirt guys "Nick and Bob," still cemented to their bar stools. Her stomach bottomed out as she tried to make eye contact with Michael, but couldn't. George, who was standing next to Michael, was shamelessly blowing kisses to Diane, so there was no way Michael didn't know they were there, Maggie thought.

The music began with a few delicate piano notes. Diane had brought her own copy of the song by a largely, unknown Denver band, The Fray, with which Diane had become infatuated. On Shots' karaoke stage, a giddy Diane went first, happily belting out the first few lines of her designated part of the song, "How to Save a Life," in her high-pitched but not entirely off-key voice, just the way she and Maggie had done a number of times in Diane's kitchen during recent play-dates:

"Step one you say, 'We need to talk.'"

He walks. You say, 'Sit down, it's just a talk.'
He smiles politely back at you.
You stare politely right on through."

Maggie, brimming with beer-fueled courage closed her eyes, gripped her mike and boldly sang her lines at a much lower pitch than Diane's, hitting the notes expertly and lingering at the end of each line, a better natural singer than Diane, though Diane clearly cornered the market on enthusiasm. They sang the chorus in unison, creating a rough kind of urgent harmony:

"Where did I go wrong? I lost a friend
Somewhere along in the bitterness.
And I would have stayed up with you all night
Had I known how to save a life."

Maggie experienced a rush of self-consciousness. She hadn't sung karaoke in front of people in a bar in quite some time. The last time was well before she was pregnant with Jackie. This wasn't the same as singing obnoxiously loudly in the kitchen or the driver's seat of her minivan or at Diane's house. Seeking reassurance, Maggie looked for Michael the way a child looks for a parent in a crowd, hoping to get a comforting nod or wink. Michael, however, wasn't looking even ambiguously in her direction. He'd missed his wife's smooth gesticulating and was instead looking up at the tight Broncos-Cowboys game playing on all the TVs above the bar.

Maggie's tiny glimmer of anxious excitement dissipated. Her jaw stiffened and she clenched her body, halting the small swaying she'd been doing while Diane's hips swung back-and-forth like a pendulum. Eyes pooling, Maggie began to semi-shout her lines into the microphone, chopping notes of the words off abruptly as though the viciousness with which she treated the notes could snap Michael to attention, literally turn his face toward her with the blunt force of her vocal chords:

"Lay down a list of what is wrong,
The things you've told him all along

And pray to God he hears you
And pray to God he hears you!"

Confidence waned with each syllable that passed through her lips. Maggie watched as Michael remained apparently riveted by a replay of a blown 34-yard field goal that would've given Dallas the lead. The play had energized the assembled Cowboys haters at the bar. The color TV commentator was dissecting the play in minute detail when Michael felt his BlackBerry vibrate inside his beer-dampened pocket. Maggie watched as Michael pulled out the handheld device, read the screen (it was Sam Young calling), answered the call and walked away from the bar, out the door and into the parking lot where the music and the crowd became a blur of white noise in the background.

Maggie's ability to push clearly formed words out of her mouth declined even further. Eyes now glazed, she gawked at the door, which was covered with a large black and orange poster promoting a locally brewed malty caramel Oktoberfest beer that Shots now had on tap. The next stanza she was supposed to sing came out in nearly a flat whisper:

"He will do one of two things.
He will admit to everything.
Or he'll say he's just not the same
And you'll begin to wonder why you came."

The 4-minute-22-second song now seemed like a lengthy opus to Maggie, who was trying to concentrate on simply standing upright until the last line had been sung. Diane was either oblivious to what was happening with her singing partner or immune to the dark clouds that always seemed to be swirling around Maggie because she wildly pumped her fists as they reached the end of the song, utterly pleased with the performance. "Awesome!" Diane said perkily into the microphone, bowing to the applause punctuated by appreciative hoots from George who had removed his cap and was swinging it above his head in a circle.

"THAT," George shouted, "is MY wife!"

Diane struck a coquettish hands-on-the-hips pose for George's benefit, flipped her hair to the side with a toss of her head, fluttered her eyelashes, puckered her lips toward him and curtsied, in quick succession.

Maggie bounded off the rickety stage with fierce determination, headed for one place: That spot at the bar next to Nick and Bob. Forcing herself through the crowd, she grabbed the edge of the bar and held up two fingers to the bartender. "Hey!" she yelled when the bartender ignored her. "Hey! Two drafts!" But she couldn't be heard after the crowd loudly groaned following a Denver penalty.

CHAPTER TWELVE

WHY DO I EVEN BOTHER?
File under: I'm in a sucky mood, how 'bout you?

Thanksgiving.

Total disaster. But, hey, at least no one died. I should've done what I wanted to do all along, just grab my kids and snuggle up with them on the couch instead of trudging through all the crap we had to deal with.

Where to start? With Her Excellency Benita making my life hell, ridiculing my parenting, my lack of dedicated wifeliness, my general incompetency and whether I can get my own clothes onto my body in the mornings without assistance? With the fact that my weak ass father and dolt of a drunk ass brother drove me from my childhood home (the brother wouldn't stop smoking in the house and in front of the kids, didn't matter how many ways I asked him to stop he just wouldn't, while my old man did nothing)?

But no, I'm gonna start with the Wannabe-King. Yes, I'm back to calling him "Wannabe-King." Sweet Lips, as far as I'm concerned, is dead. I have no idea where that guy went. Maybe Sweet Lips was murdered by someone, like my relationship with everyone (except maybe with Thing I and Thing II) seems to be right now. And aside from one bitchy little incident I had with Thing I at a high school football game we went to on Thanksgiving (I was thrilled my brother's team lost, the bastard deserved it), the kids have been pretty awesome. I should buy them some ice cream for being bright spots in this darkness. Yo, that's it. I've decided. After I hit "publish" on this post, I'm taking them to Friendly's for ginormous ice cream cones. With sprinkles, or jimmies, whatever the hell you call 'em. I don't care if it spoils their dinner tonight. Let Wannabe-King figure out why no one wants to eat Benita's sainted leftovers that she packaged up for us after the kids have eaten gallons of ice cream. Yes, I am a bitter bitch and I don't fuckin' care.

What did the Wannabe-King do to kill the "Sweet Lips" name, you ask? Well, why don't we talk about he DIDN'T do? We'd had words, a couple of real big arguments during our time at Bleak House. We were both tense. I wanted to run fleeing out the front door several times. But I was trying, I really was, to get past all of the uncomfortableness and wanted to connect with my husband on Thanksgiving. So I suggested that we go out on Thanksgiving night, leave the kids with my father (even though it meant the kids spent more time in the smoke-filled house, I know, Bad Mom, but I was desperate) so we could dance and flirt as though we actually give a crap about one another. I even wore that stupid push-up bra I mentioned in that blog post last month (the one with the black polka dots, the one he said he really liked when I wore it that time. Link to that post is HERE.) under the black turtleneck sweater that he has said he also liked because it's form fitting. I kissed him on the dance floor. I took the lead. Did all the work. Even made an ass of myself, getting up to sing one of our new favorite songs up on a karaoke stage. Tried to sing to him like you see in the movies, in those romantic scenes where suddenly the clouds part and all the crap falls away and the two star-crossed leads forget everything they've been fighting about and melt into one another's arms. I was planning on swinging my booty and making him laugh, which would, in my mind, lead to, well, you know . . .

And what did that get me? He never even looked at me. Then he walked out when I was in the middle of my song. Left the freakin' bar. Literally. Out the door. After not even looking once in my direction when he KNEW I was up there on stage. He took a work call. (He later explained that it was crucial to his project, blah, blah, blah. I've heard it all before. Don't care.) Not that he was watching me BEFORE the call came in. But those are just minor details, right? He was watching football on TV. (He tried to say, "It was a really close, awesome overtime game!") Other than his lame explanation about why the game was more interesting than his horny wife, we haven't really talked about that night. Not during the car ride up to Her Excellency Benita's house in New Hampshire, something I agreed to do as a way of apologizing for how my nitwit family behaved (like totally self-absorbed jerks who don't care about anyone other than themselves).

But the Wannabe-King spent all his time on his BlackBerry, on his laptop, talking to everyone. 'cept me. He never even acknowledged that I sang on stage. Just walked out in the middle of my song. Did I mention that? That he left when I was singing? That's when his eyes weren't glued to the fucking football game.

Look, I get that having Thanksgiving at Bleak House wasn't any fun for him. It definitely wasn't fun for me either. I also know he's under a lot of pressure with his king of the universe project. But all that work stuff is not my fault. Neither is the fact that my family acts like buffoons. I gave him HIS time at his mommy's house and put up with her bullshit attacks and lectures (all aimed at me, not him, her perfect son whose only flaw was marrying me) about the dangers of letting my kids spend time around people smoking in their presence. She started blabbing about this as soon as we walked into her house Thanksgiving night and she smelled it on us. Then she scolded me for "smelling like a brewery" and went on about how I should've listened to her son and left Bleak House right after dinner instead of selfishly going out to a bar and putting my children's health at risk by having them spend more time in a smoky house. She then asked me what I'd made for Thanksgiving dinner and proceeded to grill me on how I prepared it — "Was it homemade?" which is code for "Was it full of killer chemicals and preservatives that will give my son and grandchildren cancer, you imbecile?" — even though, at that moment, I'd had so many beers, my head was a bit fuzzy and I felt like I was going to hurl on her gleaming kitchen floor and her shiny Easy Spirit loafers.

Speaking of Thanksgiving dinner, I let the Wannabe-King stay outside with the kids all day, or sit in the minivan, while I was making dinner like an unpaid servant. I let him work and talk and text. My dad and brother watched football then I cleaned all the dishes afterward. The only thing, the one thing I wanted was to dance at the bar *where the Wannabe-King and I went the first night we had sex. (No, we didn't have sex in the bar all those years ago. The sex happened after we'd been dancing at the bar.)*

And he walked out on me.

I don't even know what to say to him. When we got home from Benita's today, he informed me he had to work to do and disappeared into his office. He's there right now as I write this while I'm sitting on our bed. It's Thanksgiving weekend. And I'm up here alone. It's ice cream time. Maybe some fudge and whipped cream and peppermint ice cream will make it all better.

P.S. — Forgot to add . . . the whole reason we supposedly HAD to go Benita's, even though it wasn't her turn this year to have us over for Thanksgiving, was because her sister Susan, who we haven't seen in a long time, was supposed to be there. Benita demanded that the Wannabe-King show his face at her house on Thanksgiving night to see his aunt before she left the next morning. But you know what? The aunt didn't even show up to Thanksgiving. Got a flat tire on the way there. Went to a Holiday Inn dinner with her "friend" who picked her up at the airport. Never even drove up to New Hampshire. But did Benita call us to tell us that we didn't have to rush up there? What do you think?

Just a few more changes, a little tweaking, Michael thought, and this baby'll be ready for submission. Michael reviewed the plans he had spread out across his desk. He didn't even know if they, or his lengthy analysis, made any sense any more. He was so tired after having stayed up all night at his mother's house working on them. Sam Young said if they could get the application for the variance for the Bypass submitted by the Monday after Thanksgiving, he'd heard from one of his country club mates who had connections in the state Department of Environmental Protection's office that they'd be likely to see action on it before the end of the calendar year. Despite all the bad publicity the project had received and the flak Michael had personally weathered, Sam told Michael that he was impressed by his commitment to this project and strongly hinted that, if things worked out, that he'd consider promoting Michael, a promotion that would afford Michael more control over his projects, over scheduling and what assignments he pursued. It would also come with more money, a company car and greater flexibility. And the way things were going at home right now, Michael thought, all of that would be welcomed, especially the flexibility and scheduling parts. But it wasn't a good idea to get ahead of himself. First he had to finish working on the proposal. Everything seemed to hinge on how the ENY plan addressed the environmental impact of a small, half-mile tract of wetlands that went through Westbrook and how the state officials responded to the plan.

"Michael!" Maggie shouted through the closed door to his office.

Michael weighed whether he should reply. She'd been like a one-woman cold front since Thanksgiving night and had been treating him and all his belongings with disdain, chucking his work papers, his laptop and his BlackBerry onto the kitchen floor when they got home from Frank and Dorothy's. (Michael nearly had a stroke when he saw her toss the laptop, even though she did plop it on top of a stadium fleece blanket she'd thrown down onto the floor first.) He was in the midst of this one last calculation and didn't feel much like dealing with more Maggie drama right now.

"When this is done," he whispered as he hunched over his laptop, "everything will be better."

"Hey! I was calling you!" screamed Maggie who was now standing in the doorway of his office, visibly startling him. "We're going out. Don't know when we'll be back. If you want dinner, you can eat leftovers. I'm done cooking for this weekend."

Michael wanted to utter some snide reply about how

nice it must be to go out whenever you wanted and not to have a multi-million-dollar project hanging over your head, how it was *his* hard work that was paying for her to go out and pay for whatever it was she was planning on buying, but he held his tongue. "Fine," he said without looking away from the computer screen.

Maggie waited a beat for something more. When there was nothing else forthcoming, she parroted back, "Fine," and left as stealthily as she had arrived.

When he heard the garage door open and close, Maggie and the kids now on their way to wherever it was that they were going, Michael's BlackBerry began buzzing around on his desk, rattling the two black ballpoint pens lying next to it. Hoping it wouldn't be Maggie with another demand or directive, he glanced at the screen and saw it was Dorothy calling. He could avoid the call, but that meant that his mother would just call the house phone next, then Maggie's cell phone. Dorothy usually tried all three numbers in that order if she couldn't get Michael immediately, knowing full well that she'd hear from him soon after she harassed Maggie about her husband's whereabouts. If he ducked Dorothy's call now and she phoned Maggie, his wife would flip out and go on another anti-Dorothy rampage like she had done on the ride home from New Hampshire and he just didn't have the energy to deal with both of these high maintenance women right now. However, he figured that his mother would be more rational to deal with than Maggie at the moment.

"Hello Mom," he said, leaving the BlackBerry on his desk and hitting the speakerphone button.

"Michael, am I disturbing you? Are you and Margaret heating up those leftovers for dinner? I don't want to interrupt a family meal."

"No, Mom. Not right now. I'm working on that application for the Bypass plans in my office. In the house. Maggie and the kids just left to go someplace."

"They just left? It's 5 o'clock. Isn't it dinner time? That

doesn't sound like a very good time to go out with young children. They should be getting ready for dinner. Children tend to act-up at this time of day. They need a firm routine."

Michael didn't take the bait and continued typing on his laptop, wondering why she called now if she was so worried about interrupting their dinnertime.

"Is that the keyboard I hear? Are you typing while you're talking to me? You know I hate that," Dorothy said, feeling snubbed. Out of the corner of her eye, she saw Frank—who'd spent a large portion of Thanksgiving weekend secretly thanking God for flattening his sister-in-law Sue's tire—shake his head disapprovingly. "Hold on a minute Michael," she said, directing an angry glance at her husband, "I'm going to go upstairs."

She retreated to the privacy of her shrine to Laura Ashley, otherwise known as her bedroom, prominently decorated in a bright blue and green floral pattern dotted with plump little berries, which inspired Frank to nickname their bedroom "the fruity room." Sitting down on the white wooden rocking chair cushioned by two "Bramble" patterned pillows—which matched the comforter, pillows and curtains—Dorothy now felt as though she could talk freely, without Frank's non-verbal commentary. "Would you mind stopping the typing for just a second please while we talk? I won't take long."

Michael removed his hands from the keyboard growing weary of people placing demands on him. "There Mom. Stopped. I stopped!" He paused and then lowered his voice. "What can I do for you?"

"Well, first . . ."

"First?" Michael thought. "Nothing that starts with 'first' is going to be brief."

". . . I wanted to apologize for Aunt Sue. She'd promised she was going to be here on Thanksgiving. I don't know how things got so confused. First she called to say she'd gotten a flat tire on the way from the airport. Then she called to say she and her friend had the car towed to a gas station in Enfield to get a new tire. Did I mention that the spare tire in her friend's car was missing? I can't see how a responsible adult could drive without checking to see that she has a proper spare tire in her trunk in case of emergencies."

"Mmm, hmm," Michael said, aggressively cracking his knuckles as he opened an e-mail that'd just popped up on his laptop. He moved the mouse as quietly as he could so his mother wouldn't hear him, reminding him of the times he tiptoed into the living room on Saturday mornings when he was a little kid to watch as many cartoons as he could before Dorothy woke up and snapped off the TV.

"I don't know why she didn't just cancel right then and there, but she kept us hanging for a long time saying she had no idea when she was going to roll in. I didn't know that she'd decided not to come to see us at all and stay in a hotel in Connecticut until shortly before you and the kids got here. She just went to Rhode Island the day after Thanksgiving instead." She waited for Michael to say something affirmative, perhaps acknowledging how disappointed Dorothy must have been to have been blown off by her sister. When Michael didn't pick up on that hint, to her disappointment, she plodded ahead, "Well I didn't want you and Margaret to think that I made the whole thing up about Aunt Sue coming."

"We didn't think that," Michael said, distractedly as he scanned the new e-mail, pleased that Sam had ended it with, "After you send me those last changes, stop working you idiot. Have a beer. You've earned it."

"Well . . . I didn't get that impression from Margaret. She acted like she didn't believe me. I just wanted to make sure you didn't think that too."

"No Mom, I don't think you made it up. Maggie didn't either. She'd had a long, terrible Thanksgiving at her dad's. She was tired. I'd just write it off as holiday pressure. Don't take it personally."

"'Don't take it personally?' Margaret called me the 'health

Nazi' when you arrived! She threw her hands up into the air and stormed off to the guest room without even saying, 'Goodnight' or 'Happy Thanksgiving.' She made it pretty personal Michael . . ."

Ah, the real reason for the call, Michael thought.

" . . . How can you just ignore how she treated me after I'd spent the whole day trying to make a nice holiday for my family?"

"You had just finished yelling at her and blaming her because her brother had been smoking. That wasn't her fault. SHE wasn't smoking. She asked him several times to stop."

"But it *was* her decision not to put her children's health first. As soon as Luke started smoking, she should've insisted that he stop. If he didn't, she should've taken the children out of there immediately. You all could've had Thanksgiving dinner with us. There was plenty. But she didn't. And then she made my grandbabies stay at that smoky house even longer while she insisted on boozing it up at a bar. You'd told me on the phone that you'd probably leave their house right after dessert. Then you wound up going out and arriving here quite late. I swear, Margaret looked and smelled like she'd drunk an entire keg of beer by the time you got to my house."

"I . . ."

"Now I know you went out too, but you were just trying to be nice to her. You're really nicer to her family than is really necessary. Molly's been gone too long for you to continue this pity party where you have to tiptoe quietly around her beer swilling family, letting them walk all over you, while she mopes like she's the only person in the world whose mother isn't around anymore. I know you don't agree with me, but I still say that Margaret's still acting out her unprocessed grief all these years later and that you should seriously think about having her see a therapist. I've asked the school counselor about it and she agrees with me. Margaret's troubled. You can just see it in her eyes. Even still, that doesn't justify leaving my grandbabies in the smoke . . ."

"Mom, we covered this already. I can't keep talking about this subject with you over and over. I don't want to keep reminding you that I can't have you talk about Maggie this way. We heard what you said about the smoking. And you're right about that. We'll figure out a plan to make sure this doesn't happen again. Maybe all the Finn family dinners will be held here at our house where we don't allow smoking. We'll work on it. As for calling Maggie 'troubled' and all, and what, having crazy eyes or something like that, I don't think that's fair of you to bring that up. It's not something we're going to talk about again. Now, you said you had another thing you wanted to tell me, or ask me. What was it?"

Dorothy, put off by Michael's directness, was uncharacteristically silent, miffed. She wasn't accustomed to being spoken to in this fashion by her son, to have her concerns brushed aside like lint on a sweater. Surely Margaret had poisoned her son's mind, made him lose sight of things. She absentmindedly picked at the tag on the pillow that she'd pulled onto her lap.

"Mom? . . . Hel-lo?"

"Sorry," she said, although she wasn't. She spread a blue blanket across her legs to counter the chill that was spreading across her body. Frank always set the upstairs programmable bedroom thermostat at a brisk 59 during winter evenings. "The other thing I wanted to discuss with you was about Christmas, your Christmas plans. We've got to start figuring that out now so we don't have a repeat of this kind of holiday debacle."

CHAPTER THIRTEEN

When he finally took the time to carefully observe Sarah Monroe, Michael decided that he found her enthralling. In fact, when he really paid attention to her, he couldn't, for the life of him, understand how he could've missed seeing her the first dozen times they had been in the same room and he had shared the same air with this fascinating creature.

Tall and slender, Sarah wore her icy blonde hair in a short pixie cut and applied little make-up other than mascara and a hint of blush on the apples of her pale cheeks. What intrigued Michael the most was the way she moved. She had a strangely languid yet fluid way of carrying herself, as if she were wearing a noise-deadening cloak with silent stealthy powers. She had an uncanny habit of appearing behind people before they even realized she was within their vicinity, sometimes catching them saying something they wouldn't have said had they known she was listening. However the hushed nature of her gait was counterbalanced by the volume of her opinions, which she offered fearlessly and liberally whether people wanted to hear them or not. Sarah was skilled at the art of persuading her peers to buy into her well crafted opinions on a wide array of subjects, as if she was an intriguing, fast-talking saleswoman from whom you'd unwittingly agreed to buy an overpriced lemon of a car that was likely to break down on the way home, only you didn't really care about the condition of the car when you were the focus of her undivided attention and gaze of her brownish-green eyes. On occasions when people found Sarah's aggressiveness off-putting, which happened with some people, she'd eventually win over most naysayers, but no one was quite sure how, though they speculated that it had something to do with pheromones or some elusive seductive trait they couldn't quite put their fingers on.

Michael didn't initially notice her when he first walked into Professor Perry's American Romanticism class at Boston University during the first week of his junior year and sat down at a desk near the back of the room. He was preoccupied by the fact that he hadn't wanted to take this class. Michael wasn't a fan of English lit classes, but needed to fulfill a graduation requirement to take two of them and this course fit into his schedule well, plus he'd heard good things about Professor Perry. Even after the obligatory go-around-the-room-and-introduce-yourself first day of class routine, Sarah's presence didn't really register with Michael. It wasn't until October, during a discussion of Henry David Thoreau's *Walden* when Michael was astonished to find himself suddenly smitten.

"He was nothing more than a mooch!" Sarah declared as she draped her long, thin arms casually over a bent knee which she had drawn up in front of her, resting her foot on the edge of the seat. "He *said* he lived off the land, but in reality, he lived off the generosity of other people. Most everything he had belonged to someone else, was the fruits of someone else's labor or was just given to him."

Michael, who'd been surprised that he actually enjoyed reading *Walden*, thought Sarah was simply being provocative out of boredom. "Thoreau wasn't a 'mooch'," he said, speaking up for only the second time this semester as he made air quotes with his fingers around the word "mooch." "He was a living example of rugged individualism, Yankee spirit. He used found objects, things that weren't used. He wasn't stealing."

"No one said 'stealing,'" Sarah interrupted, as she too used air quotes, albeit in sarcastic response, as she aimed a searing stare in his direction. "But if you can tell me how, exactly, Thoreau actually did anything to support himself that didn't come from the sweat of someone else's brow, then please, be my guest."

As he looked into her eyes, Michael felt as though he'd fallen into a pool of warm water and was under the spell of a mermaid who'd bewitched him.

"Mr. Kelly? Hel-lo? Care to respond?" Professor Perry asked while Michael sat mutely in his seat, continuing to unabashedly gaze at Sarah. She refused to avert her eyes despite the fact that others in the classroom were growing uneasy by their impromptu staring contest. "All right then," Professor Perry said before he cleared his throat, "let's move on to another aspect of Thoreau's experience while writing *Walden* . . ."

It wasn't until Sarah and Michael verbally tangled again in class a week later, this time over whether there's a modern day equivalent to a scarlet letter — she said Nathaniel Hawthorne was a man ahead of his time by "deconstructing the sexist, patriarchal practice of shaming women for expressing and enjoying their sexuality," something for which she asserted that women are still punished and shamed for, while Michael countered by saying that he didn't really believe such a level of social ostracism existed in the present day "exhibitionist, post-Madonna culture" — when the two finally exchanged words about something other than storied, long-dead writers. After the Hawthorne discussion, Sarah stood up to adjust the cuffs on the oversized yellow and red flannel shirt she was wearing unbuttoned over her dingy white cotton camisole and black jeans when Michael placed his left hand on her right shoulder.

"Hey, do you want to grab a cup of coffee and discuss whether we're better off now than we were in the 1800s?" he asked. He slowly removed his sweaty hand from her as he lost his nerve and crammed his fingers into the pocket of his creaseless jeans.

"No," Sarah said curtly as she slung her faded black Eastpak backpack over her left shoulder, over the spot where Michael's hand had just been.

A moment of awkward silence lingered. Michael shifted his weight from one foot to the other, nervously fiddling with the strings on the hood of his new cherry red BU sweatshirt. As the heat of his embarrassed blush started creeping up his neck and his ears, then radiated across his face like streaks of pink-red light in the sky at dusk, he said, "Oh," and slunk away, defeated and confused.

He was halfway down the hall when he heard her voice behind him. "But I *will* go with you to get a grilled cheese and tomato, a Diet Coke and giant fries with loads of ketchup while I tell you the 147 ways that you're dead wrong about Thoreau and Hawthorne."

Redeemed, Michael pulled his shoulders back and stood tall — even though Sarah was taller than him — and pretended not be fazed by her confidence. "You're on Monroe," he said, voice heavy with false bravado.

Fiery debates over 19th century writers morphed into late night rhetorical battles of wits about everything from whether women suffered from unfair career penalties once they become mothers (Sarah, channeling her sociology professor, said they did because the mere fact of their maternity made them less likely to get promotions, raises or to re-enter the workforce after childrearing, while Michael asserted that having a child is a choice, plus he threw in the fact that his mother had two kids and was doing well with her job as a school nurse), to whether the designated hitter should be abolished in the American League (Michael said it should be eliminated and called it "an absurd crutch for overweight tub of lard hitters who should just retire," as Sarah asserted that American League pitchers were stronger and lasted longer during their games because "they don't have to tire themselves out by hitting and dealing with batting practice; they just focus on pitching."). The verbal tussles eventually evolved into playful physical wrangling, then led to sex in Sarah's dorm room, a cozy spot of privacy she had all to herself because she was a Resident Assistant, charged with keeping watch over the students on her floor. Soon, Sarah and Michael could be found bickering about politics, literature and sports all around the city of Boston, on their way out of an REM concert, on the T (Boston's subway), over coffee at Dunkin' Donuts, in a BU student parking lot as they were unearthing their cars from mounds of snow, nailing one another's heads with snowballs and having a ton of sex in her bed.

On New Year's Eve, a few weeks after they started officially dating, Michael invited Sarah to join the Kelly family for their annual New Year's Eve meal of lobster, steak and champagne (the hooch was only for the 21+ crowd, which excluded Michael's brother Joseph). This was the first time someone other than an individual with Kelly blood running through his or her veins had been invited to join in on the festivities, and Dorothy, who was not at all thrilled Michael had invited Sarah without asking her first, decided to play nice as this was the first girlfriend Michael had brought home from college. This would provide her with an opportunity to make a first-hand assessment of this girl that Michael had been raving about. However after Dorothy pointed out that the weather forecast called for heavy snow on New Year's Eve, Michael started to worry about Sarah driving all the way from her home in Enfield, Connecticut — just over the Massachusetts border — to New Hampshire, so he volunteered to pick her up.

"You're just being overly protective and kinda sexist there Kelly," Sarah told him over the phone that morning. "I've been a New Englander all of my life. I can handle a few inches of fluffy flakes. They don't scare me."

A little more than an hour after Sarah was slated to

arrive, Michael was pacing around the kitchen, repeatedly looking out the window at the six inches of heavy snow that were now coating the driveway, hoping to see Sarah's beat-up gray Toyota Tercel pulling in any second. "I knew I should've just gone to pick her up anyway. I knew it!" Michael muttered to himself.

He heard Dorothy tsk when he finally caught a glimpse of Sarah's car slowly rolling down Arbor Way toward house number 17, a modest, neat-as-a-pin, modified two-bedroom blue Cape style home onto which Dorothy and Frank had added a den/sunroom more than a decade ago. (Dorothy was now working on Frank to add on a first floor half-bath.) Michael slipped his boots half on and eagerly ran outside without donning a coat to greet Sarah, as snow spilled into his boots and he got his socks wet. Peering out the window, Dorothy flinched as she saw her son give his girlfriend a deep kiss and wrap his arms around her. Rattled, Dorothy turned away from the view and decided to fill the crystal pitcher with a tad more ice water.

"I'm so glad that you're finally here," Michael said as he led Sarah into the house by the hand, absentmindedly leaving the door open and filling the toasty kitchen with a rush of winter chill. He also forgot to remove his boots, as was customary in his house, and Dorothy noticed that Michael and Sarah were tracking snow and rock salt all over her clean kitchen floor. "I was really worried about you."

He leaned in to kiss her again.

"Careful, careful Mike," Sarah said, as she came up for air. "Your sweater's caught on my earrings!"

"Oh! Right!" Michael said as he attempted to extricate his new gray wool L.L. Bean sweater — a Christmas gift from Dorothy and Frank — from the three silver hoop earrings in her left ear.

"Here, let me help!" Dorothy said, as she made a mental note of Sarah's well worn and fraying black pea coat. ("How old is this coat?" Dorothy thought, figuring it was likely from a thrift shop.) Once Sarah unbuttoned her coat Dorothy assessed Sarah's ensemble: A faded black T-shirt that said "Dead Kennedys" in white lettering, and skin-tight blue jeans which had stringy rips at the knees.

Dorothy took a dramatic, almost theatrical, step backwards, and stood in the middle of the kitchen with her hands clasped in front of her waist as if she was waiting for something to happen. Sarah inserted herself into the lull and stuck her right hand out toward Dorothy. "Dot, it's nice to meet you. Mike talks about you often, especially after he comes back from a weekend at home of getting his laundry done and he has your famous carrot cake cupcakes and pumpkin bread with him." Sarah smiled as she tried to casually size up the room and its occupants. "He's the only one I know whose mom irons his jeans. No one in my house irons anything."

Dorothy slowly extended a limp hand toward Sarah, thinking it odd to be shaking hands rather than embracing. "Yes," she said, "Michael," she paused after enunciating each syllable of her son's name, "has spoken about you a great deal too. He's quite fond of you." Dorothy swept her arms through the air, gesturing for them to venture deeper into the kitchen. "Welcome, please come in."

"Thanks," Sarah said. As she followed Michael through the blue and white plaid wallpapered kitchen and into the cream colored living room, Sarah left black scuff marks on the floor with her thick-soled shoes.

"Oh, and if you don't mind Sarah," Dorothy called after them, Sarah turned her head as she continued to walk, "it's 'Mrs. Kelly' or 'Dorothy,' not 'Dot.' Thanks."

During dinner, Michael and Sarah had a lively dialogue about tenure for secondary school teachers: He was firmly against it. She, the child of a high school English teacher, was for it, saying, "You've gotta protect yourself from the jack-booted thug administrative bean counters who just love to crush innovative teaching techniques if they make the teeniest bit of controversy, right Dot?"

Dorothy managed to put a phony smile on her face as she wrung her blue and white cotton napkin between her fingers. "Anyone ready for some coffee and dessert?" she asked in a pinched voice as she gathered some of the plates from the table and excused herself from the room.

"I am! Thanks hon!" Frank said. He got up from the table and walked into the adjoining living room to stretch out in his chocolate-colored leather chair, where, after eating too much cheesecake later in the evening, he'd fall asleep well before midnight with his reading glasses still perched on the tip of his nose. As Frank slipped into his fatty-food-induced slumber, everyone else gathered around him and watched on TV as the famous New York City crystal ball dropped in Times Square. In between snarkily commenting on the mediocre musical performances, Michael and Sarah continued their good-natured ribbing while they intertwined their arms and Sarah occasionally rested her hand on Michael's thighs. Michael's younger brother Joseph, amused by watching his mother's reaction to the young couple, retreated to his bedroom at exactly 12:01 a.m.

Soon afterward, Dorothy stood up and kicked the bottom of Frank's feet as he snoozed in the chair, "Come on Frank! Time to go to bed." A few minutes of grumbling later, she finally coaxed Frank out of his chair and directed him toward their bedroom. "Good night. Happy New Year," she said to Michael and Sarah as she followed Frank down the hall. Once she removed her make-up, applied her face cream, combed her hair and donned her new black and red flannel night-gown and climbed into bed next to Frank under their navy blue down blanket, Dorothy realized there was absolutely no way she was going to be able to go to sleep any time soon. She sat up on her side of the bed and pretended to read one of Frank's new biographies, straining to hear what was happening in the living room. She'd made it clear before Sarah arrived that the girl would be expected to sleep on the pull-out couch in the living room. Alone. Michael would sleep on the pull-out sofa in the den. Alone. Michael was explicitly told that he was expected to sleep in the den. Dorothy prayed that she wouldn't hear Michael and Sarah fooling around, in which case she'd be forced to go into the room to make sure they didn't do anything they'd regret. By 1:30 a.m., Dorothy was finally starting to feel drowsy and struggled to keep her eyes open when Michael walked down the hall to the den and closed the door behind him.

"Michael!" she said in a loud stage whisper outside the den as she quietly knocked on the door, startling her son who knew Sarah was in the bathroom. He thought everyone else was asleep. "I need to talk to you!" He opened the door and his mother entered the still-darkened room giving off a palpable sense of urgency. She softly closed the door behind them and pushed the button on the door knob to lock it.

"What Mom?" Michael asked, emitting a warm buzz, fueled by new love and champagne, which seemed to really irritate Dorothy. "Why are you still up? I thought you went to bed over an hour ago. Wait, you didn't think Sarah and I were going to mess around did you, because we wouldn't do that . . ."

"Michael," Dorothy said, "please, sit down." She smoothed the front of her nightgown before she sat down on the denim comforter on the creaky pull-out bed, patting on a spot next to her and signaling for her son to join her. "We need to talk about Sarah. I'm going to be blunt here because it's so late and I'm so tired from putting together this big meal, but, are you serious about this girl? I hope you're not serious about this girl."

Michael sat down next to her, now acutely aware that the heady glow he'd been enjoying was going to be doused. "We've been dating for almost three months. Why? What's wrong with her? You don't like her? How could you not like her? She's smart and pretty . . ."

"Michael," Dorothy said, stepping on what she was sure would be a wide-eyed avalanche of compliments, "she has no respect for anything. She won't call me by the name I asked her to use. She kept calling you 'Mike' or that god awful 'Mickey' when I made it clear that you're called 'Michael' here. She didn't lift a finger to help me with dinner or dessert or the dishes or the coffee. Never thanked me, or your father. Do you know how much this meal cost tonight? Lobster and champagne and steak for five adults? She could've at least . . . "

"Mom . . ."

"Please, let me finish. She insulted, well, not insulted exactly, but . . . but . . . well I found her T-shirt extremely distasteful, particularly to wear to a nice dinner at the home of your boyfriend where you're meeting his parents for the first time. We were all wearing nice clothing, appropriate clothing for a special meal. But she was in a T-shirt that made fun of the assassinations of the Kennedys. We live in New England for goodness sake! She had ripped pants that were so tight I'm surprised she could sit down."

"Mom, the 'Dead Kennedys' is a band. The T-shirt was about the band, not the Kennedy family."

"Oh." Dorothy briefly considered apologizing for disparaging Sarah on the "Dead Kennedy" matter in light of the new information but opted to press on. "I just get a very bad feeling about her. I get the feeling like nothing's important to her. Did you hear the way she spoke about her family? Making fun of her mother? Saying that no one there cooks or irons or eats meals together? What kind of a family did she come from?"

Michael rubbed his hands back and forth over his hair as though rubbing a magic lantern hoping that a genie would soon appear and shut his mother up. "She's just got spunk, Mom. She's different and exciting and smart and we really have a great time together. She challenges me. We talk about all sorts of things, things I hadn't even thought of until I met her. She wants to be a high school English teacher, just like her mother. She's been involved in the Big Sister Program in

Connecticut for years. She tutors freshmen at BU for the writing center . . ."

"Michael, I'm not saying she wouldn't be qualified to teach English or head up the debating team. I agree with you that she's smart, but she . . . "

"You're not being fair!" Michael shouted, shocked that his mother was dumping on the first girl he'd ever been really interested in. The rich meal he'd eaten started to curdle in his gut. "You're just not used to girls being so confident and aggressive is all. She's got kind of a punk edge to her, so what? Why should that bother you? I'm the one who's dating her. It feels good, I feel good when I'm with her."

"She's *not* confident Michael. She's not, believe me. She's arrogant and rude and selfish and careless. There's a difference between being confident and being rude. She even called you 'Chump' more than once. Doesn't she care what we think of her? I know that I really wanted to make a good impression when I met your father's parents for the first time." Dorothy paused to catch her breath and realized she'd been pressing her fingernails into the palms of her balled up hands and now her palms hurt. "She called your brother 'Chump Junior' and she doesn't even know him."

Michael smiled, shook his head and crossed his arms in front of him tightly. "Joseph thought it was funny."

"I don't care if Joseph thought it was funny. Joseph is in *high school* and thinks MTV's *Real World* is classy entertainment. What does he know? I realize that you're almost a grown man with a year and a half left of college before you graduate, so I can't tell you what to do, but, mark my words honey, you're going to get hurt by this girl. I just don't trust her, not with your heart. I think she'll be careless with it."

Michael closed his eyes and thought hard, then decided to rise above what he saw as his mother's irrational broadsides against the woman he loved, attributing it to her fears of losing her first child to another woman. As he came to the conclusion that she was, ultimately, motivated by love and concern for him, he softened his response. He put his arm around Dorothy. He was so much bigger than her now that he'd finally grown to 5'9 and change. At half-a-foot shorter, Dorothy seemed smaller, more fragile than he'd ever noticed before. "Don't worry. I trust her Mom. I'm fine. I'll be fine. But thanks for worrying about me."

"I hope you're right," she said. Dorothy rose to her feet, gave Michael a concerned look, then kissed him on the forehead.

Nearly a year later, Sarah was still living in the same single BU dorm, Room 334, as a Resident Assistant. It was a place where Michael wanted to spend the bulk of his days during his senior year. Sarah and Michael's relationship was still populated by thoughtful debates about the day's news, but their discussions had lost some of their original spark as Michael had been pulling his punches with Sarah, frequently allowing her to think she'd won. He'd just give in, surrender and end each debate with a tender hug, something Sarah was finding more and more unattractive as time wore on. Citing a hectic course load and work schedule, Sarah had become less and less available to Michael, saying she had papers to research and shifts to work at the Residence Life office. One October Monday afternoon, a day shy of the one year-mark of their first debate about Henry David Thoreau's *Walden Pond* in Professor Perry's class, Michael showed up unannounced to Sarah's room bearing goodies: A bouquet of bright yellow and white mums he'd picked up at a Norton farm stand on his way back to BU after spending a weekend at home, two loaves of pumpkin bread Dorothy had baked specifically for Michael but that he planned to give to Sarah because she adored freshly baked goods, and a gently used copy of *The Portable Thoreau* tied a yellow ribbon, which matched the color of the mums. As he walked down the hall, he saw that Sarah's door was open and he could hear her clearly as she chatted on the phone with a friend.

". . . It's just so pathetic. Freudian almost. I'm really, *really* tempted to write my psychology paper on them . . . No, I haven't . . . Well how can I tell him *that* without having him flip out? What, I'm supposed to take him out for drinks and say, 'Hey Mike, you're unhealthy attachment to your mother has become a huge turn-off? Perhaps you'd be happier if you crawled back up her pussy and into her uterus again?' Or tell him that mama's boys make bad lovers? That it's weird that he can't go more than two weeks without having his Mama fix? That I seriously have trouble getting off because of this, wondering what their weird connection is?" Sarah paused to chuckle aloud then continued. "I just don't see this going on much longer. It's kind of sad. We used to have such a strong, sexy connection. I don't know what happened . . . He's so just pathetic."

Sarah got up to fetch a Diet Coke from her mini-fridge and recoiled when she saw a crimson-faced Michael standing in the doorway holding the flowers, the tin-foil covered pumpkin breads and the book. He dropped them all in a heap at the entryway and walked back down the hall.

CHAPTER FOURTEEN

CHRISTMAS CARD PHOTO DISASTER
File under: Holiday madness

I was trying to capture the innocence and breathtaking cuteness of Thing I and Thing II in a photo for our damned Christmas card yesterday when disaster struck. Not kidding. Here's the gory story:

I bought the kids matching red sweaters (on sale at Baby Gap!) and khakis. Found Thing I a sparkly red headband (25 percent off!) which looks great in her dark hair. Took the kiddos for haircuts over the weekend all in preparation for today's photo session.

When Thing I got home from school, I fed both of my kids their favorite snack (fresh brownies — yes I baked them myself *rubbing nails triumphantly across chest*— with vanilla ice cream on top) in order to bribe them into letting me take their photos. They put on their sweaters and pants without complaint, a minor miracle. This was shaping up to be way easier than last year where the only photo I got had Thing II crying his eyes out.

"Say 'Santa Claus'!" I said with fake happiness, after positioning them in front of our sad looking Christmas tree. (Thing II just won't leave the ornaments alone — keeps hiding them, breaking them, etc. — so I had to move most decorations up to the top third of the tree. Now the tree, naked on the bottom half, looks like it has been ravaged by raccoons.)

It was about this time for everything to start falling apart.

Things I and II quickly grew bored and wouldn't cooperate. Someone was blinking, sneering, fleeing or turning away in every shot, no matter how nicely I spoke to them or how much I tried to bribe them with the promise of candy for compliance. My pleas of, "Look here honey," had gone from fake happy, to an order given through gritted teeth. I took, I dunno, 30 or 40 shots and even gave them a break while I inspected each image in my digital camera. I didn't find a single one that was usable for our Christmas card. It was December 10 and if I didn't get this done we wouldn't have a photo like every other Christmas-celebrating family in the Commonwealth of Massachusetts somehow manages to do. Except for us. The Loser Family. The Procrastinators.

After I'd given each kid a candy cane, I tried a second time to get a halfway decent photo, figuring they'd still look cute and festive while holding candy canes. But it turns out the candy canes were a bad idea. Really bad. Epically bad. The candy gave the kids sticky, reddish rings around their mouths. In order to get that goop off their faces, I had to use a lot of elbow grease and their faces wound up getting rubbed a little reddish raw when I used the baby wipes to clean them up. But I couldn't completely remove the stickiness from their hands by just wiping them down with wipes. (I didn't want to wash their hands at the sink because I was worried they'd get their pants and sweaters wet, and if I removed the clothing I'd never get the kids to put them back on and this photo session would be over.)

While I was trying to decide what to do next, Thing II decided to grab two fistfuls of Thing I's hair and spread the candy cane slime all over his sister's head and her new headband. She responded by shoving him to the floor. As he was down on the floor, Thing II picked up the half-eaten candy cane he'd dropped when he fell, leapt up and went after his sister with it, using the candy cane like a dagger. But she was too quick for him and she pushed Thing II back down onto the rug again. Thing II was still clutching the candy cane when he fell to the floor that second time. He'd braced himself for the fall by putting his hands down in front of him. His right hand was holding the sharp candy cane tip that was sticking upward . . . it's too terrible to write. . . well, it wound up going into his nose. His right nostril to be precise. When he panicked and tried to roughly pull the candy cane out of his nose, a piece of the candy broke off and was lodged way up there.

The rest is kind of a jumbled, horrifying mishmash of recollection:

There was blood and screaming followed by a frantic visit to the ER where I was carrying one howling kid and forcefully dragging a sullen one around by the lapel of her winter jacket into the exam room. I hadn't been able to fish the candy out of Thing II's nose at home, what with all that blood oozing out and his squirming and complaints that his nose was stinging. (Peppermint oil in the nasal cavity, particularly one with an open wound, will do that to ya, sting that is.) I didn't want to poke at his cut and make it worse. Plus he kept screaming and I wasn't sure if I was hurting him or if his screaming was from the initial incident. Best to seek professional help.

Long story short: He wound up being okay. An amused doctor (he seemed amused to me which, I suppose, is better than him calling the child protection people) gave Thing II a local anesthetic while a nurse and I held Thing II down and I cried. Thing I was blasé about the whole thing as she drew pictures of Christmas trees decorated by candy canes on the pages of a small notebook I had in my purse. The doctor used some special tweezers and pulled out the chunk of bloodied candy. (I'll never be able to look at candy canes in the same way again.) He stitched up my baby's wound inside his tiny little nostril then said, "Off you go," in a crazy chipper way that kind of irked me, because I was in no mood to feel chipper.

Yes, I know I should've planned my Christmas cards ahead of time, way before the holidays approached, as my best gal pal did. (She took photos of her kids just before Thanksgiving dinner when everyone was already dressed up. Her family's Christmas card arrived on the Tuesday after Thanksgiving. Good old Do-It-All-Diane.) But I'm not as organized as she is. Everything's on the fly around here. And now I'm paying the price or Thing II is paying it with his terribly swollen nose which I don't want to commemorate in a Christmas card photo. I keep getting all these Christmas cards in the mail and I haven't a clue about what to do with ours. All I need to do is get a good photo, then run it over to CVS and order those Christmas photo card things.

Maybe I should just take a photo of the piece of candy cane that the doctor pulled out of Thing II's nose (Yes, I kept it. It's in a crinkled, bloody plastic baggie.) and send a card that says, "Merry Bloody Christmas." I'm going to finish off my morning coffee (my second cup, actually) and ponder this idea. Ciao Internet.

The day after the candy cane incident, Maggie's blog post went, as they say, viral, generating a huge buzz on the Internet. A popular parenting blogger, Mamma Rule, who ran a blog that regularly had tens of thousands of readers a day, had stumbled upon Maggie's candy cane story while writing a larger post about other parents' Christmas photo exploits. She decided to dedicate an entire post to *Maggie Has Had It* and the candy cane tale. Bloggers who routinely checked in with *Mamma Rule* — as she was considered a must-read among the burgeoning mom blogging set — also wrote their own posts about the candy cane incident, linking back to Maggie's original entry on *Maggie Has Had It*. When Maggie checked her blog the day after she published the "Christmas Card Photo Disaster" post, it had received 547 comments, well exceeding any number of comments she'd received on any of her other posts.

"Whoa!" she said in a murmur as she scrolled through the comments, mostly from sympathetic parents who wanted to share their own Christmas card photo horror stories. Sandwiched between a comment from "RiotEr4EVA," who called her a "stupid, lazy bitch who let a 3-year-old run around with a candy cane," and a complimentary one from "AmyJennySallysMom," who wrote, "My youngest, Sally put a green Christmas M&M up her nose on the same day and we went to the ER too!" was a comment from someone who claimed to be a *Boston Journal* reporter, Lesley Fair, who said she wanted Maggie to contact her. "Can't find your e-mail address on the blog, but am working on a story about the growth in the number of New Englanders who write about their personal lives on blogs. Would like to interview you about your blog. Please e-mail me."

Maggie pushed her chair away from the kitchen table and was disappointed when she went for a third cup of coffee only to find that there was only a quarter-inch of java left in the her coffee pot. She poured the now-bitter and burnt-tasting, overheated dregs of coffee into her Red Sox mug and dumped a bunch of sweetener into it as she considered this Lesley woman's request. What were the upsides of contacting this reporter? The downsides? If she did this interview and her blog's address was mentioned in the article, that could direct a lot of new readers, hundreds, thousands, maybe more, to her blog, increasing her Internet traffic. This was something Maggie had already been thinking about anyway, trying to stimulate more traffic so she could start selling ads on her web site, turning her hobby into a potential money-maker. She'd heard that Mamma Rule was able to quit her day job thanks to the ad revenue she'd earned from her blog, which featured photos of Mamma's family and a daily chron-icle of life with her wild toddler son, Eric and their border collie they'd named Lassie. If Maggie didn't respond to the *Journal* request, another blogger would take her place in the article and then *that* person's blog would get a bump in traffic instead of hers. To not respond, Maggie thought, seemed stupid if she looked at it in terms of Internet traffic. She wanted to get out there now, before there was a stampede to climb aboard this Internet blogging train, needed to establish herself before wannabes saturated the personal blog market. This was the time.

Maggie re-read the reporter's comment and then scary thoughts crossed her mind: What if someone like "RiotEr4EVA" wanted to make her look like an idiot by impersonating Maggie in an e-mail to the reporter? Or what if the "reporter" wasn't really a reporter and was just a commenter pretending to be a reporter? If she replied and answered questions, this person could then portray Maggie as a gullible moron.

She stared at the computer screen for a moment before she typed "Lesley Fair's" name and e-mail address into Google. "Lesley Fair" popped up right away. The first item was a *Boston Journal* article she'd written about the growth of dog walking services for dual-income families who didn't have time to walk their dogs and who had hired people to take care of the canines during weekdays. When Maggie clicked on Lesley's name, which was highlighted, she was taken to a list of *Journal* articles Lesley had written, mostly lifestyle stories about quirky trends, all of which ended with the same e-mail address that had been left on Maggie's web site. At least Lesley Fair was a real person.

Maggie decided that she had to control how people saw her, so there was no choice but to contact Lesley and prove she was the one and only creator of *Maggie Has Had It* by putting something directly into a new blog entry, which mere commenters didn't have the power to do. Plus, she'd use her "maggiehashadit" e-mail address — the one listed on her "About Me" page as her contact e-mail that Lesley could've found if she'd actually done a thorough reporting job — which would further verify her identity. As her concerns percolated, Maggie decided to phone Diane.

"Hey Di. Glad I caught you. Ya busy right now?"

"Nope. Lily's down for her nap. I don't have to pick Zoë up for another hour. What's up? Is it all those comments on your candy cane post? That's still an unbelievable story. I can't believe Tommy and Jackie did that. I must've told 15 people about what happened and they just could not believe it. George said he was lucky it didn't go into one of his eyes instead of his nose. How *is* Tommy?"

"He's okay now, feelin' all proud now because the doctor called him 'brave.' He told his teacher this morning that he's the 'King of the Candy Canes.' That's a nickname Michael came up with. And George is right, by the way, I can't believe how lucky we are that it didn't hit an eye or go through his nose to his brain or something like that. Who knew candy canes could be so dangerous?"

"What did Michael say? You never wrote about his reaction."

"He was at work when it happened, and I didn't have a chance to call him until we were already sitting in the waiting area of the ER. He thought I was joking at first, then he started rattling off all kinds of questions for me to ask the doctor when we were called into an exam room by a nurse and I had to hang up. We only had to wait about, I dunno, 30 minutes or so, which wasn't that bad at all. I was surprised at how quickly we were seen by doctors 'cause I'd heard all sorts of horror stories. Jackie was totally quiet the entire time. Anyway, Michael was mostly worried about whether Tommy had any serious damage inside his nose. He was home, waiting for us with a pepperoni pizza when we came back. After the kids went to bed, we actually started laughing about how crazy it all was. It was the first real laugh we've had since Thanksgiving. He even said that we should buy candy cane-themed Christmas cards, tape one of the bad photos inside the card and type up a note telling the entire disgusting tale."

"You know, that's actually a good idea. It would definitely stand out from all the other Christmas cards."

"I can only imagine what Dorothy would say."

"Oh my God. She'd go nuts. Didn't she get upset by your cards last year, when you took a photo of all you guys in those Groucho Marx glasses, with the big mustaches and huge noses? What did she say again?"

"She called us the day she got it in the mail and said, 'I don't find this very funny. Christmas is a holy holiday filled with joy, not jokes.' She said she was too embarrassed to put it up her mantel with her other Christmas cards, those other 'nice family cards.' She said it was 'disrespectful' to Christmas and asked why we couldn't have a nice card like everyone else."

"Mother Christmas."

"Hey, did you see the comment on the blog from that *Boston Journal* reporter. She wants to interview me about my blog. Do you think I should contact her? If she mentions *Maggie Has Had It*, that could help my traffic."

"I don't know Mags," Diane said, pausing as she mulled. "What if she wants to know your real name, town and everything? You can't let that out. You've written some pretty bad stuff in there. You can't let her say who you are. That would be *bad*."

"Oh, no, no, no, no, no, no. There's no *way* I'd do it if she identified me by my first and last name. Or my town. It would have to be anonymous all the way. That's the first condition or I'm not doing it."

"Well how are you going to contact her anonymously? If you e-mail her, she'll see your name, unless you make up a fake e-mail account."

"I've got that covered. I already have an e-mail account under the name, 'Maggie Has Had It.' I send out e-mails on it all the time. The e-mail address is actually listed on my blog's 'About Me' section, but apparently crack reporter Lesley Fair didn't think to look there. I could e-mail her on that e-mail account and have her call my cell phone."

"I guess you *could* do that, but how are you going to know you can trust her? How can you be sure that no one will be able to identify you? If Michael finds out . . ."

"I'll make conditions for the interview. If she doesn't agree to them, I won't do it. I also won't tell her where I live. I'll say, 'in the Boston area.' There are tons of Maggies in this area. I never mention Michael's name, the kids' names, our town, Dorothy's name."

"I don't have any experience with reporters. Aren't they kind of vicious, like, looking for something to, like, slam people with? What if she investigates or something?" Diane could tell that Maggie didn't really want her honest input; she just wanted to make her arguments out loud and have

Diane serve as a sounding board. Maggie had already decided to do this. If Diane kept pushing the "this is a bad idea" point of view, Maggie would just come up with an excuse to get off the phone, Diane thought.

"Why would she do that? It's not like I'm accused of embezzling money or some sort of crime. There's nothing here to investigate. She's writing a story about bloggers who write about their personal lives. What's more innocent than someone like me, who writes about her kids and being a mom most of the time? I'm not writing about politics. She has no reason to 'investigate' me . . . so, you *don't* think I should do it?"

"I didn't say that," Diane hesitated again, still reluctant to give Maggie the rubber stamp of approval she was desperately seeking. "I'm just saying I'm not sure. I think it could be trouble. You could find other ways to get more people to see your blog."

Maggie glanced at Lesley Fair's bio and photo on the *Journal's* home page again. "Lesley looks trustworthy. Her last story was about dog walkers. And her story before that one was on people who had, like really old cats. And besides, if I don't talk to her, someone else will and *they'll* get the boost in Internet traffic, not me."

"Just be careful Maggie."

"No worries," she said, as she slurped down the cold coffee. A few, annoying bits of coffee grinds that had been lurking in the bottom of her mug left a bitter taste in her mouth.

CHAPTER FIFTEEN

Maggie made contact with Lesley Fair via e-mail and then, to establish that she was THE Maggie of *Maggie Has Had It* — which Lesley said via e-mail was unnecessary — Maggie wrote a blog item telling her readers that she was going to do a *Boston Journal* interview and promised to post a link to it when the story was published. In her e-mail, Lesley had agreed to all of Maggie's conditions: Anonymity, she'd just be called "Maggie," and she'd be said to live "in a western Boston suburb." Lesley called Maggie's cell phone at the appointed time that afternoon, when both kids were still in school and Maggie was sure that Michael had a meeting in Boston and wouldn't come home early.

Lesley sounded upbeat as she began the interview: "My story's going to focus on why people blog about their families and tell personal stories about them. I'm looking to use the voices of some local bloggers about why they're revealing themselves in blogs. After reading about your candy cane Christmas card story with your son and the candy up his nose, I really wanted to include that anecdote and mention you in the story. I've got no interest in telling people where to find you, your kids, your husband, or even your mother-in-law, who, from the sounds of your blog, seems like a real character."

Maggie laughed as she sat at her kitchen table, jiggling her right leg against the table leg as she gazed at her blog on the laptop, wishing she had a glass of wine in hand to calm her nerves, "You have no idea. I don't even blog about half of the things that go on with her."

Maggie could hear rapid keyboarding as she spoke. It was surprising to Maggie, realizing, suddenly, that everything she was saying was being transcribed. But she shook her head and tried to focus on being witty so she'd make it into Lesley's story, get lots of hits and then get to sell some advertising.

"So, why don't you tell me about why you started the blog in the first place? Um, was there a specific incident or, you know, one specific reason for why you, uh, decided to blog?" Lesley asked after a lengthy pause once she'd finished typing.

"My friend Di-, oh, sorry, um, lemme start again . . . A good friend of mine suggested that I start it. She'd, like, well, she'd read somewhere about people who wrote personal blogs as a way to get their frustrations out, like you said, a kind of diary, only other people can read the diary and can help you out. It's kind of like a, a, um . . . a catharsis. I started writing it after my second kid was born and I really missed working. I really loved talking to people at my office but then, after I decided to stay at home with my kids, I, uh, well, I didn't have the chance to have real conversations with anyone anymore about my day, didn't have the chance to bitch about stuff to my friends at work over lunch. You know what I mean. And I felt, well . . . lonely. Everywhere I looked, people, moms, seemed to have it all together and were happy. But I didn't."

"You wish you were still working? Why don't you just go back to work then?"

"Yes, well, wait a sec, wait a sec. I need to say, well . . . I need to say that I feel lucky to be home, to be able to be home with my kids. They're still little. I think that it's better for them at this time in their lives that I'm home with them. For now. I do work part-time though. I do Memory Makers home parties, the scrapbooking stuff, selling products at home parties and at events, but it's not the same as going to an office where you get dressed up in professional clothes every day, where people listen to you, you go out to lunches, real lunches, not PB&J or mac-n-cheese. No one's throwing up on you or needs a diaper change, or tells you that they hate you because you won't let them watch TV. The blog was a place for me to, uh, you know, uh, vent about not being the perfect parent, not loving being at home, even though I love my kids. I do! So please don't write that I don't love them, 'cause I really, really do."

Typing, furious typing was all Maggie heard in response. The typing went on for so long that it unnerved her, that and the fact that Lesley wasn't saying anything was starting to make Maggie feel uneasy. "No, no, Maggie," Lesley said after a lengthy period of silence and she'd stopped typing. "I know you love your kids. I don't think anyone who reads your blog would think that you didn't. But one of the big questions I have for you though is why don't you write about the day-to-day stuff about parenting, like more about potty training or trying to feed picky eaters, stories that other moms in your position might be able to weigh in on. Why do you write about some of the more personal parts of your life, like your sex life and stuff about your mother-in-law? Why not stick to the mommy stuff? Doesn't your husband or your mother-in-law get upset with what you write?"

"They don't know I'm writing the blog."

"*Real-ly*?!" Lesley said, intrigued. "So *that's* why you wanted anonymity, not so crazy readers wouldn't be able to track you down. Huh . . . okay, so they don't know you're writing about them?"

"Well, the only person who knows is my friend, Di- . . . um, the friend who first suggested I write a blog. She thought it'd be good for me. I don't use names or anything that would identify me or anybody. They're anonymous. I don't say where I live and I'm not identified other than my first name and that I'm in the Boston area."

"But some of the stuff you write in here *is* pretty uniquely detailed, pretty, uh . . . revealing, um, when you wrote about

Thanksgiving night and going to the bar and singing karaoke and how your husband walked out during your song, that your mother-in-law folded your underwear, about a time when your husband didn't, uh, didn't, uh, what's the word, *please* you in bed. Don't you worry that your husband will find out? Won't your mother-in-law go crazy if she finds out you've nicknamed her after an Italian dictator's wife?"

Maggie realized that her hands were getting sweaty. She shifted in her seat. This wasn't going in the direction she'd expected. Something in Lesley's tone was setting off a thousand red flags, flags that were blinding her. "Damn! Diane was right," she thought. This was a mistake, but there was nothing she could do about it now except press on and make her case. It was too late now.

"No, I don't, I don't . . . look," Maggie said, verbally flailing, reminding herself not to sound defensive. She placed her open left palm over her heart, closed her eyes, drew in a deep breath and focused. She tentatively continued, "I write about some really personal things because life *is* personal. If I only wrote about one portion of my life, told everyone I know that I was writing this blog and then had to hold things back so I wouldn't hurt their feelings, what I write here wouldn't really be true. It'd be half-truth, or quarter-truth if I had to gag myself and censor bits of my life from my blog and that's what I'd have to do if people knew I was a blogger. This blog is about my life, my perspective, *my* experiences. It's not about them. It's about *me* and my life *with* them. I think that's why so many people read my blog, because, you know, because of the details I include. Um, well, they see that they're not the only ones whose sex life has fallen apart after having kids, you know? True stories about that are uncomfortable but real. When I write about my marriage, I know other people will identify with what I'm sayin', but only because I don't have to worry that my husband's gonna read what I write and we'll wind up fighting about what I wrote. There are people who've e-mailed me and told me that they've had the same things happen to them that've happened to me, especially with their sex lives or trouble with their parents or in-laws. It makes me think that, as bad as things sometimes get, what's happening to me and my husband isn't new or unique, it's just marriage, just life, ya know? This stuff eventually passes and can be gotten over . . . or, no, no . . . they can be overcome, yeah, 'overcome's' a better word than 'gotten over.' Please don't use 'gotten over.'"

"Yep," Lesley said mechanically, as she was madly typing at her computer trying to keep up with Maggie. "Could you hold it there . . . one . . . more . . . second [long silence]. Okay! What else did you want to say?"

"Well, hmm, well, when I write about my mother-in-law, who tries to run my life and my husband's life as you might've noticed, there are tons of other daughter-in-laws who get it, and have the same sort of thing happen to them too, sometimes with their father-in-laws. It's not that they hate their in-laws or anything, they just don't like fighting for control. And when I write about my husband's long hours and how I didn't expect I'd be a kinda single parent because he's never around and it gets lonely, there are plenty of moms, and some at-home dads too, who get that, who are at home all day with the kids and wonder how they got to that place."

Maggie's face flushed as she gained speed and confidence, feeling as though she was bulldozing through Lesley's skepticism, knocking down each of Lesley's negative assertions: "Everybody goes through this at some point after they have kids. Their lives change, in good ways, of course. We all love our kids. But when it comes to what happens to a marriage *after* kids, that's what I didn't expect. I feel like no one told me that my marriage would change so much. That's what I write about. And when I'm blogging, I'm hoping that someone out there will explain to me how marriages survive this stuff, this hard child-raising part, or what to do when you feel like you're losing one another because you're changing diapers or getting snacks for the soccer team, or working a bazillion hours. What have other couples done to get past this hard part? At the very least, writing about this stuff, and getting comments from people, makes me feel as though my situation isn't just me and my husband. And that's helpful to me at least, and maybe to other readers too."

It took a while before Lesley stopped typing. Maggie decided to stop talking, got up, walked to the fridge, opened up and proceeded to empty half of a can of Diet Pepsi into her mouth.

"By writing in the way you do," Lesley said as she shuffled through some questions she'd written beforehand in a notebook and repositioned the telephone receiver on her other shoulder, "being totally open, without shame when you're blogging about intimate, personal things, you think that encourages other people to open up to you and share their experiences?"

Maggie was trying to get a clear read on Lesley's tone. Was she coming around to Maggie's point of view? "Yes," she said slowly, warily. "Yeah, that's true. If you put out truth, that's what you'll get back."

"Don't get me wrong . . ." Lesley said.

Oh boy, Maggie thought, here it comes.

". . . but, after reading months and months worth of your blog entries here, it almost sounds as if you're kind of depressed and putting your depression out there, crying out for help. What's your take on that theory?"

"Are you serious? Depressed?!" Maggie replied in a half-shout, dumbfounded. She hadn't seen that one coming.

"Well, yes."

Maggie angrily broke off the metal tab on the soda can and chucked the can across the room where it ricocheted off the edge of the kitchen counter, hit the dishwasher and fell to the floor, sending drops of sticky brown cola into the air. "Look, if you think that writing truthfully about your marriage and the things you're disappointed about equals depression, then I can't stop you. But, the way I see it is that I don't think

I'm alone and I think many people go through something like what I'm experiencing. I'm just writing about it while everyone else is livin' it and not talkin' about it on the Internet. I wouldn't call it 'depression.' I'd call it disillusionment. That's probably a better word."

Typing, typing. "Okay, okay Maggie. I'm off the depression issue. Sorry, didn't mean to insult you. Oh, what else, what else . . . oh, yeah, I know what I wanted to ask. Those people who post comments, I wanted to ask you about them. As I was reading through blog entries, I found that while you get a lot of comments from regular readers who seem like real fans, there are some people who are outraged and pissed off by what you write. How do you deal with the negative comments, including the name-calling ones?"

"It's hard," Maggie said, wondering if Lesley was a closet nasty commenter herself. "Sometimes I take some of the comments too personally and feel heartsick about them, even though I know I shouldn't because there are all kinds of nut jobs out there who just like to make trouble and take advantage of people who make themselves vulnerable and swoop in for the kill. It's really easy when they can do it anonymously. Like when people say I don't deserve my husband or my kids because I'm unhappy about something, especially the ones that question whether I love my kids because I tell the truth that sometimes I hate being an at-home mom, because sometimes it sucks and I wanna run away. That's a natural, normal reaction. But the fact is, I don't run away. I don't leave my kids. I don't leave my husband. I love them all and take care of them. I love my husband and try my best to be a supportive wife. On the blog, it's a safe place for me to write about the not-so-nice feelings we all have and deal with 'em there. On the blog, I don't have to be nice and take care of everybody. I can put my bad feelings into words and get 'em out of my head. I doubt there's anybody out there who hasn't had bad thoughts about their husband or wife. I'm trying, every day, to be thankful that I'm married to my husband, but if I just wrote all the good things that happen, that would be really boring. Who wants to read that Mi- . . . wait, um, who wants to read that my husband ran out and got me a Dunkin' Donuts hazelnut coffee and everything bagel with cream cheese this morning before he left for work? Or that, a few days after that big fight we had on Thanksgiving that I wrote about on the blog, he bought me a huge bouquet of orange colored roses and wrote a note saying he was sorry and that he knew it was a rough time for me and promised that things would get better once something he's been working on at his work is finished? That's not what people want to read. It's too sickly sweet. Boring."

All she heard was keyboarding. Maggie got up from her chair again, swung open the fridge and grabbed a second can of soda, desperately wishing this interview were already over. Didn't Lesley have enough material yet?

"So people only want bad news? They only want you to blog about your problems?" Lesley asked, clearly goading her now.

"What do you put in your newspaper? Unicorns and rainbows? Most of the stuff in your paper is bad news, isn't it? Scandals and crimes and stuff that'll sell more papers and ads? Most of the entries in my blog are me working out my problems and that's more interesting, at least to me, than a bunch of fake Hallmark-y stuff about how to make things perfect, or how they supposedly are perfect. I do, sometimes write sweet, sentimental blog posts, like how I ran a photo of the Santa picture my daughter drew last week. I wrote about how my son has slept with the little football his grandfather bought him over Thanksgiving and how he says he's going to grow up to be a 'quarfer-quack' when he grows up while his Pop-Pop watches him from the stands. Now that's cute, but cute doesn't help people figure out the hard parts of marriage and parenting."

"So most of what happens in your house is bad?"

"No! That's not what I said at all!" Maggie was getting

frustrated. "As I've already said, I only write about a fraction of my life in this blog. I only occasionally write about the good stuff, but most of what I write is a way for me to work out my problems with the readers or just vent. We help each other through this stuff."

"Like a big, public therapy session?"

"Yeah, kind of. Except I don't think there's a ton of judging or name-calling in therapy. Online, you sometimes get those troll commenters, the people who think I'm awful for writing what everyone else's thinking but not saying . . . that wouldn't happen in therapy I don't think."

"Well thanks Maggie," Lesley said, sharply interrupting. "I think I've got what I need."

After all the insinuations and tough questioning, Maggie felt this was a jarring, almost rude conclusion to their chat. "Oh, okay," she said quietly like a chastened grade schooler who'd been told to stop talking in class. "Wait, when will this be in the paper?"

"Next week sometime, depends on what my editor says and what else is happening that day. I'm never sure."

"Could you e-mail me a link so I can publicize it on my blog?"

"Sure."

CHAPTER SIXTEEN

It was a postcard-perfect late Saturday morning in May. The sun was shining through a smattering of brilliantly white, puffy clouds that looked so perfect that they seemed as though they'd been cut-and-pasted from a TV meteorologist's forecast graphic. After several dry, sunny days where the temps had been in the 70s, the ground had finally firmed up and was no longer sloppy and muddy. That was the trouble with spring in New England, it was typically messy, kind of chilly and too brief to really enjoy. There was usually a long, hard winter where it seemed like everyone's cars wore a constant white coat of salt and sand, and people had to keep their boots on hand through March, maybe even April. Spring was, essentially, all about mud. Then, before you knew it, the summer's heat and humidity would descend without a gentle transition in between the seasons. "What happened to spring?" people would marvel to one another each year on the first day the mercury hit 80 degrees and there was a touch of humidity. So on a spring day when the weather was warm and the mud had dried up, people tended to flock outside to soak up the rays like prisoners who'd been deprived of feeling the unfiltered sun on their skin for more than five minutes at a time.

Such was the case for 6-year-old Michael when he and his mother Dorothy went to the Curtis Corner playground near their house, while Michael's father Frank had taken 3-year-old Joe to get his hair cut at Ron's Barbershop, a place

Frank had frequented for years. The plan was for all four of them to meet up afterward at Friendly's for lunch. The trip to the park had been prompted by Dorothy who feared that she was precariously close to losing her temper with everyone, her sons in particular. She really needed Michael to burn off some energy and needed to take a breather herself, to regain her composure while sitting on a sunny park bench. That wouldn't happen if they stayed home on Arbor Way. She needed to get out of that house. Immediately. Plus there were working bathrooms at the playground. At her house, not so much.

The morning had been insane and had pushed every one of her buttons. The boys, who'd risen in the 5 o'clock hour for no apparent reason, had knocked over and trampled on a large potted fern that Dorothy had been nurturing for years. They ground half of its delicate leaves into the floor with the soles of their sneakers. While Dorothy was busy sweeping up the dirt and assessing whether the plant could survive, Joseph ran into the bathroom and tried to flush one of his plastic drinking cups down the toilet, just because he could. The cup was precisely the right size to plug up the toilet bowl opening. After a sweat and expletive-fueled 15-minute effort, neither Dorothy nor Frank could get it out, after trying various tools and kitchen utensils to extricate it.

"We have to call someone," Frank said after he'd tried and failed to slip a thin knife blade in between the cup and the porcelain in an attempt to pry it out. "I'm afraid I'll strip the bolts on the bottom of the toilet if I try to remove them. They're pretty much rusted on there. I can't do this on my own."

"Great! How much is THAT going to cost us?" Dorothy asked angrily, noticing, out of the corner of her eye that Joseph and Michael were now playing with the ruler she'd already stuck in the toilet trying to dislodge the petite cup. "Stop that! That's dirty! It's been in the toilet! Argh! Come with me!" She grabbed the collars of their shirts, cringing at the thought of what manner of germs were all over their hands, and marched them to the sink. She lifted them up around their waists, one by one, so their hands could reach the water and they half-heartedly washed themselves, giggling as they clandestinely flicked water into one another's faces, something their mother didn't happen to notice as she was in her own world. "Can't you think of any other way than to pay someone to get that cup out?" she hollered to Frank.

Frank, ignoring his wife's question, said, "I'll call James. James Fletcher. He'll do it for nothing. I'm sure of it. Plus, he owes me a favor anyways."

A little while later, after speaking with James on the phone, Frank found Dorothy in the kitchen angrily scrubbing scrambled eggs, bacon and cinnamon toast debris from breakfast dishes while the boys were coloring in Superman coloring books and, unbeknownst to the distracted their mother, were intentionally getting crayon marks all over the kitchen floor and snickering. "James thinks our best bet is to remove the entire toilet from the floor, making sure not to strip the bolts, that's a big worry. He said he and I could do it. He's got all the right tools and everything. He'll be over here at around 5 today, maybe earlier. He's got another job he's already scheduled."

"So what are we supposed to do for a toilet until then?" Dorothy asked, hands on her hips, trying not to burst into tears out of sheer frustration and exhaustion. She hadn't slept much the previous night because Joseph had jumped into Frank and Dorothy's bed at around 2 a.m. and refused to leave. Yesterday morning, both boys were up and playing by 5:30. She was too embarrassed to admit — particularly to her own mother, Sophie, who was a firm believer in adhering to strict household — that she'd been unable to get Joseph on a sleeping schedule and that, on most nights, he wound up in Frank and Dorothy's bed because Dorothy didn't have the heart to give him the boot. Frank was usually unfazed by the whole thing, snoozing his way through each night like he'd done every night of his life. But because Dorothy was such a light sleeper, she had been sleep-deprived for what seemed like years. Despite her fatigue, she was the one who got up early to get ready for work, made breakfast for everyone, lunch for Michael, Joseph, Frank and herself, tidied up afterward and ironed everyone's clothing for the day before her mother came over.

"Well, the boys and I will have to go outside in the woods and you, well, you'll have to hold it," Frank said grinning devilishly as he awaited her response, expecting it to be entertaining.

"In the woods? I won't have my children using the out of doors when they have to go to the bathroom! And I won't be 'holding it' until 5 o'clock, I'll tell you that much. I've had three cups of coffee this morning Frank!" she paused, getting herself more agitated the more she played out the rest of the day in her head. "Knowing your friend James, it'll probably be closer to 6 by the time he strolls in the door. It's 10:18! That's absurd to think that we'll, or *I'll* hold it all day!"

"Why don't I take Joseph to get his hair cut? He needs one anyway, plus I could stop at the hardware store first to pick up a few things," Frank said. "We could all go to Friendly's for lunch afterward. They have bathrooms there. And at the barber shop. Then we could stop off at the bookstore on the way home, they've got a bathroom there too, and, boom, we've almost made it to 5 with bathroom facilities at our disposal all day."

Dorothy folded her arms in front of her. "And what am I to do with Michael while you're out with Joseph? What if he has to go to the bathroom too? Couldn't you take him with you?"

"He doesn't need a haircut," Frank said. "He'll be fine with you. He's older."

"Michael, get your things, we're going to Curtis Corner," Dorothy announced, looking over her shoulder at Frank and muttering, "There are bathrooms *there*. And it's a lovely day to go to the park."

Frank and Dorothy each climbed into separate cars, with a child in tow and plans to meet at the restaurant. When Dorothy pulled into the playground parking lot and turned off the motor, she told Michael, "Go on. Go play. I'll be right behind you."

Michael, clad in pressed navy blue dungarees and a short-sleeved royal blue collared cotton shirt, made a mad dash for the jungle gym, while Dorothy exited the vehicle slowly and took a leisurely stroll over to the wooden park bench located in a spot of sun. She smoothed down the hemline of the skirt she'd made herself, adjusted her blue and white striped blouse and opened the latest issue of *Ladies Home Journal* in an attempt to calm herself down from the morning's events.

"Mom! Mommy! Watch me! Watch me!" Michael shouted to Dorothy as he scaled to the top of the tangle of metal on the jungle gym and carefully creeped across to the middle of it.

"Nice Michael! Nice! Be very careful up there. No jumping," Dorothy said in a checked-out kind of voice. She tucked her near-black bob behind her ears and started reading an article about whether margarine was healthier than butter. As Dorothy scrutinized the piece, which cited a medical study saying that it hadn't been proven that margarine was better and that some nutritionists and physicians had raised concerns about its chemical components, she felt vindicated. For weeks, she'd been arguing with Melissa Tippen, who ran what Dorothy considered the abysmal lunch program in the school where Dorothy worked, about this very issue. Melissa wanted to replace all the butter with margarine, saying that experts were reporting that it was healthier, but Dorothy said that it'd be better to stick with all natural products instead of synthetic food, which she believed was bad for children's growing bodies. The fact that Melissa fed the students of Franklin Middle School a steady luncheon diet of fatty, bland meals and then had the nerve to claim that *she* knew what was best for the children, enraged

Dorothy. The Franklin Middle School principal, the doddering Charles Martins, refused to dip even one toe into the middle of the argument, even when Dorothy cornered him and reminded him that she possessed a degree in nursing while Melissa had barely finished high school with passing grades. Dorothy had been collecting articles which were skeptical about margarine's so-called health benefits in a manila folder for some time and planned to present them to Charles and the school board once she felt as though she'd gathered sufficient evidence to prove her point. She still planned on writing letters to some college professors currently studying the matter to solicit their input. She was convinced they would agree with her.

"Moooomy! Moooommmy!" These shouts had a different tone than the previous ones. Unlike Michael's previous bids for Dorothy's attention, the latest ones carried the distinct tone of alarm, shaking Dorothy from her margarine-versus-butter fog. She glanced in the direction of the line of swings and saw Michael lying on his back, rolling from side to side on the dirt, clutching his right leg tightly to his chest and sobbing.

Dorothy leapt up, dropping the magazine and her purse into the dirt as she ran to Michael's side. "What happened? What happened?"

"I fell," he said threw his tears. "I fell. My leg hurts."

"You fell?"

"Jumped," he sniffed, "jumped off. Owww, Mommy! Don't touch my leg!"

Three-and-a-half hours later Dorothy and Michael left the Nashua Regional Hospital's Emergency Room where a doctor had set Michael's fractured right tibia in an off-white, plaster cast, and handed Dorothy a prescription for pain medicine and a set of impossibly small crutches.

"Mommy, it still hurts," Michael whimpered in a small voice, burying his face into her shoulder while she carried the 48-pound boy, the crutches and her purse to the car.

Dorothy gently deposited her son into the back seat. "I'm sorry honey. I'm so sorry," she said, her voice choking. The ends of her hair skimmed Michael's face as she leaned in to kiss him on both of his cheeks, which still contained some remnants of baby fat, enough to make his face feel cushiony and supple when she kissed it. The hospital scenes she'd just experienced kept playing over and over in her head like a movie as she drove home, specifically when Dr. Melvin X. Fisher ignored the fact that she was a registered nurse and repeatedly asked her to explain the circumstances surrounding Michael's fall, not so obliquely probing whether she played any role in her son's injury.

"Weren't you *watching* him?" Dr. Fisher asked as he gripped his clipboard with one hand, his pen poised expectantly in the air as though he were about to inscribe her every utterance into some sort of permanent, condemnatory record. "You said, let me look at this chart again, yes, yes, you say that you didn't see exactly what happened? Why not? What *were* you doing?"

Dorothy, who didn't believe she'd done anything wrong at the park, nonetheless felt as though she was under attack. "I was sitting on a bench next to the jungle gym. I wasn't looking at him when he fell off the swings. I told you, I don't know how high he was swinging. I was reading a magazine article," she said defensively. "That doesn't mean I'm a bad mother, Doctor. Accidents happen. I see accidents every day at the school where I work as the school nurse."

"I'm not saying you're a bad mother Mrs. Kelly," Dr. Fisher said carefully and slowly, as though talking to someone who wasn't in total control of her mental faculties. The gray-haired sixty-something doctor looked at Michael's chart again. "I'm saying that perhaps this whole thing could've been avoided if you'd been looking out for your 6-year-old son and paying more attention to him than to your *Good House-keeping Magazine*. A child his size shouldn't have been swinging so high that a fall would fracture his leg."

"It. Was. *The. Ladies. Home. Journal*," Dorothy said, employing the same simpleton, over-enunciation that the doctor had used. "And I *was* there with my son, Dr. Fisher. This was an accident that I doubt even you could have prevented, even if you were there watching him. And he *was* using the playground apparatus appropriately."

"How would you know that for sure Mrs. Kelly?" Dr. Fisher replied acidly. "Your nose was buried in your ladies' magazine."

When she got to the stoplight after leaving the Emergency Room parking lot, Dorothy peered at her son who was lying across the backseat of the car looking small and scared. She couldn't help but feel as though this *had* somehow been her fault after all, despite what she said to Dr. Fisher. She needed to focus more on Michael, she thought. And Joseph too. Maybe the pompous doctor was right and that if she'd been more attentive, watched her children more, there wouldn't be a powder blue drinking cup stuck in the toilet or a shredded fern clinging to life in her foyer or a child with a cast on his leg sitting in the back of her car. "I'm going to look after you much better from now on Michael, much better," she said, tears leaking from her eyes as Michael reached out his arms in her direction but couldn't quite make contact with her. "Don't you worry. Mommy will look out for you. I don't want you to get hurt again. I'll protect you sweetheart."

When she and Michael arrived home, Frank met them in the driveway. Dorothy was still fuming with a mixture of guilt and anger while she told him what Dr. Fisher had said to her. Frank shook his head to indicate his disgust with the physician, then tenderly carried their sleeping child into the house and lovingly stretched him out on the roughly textured green sofa, next to the matching green recliner where Joseph was already napping in front of the TV as cartoons continued to play. Frank and Dorothy silently gazed at their boys until Frank took her hand, led her to the kitchen and poured them both a large drinking glass filled with the white wine he'd found in the fridge. She waved it off. "I can't have anything now," she said, wringing her hands together fiercely. She collapsed into a chair next to the kitchen table, covered by a gold and blue paisley pattered plastic tablecloth, and put her face in her hands. "I don't deserve anything."

Frank crouched down next to his wife's chair. He put his hand on her shoulders and said, "You did nothing wrong here. Nothing! You hear me? I broke all kinds of bones when I was a kid at much younger ages than 6. And my mother was a saint. Didn't you break your arm when you and Sophie were clearing the driveway of snow when you were, what, 10?"

"Eleven."

"Okay, 11, then. Do you think Sophie was an inattentive mother? Negligent?"

"Of course not."

"Well neither are you. Neither was Sophie or my mother. We can't protect our kids all the time. That's just a fact. And we shouldn't. How else would they learn things?"

"But we can try," Dorothy said. "Can't we just try?"

CHAPTER SEVENTEEN

Maggie felt anxious for the rest of the week, emotionally drained by a constant sense of impending dread over how she'd be portrayed in the *Journal* article by Lesley Fair, who, by the sounds of her commentary during the interview, clearly didn't like Maggie's blog. Would the article draw or alienate readers? Why had she gone and announced on her blog that she'd done this interview? Now she would have to post the link to it once the article was published. If she came off like a total imbecile, all her readers would see that. "Moron," she said, mentally kicking herself.

Luckily for Maggie, the messy details of Christmas planning were also bearing down on her and provided some degree of distraction from the agonizing wait for the article's publication. The Christmas cards still weren't done, weren't even started, actually. (She was still traumatized by the candy cane incident.) She hadn't tackled any Christmas shopping yet, plus Jackie and Tommy hadn't written their letters to Santa. Those letters would inform Maggie of what she needed to buy, provided that they didn't ask Santa for a toy that had sold out of the stores already. On top of that, she and Michael still hadn't figured out what was going on with Christmas dinner yet. Maggie wanted to have Christmas at their house with just the four of them, and then invite Dorothy, Frank, Joseph (as if he'd come), Luke and Rob over to their house *after* dinner for dessert and drinks and to exchange gifts. But she wasn't sure if Michael was on board with this plan which she saw as a generous compromise, especially after the Thanksgiving debacle.

Meanwhile, Maggie was annoyed by recent developments at Jackie's school: Last week, she received two e-mails from the room mothers, Hope and Ally. In the first e-mail, they asked for donations of $20-30 per family in order to buy Mrs. Stone a "holiday" gift on behalf of the class, though they said the amount listed was just a "suggestion." The second e-mail was a list of items they said Mrs. Stone needed for the class "Winter Celebration," otherwise known as the Christmas/Hanukkah/Ramadan party, though the school couldn't explicitly say the party was marking those holidays lest they be tagged as politically and religiously insensitive or non-inclusive. The list requested: A couple boxes of doughnuts, hot cocoa for 40 (for both parents and kids), bottles of water, several trays of fresh fruit (no melon though because one of the students had a melon allergy), "winter-themed" paper goods (the e-mail explicitly said there were to be no Christmas paper goods so as not to offend non-Christian families) and gingerbread cookies (still in the box so the school nurse could read the ingredient label in search of allergens to which a few other children are allergic), to be consumed while reading *The Gingerbread Boy*.

The same day she received the "shake-down e-mails," as she called them, Mrs. Stone also sent a note home in the students' backpacks, printed on cobalt blue paper decorated by two stickers featuring pleasant-looking snowmen:

"Dear Families,

Our class will be having a Winter Celebration on December 22nd at 1:30.

We would like to ask that every family purchase and WRAP a new book ($10 limit) for our party. We have attached the book order form — where you can select the book you want and enclose a check — as a simple way of ordering a book for the Winter Celebration. Please select a book that would be enjoyed by either a boy or a girl. Please bring the wrapped book to the Winter Celebration.

The room mothers will be contacting you in an e-mail regarding food and supplies we will need for the celebration.

Sincerely,

Mrs. Stone."

Maggie was annoyed that on top of her existing Christmas "To Do" list, she now had to buy and wrap a book, write out a check for Mrs. Stone's gift, as well as buy and send in something to contribute to the Winter Celebration, an event which she had prominently highlighted on the family calendar in bright red marker so that there was no repeat of the Halloween party incident. She hadn't heard from Tommy's preschool teachers about his class' holiday celebration, but figured she'd be called upon to buy or contribute a gift for each of her son's three teachers plus the young class room aide. Oh, and she couldn't forget to buy a gift card for Jackie's bus driver who was kind enough to frequently idle the bus in front of their house when Jackie was running late, which happened more times than Maggie was willing to admit.

"Shouldn't the schools be teaching the kids about recycling and re-using stuff?" Maggie asked Michael whom she'd called while she was making dinner and he was still at the office. "Who do they think they are demanding that we go out and buy a stupid book? We're going to be spending money on the party stuff, on the teacher gift. We spent, what was it, something like $40, or something like that, on 'mandatory' classroom school supplies at the beginning of the year. We were guilted into buying gift wrap during that fund raiser in October that we were told was 'crucial to help fund our quality educational programs.' Luckily I caved and bought snowman themed wrapping paper and gift bags, so I don't have to go out and buy new wrapping paper for this stupid Winter Celebration book swap. There've been winter coat drives, Thanksgiving food drives, calls for antibacterial gel and tissues for the classroom. All of this adds up ya know. It's really hard to keep on top of all of this, especially with more than one kid in school now."

"Mmm, hmm," Michael said, trying to feign a modicum of interest in the grade school drama while he was actually focusing on an e-mail, another "urgent" one that ENY's attorney had sent to a Mass Highway official to make sure everything was in order with the Bypass's environmental variance application. Normally he wouldn't have taken Maggie's call when he was under the gun and had to double-check the application and all the supporting documents. He needed to focus. But he took the call hoping that by letting her vent about whatever she wanted to vent about (when she called him after 5 p.m. — when she knew he was getting ready to go home — it was most likely so she could complain about something), she could purge the irritation from her system before he set foot in the kitchen. Tonight, he didn't want her to be in a bad mood.

"Well, I'm gonna write an e-mail to Mrs. Stone, suggesting that she offer parents another option, like taking a book the kids've already read, something 'gently used,' and wrap it with homemade wrapping paper made out of paper grocery bags, instead of demanding that everyone march out to the store and buy a new book and use new wrapping paper. That would teach the kids some good lessons and not cost anyone a dollar, right?"

"Great idea honey," Michael said. "Very environmental of you. Al Gore would be proud."

"Thanks!" she said, pleased. "I'm gonna go and write that e-mail. Oh, and I need to confirm the date of the Memory Makers event with Lisa Slate for next Thursday night. That's still okay with you, right? You'll be home to watch the kids?"

"Hold on, lemme check my schedule," Michael said, pulling up his calendar on his laptop. "Next Thursday night is all clear work-wise. I'll block it off on my ENY schedule so no one signs me up for a meeting . . . I've gotta go and finish up a few last things as well. I'll be home soon! Promise."

Maggie sat down in front of her laptop and quickly dashed out an e-mail to Lisa to verify next Thursday's event and that she was expecting about 20 people to attend the home party. She needed to fit in one last Memory Makers event before Christmas to unload the boxes of inventory that were sitting atop the wall-mounted shelves in her garage. Multiple times a week when they were walking past those shelves to get from the garage to the kitchen — particularly since she got her latest shipment of 12X12 inch scrapbooks, decorated papers and square hole punchers — something from her Memory Makers' stash always seemed to be accidentally knocked off the shelves and came crashing down onto Michael or Maggie's heads, shoulders or backs. Whenever they tried to place the kids' shoes, backpacks, mittens and hats onto the kids' designated shelves beneath the Memory Makers shelf, they risked sustaining an injury. Michael had installed the shelving the previous year with the express purpose of getting a handle on the kids' clutter and the crush of Memory Makers products which had previously been stacked all over the house. But every day, the kids thwarted Michael's organizational attempts and they chucked their belongings under the shelving unit or into a heap at the bottom of the stairs. It drove Michael crazy that Maggie did not insist that the kids place their belongings on their designated shelves when they got home from school each day, but he had made the conscious choice not to harass her about it until after the new year. "Maybe she'll sell enough product at this next party that will wind up clearing that junk off those shelves," he hoped, when he'd hung up the phone in his office.

Later that evening, shortly after getting out of his car and maneuvering himself around the garage with his briefcase, Michael picked Jackie's soccer cleats off the floor and placed them on her shelf, jostling the shelving unit just enough to cause a maroon scrapbook — which had been stacked haphazardly atop some three-hole punches on the top shelf — to tumble down from its perch and hit on the back of his head, corner first. He swallowed his pain in silence.

When he walked into the kitchen where his family was already eating dinner he said, "You've got to really sell those huge scrapbooks Mags. I'm afraid that one day I'm going to be knocked out or lose an eye or something."

He washed his hands and joined them at the table, where Maggie had already fixed him up a plate with salad and a bean and cheese burrito, Jackie's favorite meal. He reached behind his neck and massaged a spot on the edge of his hairline where a small goose egg had risen. "One of those books got me on the back of the head just now," he said. "I've got a bump."

"Poor Daddy!" Jackie said, jumping out of her chair and skipping over to her father to examine his injury. She roughly parted and pressed apart his hair in search of a bump. While Jackie indelicately manhandled his scalp, Michael felt something warm and slimy. "What the?" he asked. He touched his head and discovered something warm and paste-like on his hair. "Jacks do you have refried beans on your hands? Are you getting it all in my hair?"

Jackie — decked out an outfit of her own creation: purple fleece pants and sweatshirt, accented by orange socks and a red headband — instinctively clasped her hands behind her back, pursed her lips and looked down at the floor as though she hadn't heard him. Michael patted his head and found more refried beans smeared in various other places atop the stiffness of his tufts of gelled hair.

"Errrr! Whaddidyado?" he shouted. He hated it when the kids soiled him or his clothing. It made him irrationally crazy, and while he recognized that he had a tendency to overreact, he firmly believed that the children needed to be more careful about how they handled other people and other people's things, regardless of how lax Maggie was about it.

Maggie winked at Jackie, grabbed a couple of white and blue "Home is Where the Heart is" paper towels from the roll that was already on the kitchen table because the kids were so messy when they ate burritos. She moistened a few of them at the sink and attempted to remove the globs of beans from Michael's hair, only to discover that she was making things worse, leaving behind shredded bits of paper towel on his head. (The paper towels had been sliced into pieces by the sharp points of Michael's gelled hair.) Abandoning the paper towels, she started removing bean-covered paper shreds from his do with her fingers.

"It'll be okay Daddy. Jackie didn't mean it. It was an accident. *Riiiight Jackie*? You were just trying to help?" She looked over at her daughter while nodding her head vigorously and raising her eyebrows, trying to will Jackie to apologize without being explicitly told to do so.

"Right Mommy," she said, bowing her head down again, scrunching up her face as she held back tears. "Sorry Daddy."

Michael noticed that Tommy's eyes were also brimming with tears and he'd slumped down in his seat. "Guys, I'm sorry I yelled. Sorry," Michael said.

"s'okay Daddy. The kids understand that you've just had a long day. He's not really angry, guys. He just sounds like a crazy monster when his nice hair and clothes get all messed up," Maggie said, sounding as though she wanted to laugh although she was pretending to be serious as she extracted the remaining beans and tried to ignore the powdery remnants of the disturbed nest of dried gel on her husband's head.

Listening to Maggie make excuses for him to the children only made Michael feel worse. "Thanks," he said, looking up at the smirking Maggie, wrapping one arm around her hips and giving them a squeeze. "Come over here guys." Michael patted his lap and gestured to Tommy and Jackie to climb onto him. After looking momentarily uncertain, they piled on top of him.

"Look, everybody, I want to tell you that I'm sorry if I've seemed distracted and not very nice to be around lately. I know it's not fair to be so grumpy to you guys. I've been having a hard time at work, but that's about over. Almost over. The Daddy you know and love will be back."

"No more yellin'?" Jackie asked, as Michael noticed that she got refried beans on his pant leg. Instead of loudly sighing or shouting at the child, Michael grabbed another paper towel and wiped off her hands and his pants without saying a word.

"No more yelling . . . unless you do something nutty, like shove your brother again." Then he got in Tommy's face in a quasi-playful way. "Or if you try to hurt your sister with a sharp candy cane."

"There will be no more candy canes in this house for a long time," Maggie said.

"Hey, Mags, isn't that Charlie Brown Christmas special on tonight? In about," he looked at his watch, "25 minutes? Why don't you guys run upstairs and get into your pajamas, brush your teeth and play in Jackie's room for a little bit. Mommy and I will come and get you when it's on."

The two kids enthusiastically scampered out of the room, the sound of their stomping feet fading as they disappeared up the stairs.

"Do you really think that Tommy's gonna put his pajamas on if one of us is not standing there, watching him or actually physically putting the clothing on his body?" Maggie asked. "He'll just roll around the floor for 10 minutes then come downstairs and whine at us, not wearing his pajamas, and without having brushed his teeth."

Once he was sure the kids couldn't hear him, Michael said, "I just wanted them to go upstairs for a minute. Come with me." He took her hand in his and pulled her toward the garage, forgetting, temporarily, all about the refried beans in his hair and the bump on his head.

"But what about all this food? We can't leave it all out here on the table," Maggie protested, gesturing toward the ransacked kitchen. If she had been alone with the kids, she likely would've left the food on the table and gone upstairs to get the kids ready for bed, maybe read them a few books before returning to the kitchen to clean up, but because

Michael was home, she wanted to at least appear conscientious about keeping things tidy and pretend as though she cared about promptly cleaning up.

"Where're we going?" she said.

Michael smiled as he led her down the stairs to the garage.

"What? Are you going to show me the exact spot where the scrapbook hit you in the back of the head? I told you, I'm putting them on discount at the Slates' house to move 'em."

"Shhh," Michael said, "keep quiet."

He guided her past all the stuff that lined the walls of the garage — the scooters, bikes, plastic playground balls, rollerblades, ice skates and the winter jackets that were slumped beneath their designated hooks and shelves and lying on the dirty concrete floor — and they tried not to brush up against Michael's Accord, which was covered with salt and sand from driving on treated streets after a recent ice storm. Maggie's minivan was parked outside in the driveway because she could no longer park it in the garage without someone dinging Michael's car when he or she opened the doors.

Michael's dimples looked as though they were about to pop off his beaming face as he looked back at Maggie, who was also smiling only she didn't know why, just that he was, and he hadn't been doing that a lot these days and it was kind of contagious. The only thing she cared about right now was the fact that she was getting her husband's undivided attention when she was still wide awake and alert. Michael opened the passenger door of the Accord and gestured for Maggie to climb inside.

"What? Get in the car? What, are we going to do, go 'parking' in our own garage?" she joked, as the door closed behind her, a bit thrilled by the thought of steaming up the windows of that Accord. Michael walked around the other side of the car and slid into the driver's seat. Once all the doors were closed, Maggie thought she heard a soft noise, almost a whine, coming from the backseat.

"What the hell? Is something in here? I heard a noise!" she asked, alarmed that maybe the mice that had infested their garage last year had returned. The rodents were quite fond of the snack-sized bags of cheesy popcorn and apple juice boxes the kids tended to leave on the garage floor mingling with the haphazardly discarded footwear in the shoe heap. Last year, a small community of gray mice somehow made their way into Michael's old Accord sparking contentious conflict in the Kelly house with Michael saying that Maggie's laissez faire attitude toward cleaning was akin to issuing an engraved invitation to the pests to invade their domicile. A return of the mob of mice would definitely put an end to this tantalizingly, mysterious moment, Maggie thought, certain that Michael would blame her slovenly ways for luring the mice back into their garage like the Pied Piper. But instead of cringing about the possibility that the vermin had returned, Michael just laughed. This reaction struck Maggie as odd. "What's going on?" she asked, excitement now gone. Did that scrapbook bonk him on the head too hard?

"Well," he began, grinning so hard that his cheeks were beginning to hurt. He took her cold hands in his warm ones, "You've been so awesome through all of this, the Bypass project and all. You've been here with the kids, making and eating dinners, alone a lot of the time. You get Jackie ready for school each morning and help her with school stuff, go to all the teacher meetings, buy all the stuff she needs for school and bring her around to playdates. And with Tommy, well, you've potty trained him practically all by yourself, taken care of his school stuff. And you've taken them to the ER and all their doctor and dentist appointments . . ."

Another high-pitched noise emanated from the backseat, this one louder and more insistent than the first. Maggie turned around, wide-eyed, and peered into the darkness, cautiously pressing her back against the car door in the opposite direction of the noise. "What IS that? Have you checked for mice recently? Do you think they're back?"

Michael remained uncharacteristically calm. He patted her hands and continued: "Anyway . . . you've done all these things, taken care of our kids, dealt with all the Thanksgiving craziness while I've been off with Sam Young, Rick Strong and the ENY guys and the Mass. Highway guys. You've supported me and made it possible for me to become a junior partner at ENY. Junior partner! Just found out this afternoon. And because I owe it all to you, I wanted to do something for you, give you something you've talked about for a long time. It's an early Christmas present. But to get what I wanted, I had to get the gift now and give it to you now, rather than in two weeks."

Michael reached into the back of the car. Maggie heard the rustling of what sounded like cardboard or papers being scratched. Then she saw Michael lift a light object about the size of a young child's playground ball, over the front seats.

"Meet your new puppy! It's a boy!" Michael said, presenting to his wife a wriggling mass of fuzzy, apricot hair and four tiny, scratching paws. She passively accepted the toy poodle puppy onto her lap. It looked just like one of Jackie's stuffed animals. Maggie was so stunned that her mouth fell slightly agape. The pup got up on his hind legs, reached his front paws toward Maggie's hair and nuzzled his soft, slightly dampened face into the warm comfort of her neck.

"Well?" Michael said expectantly, "whaddya think? I know I said I *never* wanted a dog, that they're messy and dirty and track dirt and get ticks and all that, but I know you loved your dog Snickers when you were a kid and seemed really upset when I said I didn't want a dog in the house. But after all you've put up with over the past year, you deserve it!"

The dog seemed keenly interested in Maggie's face. He licked her dry cheek then nipped at her eyelashes. "I can't believe it," she said, in tone that was difficult for Michael to gauge.

Michael felt slightly nauseous. Had he misread her? Did

she NOT want a dog after all? He remembered, with crystal clarity, that one afternoon in May a few years ago when they were picnicking at the Arnold Arboretum in Boston during the lilac festival, one of Maggie's favorite events. Maggie, Michael and Jackie were sitting on an old baby blue cotton blanket next to a huge lilac bush filled with sweetly fragrant deep purple blossoms, and dining on a lunch of peanut butter and jelly sandwiches, green grapes and a fresh canister of Pringles potato chips as Tommy napped in his stroller. While reaching into the cooler to get Jackie a juice box, Maggie had noticed a young family playing with a friendly, tan mutt of a dog. The scene reminded her of her childhood dog, a black and tan Cairn terrier named Snickers and she started talking about how much she loved it when Snickers would snuggle up next to her on her bed when she was reading or doing her homework, her constant companion. Maggie regaled Jackie with Snickers tales like the time Snickers ran off with a gray, mangy, one-eyed dog of an indiscernible breed who lived a few doors down from the Finns on Oak Terrace. Jackie nearly snorted apple juice out of her nose when Maggie told her about how Snickers used to pilfer Luke's crayons — especially the purple ones — peel them, spit the paper wrapping out, eat the colored wax and then leave multi-hued poop nuggets all over the Finns' lawn. Michael listened to Maggie's stories without comment, recalling how, by contrast, he'd been raised to think of dogs as smelly disease carriers who licked their excrement-covered behinds and he wanted nothing to do with any of them. The only pet he ever had as a child was a goldfish named King Lear — Dorothy came up with the name — who lived a little less than a year and bored Michael to tears because it wouldn't do anything and didn't really swim around his small fish bowl all that much.

"Just this past summer," Michael thought, growing defensive, "we saw the Finch family with their collie when we were taking a walk around the block and Maggie said that their dog was 'beautiful,' that the Finch kids looked like they were having a blast tossing the tennis ball to him." Maggie's non-reaction had thrown him.

"What do you think, Mags?" he asked, as he leaned over and scratched the dog behind his minuscule ears. "You DO want a dog, don't you?" There was a long, uncomfortable pause. "Did I screw up here? I mean, you're not saying . . . ANYTHING."

Maggie snapped out of her daze and held the puppy aloft in front of her face, watching as its legs flailed, like it was searching in vain for the pedals of a bicycle. She hadn't expected this. Not in a million years. She didn't know what she was feeling.

"Michael, I don't understand," she said, putting the dog down on her lap and watching as he got a sudden surge of energy, climbed out of Maggie's lap and bounded around the front of the car, "I thought you hated dogs. Never wanted one. Ever. How is this suddenly okay with you?"

"I changed my mind."

"But . . . I'm just . . . just, uh, confused is all. Aren't you going to be miserable with him being here? He's going to pee and poop and scratch and chew stuff up. We're going to have to paper-train him, *and* finish potty-training Tommy while we're at it. It was nice of you to say that I potty-trained him, but he's not quite there yet. And puppies, well, they chew up furniture and shoes. They make huge messes and they bark and whimper, especially when they're young. They need to be brought outside in all kinds of weather, the rain, the snow . . . You're up for all of that? I didn't think, well, you're, you're so . . . uh . . . into things being clean that I can't see you wanting to deal with the mess of a puppy. Our kids are already human wrecking balls, and that drives you crazy. Like tonight, with the beans, or the scrapbooks and shoes all over the garage. Those things make you crazy. How can you accept a dog?"

"Because," he said, leaning forward to kiss Maggie on the forehead, "because it makes you happy. And I want to make you happy. It's not all about me."

As if on cue, the puppy, who'd scrambled onto Michael's lap, peed about a shot glass full of warm liquid onto Michael's pants, leaving a wet spot next to the faded stain left behind by Jackie's refried beans. Instead of jumping up and running into the house for the paper towels and antibacterial gel, he smiled and said, "See? See? I'm not freaking out over the fact that puppy boy here just pissed on me. Life's messy, as you're always saying. And that's okay."

"Who the hell are you?" she said with a laugh as she started to let the magnanimity of this gesture sink in. Maggie then jerked her head backwards and blurted, "Oh my God! You made junior partner? You made junior partner!"

Michael glowed, feeling all Zen-like as he pretended as though he was unfazed by the fact that he'd just been urinated on or by the fact that it had taken his wife a few minutes to acknowledge his huge promotion. "Yup. Sam let me know today. He took me out to lunch at the Capital Grille and told me. He said my work during Thanksgiving was, and I'm quoting him, 'above and beyond what anyone at your level has done' and that it proved my willingness to be dedicated to ENY."

"So you knew about the promotion when I called you to bitch about the stupid book thing in Jackie's class? And you didn't tell me?"

"Didn't want to spoil the surprise. And I wanted to tell you when I gave you this little guy," he picked up the dog, who'd insinuated himself beneath the gas and brake pedals. Michael hoped the pup wouldn't pee again on his new floor mats. He'd never be able to get the smell out.

CHAPTER EIGHTEEN

Rob was trying not to let the sweat — which was starting to pool in his blistered, burned hands — cause him to lose his grip on the old, battered gray air conditioner that he was lugging from its winter resting place in the cellar all the way upstairs to his bedroom. He wanted to surprise Molly, who'd recently started to complain about the early summer heat and humidity as her pregnancy entered its seventh month, by installing their lone air conditioner in their bedroom window and crank it up at full blast. Rob had planned on surprising Molly, who'd taken Maggie out for soft serve at the Ice Cream Igloo, by installing the AC and moving the extra black and white TV they had in the kitchen into their bedroom with the idea that Molly would be able to lie down, cool off and watch her programs. He wanted her to feel as content and safe as possible, given what happened last year when they lost the baby at this same point in the pregnancy. Molly spent the weeks after the baby died sobbing into her pillow, leaving the then-5-year-old Maggie wondering what she'd done to "make Mommy so sad."

Rob had felt helpless as Molly, normally very upbeat and positive, retreated to her bed and stopped eating anything other than bowls of Frosted Flakes washed down by glasses of strawberry Kool-Aid, which Maggie would insist upon making for her mother out of a powdered mix, leaving a sticky, gritty residue all over the kitchen counter and floor. Nothing Rob tried to do to ease her anguish seemed to make any bit of difference. He enlisted the help of his mother-in-law Emily, who also lived in Eastborough, to babysit Maggie while Rob tried to distract Molly by taking her out to dinners at The East Garden Chinese restaurant for chicken chow mein or to the Hilltop Steak House for sirloins, followed by a whole lot of movies at the Showcase Cinema, mostly comedies, like *Foul Play* and *Heaven Can Wait*. Rob even suffered through *Grease* hoping it'd get a smile out of Molly since she was so fond of musicals, but no dice. He frequently bought her bouquets of daisies to perk up the kitchen table each week. Rob even found a daisy print dress at Bellman's that he thought would fit Molly once she lost the rest of the baby weight. But that dress remained hanging in the closet, price-tag still intact.

For Rob to call Emily and ask for her help so frequently was an indication of how concerned he was about Molly's emotional state. Emily and Rob didn't get on so well, never did, even from the get-go. Quiet and genteel as a starched lace curtain, Emily — who worked as a nanny for a Newton surgeon's family where she watched over their set of twins and did housework — was perceived by Rob to be savvy and manipulative when it came to her one and only child. But despite his aversion to inviting Emily into his marital affairs, Rob thought that maybe she could give Molly some comfort that he couldn't, seeing as though Molly revered her mother and did virtually everything she told her to do. The lone exception came on the subject of housekeeping, a discipline to which Molly was stubbornly indifferent. When Emily would offer her advice on how to keep her home, Molly would smile and tune her well meaning mother out. Not that Emily was one to talk, seeing that she was so busy tending to the Smiths' children and five-bedroom home while Molly was growing up, that Emily rarely had time to do more than a cursory cleaning of the surfaces of her own home, saving thorough cleanings for holidays or for when company was coming over. Oh, and then there was that one other occasion when Molly didn't exactly to the advice proffered by her mother: That she not marry Rob.

When Molly started dating Rob during their sophomore year of high school, Emily was not at all thrilled with the match. During his visits to the Mahoneys' home, Rob was unnervingly quiet, almost completely silent, declining to say much at all, regardless of Emily's efforts to coax him out of his protective shell, which left her wondering if he was just naturally a nervous person, was hiding something, was just plain stand-offish, or, perhaps, was as dumb as a dial tone. Even plying Rob — who perpetually looked like a ravenous, abandoned hound — with rich, homemade meals and baked goods (popovers were Emily's specialty) didn't loosen his tongue or make him seem at all comfortable in their presence. Emily was initially convinced that this romantic pairing would be short-lived. "They have little in common, really, if you think about it," Emily remarked to her husband Elliot, whom she called Eli, as he nodded his head in agreement. "It won't last. It's a fling. He's taking her out, giving her flowers now, but that'll get old soon, especially since the boy doesn't even talk. Molly'll get bored of feeling like she's talking to a brick wall, to someone who just nods at everything and seems like he has no feelings at all."

However when Rob, then 17, insisted upon moving in with his Aunt Stacia in Eastborough when his parents, Hal and Evelyn announced that they were moving to California, Emily became very concerned. "What kind of parent leaves her child behind and moves across the country?" she vented to Molly. "Honey, honestly, don't you think it'd be better for Rob to live with his parents?"

"Mom," Molly said with a twinkle in her eye, "his whole life is . . . *here*. In Eastborough."

"Molly, you're far too young to just date one boy," Emily said, not at all liking that look in her daughter's eyes. "You've never dated anyone else. You don't want to limit yourself to just him and then, 30 years later, regret that you never had a chance to date other people and experience other things. I dated several different boys and I'm glad I did because when I met your father when I was 25, I knew right away that marrying him was the right thing for me and that I wouldn't regret it at all."

"Mom, I'm not you and we're not you and Dad," Molly said. "We're just . . . us."

Emily entered full panic mode when Molly and Rob shocked everyone by announcing their engagement on the day after their high school graduation ceremony. Hours after Rob proposed during a picnic lunch in a field of wildflowers — without first asking Elliot's permission, something which galled Emily — Molly sat her parents down at the kitchen table and told them the news. Elliot, unsure of how he was supposed to react, uneasily unwrapped a couple of Mary Jane candies which he'd taken from their omnipresent candy dish — he was always bringing home treats from NECCO, the New England Confectionery Company candy plant where he worked — and popped them into his mouth so he didn't have to talk, while Emily wore a disingenuous smile.

Fearing the premature death of all the dreams she had for Molly — that she become educated, maybe marry up and possibly enter the world she'd observed in Newton where her employers, Dr. Smith was a surgeon and his wife Cordelia was a well-read society lady who was active in several charities — Emily blurted, "Sweetie, don't you think that you'll be limiting your . . . your life, getting married so early? Is there any way of . . . uh . . . I don't know, maybe you could be engaged for a while, while you go to school? Not get married right away?"

Molly was barely listening or even looking at her parents for that matter. She was distracted by the small diamond engagement ring she'd received from Rob earlier that day, the one onto which he'd tied a daisy he'd plucked from the field, telling her that she was *his* ever-blossoming flower, the single most romantic thing he, or anyone else for that matter, had ever said to her.

"You've talked an awful lot over the years about going to college, maybe becoming a teacher," Emily said, her voice kicking up an octave as she tried to sound hopeful. She took a sip of iced tea to soothe her dry throat. "If you get married right away and have babies, that won't happen, none of it will. You'll never go to school or teach. And what about Rob, is he going to be an auto mechanic at Sam's, where his father worked before his parents moved to California?"

"Oh Ma, I love you," Molly said, her lilting voice brimming with a combination of misguided teenage hope, dreams and lust. "I know you love me and want me to get educated and all that, but Rob loves me too. This *is* the right thing for me, Ma. It is. I feel it. In my heart." She patted her chest with her right hand for emphasis. "We can't wait to give you grandchildren. You'll be a *best* grandmother."

"You're not pregnant are you?" Emily blurted, causing Elliot to accidentally swallow a half-chewed candy, his third. It felt like it got stuck in his throat. Elliott started to turn red as he coughed roughly and repeatedly until he dislodged the candy. After stealing a sip of Emily's tea, he pulled out his cigarettes.

"No!" Molly shouted, insulted at the insinuation. Here she was talking about the endless possibilities of true love and Emily was someplace else entirely talking about lost opportunities in the work world.

"Well, that's good," Emily said, mentally crossing herself with the Father-Son-Holy Ghost gesture. "You're only 18 years old Molly. You still need to live your life before getting all tied down to babies right away. Didn't you read that book that I left on your bed a few weeks ago, *The Feminine Mystique* one I borrowed from Mrs. Smith? Honestly, you're too young to become a housewife, too smart, too talented. You should go to college. You give me grandchildren later."

Molly continued staring at the sparkling glint on her left hand, mesmerized.

"Are you sure you don't want to consider becoming a

teacher? You've always been so good with children, like when you've helped me out taking care of the Smith boys or even the Weston children. I could see you doing well as an elementary school teacher. Surely Rob would support that. Your father and I could pay for your schooling if money's the issue. You could go to Worcester State College, live here and *still* be engaged." She elbowed Elliott, waiting, with growing irritation for him to say something.

"I think," he said, clearing his throat again after a deep inhale on his cigarette, "that your mother's right. I think it'd be a big mistake for you to not go to college. No one's telling you not to love Rob, or not to be engaged to him, but if he loves you, he'll wait. Marriage can wait. If it's real love, it'll keep. It's better to know if it's real now, rather than later, don't ya think?"

Molly smiled even wider than seemed possible. She rose from her chair and planted a sloppy kiss on her mother's right cheek, touched the top of her father's hand lightly, then eased herself into Emily's lap, her legs dangling off awkwardly, as she wrapped her arms around her mother's neck, hugging her contentedly the way she used to when she was a girl.

Emily sighed, realizing, that she should've had this conversation years ago, after she saw that that same look on Molly's face when she came home after her first date with Rob. "What if you get married, get pregnant and he gets drafted Molly, sent to Vietnam and gets killed? What then? You don't want to be a young widow with a baby and no education do you? That would just break my heart."

As soon as those words crossed her lips, she realized this might've been a step too far, that she was doing her side of the argument no favors. But she was desperate.

The possibility of being a Vietnam War widow didn't wipe away Molly's grin. "I've already told you Mom, Rob's doctor said he'd get a medical deferment because of his asthma. Dr. Welch has already written Rob a letter saying that he's not healthy enough to serve, just in case he gets called up. We have nothing to worry about. You're the only one who's worrying."

Though Molly never did tell Rob that Emily had tried to talk her out of marrying him, she did, in fact, heed her mother's advice. She and Rob remained engaged for four years, while Molly lived at home with her parents and earned a bachelor's degree in education from Worcester State College. She married Rob in August of 1971, a few months after her college graduation. Elliot, who'd had difficulties walking Maggie down the aisle due to his worsening emphysema, died at age 52, the week before Thanksgiving.

Despite never having been told about the conversation Molly had with her parents after he proposed, Rob always sensed his mother-in-law's disappointment at how her daughter's life turned out. It was only after Elliot's death that Rob felt Emily slightly soften her attitude toward him, although she remained relatively cool. She couldn't help herself, really, despite the fact that Rob did all that handiwork around her house, mowed her lawn, raked her leaves and shoveled the snow off her driveway. It was as though she kept an invisible, stiff arm extended out between her and Rob, keeping him as far away from her as Rob did with everyone else. There was only one person who Rob had allowed to truly gain access to his heart, and that was Molly, to whom he was devoted. With everyone else, even his own parents, Rob maintained a solid wall around him that his buddies weren't able to crack, even after a couple of pitchers of beer. Sure, he'd amiably chat about the day's news, diligently attend to his long-distance son duties, but he was only real with his wife.

Until Maggie came along.

When Maggie was born, Molly and Rob simply couldn't get enough of her. Their passionate marriage bed became a gleeful family bed with Maggie snug in between her parents' loving embrace. They lavished their first-born with hugs and giant, toothy smiles. Rob absolutely fell in love with this little girl with the deep brown eyes and round little belly. Watching her husband with the baby made Molly fall for Rob all over again, even harder, not that she ever dreamed that could be possible. To see Rob toting Maggie around the house, enveloping her in the crook of his tanned, freckled arms, made Molly want to abandon everything she was doing and just watch them, as though they were a flesh and blood Mary Cassatt painting, only featuring a father and child, instead of a mother and child. Even Emily, who gave Rob and Molly an extraordinary amount of help and support after Maggie was born, surprised herself by observing one day, "Fatherhood becomes him."

"Yep," Molly replied, "really does."

Molly and Rob loved parenthood so much, that, within a year of Maggie's birth, they tried for baby number two, but Molly didn't get pregnant right away. They dismissed their disappointment by saying that they were young and had lots of time. They were confident it'd happen. Five years later, Molly was finally able to tell Maggie about how, after many years of begging for a baby brother or sister, she was finally going to get one. Molly taught Maggie how to diaper and feed a baby using Molly's dolls for practice. "You'll help Mommy," she told her daughter. "It'll be really fun." As Molly's belly swelled and the baby's kicks grew stronger, she'd grab both Rob and Maggie's hands and place them over her taut skin so they could feel the baby move too. It became an evening ritual: Every night after dinner, Molly would eat a piece of chocolate and wait for the baby to kick. Rob and Molly would allow Maggie to be the first one to announce that she felt something. "I felt it! I felt it! Right here!" she'd exclaim.

"You found it again Mags!" Rob would say. "This baby sure does love you. I'll bet he or she can't wait to meet the big sister."

Then came the day when the kicks ceased.

"Mama, why no kicking? Is baby sleeping?" Maggie asked, sliding her hands all over her mother's belly searching in vain for the sensation of motion beneath her mother's skin. Not long afterward, Molly's doctor told her why, in a series of clipped phrases: Fetal death, no heartbeat, unknown cause. For weeks upon weeks later, Molly did little else but sob in her bed, wail really, on and off for hours, and saying very little to anyone while Rob felt powerless as he too grieved his lost baby in silence while trying to maintain a cheerful façade for Maggie's sake. Most of Maggie's caretaking during that time fell to Rob and, when Rob wasn't available, to Emily who, seven years after telling her daughter not to marry Rob, was beginning to think that perhaps Molly hadn't made such a bad choice of a spouse after all.

When Molly got pregnant again within the year, Rob wanted to place her inside a protective bubble and do everything he could to head off anything that could potentially harm her or the baby. Molly, who'd snapped out of her melancholy the moment the pregnancy test indicated she was pregnant, was determined to act normally, not like she was some kind of fragile creature. She strenuously rejected Rob's help at every turn while declining to talk about "that bad time," as she called it, or to even acknowledge that she'd lost a baby, which made Rob, who was still quietly mourning, angry. But if she needed to stuff her grief into a box, compartmentalize it in order to function, Rob would reluctantly go along with it, with whatever helped her get through the day. But he wouldn't tolerate Molly's refusal to take it easy on the housework front. Rob repeatedly told her she was under direct orders from Emily to relax but, in some strange kind of push-pull reaction, the more he insisted that she take it easy, the more she'd try to do.

Hours before Rob installed the air conditioner in the bedroom, he'd tried to come to Molly's aid after he walked into the kitchen and saw her leaning over awkwardly trying to pull a heavy casserole dish out of the oven. Without even thinking, he raced over to try to wrest the dish from her, completely forgetting to don oven mitts or even grab a dish towel.

"Damn it Rob! What's the matter with you?" Molly yelled

as her husband vigorously shook his hands which were stinging, terribly burned, from unwisely grabbing the scalding Corning Ware dish and dropping it onto the stovetop. Molly waddled over to the freezer, grabbed the ice cube tray, twisted it, dumped a few cubes onto the counter, then pressed them into his hands. "You've got to stop this! It's gonna be fine. I know it. I feel it."

But Rob couldn't listen, wouldn't listen. It was *his* job to look out for her, no matter what anyone else said. He saw what could happen when he didn't. If that meant out-hovering even his hyper-vigilant mother-in-law, trying to get Molly to buy more frozen meals so she wouldn't have to cook, to let him do the grocery shopping, and even forgoing sex so that neither Molly nor the baby would be injured, so be it. Rob was convinced that having sex with his pregnant wife would jeopardize the baby's health so he refused to have relations with her, and, of all the things he was trying to do to shelter Molly from possible injury or stress, this was the one thing that irked her the most.

Some 10 days before Rob installed the air conditioner, Molly had her doctor telephone Rob at home one evening to inform him that it was perfectly safe for Rob to have sex with his wife. Rob listened patiently, then, after he hung up the phone, he shook his head. "No Molly! It's not worth it," he said. "And I can't *believe* you told the doctor! This is private. I don't want to discuss this anymore. We can wait." And with that unilateral decree, Rob walked over to his wife, pulled her light, bushy hair out from behind her ears, tousled it a bit and kissed her on the tip of her nose.

When hearing from the doctor's own mouth that intercourse was safe did nothing to persuade Rob to abandon his self-imposed abstinence, Molly allowed Rob to think that he'd won, even though her pregnancy was stirring up vast, insistent amorous feelings deep within her, needs she felt compelled to have satiated by someone other than herself.

After Rob burned his hands by grabbing the scalding

casserole dish from Molly, she became so irritated with his over-protective behavior that she decided to go over his head and call her mother. She specifically wanted to know what Emily thought about Rob's refusal to sleep with her until the baby was born. For all the worrying Emily was prone to do, she did believe, very strongly in fact, that keeping Molly happy and content was healthy for both mother and baby. When Molly pleaded for her opinion on whether she and Rob should have sex — especially when the doctor said there was no reason for them to abstain — Emily hesitated. "Well, honey, shouldn't you just err on the side of caution? Just not have, uh, *relations* for, what, a little more than two months more? It's not really that long honey, you can handle that."

"Mom!!" Molly whined, stretching the curly phone cord out as far as it could go in order to continue her whispered conversation without being overheard by Rob who was watching the NBC *Nightly News* on TV in the next room. "There's just no medical justification for . . . for . . . not having, *relations* as you said. I can't believe I'm even talking about this, with my mother, but I'm at my wits' end. I think Rob's being ridiculous. I'm not a child. We're man and wife. We're supposed to have normal, healthy . . . *relations*."

"I know but . . . the last time . . ."

"The last time I was pregnant with Maggie, Rob and I made love all the time. He wasn't afraid of me being pregnant. It brought us closer together."

"No, no, dear, I'm talking the last time . . . the *last* last time," Emily said quietly.

Molly took a deep drag on her cigarette. She felt the swirling comforting motion beneath her sweaty skin, the baby, kicking or elbowing around in the ever-shrinking pocket of space inside her womb. Her hand automatically went to the location of the movement, feeling the pressure of one of the baby's extremities pushing outward, like he or she was trying to grab for the phone to add something to the conversation. She wasn't quite sure if it was a hand or a foot.

As ashes hung precariously from the end of her cigarette, Molly lifted up the front of her yellow maternity shirt and peered down at her abdomen, examining the outline of whatever was pushing outward, tracing it with the fingertips of her left hand.

"Ma, I've gotta go now, Maggie needs me, she's crying," Molly lied. "Talk later."

She extinguished her cigarette in the green ceramic ash tray on the kitchen table and headed to the living room. Molly placed her hands on either side of the door jam and said, "Who wants ice cream? Ice Cream Igloo. I'm roasting hot and still hungry."

"Oooh! Me!" Maggie said as she leapt off the couch and extended her arms out as far as she could around Molly's stomach, clutching the yellow fabric between her fingers.

"How 'bout you Rob?" Molly asked as she grabbed her cream colored crocheted purse, the one with the wooden handles, off the coffee table and checked her wallet for cash.

"Naw," he said, "I'm gonna pass. Got some things to do around the house."

"Fine then," Molly said, stepping forward to kiss Rob who was sitting upright, as opposed to reclining, in the Lazy Boy. "Come on Mags."

As soon as he heard the car engine, Rob headed to the basement to get the air conditioner, hoping to turn the bedroom into an icebox as soon as possible. After brushing the cobwebs off the front of the unit and lugging it up the stairs, Rob shoved the AC into a safe, secure position on the window ledge. He crossed his fingers as he turned it on — hoping it wouldn't blow a fuse — and breathed in the stale, slightly burnt smell that emanated from its vents as it came to life for the first time in 10 months. That staleness dissipated after a minute and the appliance started to push cool air into the room. Rob, wiping the sweat from his forehead with the back of his hand, walked over to his dresser to make room for the kitchen TV when the telephone rang. He wiped his hands off onto the thighs of his faded, dust-covered blue jeans, exhaled and semi-jogged down the hall to the kitchen.

"Yep, uh, hello," he muttered into the phone.

"Rob, it's Emily here. I hope I'm not catching you at a bad time dear. You sound out of breath."

"No, it's fine Emily. Fine. Molly just took Maggie out for ice cream and I just put the air conditioner in the bedroom window, you know, so Molly can cool off when she's in bed. She's been complaining about being really hot with the baby and all. What can I do for you? Everythin' okay?"

"Well I wanted to talk to you about Molly actually."

"To me? What about Molly?" he immediately felt a little panicky.

"She called me earlier and asked me my advice about something and I don't think I gave her the answer she was looking for."

"What? I didn't know she called you," Rob said, curious. He plopped himself down onto a chair waiting for Emily to fill him in, but he couldn't hear anything on the other end of the line. "Emily?"

"Well . . . and I don't want you think I'm sticking my nose in where it doesn't belong, Rob but Molly is really upset. Being upset isn't good for her or the baby. We've got to keep her happy and calm."

Rob was getting impatient. "About what? *What's* upsetting Molly?"

"About what goes on in your bedroom. Or . . . what's *not* going on."

"The air conditioning?"

"No Rob . . . *bedroom* things."

Rob blushed deeply. His breath was coming out of his nose so hard that it sounded as though he was huffing.

"I'm . . . oh, I'm sorry Rob," Emily said genuinely. "I didn't mean to upset you. I know this isn't my business and I know that you just want her and the baby to be safe, but if the doctor says it's okay . . ."

Rob stood up tall, gripping the phone tightly and said, "Emily, thanks for your call. 'preciate it. We're fine. We're all fine. I'll talk to you later. Take care." Then he hung up.

The gals breezed in a short while later, giggling, smears of chocolate from the chocolate dip that had coated their vanilla soft serve ice cream cones still a bit visible on their faces.

"Who's there?" Molly asked playfully, casually tossing her purse on the kitchen table.

"Chicken," Maggie said, trying to stifle a laugh but not succeeding.

"Chicken who?" Molly asked as she pulled her little girl onto what was left of her lap as they dropped into a kitchen chair together.

"Chicken nobody!" Maggie said, bursting with laughter.

Molly laughed too, in spite of the nonsensical knock-knock joke. She looked over at Rob to share this goofy moment with him, but he was stone-faced. "Hey, do I hear the air conditioner?" she asked hopefully, ignoring his frown.

Rob got up, took Maggie's hands in his and said, "Can you show me what a big girl you are and go to your room and get on your pajamas? I need to talk to Mommy for a minute."

Rob watched her go down the hall. When he was sure she was in her room, he drew a chair up next to his wife and spoke in a low, menacing tone. "You told your *mother* that we weren't having sex? You went to her with this?"

Molly raised her eyebrows and rubbed her belly, more out of habit than because the baby was moving.

"Didn't I ask you not to tell anyone?"

Molly didn't like the way he was speaking to her. It was very unlike him. Rob so rarely lost his temper, hardly ever shouted, so she wasn't sure how she was supposed to react.

"Do you know how humiliating this is to have not just your doctor, but YOUR MOTHER telling me that I should have sex with my wife? Like I don't want you or something? Like I'm not a man or something?"

She just kept looking down at her stomach, mentally grasping for the right words.

Rob roughly grabbed her chin and pulled her head upward to face him. "Look at me Molly!" His damp fingers, covered with dust and cob webs from the air conditioner, felt uncomfortable on her face. "You made me look like less than a man. In front of *everyone*."

She angrily pushed his hand off her chin. "First of all, it's not 'everyone.' It's my doctor and my mother. That's not 'everyone.' Both of those people have seen me naked so it's not like I went to the town green and asked everybody there what they thought or took an ad out in the paper or something. And second, *you* don't get to make this decision for us. It's not fair. There are two people in this marriage. We *both* get a say!"

"Do we? How can you sit there and say that we both get a say when you went behind my back and told everyone I wouldn't screw you?"

"What other choices did you leave me? None!"

"I've been very, very patient. You're not the only one who doesn't get what he wants."

"What the hell are you talking about?"

"I'm talking," he stood up straight again, turned away from her, walked toward the refrigerator, then abruptly stopped and whipped back around to look at her, "about how you're pretending like you're the only one who lost a baby and like all that . . . that . . . that nightmare last year never happened. I'm supposed to act like it didn't happen, no matter how I feel. You won't talk about it, even *now*!"

His words took her breath away.

"Say something dammit! How can you be so selfish about this one thing, the *only* thing I've ever asked of you, when I've done *everything* you've wanted? It's not even *for* me."

Her face reddened. She felt sick.

"You only care about getting what *you* want, to hell if it may or may not hurt our baby?" he yelled. "And you tell everybody about it?"

The sound of a plastic cup falling onto the floor in the hallway interrupted the squabble. Rob and Molly turned to see a teary-faced Maggie sitting, cross-legged in the doorway to her bedroom, her red cup still slowly rolling away from her. The girl looked as though someone had just told her that Christmas was going to be canceled this year.

CHAPTER NINETEEN

Although he'd just been anointed as a junior partner and was very close to the finish line for the Bypass project, Michael did not in any way feel as though he could ease up now. After Michael and Maggie introduced the puppy to Jackie and Tommy and the kids christened him "Rudy" — after "Rudolph the Red Nosed Reindeer," their favorite Christmas carol with which they'd been obsessed and had been singing, almost non-stop — Michael told Maggie that he'd be leaving for work extra early the next morning to put the final touches on the variance application. And because forecasters were calling for "a whopper of a Nor'easter," in the words of the shiny-headed, gap-toothed meteorologist from Channel 4, Michael knew he'd have to tack on an additional 40 minutes to his morning commute, at the very least. In the unlikely event the storm was as bad as Channel 4 predicted, Michael tossed a change of clothing, his toothbrush, a tube of travel toothpaste, deodorant and hair gel into a gym bag, just in case the roads were in lousy shape and he needed to stay near the city, something he'd done once before during a fierce winter storm.

Before leaving the bedroom, casually attired in his "good" jeans and a blue fleece pull-over atop an L.L. Bean monogrammed white turtleneck, he looked at the sleeping Maggie, whose head was lying on the mattress while she was holding her pillow in a death grip between her arms, fists balled up. Michael was pleased about the way last night's surprise was eventually received, despite its bumpy start. The puppy, the promotion, it was all melding together to create a warm, feel-good aura for him, except for the peeing on the leg part. The kids had gone wild when Maggie and Michael brought the dog into the house. They showered him with kisses and too-tight, nearly choking hugs and went to bed way past their bedtime, forgetting all about the fact that Michael had mentioned that the Charlie Brown special was on TV. Maggie and Michael made love on the sofa after the kids were asleep and Rudy was curled up in his new crate which Michael had hidden in his car trunk until after he'd given Maggie the dog. Things were good, Michael thought, despite the fact that there was already six inches of snow outside. On his way out of the house, Michael peeked inside Rudy's crate in the corner of the kitchen and saw that he was sleeping, then snagged a scrap piece of paper and scrawled a quick note to Maggie: "Thanks for last night. Love ya! Keep warm!" He propped it up against the Red Sox mug, mostly filled with empty pens and dull pencils, on the kitchen counter.

Maggie was still clutching her pillow, sound asleep when the phone call came at 6 a.m. Her hand fumbled along her nightstand for the phone as she knocked over some magazines and the TV remote before grabbing the handset and heard the dull voice of the school superintendent on an automated message alerting parents that "due to the severity of the weather forecast, school is canceled today." Jackie and Tommy, who were already awake in Jackie's room playing "guys" (action figures) and Barbies, raced into Maggie's room after hearing the phone ring and climbed into her bed, bringing with them a half-dozen plastic figures with pointy little fingers and accessories.

"Who was that? Who was callin'?" Jackie asked.

"No school today Miss Jackie," Maggie said as she slid out of bed, opened up the curtain and saw nothing but blinding white snow blanketing everything in sight. She couldn't see her driveway, save for the quickly fading tire marks left from Michael's car when he left an hour before.

"Whaddaboutme?" Tommy asked as he made one of his *Star Wars* droids viciously slam into another atop Michael's pillow.

"Well, if Jackie's school's canceled, so is yours buddy!" Maggie said, rubbing her eyes and wishing she had a coffee service in her room. She shivered. Michael always set the programmable thermostat to go down to 54 degrees at night and it didn't kick up to a "balmy" 64 until 7 a.m. Pulling on the gray Framingham State sweatshirt, which she found lying inside-out on the floor next to her bed, over her white tank top and black, stretchy workout pants, Maggie sleepily shoved her feet into the grocery store-bought navy slide-on slippers, the ones with holes on the inside corners next to each big toe. "Who wants breakfast?"

It was only when they got to the kitchen when Maggie remembered that they now had a dog. Rudy emitted crisp little barks that seemed so impossibly petite that it was easy to imagine that they'd come from some kind of wind-up toy. He was standing on his hind legs on two towels that he'd balled up overnight as he excitedly scratched at the side of his crate and wagged his tail wildly.

"Oh yeah!" Maggie said. "Rudy."

"Midget!" Jackie said. "I still think we should call him Midget!"

"No way," Maggie replied, as she began the task of preparing her coffee, not yet ready to allow Rudy to be loose yet.

"Elmo!" Tommy said as he lowered his face in front of the crate door and Rudy tried to lick Tommy through the thin metal bars. Tommy laughed and wiped the puppy spit onto his solid blue footie pajamas that Dorothy gave him on Thanksgiving. Jackie opened the crate door and awkwardly took Rudy out and watched as he skidded around the floor.

"You guys want cereal or waffles?"

"Waffles!" they shouted in unison.

Once the kids were settled in at the kitchen table with their waffles and the coffee was brewing, Maggie cleaned up the first of what she knew would be a multitude of puppy mistakes from the kitchen floor. The scrape of what Maggie hoped was a town plow lured Maggie to the front window in the living room where she noticed how intense the snowfall had become in such a short time. Michael's tire tracks had completely vanished. There was certainly no way that their newspaper carrier had been able to deliver the paper, Maggie thought. Even if her newspaper had been thrown onto her driveway, she wasn't going out there to hunt around for it. She pulled her laptop across the kitchen counter, plugged it in, turned it on and smiled as she re-read Michael's note for the third time.

"We're done. We're gonna go play with Rudy," Jackie said, sliding the back of her hand across her syrup-covered face and giving Rudy a hug so tight that he yelped.

"Hold on! You can't go getting syrup everywhere. Think of what Daddy would say!"

After wiping the kids' hands and faces clean, Maggie told them to keep Rudy in the living room, fixed herself a cup of coffee and plopped down on the stool in front of her computer. Rudy, the kids following closely behind, batted around a soft ball and looked truly surprised each and every time it bounced back at him after it hit a wall or Tommy roughly rolled it back. Maggie checked her e-mail, something she did compulsively and frequently throughout the day, reading her personal e-mails first, then e-mails sent to her blog's e-mail address. Seeing nothing in her personal e-mail account — "It's not even 7 o'clock yet," she thought. — she went to her *Maggie Has Had It* e-mail address and was astonished to find that she had 201 new e-mails since she last checked at 5 p.m. the previous day.

"What the?" she muttered. She scrolled through the e-mails and found that many of the subject headings included the words "*Boston Journal*" and some form of obscenity in the subject line. "Oh my God!"

The small bit of coffee she'd already sipped started to feel as though it was eating away at her stomach lining. Palms sweaty, she went onto the Internet and typed in the *Boston Journal's* web address. There was no need to put Lesley Fair's name into the search engine to try to locate the story as it was promoted on the top of the home page under the head-line, "No Holes Barred: Many Bloggers Rip Their Families to Shreds Online."

"Oh. Shit," she groaned, closing her eyes as she clicked on the headline which took her to the story:

"Maggie doesn't want to disclose her surname. Who can blame her? She writes on a daily basis about every aspect of and the people in her life: Her kids, her husband, her neighbors, her friends and her mother-in-law from hell. She reams and mocks them, tells the world that her husband doesn't please her sexually, jokes about how unhappy being a stay-at-home mom makes her and complains about how her mother-in-law is just this side of being an Italian dictator. Who would want their real name associated with such frankness? Not her.

Maggie is the woman behind a popular web log — known as a 'blog' — called 'Maggie Has Had It' (www.maggiehashadit.blog-spot.com), one of hundreds of personal, online diaries written by locals that are generating substantial Internet traffic and reader interest with their brutally honest, scathing and oftentimes profane content about their families, content that has raised concerns among some psychologists about their destructive tell-all nature.

A year ago, Merriam-Webster declared the word 'blog' the top word of 2004. Now, thousands of blogs, mostly written by untrained citizens, hobbyists and stay-at-home moms, are getting widespread attention for peddling anecdotes that were, in the pre-Internet age, considered grist for private diaries or discrete chats with friends over cocktails or coffee, not for public disclosure, accessible to Internet users around the globe.

'On the blog, it's a safe place for me to write about the not-so-nice feelings we all have,' said Maggie, a married mother of two

children — ages 6 and 3 — who would only say she lives in the greater Boston area. '[Blogging is] different from my actual life where I'm doing laundry or making dinner or making the beds for my family. On the blog, I don't have to be nice and take care of everybody. I can put my bad feelings into words and express them . . . Most of the entries in my blog are me working out my problems and that's more interesting, at least to me, than a bunch of fake Hallmark-y stuff about how to make things perfect or how they're supposed to be perfect.'

What kind of 'interesting' stuff? Tales that experts say could permanently damage personal relationships, including the bonds of trust between husbands and wives, as well as parents and children once those offspring grow up and read blog entries that eviscerate them, their spouses and families.

Alongside her rants about the 'annoyingly perfect' parents of her daughter's first grade classmates and entries about her daughter's 'never-ending-pit-of-need-sad-sack of a teacher,' Maggie's two prime targets, like many of her blogger peers, are her spouse and her mother-in-law. While she writes extensively about her married sex life — including how she says her husband can rarely get her to achieve orgasm — she frequently grumbles about her husband's late nights at work. Writing about her husband, who she nicknamed the 'Wannabe-King,' she was angry that one evening he had to get off of the phone with her in order to rejoin a business meeting: 'He f——— hung up. He was probably terrified I'd reach through his BlackBerry — which is like his second d——— that he fiddles with all day — and rip his head off. (Pun intended.)'

Her mother-in-law — to whom Maggie refers as a multitude of nicknames ranging from 'Torturer-in-Chief' and 'Excuse-Maker-in-Chief' to 'Benita' (as in Mussolini's wife) — is likewise spared nothing on the blog, portrayed as a meddlesome, interfering shrew who hates her daughter-in-law. In one entry Maggie was unhappy that her mother-in-law, who was babysitting for Maggie's children, decided to do some chores around the house, including the laundry, after the children went to bed:

'And what had I left in the washer when I left the house, you ask? My lone pair of thong underwear. Of course. The one and only pair. And SHE had to see them. Handle them. Excellent. When I realized what she'd done, touched the thong underwear (and put them on top of my clean laundry pile so that I could feel her disapproval in the way she folded the item), I burned it. Literally.'

Maggie's blog recently created substantial Internet buzz when she wrote about an incident where her 3-year-old son — whom she calls 'Thing II' — was seriously injured when, during a scuffle with his older sister while Maggie was trying to take a photo for the family Christmas card, he fell on a candy cane and it went up his nose. 'Maybe I should just take a photo of the piece of candy cane that the doctor got out of Thing II's nose (Yes, I kept it. It's in a crinkled, bloody plastic baggie.) and send that out [to Christmas card recipients] saying, 'Merry Bloody Christmas.''

When asked about whether she worried about being so blunt, Maggie, who told only one close friend that she's writing this blog, said she isn't concerned about airing her family's dirty laundry. 'I write about some really personal things because life is personal,' she said. 'If I only wrote about one portion of my life, told everyone I was writing this blog and had to hold things back so I wouldn't hurt their feelings, what I write here wouldn't be true. It would be a half-truth. Or a quarter-truth if I had to gag myself and censor bits of my life from my blog, and that's what I'd have to do if people knew I was a blogger.'

'Maggie Has Had It' is not alone in its harsh assessment of modern family life. Other blogs recently started by Boston area bloggers — notably 'Nasty New England Mama' (www.nastynemama.com), and 'Blasphemous Breeder' (www.blasphemousbreed.com) — are just as frank. Personal blogs like 'Merrily We Go, NOT' (www.merrily-gonot.com), which doesn't use salty language, seems to buck the trend.

Belmont's Michelle Monson, the 'Nasty New England Mama,' said that if a blogger wants her blog to have 'significant web traffic' then 'You've got to be honest. Without harsh honesty, you might as well just turn on Lifetime TV.'

'Raising kids is messy and ugly and if you don't write about all of it, you're basically lying,' Monson said. 'I write the bare-bones truth *and if people can't handle that, that's their problem.' Monson recently called her brother a 'selfish, thumb-sucking lout' for refusing to babysit so she could attend an early evening parent-teacher conference and said her husband Lou won't stop teaching their three boys how to fart on command. 'His favorite game, if you can believe this, is the old 'Pull My Finger' game,' Monson wrote recently. 'Is this appropriate behavior for a lawyer who argues cases in front of the Supreme Judicial Court?'*

Cambridge's Robert Black — a.k.a. the Blasphemous Breeder — echoed Monson's sentiments, saying that if bloggers don't talk about their lives in a realistic fashion, they'll lose their readers and the important emotional punch delivered by their raw daily prose which, in the case of Black, includes profanity-laced posts about his four favorite topics: His two children, the New England Patriots, the Bruins and Bay State politics.

'If you start shelving stuff that really matters to you because you're afraid you'll hurt someone's feelings by blogging about it, you're not talking to your readers truthfully and they get that, the readers, when you're not being truthful, and they won't read you anymore,' Black said. 'I look at these blogs as serving the function that corner, neighborhood bars used to be for guys who worked in cities, places where they stopped by for a beer on the way home from work to shoot the s—- with one another. We're [bloggers] doing the same thing except we're doing it on our blogs on the Internet and no one's serving us beer and peanuts, unfortunately.'

Gil Hastings, a Sudbury third grade teacher and dad of one who writes 'Merrily We Go, NOT,' said he's an exception to the 'tell-all blogging culture.' Hastings believes his readers prefer that he keep it clean and 'not write anything that I wouldn't want my boss, my students' parents or my grandmother to read.'

'Maybe that means I won't get as many hits [Internet visits], as other bloggers who swear and write about their sex lives and trash their spouses,' Hastings continued, "but, 20 years from now, I won't have to worry about my kids hating me for what I wrote or getting fired for something inappropriate that I wrote. It's just a blog. It's not worth it to me to expose everyone I love to public scrutiny.'

Monson, who said her husband knows she's writing the blog, said her entries about their different parenting styles and decisions regarding raising their children have prompted quality discussions and helped the couple understand each other's point of view more clearly. 'Sure, I may call him a 'knucklehead' and make fun of how he's secretly afraid our 12-year-old will soon be able to beat him at basketball, but I e-mail him a copy of each entry before I post it and he's mostly fine with what I write.'

Several psychologists who spoke with the Boston Journal said that graphic and public revelations about one's family are bound to erode trust within marriages and families, and make children feel as though their blogger parents are exploiting them.

'Would you want to be the 14-year-old girl who finds out that her mother trashed her father's sexual abilities online and that her adolescent problems were written about, in great detail, in a popular blog read by thousands of strangers?' asked psychologist Neil Marketta, of Wheelock College. 'How would you feel to know that your mother or your father was secretly putting into the blogosphere everything about you and your family without your permission? You've got a recipe for some serious family dysfunction in the future. The children of these bloggers are likely to develop trust issues.'

Although Monson's husband okays his wife's blog entries, many bloggers do not ask or even inform their spouses that they're writing blogs, like Maggie, according to blogging expert Chester Myable. 'Those so-called 'anonymous' bloggers, with online personalities and whose husbands or wives don't know about their blogs, feel like they can be uninhibited because there's no cost for telling the truth,' Myable said.

But there is a cost, says Meryl Rye, author of 'In Families We Trust.' 'When the sacred vows of marriage are subverted by the venom of nasty blog entries such as these, there will be a price to pay eventually,' Rye said. '. . . Betrayal and the feeling that you can no longer trust a spouse who savaged you and your character in front of others is one tough hurdle for any husband or wife to overcome.'

'I honestly don't see how marriages that have been violated in this way can last, at least not without counseling,' Marketta added. 'Even then, you have to remember that serious damage has been done.'"

Sweat spots the size of grapefruits were visible on the outside of Maggie's sweatshirt beneath her armpits. She couldn't bring herself to even glance at the comments *Journal* readers had posted beneath the article, so she clicked back to her *Maggie Has Had It* e-mail account and scrolled through it. There was an e-mail from Lesley Fair.

"That bitch! What the fuck does *she* want? To take another whack at me? Stab me in the eyes?"

"maggie —a producer from the barry leo show from wcck wants you to be on their morning show. if you read this before 9 a.m. and you want to do the interview, give the producer, tiffany, a call. contact info below.

l"

Maggie went to the bathroom and splashed cold water on her face. As she stared at her reflection — her face and the tips of her ears still burning red — Rudy bounded into the bathroom, grabbed a tissue sticking out of the trash can and started tearing into shreds. Maggie didn't even notice. Most of what she'd told Lesley — about how much good had come out of her blogging and all her truth-telling, how it was like one big therapy session where everyone could be honest because they were exchanging ideas and support — had been left out. Anything positive she'd said, the sweet and cute things she told her about that Michael and the kids had done were absent, abandoned on the newsroom floor.

The more she thought about how unfair Lesley had been, the more she thought she should call Barry Leo's producer and defend herself. She couldn't let Lesley's hit piece get the last word and label her as someone who was willfully destroying her marriage and emotionally crippling Jackie and Tommy. The puppy, whom Maggie had been ignoring, started gagging on the tissue and spit up a small, wet hunk of it at Maggie's feet. As Maggie cleaned it up, she decided to call the radio show. Her honor was at stake.

⌇

Dorothy also received an automated 6 a.m. phone call informing her that the Norton, NH schools were closed for the day because of the Nor'easter. And, for the first time in a long time, she actually rolled over and went back to sleep until 10. She couldn't believe it when she opened her eyes and saw the hands on the Waterford crystal clock, the one her mother had given her on her last Christmas so many years ago. Dorothy usually got out of bed in the 6 o'clock hour every day, regardless of whether it was a school day, as did her husband. On weekdays, Frank and Dorothy took turns in the shower — Dorothy first, followed by Frank — before eating their breakfasts (scrambled eggs and dry rye toast, cereal with flaxseed sprinkled on top or oatmeal topped with fresh fruit) and reading the papers that Frank brought into the house from their regular spot on the end of their driveway on their quiet residential street. Dorothy would pack two healthy lunches for them both (typically sandwiches, turkey, tuna or sliced peppercorn chicken breast, occasionally leftovers), clean up their dishes and leave their orderly house spotless before ironing her day's outfit as well as anything Frank needed pressed. Then she would make their bed before taking a short drive to the town center to tend to the health needs of middle school students.

But not so this morning.

Donning her gently worn brown leather slippers and pulling her cream colored cotton bathrobe over her black and red plaid pajamas, she felt a bit lonely upon entering the empty kitchen. Frank, who adored stormy New England winter weather, had long ago gone to work, about a 15-minute drive from their house, even though it was likely that there'd be hardly anyone in the Taylor Town Hall today, save for the Highway personnel who were involved with the plowing effort. Dorothy spotted his breakfast dishes in the sink, eyeing remnants of scrambled eggs, toast with strawberry jam and an already browned apple core discarded atop a half-filled cup of Earl Gray tea. On the stove was the pan he'd used to scramble the eggs with the brown crispy edges of eggs still clinging to the sides. "Jam?" she said aloud to herself. "Well that's a change for Frank. Thought he hated that jam."

Even though she was a frugal Yankee through and through, the below-60 degree temperature in the house was too brisk for Dorothy this morning, so she shuffled into the living room, pulling her robe tightly around her and firmly rubbing her forearms in order to warm them up. Feeling indulgent, she turned the thermostat up to a roaring 68 degrees. When she returned to the kitchen, she detected the strong odor of Lysol that appeared to be coming from the direction of their downstairs bathroom, adjacent to the kitchen. "Frank!" she muttered, slamming the door shut. She found a vanilla scented candle in the pantry, placed it in the middle of her kitchen table and lit it to get rid of the Lysol stench and make the kitchen feel cozy until the furnace did its job.

Thrown by the fact that there were no newspapers sitting neatly stacked on the kitchen table ready for her to read — none had been delivered in the storm — she felt unmoored by yet one more departure from her daily routine. Dorothy walked to the side door and looked out at the driveway, straining to see if that telltale plastic bag containing the news-papers was poking out of the snow anywhere. All she saw were mounds of snow and, because the wind was blowing snow around, she couldn't even see as far as the mailbox at the end of her 25-foot-long driveway.

"A little tea," she said aloud to herself as she shivered in the untamed draft from the side door, "will do the trick."

Whistling a cheery tune, Dorothy filled her royal blue kettle with water, turned the knob on her gas stovetop to ignite the flame and placed the kettle above it, hearing the gentle sizzle of the droplets of water that had dripped down the side. With no newspaper to read, she felt restless. Not a fan of the local TV news, particularly in the morning, she turned on that radio Michael had given her for Mother's Day several years ago that she'd tucked away on a countertop in the corner. ("It's got a CD player AND a radio," Michael had told her. "You can listen to anything in here while you cook.") Dorothy had used the CD feature a total of zero times since Frank set it up on the counter, threading the wire antennae up along the side of a cabinet (in a way that Dorothy found ugly, though she didn't say so) so he could tune into Boston radio stations, especially the sports talk stations. On this particular morning, Dorothy needed some noise to fill the void. Clicking the radio on with the gray remote control Frank had left next to a pile of bills, Dorothy pulled a loaf of Stop & Shop brand rye bread from the refrigerator, removed two slices, popped them into her crumbless toaster oven (she cleaned the crumb bin three times a week) and carefully used the wire twist-tie to close the thin plastic bread bag while listening to the tail-end of the news cast on the last station to which Frank had been listening, a news talk station. There were stories related to the storm, including details about numerous traffic accidents that were littering area highways and an admonition by both the Massachusetts and the New Hampshire governors for "non-essential" employees to stay home and off the roads. She was buttering her toast as the brief news update was wrapping up.

"Your source for talk. Real talk. Real people. WCCK . . . Up next, Barry Leo talks to Maggie, a local woman featured on the front page of today's *Boston Journal*, who trashes her husband and family on the Internet in her blog. Maggie's recent story about her 3-year-old son getting a candy cane wedged up his nose while she was taking photos for the family Christmas card created a big buzz on the Internet and made her a source of controversy. It's Barry's 'Outrage of the Day.'"

Dorothy's blue and white colored dish — which had a bit of condensation on it from the heat of the two pieces of hot buttered rye toast that'd been placed on the cool ceramic plate drawn from a cold cabinet — landed on the linoleum and shattered into jagged pieces. The rye toast laid amid the shards as partially melted butter dripped off the edges of the crust just as the furnace finally started blasting warm air into the kitchen.

CHAPTER TWENTY

". . . So, Maggie, what did your poor husband do to deserve a nasty, cut-throat wife like you?"

Maggie clutched the handset, fearful she'd drop it as her hands were already moist. Holed up in her bedroom closet with the door closed — so Jackie and Tommy wouldn't hear her, or disturb her phone conversation even though they were camped out in front of a Disney movie on DVD in her bedroom and Rudy was whimpering in his crate, which Maggie had hauled upstairs — Maggie had to keep her wits about her. She was attempting to swallow any fear she might have been feeling even though she was sure, before she even exchanged greetings with the host Barry Leo, a populist talk show host in his late 50s with a penchant for shouting, that this would be a tough conversation. Although Tiffany, Barry's soft-spoken producer, had been nothing but sweet to Maggie during their pre-interview chat, Barry went at Maggie full-bore, calling her a "blogging whore" 10 seconds into the interview.

"Um . . . what?" Maggie responded, stalling for time. "What do you . . ."

"Come ON Maggie! If that IS your real name," Barry said with a larger-than-life, exasperated tone. "Whaddoyou expect? A gold star? For telling the world that your husband can't get you off?" His voice rose like a booming thunderclap.

"I'm sorry, what?" she muttered, shocked by his tone. "That's not . . ."

"Don't play all innocent now. You're no shrinking violet, Missy. Here, let me give my listeners a taste of what you've been writing about your dear husband, who you call 'Wannabe King,' the father of your two children who you call 'Thing I' and 'Thing II.' Here" — he crinkled paper into the microphone for a dramatic effect — "Tiffany printed out some gems from your blog, *Maggie Has Had It.* Folks you can just go to our web page to get a link to the blog to see this garbage for yourself. But, let me read this, lemme read this. This is from a while ago but it gives you the flavor of this stuff here on this blog. It's an entry called 'When Will I Ever Win?' where Maggie was complaining that she hadn't been, uh" — he exaggeratedly cleared his throat — "*pleased* in some time. Come to think of it, if there are any children listening right now, and there may be because of the snow-related school cancellations, parents, you should turn the radio down for about a minute. Don't want to corrupt young minds with this filth. I'll count down from five. Okay? Here goes, five, four, three, two, and . . . one. All right. I'm going to read from this blog entry here, quote:

'So what do I need to do? Start wearing that shitty' — whoops, Tiffany, bleep that out, would ya? Let me start again — 'So what do I need to do? Start wearing that bleeping Victoria's Secret crap? Put a bull's-eye on my ya-ya and say, 'Yo dude, down here!' It's not that we don't have sex, exactly, it's more that it's gotten so by-the-numbers ever since Thing II became a toddler. Only the numbers don't often add up to equal the big O very much. I can't even remember the last time THAT happened."

Barry paused, letting dead air linger so long that some people at home may have checked their radios to make sure nothing had gone wrong because a lengthy silence on the radio is unusual. The words he'd just uttered seemed as though they had been projected onto a floating cartoon dialog balloon over Maggie's head, ready to pop. Maggie — sitting cross-legged on the hair and dust covered rug in her walk-in closet next to her shoe tree, angry tears streaming down her face — felt as though her skin was on fire. She wasn't about to give in to this bullying, she thought, "I can't let him do this to me."

In a low, edgy tone, Barry asked, "How can you lie in bed next to that man and deeply embarrass him in this way? Belittle his manhood?"

"I do NOT humiliate him, if you read the whole blog, you'll see that. I love him and what I write about is . . ."

"You can't be serious!" Barry interrupted. "You DON'T think you're humiliating him with this crap? What does he say about all of this? Oh. Wait. I already know. He says NOTHING about it! Why, my illustrious listeners may be asking, why doesn't he object to this blog as any sane man would? Because he doesn't KNOW that Maggie is writing about him! She never told him! Wonder why? Why not Maggie? Why doesn't he know about it? It's because you know you should be ashamed of yourself, isn't it?"

"I am NOT ashamed," Maggie objected. She jumped to her feet and knocked a pair of black patent leather peep-toe pumps that she hadn't worn in a year off of her shoe tree. They also accidentally disturbed a dress, an aqua floral number with spaghetti straps that grazed the top of Maggie's knees when she wore it. As she watched it delicately and gracefully float down to the tan rug, she couldn't remember the last time she'd worn it. Her and Michael's last anniversary, perhaps? Two anniversaries ago?

"Well then why don't you tell him about *Maggie Has Had It,* your illicit little blog that, unbelievably, gets thousands of readers a day?"

Maggie put her hand against the wall and steadied herself. "As I told Lesley Fair from the *Journal,* I write about the truth. I write the truth about things everyone experiences every day but doesn't talk about. If I tell him about the blog, I'd wind up censoring myself, if I was worried he was reading. People tell me that they relate to the blog because I'm telling the truth about what happens to a marriage once you have kids."

There, she thought, finally got it out there. Let Barry Leo argue with the concept of truth telling.

Barry, however, wasn't buying it. "You really think people don't already know that life gets hard after you have kids? What are you saying, that moms who read your trash are too stupid to realize that or are you just using that as an excuse so you can keep on exploiting everyone you know in exchange for a lot of Internet traffic?"

Maggie opened the closet door, then closed it again and started pacing around in circles like a caged animal. "YOU are the one who's calling moms who want truth 'stupid.' I'm not. And I'm not exploiting anyone either. I'm telling my story as it is right now, the good *and* the bad. You and the *Boston Journal* are ignoring all the good stuff I write. I'm just like any other mom out there who's just living her life, only I'm writing about it on a blog. If you look at the comments I got to the story about the candy cane when my son had to go to the Emergency Room because he got a piece of candy cane wedged up his nose when he was fighting with his sister . . ."

"Ah, yes," Barry said chuckling softly, "the candy cane story. I read that. That was a touching little tale where you made a big joke about your son's hospital visit. You joked about taking a photo of the bloody remnants of the candy cane that went up your son's nasal cavity and cut it so badly that he got stitches, and you wanted to send a picture of the candy cane, which you SAVED and send it out as part of your Christmas card! I'm sure your son would find that really funny."

Now it was Maggie's turn to laugh. "Aren't you supposed to be the guy with a sense of humor, who gets sarcasm? That's what my readers appreciate, that I'm sarcastic. No one really thought I was really gonna take a photo of the bloody candy cane and mail it out to people as our Christmas card. I was writing about how I was trying to take a photo of my kids for our Christmas card and they kept fighting and then the accident happened. You can't take this out of context. That's not fair."

"You know what, it's my show Maggie, and I can take it anyway I'd like to. Hey, the phone lines are all lit up. Callers are dyin' to get a crack at ya. Okay, Chuck from Saugus, you're up first."

"Thanks Barry," the caller, Chuck, said in a deep, but commanding voice. "Look, I just took a look at Maggie's web site and I can't believe the crap that's on there about her husband and her mother-in-law. Barry, you didn't even talk about the mother-in-law, even though she does sound like kind of a psycho. Maggie, honey, what are ya doin'? This is crazy. You sound like a nice enough girl, but, and I hate to say this, but, if you were my wife, well, I'd be pretty mad at you for doing this."

Maggie continued pacing as she heard Rudy starting to howl in his crate. "Chuck," she began, "I don't think you'd really be mad if you read everything in context. Context! I love my husband and my kids. And if you read it all together, not just the angry parts, you'd get that what I'm writing about. Are you always happy with your wife?"

"'course not," Chuck said. "But I'm not writin' about our fights for thousands of strangers to read about on the Internet. That's not right Maggie. That's private."

"Thanks for the call Chuck. That's the real point, isn't it?" Barry asked. "The other bloggers, they all told the *Journal* that their families know about their blogs. They're not hiding. They're not ashamed. Now, let's go to, okay, lemme see, all right let's get a lady to chime in here. Ellen, from Stoughton, you're on with Barry from the *Barry Leo Show*. Go ahead Ellen."

"Hello," said Ellen, who sounded like a senior citizen. "Thank you for taking my call, Barry."

"Sure thing," Barry said. "What have you got to say to blogger Maggie here?"

"I just think this whole Internet, or, what are you calling it, blogs, is just terrible. Writing about your husband for the whole world to see? Telling secrets from your marriage bed? I agree with Barry. Maggie, you should be ashamed of yourself. Didn't you take wedding vows?"

"I didn't break any vow," Maggie said. She pushed her back into the wall and let herself slide to the floor. Her head felt very heavy. Where were the people who e-mailed her all the time, praising her? Why was everyone against her? "When did telling your life story, and telling it honestly, become a crime, or become cheating and breaking vows? Writers write about their families in books all the time."

The biggest fight Michael and Maggie ever had about a topic other than Dorothy or going to visit the Finns, was over a pros-and-cons list Maggie had made about whether she should have a baby. It was written in haste, in panic actually, scrawled on a fresh, new yellow legal pad that had been sitting on the counter next to the phone when she officially received confirmation from her ob/gyn's office that she was indeed pregnant, approximately eight weeks along. Her condition had already been informally established by a trio of pregnancy tests — store brand, which she had bought on sale — that Maggie had taken the week before she visited her doctor.

Unlike Diane — who was in the middle of the second trimester of her first pregnancy and had already plowed her way through several pregnancy books, picked out the baby's name with George and was contemplating three color swatches for the nursery — Maggie was thoroughly thrown by the news that she was with child. She wondered if she should be worried about the fact that she was completely uninterested in the pregnancy, motherhood and babies thing, was repelled by the thought of diapers and sleepless nights, and was loath to share Michael's attention with anyone else, seeing that Dorothy and ENY consumed plenty of his time already. Her response to hearing from her doctor's office that she was pregnant prompted her to pick up the legal pad and a pen and do what she always did when she wasn't sure about her next move at a crucial juncture in her life: She made a list.

Pros of Keeping It	Cons of Keeping It
1. Having a baby earlier is better because we'll still have the energy to keep up with it.	1. Having a baby now will ruin our social lives where we're young enuf to enjoy it. Rite now, we're going to all sorts of stuff. Loving it. Would miss it.
2. Having baby now is easier because my body's younger than if we wait 'til later.	2. Would hurt career bec. would have to cut into work hrs to drop off/pick up kid from daycare, sick days, etc. Know M won't be taking the time off to deal w/baby. It'll be me.
3. Cld raise kid at same time Diane's raising hers. Would have 1 parent/mom friend.	3. $$$!
4. Wld give incentive to buy house and move out of tiny apt ... maybe farther away from EVIL M-I-L!! (But would miss city life)	4. Don't feel ready to be tied down to motherhood!! No diapers, no sleeping late, no crazy sex.
	5. Don't know that I could luv a baby.
	6. Don't want another Dorothy or Luke in the world. What if the baby sucks & I hate it & resent it? Who wants a crappy kid?
	7. Don't want to share Michael. (M-I-L is enuf of a time hog.)
	8. Don't want to give up coffee & booze like I'd have to w/pregnancy & breast-feeding (ick!!)
	9. Pregnancy would wreck my body, stretch marks, weight gain.
	10. Would have 2 C MORE of M-I-L!

A week later, Michael was in search of some Tic-Tacs. Maggie usually bought them in bulk at BJs and kept the box of several containers of breath mints in her underwear drawer. He was looking for the breath mints when he came across the pros-and-cons list, which had been neatly folded into quarters and slipped next to the stack of Tic-Tac boxes. When Michael spied the yellow paper, it intrigued him and he was compelled to take a peek. As he scanned the sheet he felt sucker punched. He didn't know Maggie was pregnant. The things that she had written — "What if the baby sucks & I hate it & resent it? Who wants a crappy kid?" — made him wonder, "Who *is* this person?" These were not the words of the woman he thought he knew who was an energetic, life-loving ball of energy. He thought that their life together had been great and could only be made better with the addition of a baby, a physical embodiment of their love, in spite of the unplanned part. These sentiments obviously weren't shared by his wife.

He brooded about this list for some time before it dawned on him that he didn't know when it had been written. Maggie very well could've already ended the pregnancy. The number of "cons" grossly outnumbered the "pros." He could've already lost the opportunity to weigh in on this before she'd acted. There was still an hour to go before she was due to arrive home after having gone to the movies to see *Shakespeare in Love* with Diane, so he sat in the darkened apartment and stewed. Michael was pulling a third Sam Adams Winter Lager from the fridge when he heard the lock on the door turn and Maggie burst into the room proclaiming that the movie was "awesome!"

"So," he said, flipping a bottle cap onto the counter, "ya gonna kill our baby without telling me because you'd prefer booze? Or have you already done it?" He sat down stiffly upon one of the two metal chairs next to a small, round glass café table where they ate their meals.

"What? . . . Oh. . . " Maggie said eyeing the list that

Michael had picked up and waved in the air, "no . . . You're not being fair."

"Are you shitting me? I'M not being fair? How would you feel if your wife was pregnant and didn't tell you about it? If your wife considered, or already had an abortion, without even talking to you first?"

"Michael . . ."

"And I found this list, this fucking pros-and-cons list, *that's* how I found out that my wife was pregnant. I thought you were on the pill."

"I am, I was, I mean, I missed a few days and . . . well, the doctor said it must've happened because I forgot to take them during a fertile week, or something like that."

"You've already been to the doctor?" yelled Michael, his eyes widening, head nodding slowly in the affirmative. He slammed his right hand on the table and the two empty beer bottles in front of him rattled together threatening to tip over. He briefly placed his forehead in his left hand, then sat up straight, angrily grabbed the list, crumpled it up and tossed it to the floor. After a moment's pause, he took a big, loud gulp of beer. "So, have you, like, scheduled your abortion yet, or had it already?"

Maggie avoided his glare and fiddled with the strap on her leather purse which now felt as though it was digging into her shoulder.

"You didn't answer my question."

"Which question? You're just yelling at me like a psychopath."

"The one about, you know, the *abortion*," he said, stretching his pursed lips into a thin line, crossing his arms in front of his chest and holding his breath while awaiting her reply.

"No! I haven't had an abortion, Michael. God! I can't believe you think I'd do that without discussing it with you. I've just been gathering information about what's happening inside MY body. MY body, not your body. I haven't done anything other than that so you need to chill the fuck out."

"Me?! You think I need to 'chill the fuck out?' What the hell? I can't believe you! What the hell is your problem, other than the fact that you can't seem to remember something as simple as taking a birth control pill each day when you're supposed to. This is a god-damned blessing that's fallen into our laps and all you can think about is that," he picked up her list, "what, you might have to see my mother more often, oh, and give up coffee for a few months? What the fuck Maggie?!"

"You know, that's not fair," she said, dropping her purse to the floor next to the empty chair. She stood, clutching the chair back, and tried to organize her thoughts. "I wasn't expecting to talk to you about this right now. I still need to think things through. I thought this would be something we'd do a few years from now, have a baby. You're not the only one who was thrown by this. This affects me most of all. This has thrown off all my plans."

"YOUR plans?" Michael asked, voice loaded with sarcasm. "What plans were these? I don't know that I've ever heard about these plans of yours."

"OUR plans, sorry, you know I meant to say, 'our plans.' Don't be a jackass, you know what I meant," Maggie said. She clenched her jaw. "We've only been married for two years, almost, and I have a great time when I'm with you, going out places, seeing comedy shows, eating at our favorite restaurants, having sex any time here . . . I had career plans."

"You're being really, incredibly . . . selfish," he interrupted, employing a tone Maggie had never heard him use before. It was dark and cold and seemed to emanate from some place deep inside Michael that she didn't know existed. "This isn't just about you anymore Maggie, or about what just you want, or your career in what, HR? You can do that anywhere. This isn't about beer and coffee and my mother and sex. It's about us. It's bigger than us now."

"I'm TALKING about 'us!' I love our life right now. I'm

having a blast and I don't want to fuck it all up with a baby. This time in our lives, when we're young and at the beginning of our marriage, our careers . . . we can go anywhere, sleep late . . ."

"So it's worth getting rid of our baby just so we can sleep late?" Michael shook his head. "Grow up Maggie. You need to grow up."

"It's not about sleeping late. That's a cheap shot," she said. "It's not about being selfish. It's about planning for our future in a way that makes sense to both of us, not just you."

"Look, I'm just going by *your* list, your cons of having our baby that you wrote down, in your own handwriting. You wrote that not being able to sleep late and getting stretch marks and giving up coffee and booze for a little while are all reasons against having a baby. Those are *your* words. Those things aren't going to change no matter if you have a baby now or five years from now." He grabbed the list from the floor and flattened it out on the table.

"Here, number one, quote, 'Having a baby now will ruin our social lives where we're young enough to enjoy it. Right now we're going to all sorts of stuff. Loving it. Would miss it.' Unquote. Number four, quote, 'Don't feel ready to be tied down to motherhood! No diapers, no sleeping late, no crazy sex.' Unquote. Oh, here's a good one, number eight . . ."

When she listened to him read the "cons" out loud, Maggie realized that they did sound shallow, although she didn't think they fairly represented her, didn't take into consideration the conflict roiling within her and that little voice that was telling her it was too soon for her to become a mother. She had too much to do before she was tied down to all that responsibility. Again. She felt like she'd just gotten out from under all of that by moving out of the Finn household. Yet there they were, the "cons," written by her hand. She collapsed into the chair to Michael's left and grabbed his chilled beer bottle, which had been dripping condensation onto the glass table top. She took a greedy gulp then, eyes widening, she froze without swallowing. Maggie slammed down the bottle and ran to the kitchen sink where she spat out the beer. She watched the bubbly, amber-colored liquid dribble slowly down the sink, into the drain and disappear from sight.

CHAPTER TWENTY-ONE

"Oh! Man! Brutal! Bru-talll!"

"Think he knows?"

"No! No way! She's saying on there that he doesn't know, that he's in the dark. But that candy cane story is in the *Journal* and on the radio, there's no way he's *not* gonna find out."

"Colin, I just pulled up her blog. You gotta look at it. C'mere."

Colin Faraday and Greg Post, two relatively new, twentysomething ENY hires, had made it into their Boston office despite the blizzard. Most of their co-workers, however, had not. They'd arrived 30 minutes apart from one another taking the T, which wasn't too crowded. Michael Kelly was the highest ranking person who'd made it into the office. None of the bigwigs, like Sam Young were coming in, so it had the feel of a snow day. Colin and Greg — both tall, thin brunettes who could easily be mistaken for twin brothers — had spread their belongings out across the shiny conference room table. Styrofoam cups of coffee, a pink and orange colored box of muffins and a couple of newspapers purchased from the one newsstand open — just outside the subway — covered the expansive, cherry table. Their wet parkas, clumps of half-melted pieces of snow mixed with sand and salt were strewn about. Colin had turned the TV onto a local news station, muted it and put on the closed captioning, while Greg turned on the radio, as he was a talk radio fan, a habit he picked up from his mother, a major news and radio talk show junkie.

They'd caught the *Barry Leo Show* in progress and were only half-listening until they heard Barry mention the candy cane story, they both stopped what they were doing and looked at each other.

"You got the *Journal*? Where's the *Journal*?" Greg asked, shoving Colin's black canvas backpack off the table in search of the paper. And there it was. Front page. The Lesley Fair blogging story. The screaming headline.

"Holy shit! This is Michael's wife! It's gotta be!" Greg said. "He just told me about what happened to his kid the other day with the candy cane up his nose. It's exactly what it says in here. You ever met his wife, Maggie? Is that her voice on the radio?"

"Never met her," Colin said. He looked over Greg's shoulder and read the story as Greg pulled up *Maggie Had Had It* on his battered laptop and audibly gasped.

"This is serious shit," Greg said, sucking down the last of his large coffee as he scanned the blog posts. "Glad my girlfriend doesn't keep a blog."

"How do you think I know you can't screw that girlfriend for longer than 15 seconds?" Colin asked Greg. "Read it online. Erin's got a blog, dude. What, you don't know about it either? Both you and Michael are totally clueless?"

"Yeah, asshole," Greg said, lobbing his empty coffee cup at Colin's head. "Erin'd never do something like this."

Colin shook his head. "Betcha that's what Michael thought too."

"I don't even know what to say."

"What? Michael, what do you mean?"

"Don't play games with me," Michael said in a low, venom-filled voice. He'd just spent the past 30 minutes locked inside an ENY bathroom stall trying to quell his nausea, contemplating when he'd feel well enough to emerge and show his face in public, whether he could ever go home again, or whether he wanted to.

Mere minutes into Maggie's appearance on the *Barry Leo Show,* Dorothy had called Michael on his cell phone.

"Michael, are you at work honey?"

"Yeah, Mom, I got in early. It took me a while, roads were awful but . . . "

"Michael, is there are radio in your office? Turn on your radio right now! To WCCK. Maggie's on there," Dorothy sniffed, stifling a sob. "I'm so sorry. I'm so sorry."

"What? Why is Maggie on the radio?"

Dorothy swallowed hard and tried to keep herself from heaving tears into the phone. "She's been writing about you And me. And Tommy and Jackie. On the Internet, a 'blog' they call it. She's been saying awful, awful things," she said, blowing her nose into a blue tissue then tossing it onto the kitchen table where it joined a half dozen crumpled versions of its kind. "There's a story about her in the *Boston Journal* today and they're talking about it with Maggie on the radio. I just looked at her page on the Internet." Dorothy couldn't get the words out as she wept.

Michael was still sitting in his office chair like a statue, unable to compute this information as he listened to his mother cry. When Dorothy finally gathered herself, she continued, "I'm so sorry Michael. You don't deserve this. You don't deserve to be a divorced, single father, being wronged by this . . . this . . . well . . . I can't even think of what to call her. She's so troubled Michael, damaged. There's something wrong with her to do this to you. Just make sure she doesn't get to keep the children. She's unstable."

As his mother sobbed into her phone for a second time, Michael, wheeled his chair over to his computer and went to the *Boston Journal* web site and saw the headline, "No Holes Barred: Bloggers Rip Their Families to Shreds Online." "Mom, I've got to go," he said, hastily hanging up the phone without waiting for her response. He wrung his hands as he gently rocked back and forth while reading the article. At one point, he brought his right hand to his mouth, drew in a deep breath and continued rocking, picking up the pace. When he got to the end of the article, he clicked on the link to Maggie's blog, knowing that he didn't really want to see what he'd find at that web address. But he had to.

Michael lost track of how long he sat in front of the screen as he scrolled through page after page of entries from *Maggie Has Had It* when he finally heard Greg and Colin's peals of laughter from down the hall. "Did they have the radio on?" Michael wondered, straining to see if he could hear the sound of the radio. "Did they see the article? Are they laughing at me?" When he heard one of them shout, "'Wannabe-King!' Oh damn!" he knew that his humiliation was the reason for their guffaws. Michael probably would've remained hunkered down in his office and would've continued reading the blog all the way through to the very first post she'd ever written if he hadn't felt a twinge in his stomach that sent him running for the men's room, three doors down the narrow, central ENY corridor.

Minutes later, he looked at the reflection of his own peaked face in the bathroom mirror. Twelve hours ago, he'd been drinking a robust red wine and making love to Maggie in their living room atop a soft, chenille blanket, after he'd given his wife a dog she'd always wanted and told her he'd helped to secure their financial future with his new junior partnership. And that whole time, he thought, she'd been telling the world he was a selfish poser shell of a man who couldn't satisfy her in bed. He couldn't bring himself to leave this room. The moment he stepped out of it, he'd have to start dealing with something which seemed like a bad, twisted dream. He'd have to face the laughter of the likes of Colin and Greg and the shame in his mother's voice.

Michael was involuntarily forced back into reality when his BlackBerry buzzed in his pocket. Its vibrations seemed louder, more amplified in the tiled bathroom. It was Maggie calling. His rage tempted him, for a fleeting second, to flush the BlackBerry down the toilet. Or stomp on it. Refuse to provide her with an audience. Reach through the phone and strangle her. To tell her to go to hell and that he never wanted to see her duplicitous face again. But he went against his instincts, answered and was stunned when she tried to pretend as though nothing had happened. She said she'd called to see that he'd made it into the office safely and to tell him that he'd left a file in their bedroom.

"I don't even know what to say," Michael said.

"What? Michael, what do you mean?"

"Don't play games with me. I saw it. The blog. The article. I know you were on the radio," Michael said slowly, pausing for a moment to remind himself to breathe. "My mother called. She heard you."

After she'd finished the interview with Barry Leo, Maggie had wanted to erase the debacle from her mind, forget it ever happened. She'd come out of the closet, walked over to the bed where the kids were still watching a movie and planted a kiss on each of their heads. She turned to again glance out the window at all that snow that looked so pristine, so fresh, like a clean slate. Then she noticed that lying next to her foot on the floor was a big Bypass file. She decided to call Michael in case he was scouring his office in search of the missing file, though there was no way she'd be willing to drive it out to his office, not in this weather.

"Michael," she said, her voice heavy with fear, "did you, um, I mean, did you read, uh . . . *everything*? Did you see that it's not all like they said in the paper? It's not all bad or about sex. They exaggerated."

"I told you! I *read* it!" he snapped, his voice echoing off the bathroom walls. Perhaps the men's room wasn't the best place to have this conversation, he thought. He held the phone, receiver-side pressed to his chest, and returned to his office, slamming the door shut behind him. "Why?! Why would you do this to me? You told the whole world that you think I'm an asshole who can't make you come." Clamminess spread like a swiftly advancing storm front, coating his skin with cold perspiration. He doubled over in his office chair, folding himself in half, still holding the phone to his ear.

"I love you Michael. I do. You know I do. You are the center of my whole world. The blog . . . you've got to let me explain."

"No! I don't have to let you do anything! Not after the lying . . ."

"I did NOT lie to anyone. I didn't lie. Not once."

"Bullshit!" he yelled, punching his fist into the air in front of him. He bounded out of his chair and paced around for 10 seconds before sitting back down. "Look, I'm not coming home tonight. I'm going to stay at a hotel, that one over the Turnpike."

"Because of the snow or . . . because of the blog?"

"What the fuck do you think? I can't talk to you right now. I don't want to hear your voice. Tell Jackie and Tommy I love them."

He concluded the call by hurling his BlackBerry at the back of his closed office door. It fell to the ground, its screen cracked and pieces of the broken back cover landed on the non-descript gray office carpeting in a pile of high tech debris.

"Diane, tell me what to do. How can I fix this?"

Diane was cradling the phone between her left shoulder and her ear as she was fixing lunch for Max and Zoe — macaroni and cheese in the shape of Nickelodeon cartoon characters with sliced baby carrots and cubes of honeydew melon on the side — having just finished breastfeeding Lily before Maggie called. George was in their guest bedroom with his laptop, working from home so he wouldn't get stuck in the snow. The live shots on the local TV stations showed that the highways appeared largely unplowed because the harsh winds kept blowing the snow back onto the roadways after the plows went by. After placing the colorful, animal-shaped paper plates laden with food in front the kids, Diane walked into her living room and fell into her sofa, crushing some stray pieces of Cheerios that Max had left there during his morning snack.

"Hello? Diane? You still there?"

"Yep. I am. I'm just thinking," Diane said as she shook her head. She'd warned Maggie about this interview business and, had Maggie asked her opinion beforehand, she would've ardently argued that going on the *Barry Leo Show* would be a big mistake. Anyone who'd ever listened to his show would've known that that was a bad idea. Now, there was really nothing she had to offer except her willingness to listen and be sympathetic. "I don't know. Maybe just give Michael time to cool down. Finding out from Dorothy must've been awful."

"Yeah," Maggie said blankly. Jackie and Tommy were watching yet another DVD because Maggie just didn't have the energy to watch or entertain them. Rudy was curled up, napping on the sofa nestled next to Tommy after having an accident on the rug just 10 minutes beforehand. Following her brief conversation with her husband, Maggie had told the kids to go watch their DVD in the living room while she climbed back into bed and pulled the covers over her head. Breathing in her own, stale coffee-scented exhales — wondering if she'd accidentally suffocate herself this way, "Maybe that's an option?" she thought weakly — she squeezed Michael's pillow between her legs and held it against her belly. A brief slap-filled dispute between Jackie and Tommy, which she could hear, even under all that bedding, prompted her to get out of bed. After playing referee and cleaning up another Rudy mistake, Maggie trudged back to the comfort of her bed. But she couldn't just lie there. She needed to do . . . something. She just wasn't sure what, so she called

Diane, hoping to brainstorm with her.

"Wait!" Maggie yelled, throwing the covers off of her dramatically. "He needs to hear my side, but since he won't listen to me, I could write an open letter to him on my blog!"

"No, no, no, no, no!" Diane said. "That's not such a great idea Mags. He's not in the right frame of mind to hear anything from you right now. Especially, not on your blog, even if it is an apology. You just need to give him time."

"No. He will listen. He *will* hear me. If I give him time, Dorothy will be the only one who has his ear and she'll poison him against me. I've got to do this, write a note to him, make it public because he feels like he might be embarrassed."

"I think that'll make it worse. And, I hate to say it Mags, but he's probably already totally embarrassed. And besides, how are you going to get him to read it?"

"I'll figure that out later. Look, I'm going to get working on this. Can I count on you for help later today if I need it, with the kids I mean?"

"Maggie, hello?! There's a blizzard going on right now. They can't even keep the streets clean because the snow keeps getting blown back onto it. What kind of help are you talking about?"

"I dunno, but George is home with you right? I might need his help. I know it's terrible outside, but you don't live THAT far away and George has a big truck . . ."

"Yeah, but . . ."

"I'll call you back this afternoon."

She picked up the BU sweatshirt Michael had draped over the chair in the corner of their bedroom and inhaled his aroma. It reminded her of last night. Maggie wrapped it around her neck, grabbed her laptop and started writing the most important blog entry of her life.

CHAPTER TWENTY-TWO

It was 6 p.m. when Maggie set out to wage battle with Mother Nature. She'd persuaded George to drive his beat-up blue Chevy Tahoe through the snowstorm, which had greatly lessoned in intensity, over to her house. He'd agreed to watch Jackie and Tommy while she borrowed his SUV and drove to the hotel in Newton, a city neighboring Boston, instead of using her own minivan, which wasn't great in slippery conditions.

"You're insane, you know that?" George said when he walked into the Kellys' house, as the wind blew snow into the front hallway before he shut the door behind him. He stomped his boots on the doormat and tossed his jacket onto the black metal hat rack, which was tilting ever so slightly to the right. "It's not as bad out there as it was a little while ago, but it's not great either. Took me 45 minutes to get here. Usually takes me less than 30."

Maggie wrapped her chunky, popcorn knit red scarf around her neck, put her slightly pilled, knit navy Patriots hat on her head and eased into her ugly knock-off Ugg boots. "The kids have been fed already. They're playing in the living room, with Legos or something. My cell phone number is on the counter over there with the other emergency numbers. There are leftovers in the fridge, some ice cream too, peppermint stick from Friendly's. Thanks a million George. You're a life saver . . . Oh, and can you keep an eye on Rudy, the puppy? There are paper towels on the counter if he makes a mistake."

She gave George a one-armed hug, grabbed his keys from his gloved hand and shoved her laptop under her long, black wool coat to protect it from the elements as she stepped out onto her front stoop. She trudged along in snow up to her knees until she climbed into George's warm and stuffy SUV. "What a sweetheart," Maggie thought, noticing a huge cup of hot Dunkin' Donuts coffee in the cup holder with two canary yellow Post-It notes stuck to it. The first one said, "For you. Milk and two sugars." The one beneath it read, "Full tank of gas. **Be careful**. Good luck!"

Slowly, ever so slowly, Maggie navigated her way down Maple Road, then Park Street, then Main Street until she finally reached the on-ramp to the Massachusetts Turnpike which appeared to have been cleared in a pretty half-hearted way by a very tired plow driver. There was only one usable lane which was in significantly better condition than the other two which were treacherous looking. The smattering of vehicles in that one lane was crawling along at roughly 20, sometimes 30 miles per hour. Clutching the steering wheel, Maggie's whole body was one raw nerve, absorbing every bump, slip and skid through her skin and down to her marrow. She hunched forward and stared at the road through strained, squinted eyes, the highway illuminated by the two beams of the SUV's headlight which made the snowflakes glisten like the star atop her Christmas tree. She wondered how long she could drive before she'd have to pull over and chop the snow and ice build-up off the windshield wipers. She absolutely hated driving in any kind of precipitation. Even though Maggie had lived her whole life in Massachusetts and considered herself a hearty New Englander, she'd never became comfortable driving when road conditions were poor. She despised this sense of powerlessness, the petrified feeling that could overcome her in situations like this where she feared that at any moment her vehicle could veer out of control on some unseen spot of ice or packed-down snow or slip in some matter, no matter how hard she concentrated or how carefully she drove the vehicle.

As she plodded down the highway, Maggie recalled a huge argument she had with her brother one winter when she was in college and said she didn't want to drive to East-borough for their father's birthday dinner because there'd been a weather alert issued to look out for severe black ice throughout the area for the entire evening.

"Luke," Maggie said once she returned to her dorm room, tracking snow on the braided rug, "there's just no way I can make it out there tonight. You should see how thick the ice is on the streets and on my car. I was just out there. It's like the Bruins' ice rink out there."

"You're bagging on Dad? Nice. Real nice," he grumbled, pouting, because Maggie was going to be footing the bill and driving them that evening.

"You know I don't do driving when it's icy," she said, feeling herself getting emotional and defensive. "You could be driving along a street that looks like it's clear, and BAM! You hit a patch of ice. Your car spins around. Then you hit a utility pole and die."

"Give me a break. You're so much a drama queen for Chrissake. Fine, whatever. Forget about Dad's birthday then. Go back to your keg parties or whatever the hell shit you do there." With that, Luke slammed down the phone and Maggie was left to try to figure out how she was going to try to make it up to her dad.

She tried to put that memory out of her head and focus on the snow-covered road because, as much as she disliked driving in the winter, worrying about crashing was easier than figuring out what she'd say once she got to her destination. Ninety minutes after she'd left Greenville — a trip that normally took around 40 minutes — Maggie finally spotted the hotel in the distance. She'd been forced to stop twice on the side of the highway to knock the ice off the wipers, one time getting smacked by a wall of gritty, salt and sand laden snow dredged up by a car that had passed precariously close to George's SUV. The hotel made for a very odd site, hulking over the Massachusetts Turnpike like one of Tommy's Duplo block creations, propped up on two sides with a passageway beneath which provided enough clearance for his toy cars to pass beneath. Maggie had always wanted to know what it looked like on the inside, whether you could hear the Turnpike traffic rumbling below when you were on the main floor and whether the floor itself got really cold during the winter. Maggie exited the off-ramp, pleased to find that Newton's streets were in a slightly better shape than the highway. She could even see a glimpse of black pavement where snow had been cleared away. When she pulled into the hotel parking lot, some of the signs were snow-covered and there were huge snowbanks all around the area including at the entrance to its parking deck, which she wasn't sure was open. She wasn't sure where she should park and there was nothing to give her any guidance.

"Screw it," she muttered, pulling in front of the hotel entrance and parking illegally, seeing that there were no valets braving the weather to park the car for her. George's SUV skidded slightly when she applied the brakes. As a precaution, she set the emergency brake after shifting the truck into park and turning the ignition key off. "Don't need George's car rolling away," she mumbled.

Maggie took a deep, cleansing breath. She pulled out her cell phone and dialed Michael's number. "Hello, you've reached Michael Kelly. Please leave a message . . ."

"Voicemail! Again!" she groaned. She'd been trying to contact him for the past 15 minutes as she got closer to the hotel, hoping she'd be able to meet him in the lobby but he wasn't picking up. She knew he'd already left the ENY offices because she'd called there at around 5 o'clock and Colin Faraday, a new guy Maggie hadn't met, told her Michael had already left for the day.

Grabbing her laptop, purse and keys, Maggie — her sand and salt covered coat half falling off her, scarf unevenly hanging around her neck and dragging on the ground — awkwardly got out of the SUV, entered the hotel and headed to the front desk. "Michael Kelly," she declared, startling the lone, balding, middle-aged, hotel staffer behind the desk who was reading the *Boston Journal's* sports section.

"Excuse me?"

"Michael Kelly. He's a guest. What room is his in?"

"I'm sorry, but who are you?"

"I'm his wife. Maggie Kelly. . ."

The man, whose name tag read "Alfred," stood silently wearing a vacant look on his face.

"Do you want to see my ID? I'm his wife," she declared. She put her laptop on the ground and dropped her purse next to it and opened it wide while she foraged through it for her wallet. She aggressively shoved her driver's license across the counter in Alfred's direction. He picked it up and examined her photo, specifically where the left shoulder of her white shirt had been stained purple after Jackie spilled juice on Maggie seconds before the Registry of Motor Vehicles employee snapped the picture.

Alfred, appearing to be awkwardly stalling, continued to quietly inspect Maggie's driver's license. Maggie's patience was quickly evaporating. "What room is he in?" she asked.

Alfred looked at her, paused for a few beats before saying, "Mrs. Kelly, perhaps I can call up to his room. Just a moment please."

Another employee, a tall, young woman with long, sleek red hair appeared next to Alfred. "Is there a problem here Alfred?" she asked, arching one of her perfectly waxed eyebrows. She eyed Maggie, who appeared slightly disheveled and overtly anxious as she rhythmically shifted her weight from her left foot to the right foot while she bit the nail on her left pinky finger.

Attempting to be discreet, but failing miserably, Alfred leaned over and said out of the side of his mouth, "Courtney, um, well, this, ah, this lady says she's the wife of Mr. Kelly in

Room 347, and wants to go up there. Do I let her? I looked at her ID, says 'Kelly' on it."

Courtney festooned a smile on her face, the kind you get from someone who's likely going to give you bad news. She told Maggie in a cool, monotone, "Alfred's new. It's his first week. We'll be with you in a second, please excuse us." She tugged on the sleeve of Alfred's white oxford shirt and the two retreated several feet away from the counter and began whispering conspiratorially, though Maggie could make out bits of their conversation, including Courtney saying, ". . . didn't want any guests or calls."

"Forget it," Maggie said, as she bent over and collected her things. "Can you just tell me where your restrooms are? It's been a long drive in this blizzard and I need to use the Ladies' Room."

Alfred, looking relieved, smiled and said, "'round the corner over there, down the hall a bit, first door on your right" as Courtney frowned.

Without waiting for Courtney's sour retort, Maggie headed in the direction of the women's bathroom, walked into the room and stood there for a moment before realizing how unkempt she actually looked. She made some quick adjustments, smoothed her hair, straightened her hat, neatly re-tied her scarf around her neck and pinched her cheeks to look as though she'd applied blush. Slowly, she cracked open the door to check if the hallway was clear. Lucky for her, the stairwell leading up to the guest rooms was only 50 feet away on the left and she was confident she could dash to it without Courtney or Alfred seeing her. At the very least, she'd have a decent head start if they gave chase. Though the Ladies' Room door creaked loudly when it closed behind her, Maggie safely made it into the stairwell without being seen or heard. She quickly scaled the stairs, taking them two at a time, up to the third floor, her heart pounding.

CHAPTER TWENTY-THREE

In the two hours since Alfred checked him into his room, Michael had already sucked down four $14 nips of chilled vodka from the mini-bar like they were medicine, like they'd make everything that was bad seem good again. Five years ago, when he and Maggie had their first night away from Jackie, they'd taken an Amtrak train from Boston to New York City to attend a Broadway show and spend the night in a Manhattan hotel. When they returned to their microscopic hotel room, Maggie, blissfully happy to have her husband all to herself, suggested that they have nightcaps from the mini-bar. She dimmed the lights, held two nips of cognac in her hand and grabbed two glasses as she stretched out on the bed. Michael, however, dissuaded her from opening the bottles. "They're so expensive Mags. It's not worth it," he'd said.

She made a face, stuck her tongue out at him and acquiesced. "Fine, don't let me have a drink Mr. Cheap, even though we ARE in the big city for an actual date," Maggie said, putting the nips back in their place. "We should be able to treat ourselves every once and a while."

Michael thought of that moment when he looked at the collection of empty bottles and contemplated going for a fifth, even though he hadn't eaten anything since breakfast. Good sense got the better of him and he reached instead for a bag of potato chips, a veritable bargain at $5.

The TV was on. ESPN. *Sports Center*. It was the second

time he'd seen the same broadcast, same highlight reel, same wry commentary about the Celtics blowing a 19-point lead the previous night to the Lakers. He wasn't really paying attention though. He was just sitting in a hard, wooden desk chair and staring, in an unfocused way, in the general direction of the TV, unsure of what he was supposed to be doing. "Am I a wimp if I don't kick her out? A bad dad and husband if I don't give her another chance?" he thought. "But how the hell can I ever trust her again?" His thoughts drifted uncomfortably to work. Colin and Greg obviously knew what was going on based on the few out-of-context comments he'd overheard them making in the conference room. "Those two will talk," Michael thought, "like busybody old ladies who just joined the Crime Watch. They'll spread the word fast." Michael knew there was no appealing to their better natures as they were the ones who made certain that everyone at ENY heard all about the "Gel Boy" nickname once they caught wind of it.

"Does Sam already know? Rick? What'll they think of me?" Michael thought. "And God, what if that asshole columnist from Templeton who wrote about my hair finds out?" He imagined new, horrendous nicknames the man with the poison pen might concoct, like "Blog Boy." Or worse.

Michael couldn't even allow himself to consider Dorothy, who was likely driving his father insane at this very moment with her "I told you so" rants about how Maggie had never been good enough and that Michael should've listened to her and not married "that Margaret Finn." He never called her back after their earlier phone call. She'd already brought up the words "divorce" and "single father" within 10 seconds of telling him that Maggie had trashed him for the entire world to see. He clearly knew where his mother stood on this issue. Lucky for him, his BlackBerry was now busted so he didn't have to hear it vibrate with Dorothy's seething judgment and definitive declarations. He didn't have to know how many attempts she'd made to contact him.

The three brisk knocks on his hotel door startled him.

He'd hung the "Do Not Disturb" sign on the door knob. He hadn't ordered anything. He had clearly informed the clueless looking guy at the front desk to hold all calls and turn away visitors, so this had to be an error, perhaps room service being sent to the wrong room. "Idiots," Michael said as he put both hands on the arms of the chair and pushed himself up to a standing. He shuffled to the door, feeling a bit woozy from the rapid consumption of the vodka as he opened the door.

"Michael . . ." Maggie said when she saw him. He looked awful. "Please . . ."

"I've got nothing to say to you," he said angrily, narrowing his eyes and sneering. He tried to shut the door in her face.

"You don't have to say anything," she said, using one arm to push back against the door and maneuvering her body in the doorway so if he tried to close the door it would be on her. "You don't even have to hear my voice."

Michael stood there, stunned by her chutzpah, that she'd dared to show her face. Maggie pushed past him, detecting a strong whiff of alcohol along the way and set up the laptop on the desk, breathing a sigh of relief when she discovered that the hotel room had free wireless Internet access. She hadn't checked whether it did beforehand. Michael watched her from across the room, hand still on the door knob. She pulled up her web site onto the screen.

"I wrote you a note. On the blog. It's to explain to you and the readers and everyone that I'm sorry for any pain I caused. Please. Read it. We've been married for seven years and have two beautiful children. I think that those seven years warrant at least a quick read."

Michael remained frozen by the door. He squeezed the door handle wishing he could crush it in his palm. Unprepared for Maggie's forceful intrusion, his reactions a bit dulled by the vodka, Michael said nothing and simply stared at this person as though she was a stranger who'd broken into his hotel room and was trying to shove a pamphlet into his hand.

"Please, Michael. Just read it. I'm going to go back downstairs. I'll be sitting in George's SUV by the front door. I'll wait there for a half-hour. If, after you've read it, you want to talk to me, I promise I'll shut up and let you talk. If you don't come down, I'll just drive back home. Your choice."

Maggie surprised herself with the fake confidence contained in her voice — she was making this all up as she went along — and again brushed past her husband and walked determinedly down the hall. It wasn't until she got safely inside the stairwell that she let her pent-up tears start to flow.

Michael hadn't moved. The computer screen glowed on the desk, illuminating the semi-darkened room which was only lit by the thin line of light coming from the bathroom where the door was open just a crack, and from the *Sports Center* broadcast, where football experts were pretending to be soothsayers by making playoff picks. Still, there was something about that computer's bright light that lured him, like a moth to the flame. He was morbidly curious about what Maggie could possibly have said that would soothe the ache in his chest. Michael clenched his fists and his stomach as he sat down to read.

AN OPEN APOLOGY TO MY HUSBAND, WHO I HOPE CAN FIND IT IN HIS HEART TO FORGIVE ME
File under: My bad, seriously

Dear Michael (yes, readers, that's my husband's real name),

You are the man I always dreamed I'd marry. Even when I was in the worst, darkest moments of my life, I always believed there was something, someone, out there who'd be perfect for me, who'd fill the hole in my heart. You are that guy.

When you walked into my office that day that we met, you seemed too good to be true. You were smart, adorable, sexy, attentive, sweet and knew how to cook real grown-up food. (I wasn't so fond of cooking so you did it all for me.) You made my sadness disappear. You made me laugh. You made me safe. You let me tell you things, and you seemed like you really gave a shit about what I said. I couldn't wait to tell you everything, every day.

We had a really great thing going. Then we had kids, our beautiful babies who we both love more than I can say with words. You and the kids are the most important things in my world. But when they entered our world, something happened to us that changed us and I don't think I've recovered from the change. I find myself missing you like you've been away on a long trip someplace, or I've been away. You work all these long hours, tons of nights, so we can be okay, money-wise. You are under pressure as our breadwinner. (Weird word, "breadwinner.") Then, and it didn't happen all at once, but gradually things between us started going downhill. We have our moments, here and there, but it feels like we have forgotten to take care of us, Michael and Maggie, while we're consumed with dealing with everybody else, taking care of everybody else.

While you've been working, I've been trying to make myself love being at home, but I just didn't, no matter how much I tried to. I was jealous of your work. I wanted the old us back. I wasn't adjusting well and felt really guilty about it all. I love the kids, have awesome times with them, but I was starting to resent everything about my life. With you working so much I didn't think I could talk to you about it. Whenever I started to, you'd say, "But we're so lucky to have [names of our kids], aren't we?" And I felt like I had to just be grateful and shut the hell up.

So I started this blog to get through all of this stuff, so I didn't fight with you about it every time you came home. I didn't want to make the kids upset because Mommy seemed so mad all the time. I didn't feel like I could talk to people about it because they were either working and loving it, or at home and loving it. I was just this big complainer, an ingrate who must have something wrong with me for feeling this way. But here, on this blog, I posted truthful and anonymous (or so I thought) stories about my feelings and life, stuff that pissed me off and made me crazy. And you know what? Other people from all over the world started commenting and giving me the moral support I needed. They told me they were having a tough time too and some of them were just as unhappy as me and they made me feel less like a freak. Plus I didn't have to burden you with all of this.

I know that some of the posts on this blog seem really vicious to my family. And you're right, they are. And after re-reading some of them, and, seeing them through your eyes I was horrified. I have deleted them. I sincerely apologize. But please, I beg you, consider the larger context of everything here and what my intentions were. My intent wasn't to hurt you or embarrass you. I just wanted to have this open therapy session on the blog where I could be honest and other people could give me their honest input. And they helped me. Once I stopped working and we stopped having time for each other and you were working so late so much, I felt like I'd been dropped in a foreign land and I needed help to figure this place out.

I didn't tell you about this blog because if I knew you'd be reading it, or if anyone else who knows me knew about it, I would've censored, like, 80 percent of what's on here. I'd still have all those bad feelings bottled up inside and wouldn't have been able to work through them. This blog wouldn't have been worth writing because I'd have to be nice so I wouldn't hurt people's feelings. For the hurt I've caused you I'm so sorry. I didn't mean for you to be exposed to family and friends by this blog. I really thought it could remain anonymous. I never thought people would figure out who I was and link me to you. It's not fair to you that this blog doesn't represent all the awesome things you do and are. It's just a bunch of tiny bits of our lives and only from my perspective, mostly when I'm a pissed off maniac, sometimes after I've had too much red wine. I apologize for hurting you by writing this smack.

I suppose that I never should've agreed to do that newspaper interview which started all of this. If that hadn't happened, I doubt you'd have ever known about this blog and we could've just gone on and lived our lives. But I did do it. Stupid move, I now realize. And now you know and now I need to deal with the mess. Maybe, though, something good could come from this. Maybe you can find a way to get past your anger and remember that when I met you, I felt like you were someone who turned on a light in my life. These days, it's harder to find that light. It's almost like we don't even see each other really, that it's just dark all the time when we pass by each other in the hall while we're busy doing stuff. We have taken us for granted. Now that *the ugly, real me has been exposed, you see it all. This is me. And it's time you see me, even the grosser, meaner thoughts that I have. I'm sorry about the way you found out about all this, but know that I truly love you and think we can still find a way to get past this. I'm willing to do whatever it takes to make it up to you.*

Buried beneath all this crap, I'm still that girl from HR who you fell in love with and who's still crazy about you.

Love,

Maggie

Snow had completely coated the windshield of the SUV during the brief time Maggie had been inside the hotel. Instead of clearing it off, Maggie roughly brushed the snow off the door handle, unlocked the vehicle, slid onto the driver's seat and quickly turned on the ignition, clumsily dumping her purse, hat and coat in the general direction of the passenger seat. After wrenching her scratchy scarf off her neck and letting it fall to the damp floor, Maggie turned the heater up as high as it would go, closed her red, puffy eyes and leaned her aching back into the seat. In the distance, she heard the grinding metal-on-pavement sound of a snowplow, perhaps clearing a side street, or even the highway. She couldn't be sure of its location as she sat in a borrowed truck that was parked illegally in front of a hotel at nearly 8:30 at night days before Christmas, after sneaking past hotel staff to speak with a man who didn't want to hear from or see her. The love of her life. Her cell phone was brimming with scalding unheard voicemail messages from her mother-in-law who would've likely preferred that Maggie just pull the SUV into oncoming traffic and be done with it. Maggie deleted the messages — 12 — without listening to them while wondering if Alfred or Courtney had seen her when she ran through the lobby sobbing and noisily blowing her nose.

Some of the snow around the perimeter of the SUV's front window had now returned to liquid form and was starting to streak down the windshield leaving behind glossy trails on the slightly fogged windows. Maggie watched the droplets push their way through the snow which had been providing her with a camouflage of sorts, shielding her face from passersby, not that there was anyone out at that time and in that weather, save for a plow driver or, perhaps Alfred if he ever decided to look away from the web sites he was now surfing and notice the SUV parked in the fire lane.

Restless, she tried to think of something she could do to pass the time and keep her mind occupied, to stop herself from trying to bargain with God about what she'd do (or not do) if her marriage survived this. Seeing nothing in the way of amusements in the front seat — George had no magazines, CDs, newspapers in his vehicle, unlike Maggie's highly cluttered minivan — Maggie turned on the radio, flipping through the stations until she got to a pop station which was playing the latest tune from a singer whose life was being engulfed by a downward spiral of drinking and drugs. It was soothing to Maggie, in a twisted sort of way, to listen to this cotton candy confection of a song by a seemingly broken young woman and to think that somewhere out there someone had a more screwed up relationship and life than she did. A song by a new boy band came on, followed by one from a band comprised of guys who'd soon be collecting Social Security, then the station played a grating Christmas song that was so awful that it had no business being broadcast in public.

By now, the rest of the snow on the windshield had completely liquefied and Maggie had grown tired of the pop station. She tuned in a static-y independent college radio station from New Hampshire. "Who out there hates 'Dominick the Italian Christmas Donkey' as much as I do raise your hand," the DJ asked as the signal faded in and out.

Maggie, who could now see clearly through the window, raised her right hand.

"Well then I've got a better Christmas-y song to play for you, the late Jeff Buckley's 'Hallelujah.' Okay, so it's not technically a Christmas tune but hey, the snowstorm's about over folks, let's all say, 'Hallelujah' together. Keep warm and enjoy this non-donkey, non-chipmunk, non-grandma-got-run-over-by-a-reindeer song." The haunting voice of the deceased singer filled the stuffy SUV air, coupled by the simple strums of a guitar. Before she realized it, Maggie was sucked into the song's melancholy. Tears again pooled at the corners of her eyes and leaked down Maggie's face forming more salty streaks through her haphazardly applied makeup. As the singer repeated the word, "hallelujah" over and over with increasing emotion, Michael appeared at the driver's side door, without a jacket, his face just as red as Maggie's, his eyes just as bloodshot, his heart beating just as hard. Maggie — who'd yet to regain her composure — didn't open the window. Or the door. If she just stayed where she was, she thought, nothing could end. Everything would remain frozen in place.

Confused and impatient, Michael opened the unlocked door, rested his left forearm on it, glowered at his wife and then looked down at his feet. He raised his head slowly and haltingly said, "I . . . I, I've missed us too." He paused again, placed both of his warm hands against the roof of the SUV and leaned forward allowing the steamy heat from inside the vehicle to radiate against his chest and thighs. "I never knew . . . never expected that you . . . that you could be so cruel, that you said those things, felt them about me. That you were so angry."

A lengthy silence idled between them as Michael's face contorted with anguish. "I didn't know you were so miserable," his voice broke, "with . . . me. Am I such a bad guy? A bad husband?"

He sharply inhaled and paused, affording Maggie an opportunity to jump in, an opening which she was too scared to take.

"Maggie I can't . . ."

"Just tell me!" she blurted through a fresh onslaught of tears. "Are you leaving me? Have I fucked it up so badly that it's over?"

Michael stiffened. He stepped back from the SUV and shoved his hands into his pockets, again looked down at his feet as if he was rehearsing what he was going to say in his head beforehand, declining to look at Maggie's watery, anxious face.

"Well?" she shrieked, wiping her runny nose on her sleeve.

He took another long pause, "I'm so mad. I can't even tell you how mad, madder than I've ever been. And, I need to be honest with you. I can't believe I'm going to say this, but . . ."

"No!" Maggie said, sobbing, her chest constricting as though it was caving in on her.

". . . I'm not going anywhere."

— The End —

A C K N O W L E D G M E N T S

During the two year journey to write and edit this book, I have been lucky enough to receive wonderful advice and guidance from some loving, caring folks. I'd like to tip my hat to them for putting up with all of my nuttiness and helping me when I needed it. This novel would not have been published without the assistance and dogged cheerleading of the following people:

Gayle Long Carvalho, Lawrence F. O'Brien and Julie McKay generously provided honest, insightful, detailed and tremendously useful feedback about my manuscript. Gayle also proved to be an extremely patient friend and a tireless, one-woman booster club during the entire process, including the times when she fielded and replied to my desperate and snarky text messages.

My husband Scott — who should not be confused with the character of Michael Kelly as he is not Michael Kelly and Michael Kelly is *not* him — was also an extremely supportive and savvy advisor on everything from plotlines to character backstories. He frequently and unflaggingly expressed his avid enthusiasm for the project, something for which I am grateful.

Additionally, I appreciated the heroic patience demonstrated by my three children during the times when I went AWOL in order to do some power-writing to finally complete this book, including the few occasions when I was holed up in a home office for an entire weekend after issuing explicit orders to not to be disturbed . . . except if they were giving me food or coffee.

Finally, thank you to Nancy Cleary for taking a chance on *Mortified* and seeing it through to publication. I am humbled by your confidence in this book.

CPSIA information can be obtained at www.ICGtesting.com
Printed in the USA
BVOW081959140513

320717BV00001B/1/P